Jo Spurrier was born in 1980 and has a Bachelor of Science, but turned to writing because people tend to get upset when scientists make things up. She lives in Adelaide with her husband, two young sons and a formerly feral cat, and spends a lot of time playing with cars and trains ... although she still occasionally daydreams about snow.

Jo's first novel, *Winter Be My Shield*, was shortlisted for the 2012 Aurealis Award for best fantasy novel. Her first book from the Tales of the Blackbone Witches trilogy, *A Curse of Ash and Embers*, was shortlisted for best YA fantasy at the Aurealis Awards.

Also by Jo Spurrier

CHILDREN OF THE BLACK SUN TRILOGY

TALES OF THE BLACKBONE WITCHES

DAUGHTER OF LIES & RUIN

TALES OF THE BLACKBONE WITCHES

JO SPURRIER

HARPER
Voyager

Harper*Voyager*
An imprint of HarperCollins*Publishers*

First published in Australia in 2019
by HarperCollins*Publishers* Australia Pty Limited
ABN 36 009 913 517
harpercollins.com.au

HarperCollins*Publishers*
Level 13, 201 Elizabeth Street, Sydney NSW 2000, Australia
Unit D1, 63 Apollo Drive, Rosedale, Auckland 0632, New Zealand
A 53, Sector 57, Noida, UP, India
1 London Bridge Street, London, SE1 9GF, United Kingdom
Bay Adelaide Centre, East Tower, 22 Adelaide Street West, 41st floor, Toronto,
    Ontario M5H 4E3, Canada
195 Broadway, New York NY 10007, USA

A catalogue record for this book is available
from the National Library of Australia

ISBN 978 1 4607 5634 8 (paperback)
ISBN 978 1 4607 1032 6 (ebook)

Cover design and internal decorations by Darren Holt,
    HarperCollins Design Studio
Cover images by shutterstock.com
Typeset in Sabon LT Std by Kirby Jones
Author photograph by Simon Ankor
Printed and bound in Australia by McPherson's Printing Group
The papers used by HarperCollins in the manufacture of this book are a
natural, recyclable product made from wood grown in sustainable plantation
forests. The fibre source and manufacturing processes meet recognised
international environmental standards, and carry certification.

For Dad

CHAPTER 1

A man stood in the dappled shade in the middle of the road. He wore a leather hat pulled down low to shade his eyes and a printed kerchief tied around his neck. And he had a bare sabre in his hand. The blade flashed in a shaft of sunlight gleaming through the trees.

I scowled, tightening my hands on the reins. *Really?* I said to myself. *Just how long did he spend traipsing up and down this road to find the perfect spot to pose?* He was handsome, I had to admit; but the effect was rather spoiled by the smug expression on his face. I'd also bet any money he'd dressed himself as carefully as a girl going to her first village dance.

Feeling my eyes upon him, he parted his lips in a wicked smile. 'I'd stop right there, miss, if I were you.'

'If you were me I doubt you'd do anything of the sort,' I said. I dropped my hand to my side, reaching for the wand that hung there, hidden in the folds of my skirt. But before I could gather the courage to pull it out, our draught mare, Maggie, tossed her head and threw her weight back into the breeching to stop the heavy wagon. She was a gentle giant, our Maggie. Plenty of beasts would just shoulder a man out of the way, but not her. Then again, she didn't have enough sense to recognise the sabre in his hand, or what it meant. He wasn't alone out here, I had no doubt of that.

From the gleam in the man's eye, he took it as a victory. His smile deepened, crinkling the skin around his eyes, and he took hold of her bridle. I wondered what Maggie would do if I slapped the reins on her rump to drive her onwards. We hadn't had her long enough to know and, in any case, I couldn't risk him turning that sabre against her. Instead, I reached behind and rapped my knuckles against the door at my back, trying to keep the movement subtle.

The bandit didn't seem to notice. He just rubbed Maggie's long nose and gave me a sly grin. 'Well,' he said, 'aren't you a good girl?'

Lord and Lady. 'Are you talking to me, or the horse?' I demanded.

'You tell me,' he said. '*Are* you a good girl?'

I couldn't think of any way to answer that wouldn't lead to a conversation I didn't want to have, so I just scowled as he blatantly looked me over. I knew exactly what he'd make of me. A young woman in worn and mended clothes, brown hair coming loose from its braid, sitting on the footplate of a sturdy travellers' wagon. I looked every inch a maid-servant, but though I was coarsely dressed, the wagon, Maggie and her harness had clearly cost a pretty penny. I could see why they thought us an appealing target. They had no way of knowing what was behind the door at my back.

Still grinning like a fool, he came towards me, sliding his gloved hand along the rein. 'You should be careful, pretty young thing like you, out here all on your own. There's all kinds of scoundrels in these woods, you see ...'

At those words, a dozen men stepped out from behind the bushes and rocks, a few even swinging down from the trees.

'But never fear,' he went on. 'I'll protect you.'

I leaned back and this time thumped my elbow against the door. *Come on, Aleida.* My mistress was sleeping inside. Not too deeply, I hoped.

The bandit caught the movement with a lift of his chin. 'Ah,' he said, sheathing his sword. 'Or perhaps you aren't alone, after all?' With that, he put one foot to the step-iron and sprang up to sit beside me. With a yelp I tried to move away, but all I succeeded in doing was trapping my wand under me as he reached across and plucked the reins out of my grip. His other arm snaked behind my waist and pulled me close. Oh good grief, was he wearing scent? I'd half-expected the stink of someone who went weeks between baths, and honestly, I wasn't sure if this was any better.

'Who's inside, lass? Your father or your husband? Or your master, perhaps?'

'If you don't take your hands off me right now,' I snapped, 'I swear by all the demons in all the hells you're going to regret it.' With my heart beating hard, I thumped the door again. This time, there came an answering knock through the wood, and the knot of anxiety under my heart softened a little. My teacher was awake, after all. 'You really should go,' I told him. 'Before it's too late.'

The men were starting to close around us and I cast a wary eye over them. A couple of them were just young lads, close to my age. Others were older, but none of them were what I'd picture as hard-bitten criminals. They looked just like ordinary folk, with the usual complement of eyes, teeth and noses. *Of course, once we drive away from here, they might not be so lucky. Why didn't I draw my wand when I had the chance?* I could feel it half-pinned under my leg and wondered if I dared dig it out. I was worried the lout pressed against me would take the gesture as something else entirely. *Aleida is never going to let me hear the end of this!*

'Now, now, sweet,' he said. 'Why would you say something like that, when I've been nothing but a gentleman to you? Well, what *do* we have inside this fine little wagon? Perhaps you and I should take a look.' He stood, swiftly, catching my wrist to yank me to my feet.

That was all I needed to find the smooth wooden handle of the wand. I pulled it free and shoved the point of it towards his face. For a second he recoiled — just a second, and then he realised it wasn't a knife I'd thrust towards him, but a chunk of crystal hafted to a wooden shaft.

Looking puzzled, he tried to snatch it out of my hand, but the moment he touched the stone there was a flash of light and a crack like thunder. The shock of it threw him back against the door, and the air was suddenly full of the smell of burning hair and scorched leather.

Before he could recover — before the men around us could react — there came a piercing shriek from above.

Something huge and dark speared down through the trees, screeching like a demon. It was an eagle, its wingspan wider than the reach of my arms. It swooped towards us, only to flare its wings and bank hard, diving under the wagon's eaves as it reached out with taloned feet, each as large as my hand.

It slashed at the man's face and he screamed, flailing at the beast as it beat about his head with its vast wings. I ducked away from the wildly swinging arms and wings, and then I had a thought. He looked awfully precarious there, balancing on the narrow footboard.

Crouching low, my shoulder against the wall of the wagon, I shoved him with all my strength. With a strangled cry of surprise, he toppled from the seat, landing heavily in the road in a puff of dust, blood pouring down his face.

Then, behind me, the door swung open and my mistress loomed out, her black hair tousled and her dark eyes glowering, her wand in her hand. 'Get the reins,' she said to me while the eagle flapped over our heads, climbing with laborious beats of its wings, turning its fierce gaze to the man who'd taken hold of Maggie's head. The rest of the bandits were still crowding around us, one of them even climbing up to the footboard where we stood.

Aleida turned to him with murder in her eyes. I left her to it. The reins had fallen onto the shafts, down where they attached to the wagon. With a quick glance at Maggie to make sure she wasn't thinking of kicking, I slipped down to retrieve them, hearing the crackling roar of a fireball above my head and the shriek of the bandit as Aleida sent it searing his way.

She caught me by the collar to steady me as I scrambled back up. 'Get her moving! Go!'

Maggie didn't need to be told twice. I was still gathering up the reins, but it seemed the mare had decided that she'd had quite enough of all this bother. With a nicker of fright, she reared between the shafts and threw herself forward, jerking the wagon into motion with a lurch that set me and Aleida both snatching for a grip to steady ourselves.

It didn't stop Aleida from throwing another fireball at the men who rushed towards us, waving their arms and shouting as though they could stop Maggie in her tracks. 'Get out of the way, you fools!' I yelled, having a horrifying vision of what would happen if they went down under Maggie's enormous hooves, or the wheels of our heavy wagon. Amid all the confusion, something hit the wood near me with a hefty *thunk*, but it barely registered with everything else that was going on, with men running towards us or away from Aleida's fireballs, as well as the eagle circling, searching for a new target.

But there was one man not moving, seeming calm amid the chaos. He had a bow in his hands, sighting at the eagle as he hauled back the string. 'Aleida!' I yelled. 'He's got a bow!'

'I see it,' she growled, and stepped towards the edge of the footboard for a clear line to the fellow, raising her wand. The smoke-stained crystal at the tip of it glowed with a pinpoint of light in a deep, vivid green, and I felt power flex around us, thickening the air.

The bow in the bandit's hands squirmed, rippled, and then burst into life. Tiny green buds split the wood, swelling to a leafy profusion, while pale white roots swarmed from the lower length of the bow stave, questing for the ground. By the time the bandit dropped it in surprise, it was barely recognisable as a weapon.

Aleida sat on the wagon seat beside me with a thump, gripping the wood with one hand. 'Give me the reins, Dee. Check behind us.'

Now that the wagon was moving, Maggie was settling into a laboured canter, determined to leave all this vexation behind; a sentiment I shared. I handed the reins over and tried to stand, only to lose my balance as something pulled me back down. There was an arrow jutting from the wagon seat, inches from my leg. It had pierced my skirts and petticoats right through, pinning them to the bench.

I pulled it out, and Aleida snatched it from my hand, her face dark. 'Are they coming after us?'

This time I managed to stand on the rocking seat, and peered around the edge of the wagon to see just a few of the bandits left milling in the road. The rest had retreated into the trees. 'No,' I said, sitting down again. 'They've got the wind up them good and proper.'

She rolled the arrow in her hand, her face like thunder. 'We should go back.'

'What?' I said. 'No! Why?'

'No one shoots at my apprentice! I'll turn that little wretch inside out!'

I pressed my lips together, focusing on the road and Maggie's ears, still flat with annoyance. Convincing her to stop now would be no easy task. 'Let's just keep going. I reckon they've learned their lesson.'

'Mm. Maybe.' She turned to me then, and I wanted to shrink away at the anger in her eyes. 'Dee,' she said. 'Why in the hells didn't you have your wand out? You should have had it in your hand as soon as you saw him.'

I didn't ask how she knew. I just looked away, hiding behind the excuse of keeping my eyes on the road. 'You said we should keep our heads down. Try not to make it obvious that we're ... what we are.'

She snorted. 'For villages, sure. Farms, maybe. But bandits? Screw 'em, who cares what they think? If you'd pulled your wand out that idiot wouldn't have dared get close enough to grab you.'

'For you, maybe,' I muttered.

'What was that?'

'For you,' I said. 'Aleida, you *look* like a witch. I just look like a servant girl.' I glanced down at my wand, lying beside my thigh, the crystal bound to the shaft with copper wire. I'd made it myself, under her direction, but it didn't feel real. It felt like a hunk of rock tied to a wooden handle. Not like Aleida's wand of smoke-wreathed quartz. You could feel the power in that stone, radiating like heat from a fire.

'I've told you, Dee. It's not what you look like, it's

how you carry yourself. Next time something like that happens, I want your wand out right away.'

'Even if I still can't really use the damn thing?'

'Especially then. It's not going to do anything if it's not in your hand.'

'But I can't—'

'And you never will if you don't try. He saw you as a harmless little girl because that's how you were acting. You're not a servant, you're a witch. Act like it.'

'Yes, miss,' I said, scowling down at my dangling feet. 'And I'm fine, by the way,' I added, tartly.

She looked me over with flat, dark eyes. 'I know. If you weren't, those fools back there would have seen why I'm called Blackbone.'

The word made me shiver, even though it was my name now too. Aleida's old mistress, Gyssha, was the first to be called Blackbone, because all that was left of those who crossed her was a pile of blackened bones. I didn't doubt Aleida could do the same, if she was pushed hard enough. I hoped I'd never see it happen. 'Sorry, miss,' I said.

She sighed and leaned back against the door. 'Next time, Dee, next time. And I suppose there's no harm done.' Then she gave a dry chuckle. 'Well, not to us, anyway.'

It was only another hour or so before we emerged from the forest and reached a bustling little town surrounded by a lush patchwork of fields. There was a small castle overlooking it from atop a bluff of stone — at least, to my mind it was a castle, but when I called it that Aleida just gave a derisive snort.

'So,' I said, as Maggie plodded towards the village. 'Are we going straight to the old abbey? Only we should probably get Maggie's shoes checked while we can; I thought this morning her off fore seemed a little loose.'

'We'll find a smithy first, in that case,' Aleida said. 'Just in case we want to disappear once we've seen these nuns.'

I gave her a sharp look. 'Is that likely? We don't mean them any harm.'

'They don't know that,' she pointed out. 'When they find out who we are...' she trailed off with a shrug. 'I'm probably just being paranoid.'

I kind of agreed, though I kept that thought to myself. Knowing what I did of her old teacher, there were worse habits to have than an excess of wariness and caution.

The reclaimed abbey was supposedly our reason for coming to this part of the world. I say supposedly, for I'd come to the conclusion that my teacher simply couldn't bear to stay in one place for too long. Since she'd recovered from the fight that had killed Gyssha, we hadn't gone more than a few weeks without her coming up with some errand that saw us leave Black Oak Cottage and take to the roads.

We found the blacksmith's yard with no trouble, and a burly young man came to greet us as I steered Maggie through the gates. He rubbed her nose kindly as I told him about her loose shoe. 'I'm afraid you'll have a wait, miss, we've a fair few beasts ahead of you. But you're welcome to leave her with us if you've any other business in town.'

It wasn't my place to decide, so I glanced to Aleida with my eyebrows raised to find her already slipping down from the wagon's seat. 'We might as well find a spot of lunch, then,' she said. 'That fun and games on the road was enough to give me an appetite.'

The blacksmith's lad took us out to the street to point the way to the village tavern, but Aleida stopped him at the gate. There, pasted to the gate-post was a poster printed with eight wood-cut portraits of grizzled, bitter-looking men. There was a word at the top in bold letters: WANTED. And under that, REWARD.

'What's this?' Aleida said. 'You folk having trouble out on the roads?'

'Yes, miss. Lord Belmont's offered to pay handsomely for any information that leads to their capture. Truly, though, no one's seen these sods for months and months. Something ill must have befallen them, and about blasted time, too.'

I was about to protest that we'd seen them, not more than an hour before, but then I looked more closely. Each face had a name printed under it — TORO read one, and MATTOCK, another, but of the eight faces printed there, the grinning fool who'd accosted me earlier was not among them. None of the men I'd seen were — they'd all been much younger than these baleful souls.

'Shouldn't we tell someone about the bandits we saw?' I asked her once we were alone.

'Not our problem,' she said.

'But what if they attack someone else?'

That made her laugh. 'You should have thought of that before you stopped me from going after them. We witches solve our own problems.'

Her words left me chagrined, though there was no rancour in them; and I walked beside her in silence until we reached the tavern, marked with a shingle painted with a boar's head with an apple in its mouth. Underneath it was another sign, the paint bright and fresh, and on it was a strange beast — a lion's body, with the legs, head and wings of an eagle. I recognised it from one of the books Aleida had given me to practise my reading upon, a gorgeously illustrated bestiary. 'Is that a griffin?'

'Mm,' Aleida said.

Since it was a fine day, the customers were all sitting outside, clustered in small groups as they played draughts or dice. We sat together at a large barrel cut down into a table, and the custodian came over, wiping his hands on his apron. 'Welcome, mistress, miss. If you're after a meal we've got some fine pies — chicken and leek, quite fresh.'

'That'll do.'

While they spoke, I was peering through the open door to the tavern, where I could see another painting — a griffin again, this one so large it took up the entire wall.

'Why the griffins everywhere?' I asked the tavern-keeper.

'Why, miss, that's our marvellous attraction! For just one ha'penny you can see the wonder for yourself.'

'A real griffin?'

'Well, the hide of one,' he said. 'Stuffed and mounted, and so lifelike you can picture it taking flight.'

Aleida snorted, and the tavern-keeper turned to her. 'You think it's a fake, miss?'

'I've seen a few in my time,' she said.

'Perhaps you have, but this beast is real. I'd swear it on my mother's grave, only she'd slap me 'cause she's still alive. There's a nest of them, you see, up in the mountains to the north, and a few of the local lads brought one down. We bought the hide off them, and Lord Belmont took the skull and mounted it in his great hall.'

I turned to Aleida. 'I want to see it.'

'I still say it's a fake.'

'Well, I've never seen a fake griffin, either.' I felt for my purse, tucked in a pocket under my skirts. I had money of my own, for the first time in my life, since Aleida had given me a share of the profit from the unguents and oils and tinctures we'd spent the summer making. 'Are you coming or not?'

There was a door in the painted wall, locked with a gleaming brass padlock. The tavern-keeper unlocked it with a key and led the way inside, an oil-lamp in his hand, and went around lighting candles for us.

The darkness smelled like an old stable, but as the candles were lit, the dark shape in the centre of the room resolved itself.

Aleida exhaled in a puff of breath. 'Well I'll be damned,' she said. 'That's a real griffin!'

It was the size of a small horse, posed on a rock sculpted from clay. The beast was so big that the huge yellow beak of the eagle Aleida had called down an hour or two ago seemed weak and fragile in comparison. Its scaled forefeet had dagger-sized talons, the spread of them larger than Maggie's massive hooves. Its shoulders were powerful, sloped like a cat's, and its wings ... its wings were too big for the room. They'd been mounted mantled, half-spread, so I could only imagine how huge they must have been. Just one of them alone had to be as long as I was. And the eyes ... well, the eyes were just glass, but they were yellow and gold and orange, fierce and full of cold hunger. *Those must have cost a pretty penny,* I thought.

I walked around it, mouth agape, not caring that I looked like a fool

'Where do they come from?' I said.

The tavern-keeper shifted his feet, about to speak, when he realised I wasn't talking to him.

'Somewhere else,' Aleida said.

'But *where*?'

She shrugged in the dim light. 'One of the realms.'

'Like the one—' I cut myself off, glancing at the innkeeper.

Aleida made a gesture, and the man fell still. You never realise how much someone moves, even when they're standing in one place, until they stop. He looked like a doll.

'Go on,' Aleida said.

I shook myself. 'Like the one I saw when Gyssha killed that warlock?' I didn't know much about the realms — I'd only had the briefest glimpse of the worlds that lay beyond this one, and what I had seen was the stuff of nightmares.

'It's different to that one. It's windy, and full of high places.'

'You've seen it?'

She nodded. 'Just once.'

'How many are there? Realms, I mean.'

'Hard to say. Several, at least.'

'Several?' I said. 'Seriously, no one's figured it out any better than that?'

'It's not that easy, Dee. Think of it like this: you're in another world, opening a portal into ours. You could open it into the high mountains, or under the sea, or into a howling storm. Would you imagine all of those places are in the one world?'

'Oh,' I said. 'I see what you mean. But how did they get here? Could they find their own way through?'

'Possibly, if it was just one beast,' Aleida said, coming closer to examine the hide. 'But a whole clutch of them? No. Someone would have to have found them and pulled them through.' She reached up to feel the feathers on the creature's neck and shoulders, and raked her fingers through its tawny coat.

I stared at her. 'You mean a witch did it?'

'Or a wizard, or warlock. Someone with power.'

'Someone *here*?'

'Maybe.'

A short time later, we were back outside, tucking into two pies. They were very good.

'But why?' I said. 'I mean, it can't be easy, can it?'

She snorted. 'It's not like popping down to town on market day, that's for sure.'

'Then why?'

Aleida shrugged and took a swallow of ale. The innkeeper had brought us two tankards without being asked. 'Well,' she said. 'It's a bit of a laugh, isn't it?'

I just scowled at her.

'No, Dee, really. Imagine it, you turn those things loose and hang around for a bit. Imagine the tales you'd hear at the market, in the tavern. People swearing blind that they'd seen it, others refusing to believe a word. The stories would spread, too, and no one would believe it, except for people like us, who'd say, "Well, maybe". And if it was you who did it, you'd hear those tales, and you'd *know*, you'd know it was you who'd made it happen. And sooner or later, other folk with power would figure it out, and they'd tell others ...'

'So it's just a prank,' I said, unimpressed.

She laughed. 'Exactly. Like putting a horse on the balcony of a tall building. There's no point, and it's a lot of bother, but wouldn't it be fun? Just imagine the look on their face when they see it!'

'A horse on a balcony? Why would you do something like that?'

'Oh come on, Dee, it would be hilarious!'

'Please tell me you haven't done that!'

'Well, no. I always wanted to, but I didn't have any friends with balconies. Actually, I didn't have any friends, except Bennett, and if I did something like that to him, he'd just give me a look and tell me to get the beast down again ... but you have to admit, Dee, it'd be worth it.'

I took a slow sip from my tankard, thinking — not about the ridiculousness of horses and balconies, but what it must have been like roaming around the world as Gyssha Blackbone's apprentice. 'You must have been wretchedly lonely.'

She gave me a sharp look, as though none too pleased with my sudden change of subject. But then she leaned forward, elbows on the table and chin in her hand. 'You're a kindly soul, aren't you? I still don't understand why you were brought to me. I can't decide if I'm supposed to toughen you up or if you're supposed to gentle me.'

Her dark eyes seemed to bore into me, and after a few moments I had to look away. 'You sure it's not both?'

'No.' I could still feel her eyes upon me. 'But you'll have your work cut out for you if that's the case. Yeah, it was lonely, I guess, but I grew up knowing I could only rely on myself. This whole thing, me and you, it's kind of new to me. Don't go expecting smooth sailing.'

'If it's new to you, how do you think I feel? I said, and she laughed as I chewed another mouthful of flaky pastry and tender chicken. It was still a novelty, this business of eating food I hadn't made myself. 'So,' I said. 'Do you think they're still here? Whoever brought the beasts through?'

She didn't answer right away. She just leaned back on her stool, back straight and shoulders square. 'Not in the village,' she said after a moment. 'I can't feel anything nearby, except for the old abbey. There could be a hedge-witch lying low, but they wouldn't be able to open a portal.'

'But there's power at the abbey?' I said.

'Well, it's run by nuns, or so I hear, and they often have a touch of magic to them if they're serious about their business.'

That went some way towards explaining her worry about the abbey. 'What do you mean by that?'

'There's more reasons to become a nun than just being really committed to the art of god-bothering, Dee. These days it's not that hard for a low-born woman to take up a craft or run a business in her own name, but noble-born ladies are still bound to the old ways. If you're a sixteen-year-old girl of rank or money, and you don't want to be married off with no choice in the matter, running off to a convent is your best bet. I tell you, Dee, don't ever envy the noble-born. I'd rather be born to a whore a hundred times over than live one life as a princess. Once you're in the convent, though, you've got nothing but time on your hands. Plenty of nuns have a touch of magic, these days.'

I nodded, though in truth I wasn't sure I understood what she was getting at. 'All right. So if they do have power, what are they going to make of you?'

She gave a wry, humourless smile, and raised her tankard. 'Your guess is as good as mine, Dee. Might be wise to be ready for a fast retreat.'

By the time we returned to the yard to find Maggie freshly shod and waiting at the hitching post, Aleida was hobbling. She caught me watching her from the corner of my eye, and glowered. 'I know, I know,' she muttered over the ringing of hammers. 'Should have brought my staff. Here —' She tossed me a little purse from her pocket. 'Settle up, will you, and get her hitched. Time to go see the nuns.' Then she heaved herself up the wagon's steps and ducked inside.

The same burly young man came to take our coin, and he helped me hitch Maggie between the shafts again. 'She's a fine lass,' he said, patting her shoulder. 'Safe journey, miss. Take care on the roads.'

'We will,' I said cheerily. 'Good day.'

I started to climb up to the seat when a commotion at the gates made me pause. Maggie lifted her head with a snort as the blacksmith looked up from his anvil and summoned his lads with a shout. The one who'd been helping me ran off to him at once.

A team of men had appeared at the gates, all but dragging a wild-eyed horse into the yard. They had ropes on his head and around his neck, and another behind his haunches with two men to either side, forcing the beast forward step by step.

'What in the blazes are you doing?' the blacksmith demanded, though he threw himself in to grab a rope.

'We need a hand with him, Hugh,' shouted one of the men, his face red and dripping with sweat as the horse fought and plunged. 'Can you and your lads help out? We were trying to throw him down and geld him but he went completely mad and got away from us. We only got him back because he tripped over his head-rope and went down hard just down the lane.'

'Is this that wild one you caught out past Hobb's place? That beast has a screw loose, I tell you. He's not fit for anything but dog food.'

The men were fighting for every step, while the horse pulled back with all he had, his neck and sides streaked with sweat. Something about the beast put me on edge — there was a desperation about his movements, as though he was fighting for his life. I'd seen untamed beasts aplenty, I was a farm girl after all, but this was beyond an animal fighting against the first touch of a rope. This horse was frantic.

I gripped the edge of the seat to steady myself, and reached for the creature. This was the first lesson in witchcraft that Aleida had ever tried to teach me, the art of slipping into a beast's head and borrowing it — it was how she'd brought the eagle down to drive off the bandits back in the forest.

I slipped into his head, and at the first touch I felt my heart leap in echo of his racing pulse. A sick fear twisted my stomach and set me shivering like I'd been plunged into an ice-bath. That was all I managed before I lost my focus and fell away from him, finding myself back in my own body, swaying on my feet.

There was a movement above me, a swish of black skirts as Aleida came to the doorway. Her face was blank, but she had that cold look in her eyes that meant she was thinking hard. 'Aleida,' I hissed. 'Aleida! That … it's not …' It was hard to talk after borrowing, especially if you were as new to it as I was. 'That's not a horse.'

'Mm,' Aleida said, frowning down. 'I know.'

She made a small gesture and I felt her power rising, making my skin prickle.

The horse's halter snapped, and the rope around his neck parted and frayed, falling away. The horse staggered and nearly fell, and the men straining against him toppled like dominoes as the beast reared up, flailing his hooves. The men at his haunches took one glance at each other and scattered, throwing down their ropes. The horse wheeled and bolted, vanishing through the gates with a flash of hooves and a spray of sweat.

Aleida sat on the seat and beckoned me with an imperious wave. 'Up you hop, Dee,' she said. 'Time to go.'

CHAPTER 2

I was panting hard as we drove away from the blacksmith, clinging to the seat with shaking hands. My mind was racing, full of heart-stopping terror, like a beast caught in a trap.

Aleida held the reins with one hand, but she paid no attention to Maggie as she plodded along the dusty road. Instead she was focused on me. 'Breathe, Dee. Slowly.'

'I, but, I—'

'It's just an echo, your mind's playing tricks on you. Take a deep breath and hold it as long as you can.'

'I can't.' I had to run, I had to escape, I had to get out of this trap and find somewhere safe. Only nowhere was safe, not anymore. *That's not true,* I told myself. *None of it's true.* But the sheer animal panic inside of me seemed to have a life of its own, and it wouldn't be soothed.

With a sigh, Aleida grabbed my chin in one hand and pulled my head around until my eyes met hers. At once,

I felt as though she'd grabbed hold of me with magnetic force. I couldn't look away, and I didn't even want to.

'Deep breaths,' she said. 'Like this.' She took a deep, slow breath in, held it so long my head started swimming and my lungs began burning, and then let it out even slower. 'Push the panic away. It's not yours, you don't have to hold on to it. Just breathe and let it go.' We repeated the pattern a few more times, and then she released me, turning back to the road.

The moment I was free my lungs wanted to start puffing and panting again, but I made myself follow the pattern: in, hold, out. 'Thanks,' I said, between breaths.

'With better mental defences you'll be able to keep your mind separate. It's important when you do a lot of borrowing. That's something you need to work on.'

I nodded, feeling myself flush. 'Sorry. That ... that was mind control, wasn't it? Making me copy your breathing like that?'

'Yep. And how many times do I have to tell you to stop apologising? You've only been doing this for a few months, of course you've got a lot to learn.'

I grimaced. 'Sor—' I choked the word off into a cough before I got it all out, and Aleida chuckled while I felt my cheeks flush red. Back home at Burswood Farm, before I came to Aleida, it had just been easier to apologise for everything, whether it was my fault or not. I'd end up getting blamed for it anyway. I hadn't even realised what a habit it had become until Aleida lost her temper one day and threatened to bewitch me into never saying the word again. 'All right then, I'll just blame you for not teaching me better.'

That got another laugh. 'That's the spirit. Never say sorry, never admit you're wrong. Never show weakness, that's what Gyssha always said.'

I gave her a sidelong look. I was pretty sure she was joking about that. Well, not joking, exactly. It did sound like the sort of thing Gyssha Blackbone would have said.

My heart had slowed now, my panic ebbing away, but I'd bet my eye teeth that somewhere out there that not-horse was still running. 'Aleida?'

'Hmm?'

'If it wasn't a horse, what was it?'

She was silent for a moment, gazing out past Maggie's ears. 'A man,' she said at last.

For a moment I thought I'd misheard her. Then I realised she was serious. 'A man?' I repeated. 'Like, a person?'

'Mm. That's why you got so rattled trying to borrow him. You can't borrow people like you can animals, we're too similar.'

I felt myself frowning, remembering what the men had said. If he kept acting as wild as that, he'd end up butchered and fed to the pigs and dogs. 'That poor soul,' I said. 'No wonder he was so terrified. But who did it to him? And why?'

Aleida didn't reply. We were nearing a crossroads now, and she shifted the reins to the right, turning Maggie towards the old abbey, its new front gate gleaming in the sun.

'Wait,' I said, hands tightening on the bench again. 'We have to go after him! He needs help.'

'We will,' Aleida said in calm and measured tones. 'Just not yet.'

'But—'

'But nothing. Take a look behind us, Dee.'

When I hesitated she turned my way with a cool, measured gaze. 'Go on.'

I stood, balancing on the swaying footboard and clinging to the porch bracket, and peered around the wagon's high wall.

The men who'd brought the not-horse into the yard had trailed out after us, searching for their escapee. One of them seemed to be watching us while others scouted for hoof prints in the earth of the road. 'Do you know what they're saying?' she said. 'Strange that the rope should break, cursed strange. And the halter, too, just like it had been cut with a knife. Such a strange business. They're wondering if we had something to do with him getting loose,' she said, turning back to the road. 'If we go haring off after him, they'll *know* we did.'

'But—'

'People don't like witches, Dee. We're useful sometimes, maybe, but we can do things they don't understand and can't defend against. It scares people, and with damn good reason. Folk don't hunt witches like they used to in the old days, but they're not above raising a mob if they're scared enough, and I don't want to have to deal with that. We'll see to our business here and then go after him once the excitement's died down.

Besides, he's running like he's got a pack of demons on his heels, we won't be catching up with him in a hurry.'

I couldn't exactly argue with that. 'All right, but you didn't answer me. Who did it? Why?'

'Dee …' She gave me an exasperated look. 'How in the hells would I know?'

I ducked my head, but this time I managed to stop myself from apologising. 'Could it be the same one who brought the griffins here? Another prank?' I spat the last word. The way she'd talked of the beasts earlier hadn't sat well with me. The folly of putting a horse on a balcony was one thing, but it was another when folk lost the animals that were their livelihood to a winged lion swooping down from the skies. I understood why the lads who'd brought the griffin down had gone to so much effort, and taken so much risk.

'No prank,' Aleida said.

'So, what? There's an evil witch out here somewhere?'

'Don't go jumping to conclusions,' Aleida said. 'You don't know why he was turned. Maybe they had a good reason.'

'A good reason? To send him to be gelded and broken to serve as a beast of burden?' I gave her a sidelong glance. 'Wouldn't it be easier to just …'

'Kill him?'

'Well, yeah.'

'Oh, undoubtedly.' She didn't go on, leaving me to fill in the rest of the thought myself. I almost asked her what would be bad enough to decide that killing him was too easy, too simple, but I decided against it. I didn't want to know. Instead, I said, 'Could you do that?'

'Turn someone into an animal?'

'Yeah.'

Aleida shrugged. 'If I wanted it badly enough, I could probably find a way. Someone with a talent for beast magic could do it more easily.'

'But you're good at beast magic, aren't you? You're good at borrowing, you fixed up Maggie's knees, and beasts listen to you when you tell them not to wander off.'

'Yes, that's beast magic, but I don't have a *talent* for it. Look, every witch has two or three talents, things they're good at without half trying. Potions are one of mine, and I expect working with crystals will be one of yours. But a witch who sticks only to her talents will be pretty useless, and lacking talent in an area is no excuse not to get good at it.'

I nodded. 'All right. But you can undo it, right? You can turn him back?'

She gave a brief, humourless smile. 'Maybe. Depends. Put it out of your head for now, Dee. We've other matters to attend to first.'

By the time we neared the abbey, I'd caught my breath and was feeling mostly normal once again. The shining gates stood wide open, but nonetheless they were very imposing, made of stout beams and bound with bronze. *Why on earth do they need gates like this?* I thought, but I didn't ask the question aloud. My mistress had very little patience for what she considered stupid questions, which amounted to anything I could reasonably figure out myself.

The Haven was a place for women who needed shelter — presumably, those they needed shelter from would sometimes come looking for them. I wondered if they also had some way of signalling the fort, if they needed more defences than the gate and walls could provide.

Aleida guided Maggie through the gates, our wagon's roof nearly scraping against the stone.

Inside the walls was beautiful, even — my mind dredged up a word I'd first learned from the almanac, years ago, when I'd made one of my little sisters sit and read it out to me to keep her out of mischief — *idyllic*. It was full of greenery, with one side taken up by a huge garden with fruit trees growing in tight formation against the sun-drenched walls. Women and girls in wide-brimmed hats were tending rows upon rows of vegetables and herbs, with chickens and small children fossicking between them. To the other side was a pleasure-garden with rosebushes and neatly trimmed hedges, and even a patch of grass. Scattered through that garden were more folk, reading or spinning or sewing in the sunlight, including a little cluster in the shade of a tree, apparently taking a lesson from an older woman in a nun's habit.

But the sight that most caught my eye was a girl about my age, wearing skirts in a deep red hue and with blonde hair in a braid hanging over one shoulder. In her hands she held a bare-bladed sword, and she moved with fluid grace through a pattern of moves, some kind of training sequence, it seemed, first to one side and then the other.

I realised I was staring at her, and hastily looked away, though I kept watching from the corner of my eye. The girl had seen us, too, though she finished her set of moves before unhurriedly sheathing her sword.

A nun had noticed our arrival and came striding over from the garden, wiping her hands on her apron, while Aleida slipped gingerly from the footboard to the ground. She'd found her staff from inside the wagon while I'd been busy with Maggie, and she leaned heavily upon it to keep her balance.

'Well now,' said the nun, and though her clothes and boots were clearly country-quality and working class, her voice and her accent were anything but. It wasn't quite a city accent, either, though. I remembered what Aleida had said about nuns, and realised this woman was probably noble-born.

Once she was within a dozen feet of us, she stopped dead in her tracks, and her eyes narrowed as she looked my teacher up and down. I saw her eyes take in the wand at Aleida's belt and the dagger at her opposite hip. She'd cast a charm on them, so most folk didn't even notice them unless they had a touch of power. Like this woman clearly did. '*Well*,' the nun said again. 'I was about to say, you don't look like the usual sort of waif who turns up on our threshold.'

Aleida gave her a cool smile, and kept both hands on the staff. 'No,' she said. 'I don't suppose I do.'

The nun drew herself up straight. She was a tall woman, and solid, her face and hands deeply lined. 'What business do you have here, Mistress …?'

Aleida looked around. There was another nun coming towards us from the abbey's western wing, I noticed, and the one giving the lesson in the garden had passed her book to another lass and was heading our way too. The lass with the sword was standing with her arms crossed, watching the whole affair, but she was looking quite baffled by what was going on.

Aleida turned back to the nun. 'Perhaps we could just leave it as "Mistress", for the moment,' she said. 'But I promise I don't mean any harm.'

The nun gave her a measuring look, while the other two hurried to her side. 'Mother Ellendene,' one of them said, breathlessly, but the nun raised her hand to silence her. 'Will you swear it?' she said to Aleida.

'By the Lord and Lady, I swear I mean no harm to you and yours,' Aleida said.

'Then what brings you here?' one of the other sisters demanded, a tiny woman barely five feet tall. Behind them, the girl with the sword inched closer, but there was something odd about her posture.

After a moment I realised what it was. There was nothing defensive about the way she held herself, nothing protective towards the three aged women who'd come to meet my mistress. There was curiosity, yes, but aside from that she seemed … neutral.

One of the nuns glanced back to see her, too, and then shifted her position slightly as though to keep her in view as well as us. At that shift in attention, the girl stopped her approach, though she was unashamedly listening in.

'I've heard about this place,' Aleida said. 'I've heard you're doing a fine thing. I just wanted to see it for myself.

And if I like what I see, perhaps make a contribution to your efforts.'

'A contribution?' the small nun said. 'What sort of contribution?'

Aleida raised a sardonic eyebrow and glanced back at our wagon. 'Well, in my experience a nice pile of gold is always welcome.'

The small nun started to say something, but Mother Ellendene laid a calloused hand on her shoulder. 'Hush, Sister Lodova. She's telling the truth, she means no harm.'

'She's a witch,' Sister Lodova hissed.

'I know, my dear. I've met a few in my time. But magic isn't forbidden anymore, you know that as well as I do.'

'But that's not all.' The small sister leaned close, whispering something to the mother superior. I caught just a hint of the words, but that hint was enough. *She's cursed.*

'It's true,' Aleida said with a shrug. 'But that has nothing to do with why I'm here.'

Mother Ellendene lifted her chin.

'Mother Superior!' the little nun hissed again.

'Hush, sister! Haven't we sworn to take in any woman who stands in need of shelter?'

Aleida straightened at that, frowning. 'I didn't come here to buy any favours.'

'Good,' Mother Ellendene said. 'Because that sort of thing can't be bought with gold. Many other things can, though, which would make a great difference to the lives of our girls. Why don't you come inside, mistress. Come to my solar for a nice cup of tea and, as you say, see the place for yourself.'

The mother superior summoned a young lass to show me to the stables with Maggie and the wagon. I followed the shy young girl around the courtyard to the stable at the rear, which was deserted as far as I could see, empty but for an old wagon tucked in one corner. Aleida disappeared with the nuns after telling me to come find her once Maggie was settled in. At the stable, the girl vanished as well, leaving me quite alone. The place was eerie without the noise and warmth of horses and workers and dogs, the stalls all swept clean and the windows shuttered. But then I thought of the scorn my mistress would heap on me for admitting such a thing. *No, no, Dee*, she'd say. *You've got it all backwards. You're a witch, if anything about the situation is eerie and unsettling, it ought to be* you.

Still, Aleida had looked a little disconcerted herself, surprised that they'd so easily seen the curse she carried. Normally nothing ruffled her feathers, and part of me was curious to see what else they could read from her. Another part was rather worried as to how she'd react.

'Nice rig you've got there,' a voice said behind me, and I just about jumped out of my skin with surprise.

Leaning against the arched entrance to the stable was the girl from the garden, with her sword at her side and her long blonde braid over her shoulder. Her face was tanned, and the way she stood, with a thumb hooked into her sword-belt, would have earned me a clip 'round the ear back at Burswood Farm. I could just hear Ma's voice in my ear. *You look like a boy, Elodie, slouching like that. What will people think?*

'You're not here to stay, surely, with a set-up like that,' the lass said, nodding at Maggie and the wagon.

'Probably not,' I said, trying to shove Ma's voice from my mind. 'My mistress doesn't like to be beholden to other folk.'

'Someone after my own heart, then,' the girl said with a cool smile. 'So what does bring you here, if you're not another waif and stray, seeking the Lord and Lady's protection?'

I gave a shrug. 'It's my mistress's business,' I said. 'Not for me to say.'

She grimaced, looking chagrined. 'Apologies, I didn't mean to pry. It's just ... you and your mistress are the most interesting thing I've seen in weeks.'

I set about unhitching the traces again, and put out some grain for Maggie.

'Do you need a hand at all?' she said.

'I need water for the mare, could you show me to the well?'

'Sure, come with me. But are you sure it's safe to leave your wagon back there? A few of the girls here have some light fingers, I'll tell you.'

'It'll be fine,' I said with confidence. 'No one can get in without me or Aleida to open the door. I'm Dee, by the way.'

The girl clapped a hand to her forehead. 'Oh Lord and Lady, I'm such a savage, that's what Da always calls me. I'm Kara.'

She offered me her hand to shake, just like a man would, and with a laugh I took it. 'Pleased to meet you.'

'Likewise,' she said, and as she guided me back out into the courtyard I noticed her watching me from the corner of her eye.

'What?' I said.

'I heard what the nuns said, about your mistress. Is it true?'

'Is what true?' I said, playing dumb.

She gave me a mock scowl. 'Is she really a witch?'

I bit the inside of my cheek. I wasn't supposed to tell people ... but she'd heard enough that there wasn't any point denying it. 'Would you believe me if I said otherwise?'

She eyed me up and down. 'Huh. And what about you? Are you a witch too?'

I felt the weight of the belt on my hips, and the wand against my thigh. Aleida would say something tart, like *No, the wand's just for decoration.* But I couldn't bring myself to do the same. 'Not really,' I said. 'Not yet. I'm just learning.'

'Oh,' she said, and raised her face to the sky with a wistful look. 'It's got to be nice, though. I mean, you may be just an apprentice now, but one day, you'll be free to do whatever you want, go wherever you want. Free as a bird.' The longing in her voice made me remember how I'd felt, months ago, leaving home to head towards the mountains and Black Oak Cottage, not that I'd had any idea what lay in wait for me.

'So why are you here?' I said. 'You don't look like you need this place, either.'

She gave a bitter sigh and stopped, arms folded across her chest. 'You're right. I don't. We've got our own place, up in the hills; me and my da. He has to go away for work a lot, so he gave me this sword and taught me how to use it. I'm not like these other poor girls, getting beaten up by their husbands or running away from their pimps in the big cities.'

'So why are you here?' I said again.

Kara looked up at me from under furrowed brows, her eyes green against her sun-browned skin. 'Something's happened to my da,' she said. 'He goes away for work, see, but he should have been back a while ago. It happens sometimes, he gets another job right after the first one finishes, but he usually sends me word. I came to town for a few supplies and asked around to see if anyone had heard of him ... well, Lord Belmont's wretched busybody of a castellan caught wind of it and decided it's not right for a young lass to be living out in the woods by herself. Never mind the fact that I've been bloody well looking after myself since I was twelve, or that my da's missing and no one's heard of him in months, no. Next thing I knew, that brown-nosing son of a bitch was dragging me through the gates here and yelling for madame bloody superior. I've been told to stay here and let the menfolk handle it, or else.'

'Oh, Lord and Lady,' I said. 'And what about your da?'

'They don't care,' she said, voice dripping with bitterness. 'He's a caravan guard, you see. To folk like that, he's worth nothing. But he's all I have in the world.'

I bit my lip, thinking of the father I barely remembered, thinking of my ma. If she was lost, wouldn't I do everything I could to find her? 'Let me talk to my mistress,' I said. 'Maybe we can help.'

I was tense with anger at Kara's plight when I found my way to the mother superior's solar. What I saw when I reached it did nothing to soothe my temper.

Aleida was lounging on a cushioned couch with a delicate porcelain cup in one hand. The mother superior sat opposite, and if she wasn't exactly lounging she did look entirely comfortable and at home — more so than the other two sisters, who sat perched rather stiffly side by side. The room was quite lovely, a wide space with huge doors that stood open in the fine day, looking onto the pleasure garden.

'Oh, there you are, Dee,' Aleida said, and patted the cushion beside her, beckoning me to sit. 'I was wondering where you'd got to.'

'Beg your pardon,' I said. 'I got caught up talking with one of the girls.' The cushions were made of plum-coloured velvet, but the pile of the cloth had worn away, leaving them threadbare and tattered. Part of me hesitated to park my behind on this rich-looking furniture, but my teacher had told me to sit, so sit I did.

Aleida waved her cup in my direction. 'Tea, Dee?'

There was a teapot and a spare cup waiting on a tray on the little table between the couches. As soon as I picked up the cup I regretted it. The porcelain seemed as thin as eggshell, and I immediately worried that I'd crush it in my work-roughened hands.

'So where were we?' Mother Ellendene said. 'Ah yes, as I was saying, Belly is an old friend of mine, and after our troubles with that pillock of an archbishop, he offered us the abbey.'

'Belly?' Aleida said.

'Lord Belmont,' Sister Lodova said with a reproving glance at the mother superior.

'Yes, Belly,' Mother Ellendene said. 'We were childhood friends, you see, he was fostered with my family when we were little. Lovely chap, salt of the earth. Fortunately, the Lord and Lady have bestowed upon us a circle of friends like no other, and we were able to get ourselves set up out here, where we have far more opportunities for the lasses to get back on their feet and learn a trade while they figure out what to do next.'

'It must make it harder for folks to make it to your gates, though.'

'It does, unfortunately, but Lord Belmont has aided us in that respect too, as have Lady Morewind and her new husband. Thanks to them, any merchant or traveller who helps one of our ladies along their way can receive a bounty or tax concession for their service.'

'They still have to brave the bandits, though,' Aleida said.

'Unfortunately,' said Mother Ellendene with a grimace. 'Though I understand Belly has plans to do something about them, very soon. I'll admit I pray daily for his success; those dogs have fair terrorised some of our girls.'

'Can I ask a question?' I said. The two sisters perched together like hens on a roost gave me a startled look. Aleida rolled her head my way with a look that seemed to wonder what had taken me so long.

'Of course you may, child,' Mother Ellendene said.

'What if one of the women wishes to leave?'

She cocked her head to study me. 'When one of our ladies is ready to leave we have a working-bee to set her up for her new life, rather like a trousseau for a lass getting married — clothing and shoes for herself and her children, bedding and household goods — or money to buy them if she's travelling to somewhere else. Since we've settled here in Belmont the village women have taken to joining us in the work.'

'What happens if they want to leave before you think they're ready?' Aleida asked. 'Or when their husbands or pimps come looking for them?'

'Well, it's not just men who try to talk them into going back home, I hope you realise,' the mother superior said. 'We've had grandmothers and mothers and all kinds of kin turn up weeping at our gates, promising the earth and the moon. Whenever the lowest rung on the ladder breaks another one has to take the weight, you see. It really upsets the applecart.

'But when someone comes pounding on our gates demanding their little dove come home, I usually speak to them myself. They can curse and bluster at me all they like, I don't care, and the waterworks don't do anything for me either; the Lord and Lady have granted me the grace to see the truth behind their lies. And most of them have better sense than to raise a hand to an old nun. If they make more trouble, or if they hang around for more than a few days, Lord Belmont sends some men down to move them along. If the girls want to meet with their kin they can, but we won't let them be alone together. If they do wish to leave after the meeting I encourage them to pray for guidance. I spend the night in vigil with them, and ask them to reflect on what brought them here, and the lengths they went to in order to reach safety. I do manipulate them, I admit, but it's for the best.'

'And if they still want to leave?' I said. At my tone Aleida turned towards me, one eyebrow raised.

Mother Ellendene looked me over with a cool gaze. 'You've been talking to Kara, haven't you, child? She's very adept at spinning a tale, and at painting herself the innocent young girl who's been wronged most cruelly.'

'Kara?' Aleida said. 'Is that the lass with the sword?'

'That's her. I imagine she told you quite a story, Miss ...?' she let her voice drift away, and her gaze glided back to Aleida. 'I think it might be time for you to tell us who *you* are, and just what it is you're seeking here.'

Aleida drained her tea, and set the cup on the table. 'I suppose it is. But there's not much to the tale. I have some money to dispose of, and I'd like to see it do some good.'

'Dispose of?' Sister Lodova said, raising one eyebrow. 'Dirty money, is it?'

Aleida hesitated. 'You might say that.'

'Just how dirty are we talking?' Mother Ellendene said. 'Is it cursed? Like you?'

My teacher shifted in her seat, edging forward, gathering her feet beneath her. Taking my cue, I set my cup down. I wasn't sure what was going on here, but I could see that she was gathering herself. 'Not directly,' she said. 'Just ... tainted.'

Ellendene and Lodova exchanged a worried glance. 'I think we'd like to have a little more information. If you please, Mistress ...?'

Aleida sighed. 'Blackbone. My name is Blackbone. Does that mean anything to you?'

Another drawn-out silence, another significant glance. 'I've heard that name,' Mother Ellendene said, slowly. 'Is anyone going to come looking for this money?'

'Nope,' Aleida said. 'It's all mine. An inheritance, shall we say.'

Mother Ellendene frowned. She squinted at Aleida, and then leaned back, pinching the bridge of her nose as though her head pained her. 'So the old Blackbone witch ...'

'She's dead.' Aleida said. 'Took a bit of doing, I might tell you.'

'I see. So the curse ...'

Aleida shrugged and leaned back again. 'I came by it honestly.'

Sister Lodova huffed derisively, but I studied the mother superior, wondering exactly what she'd seen. The money had been Gyssha's, before my teacher had killed her. In her last act, Gyssha had cursed Aleida, her traitorous daughter in the craft. A death-curse was nothing to sneeze at, especially from a witch as powerful as Gyssha Blackbone.

'And this money,' Sister Lodova said. 'What do you expect in return, exactly?'

Aleida straightened again. 'I expect it to be used wisely.'

'For yourself,' Lodova said, her face drawn tight. 'What do you expect for yourself? I do know the name Blackbone. Your mother is dead, you say? I'm glad she can do no more harm, but if you are who you say you are, you've no small amount of blood on your hands too.'

'I'm not asking for any favours,' Aleida snapped. 'I'll solve my own problems, thank you very much.'

'Sister,' Mother Ellendene said, her voice quiet. 'Hush. It is not for us to pass judgement on the women who come to our haven.'

'But she—'

'We pledged, did we not, never to turn away a woman who seeks healing? Who seeks to turn away from a life of pain and suffering and find a new path? Didn't we, sister?'

Lodova's face looked like a thunderstorm. But she folded her hands in her lap and drew a deep breath. 'Indeed, we did, Mother Ellendene. True, it wouldn't be the first time dirty money has come into our hands, and it likely won't be the last. If you see fit to make a gift, Mistress Blackbone, it will be received with gratitude. And prayers for your soul.'

'Well then,' Aleida said, in the sort of voice that would make me choose my words with added care. 'I daresay those will come in handy.'

'But what about Kara?' I said. It felt like talking out of turn, but I wasn't about to let her be swept aside so easily.

Mother Ellendene turned my way with her mouth pursed. 'Miss Blackbone, is it?'

'It is,' Aleida said, before I could speak. 'My apprentice. She's still very green, though.'

I glared at her, but I couldn't really argue. 'Kara,' I said, instead. 'She says you won't let her leave. That's rather at odds with everything you've said, isn't it?'

Aleida gave me a look I read as amusement. In truth I half-expected her to tell me to drop it, but she held her tongue while the mother superior looked me over. I was braced for scorn, expecting her disapproval over daring to question her. But there was no rancour in her gaze. 'Well, miss,' she said. 'I'm not in the habit of gossiping about our girls, but Kara is a special case. I imagine she told you quite a tale, didn't she? Perhaps you would repeat it, so your mistress knows of what we speak?'

Now, I'm not completely dim. I realised I must have made something of a misstep, and felt a flush creep over my cheeks. 'She said her father is missing,' I said. 'No one will help her look for him, and she's being held here against her will.'

'I see,' Mother Ellendene said. 'And what did she tell you about her father?'

There was something pointed about the question, and immediately I felt on edge, worried I was about to be tripped up. 'He's ... he's a caravan guard,' I said.

Aleida shifted and gave a small sigh.

I turned to her. 'What?'

'Dee, what do caravan guards do when they can't get work?'

I gave her a puzzled look.

'Think about it. They know the roads, they know the blind corners and secluded stretches, the watering holes and the best places to stop. And the merchants. Caravan guards bleed and die so the merchants don't have to, and they get paid a pittance. And when there's no work and mouths to feed at home, what are they going to do?'

'Of course, you'd understand how it works,' Sister Lodova said with disdain.

I ignored her. 'I don't see ...'

'Dee, the caravan guards make their living off the merchants, one way or another. At heart it's a protection racket; the mercenaries are getting paid whether the merchants hand it over willingly or at a sword's point.'

I felt myself blink a few times, absorbing the words. 'You're saying her father's a bandit?'

'Probably. She'll never admit it, though.'

'That's the conclusion we've come to, as well,' Mother Ellendene said. 'Belly — Lord Belmont, I mean — agrees. Left to her own devices, I've no doubt Kara would head out in search of him, and those woods are no place for a lass of sixteen.'

'But she's got her sword,' I said, glancing at Aleida. 'And it looks like she knows how to use it.'

She shook her head. 'She'd have to sleep sometime, have to find food, water ... Wouldn't take long for those bandits to get wind of her and track her down. It's no place for a young girl alone.'

'Which is precisely why Lord Belmont had her brought here,' Mother Ellendene said. 'It was that or keep her shackled in the dungeons under the fort, which is hardly suitable for a young girl either, I'm sure you can agree. If I had my druthers, she'd have had that sword taken away from her, too, but we were afraid she'd do something drastic if we forced her to give it up. She even sleeps with the thing, keeping her hand wrapped around the hilt. She's a tough little nut, I'll grant you that.'

I frowned, rubbing my forehead. 'What makes you so sure she isn't telling the truth about her father?'

Mother Ellendene cast a grimace Aleida's way.

My teacher sighed. 'I did say she was green.'

'So you did. I know a lie when I hear one, child,' she said to me. 'It's one of the graces the Lord and Lady have bestowed on me.'

I just scowled. 'All right. So it's not safe out there for her alone. What if she wasn't alone?'

Aleida slid a foot towards me and kicked me sharply in the shin.

'Ow!'

'Dee,' she growled. 'At least let me talk to the girl myself before you start making grand plans, would you? I came here to offload some of Gyssha's damn blood money, not to start collecting waifs and strays.'

'So you're not going to help her? Ow!' I yelped as she kicked me again.

'Kindly don't put words in my mouth.'

Mother Ellendene was watching us both with disapproval. 'Clearly I can't stop you from taking the lass out of here, if that's what you choose to do.'

'Good grief,' Aleida said, 'do I look like I'm in the habit of making a rod for my own back? Well ...' she amended, casting a glance my way. '... actually, I can see why you'd say that.'

I opened my mouth to protest, only to hurriedly clamp it shut again when I saw the look in Aleida's eye. I'd gone about this all wrong, I realised, bringing it up in front of the nuns. From the way she squinted at me I could guess I was going to hear all about it later.

Once she could see the message had sunk in, Aleida's eyes cut back to the mother superior. 'Do you want any help with the girl?'

'I have the matter well in hand,' Mother Ellendene said, with the same breezy superiority I'd heard so often from my own teacher. 'But you're welcome to have a word with her, if you wish. Will you and your apprentice be staying with us tonight? You're quite welcome; I can have some of the girls prepare a room for you.' Sister Lodova looked quite scandalised at the suggestion.

'That won't be necessary,' Aleida said. 'We have some other business to attend to.'

'Well then,' the nun said, rising from the couch. She was quite sprightly, despite her age, heaving herself up with little trouble. 'Let's take a turn around the place, and you can see where your money would be going.'

Aleida all but ignored me as the nuns showed us around the grounds. For my part, I tried not to dwell on how deeply I'd put my foot in it. My new friend Kara was nowhere to be seen, and for that I felt rather chagrined. I'd liked her, following our brief exchange, and I wasn't sure I could just accept Aleida's pronouncement that Kara was lying through her teeth — she hadn't so much as spoken a word to the girl, after all. The question was answered when we returned to the wagon — Kara was in the stable, leaning against the wall with her arms folded across her chest, her face like stone.

'Kara,' Sister Lodova said with reproval. 'Aren't you rostered to work in the garden today?'

'Workers get paid,' Kara said. 'But if you feel that I'm not earning my keep, Sister Sourpuss, you can always evict me.'

Aleida looked away to hide a smile. 'Come with me, Dee,' she said. 'I'm going to need your help to lift this blessed thing down.'

She clambered up to the footboard ahead of me — and then stopped, running her fingertips over the door.

The hesitation made me look up. 'What is it?' I murmured.

She tapped her fingertip to a spot beside the lock, and a sigil marked upon the wood gleamed faintly in the darkness. Then, without another word, she opened the door and beckoned me inside.

Within the wagon, she lit a hanging lantern with a touch of her finger. 'Someone tried to get inside and set off one of the wards. Would have made a nice little flash.'

'You didn't feel it?' I said.

'Pfft, no. There was no power in the effort. I'm guessing they tried to pick the lock. Here, help me get this chest out, would you?'

Our wagon was rather nice inside, if I might say so myself. There was a little wood stove and a cabinet that latched closed firmly against the rocking and bumping of rutted roads. A bench seat along one wall also served as a storage chest, while a panel halfway along folded down to make a little table, or, more often, a writing desk. At the end opposite the door was a narrow bed, with a second tucked away underneath rather like the box bed back home at the cottage. But, at the moment, the lower bed was packed full of crates and baskets and chests. I made my bed on the floor instead, on a pad of felted wool.

The lower bed could be screened off with a sliding hatch, and Aleida slid it back to start hauling things out while I stacked them up as best I could in the narrow space. 'You think it was Kara.'

'I said no such thing.'

'But you were thinking it, weren't you?'

Aleida shrugged. 'And what do *you* think?'

With a sniff, I declined to answer, but she'd already moved on. 'Ah, here it is ... oh good gods, I can barely move the thing.'

'Let me get it,' I said. 'You're still naught but skin and bone. You don't eat enough.'

'Yeah, yeah, what are you, my mother?' Still, she shuffled back out of the way to let me reach into the cramped space. I didn't mind sacrificing the space to storage. I was afraid that if I did try to sleep in there I'd have nightmares of suffocating — and then thump my head against the roof when the bad dreams woke me up.

'But seriously, Dee,' Aleida said as I wriggled in to get a grip on the heavy chest. 'What do think of the place? How do you like it?'

'It seems nice,' I said. 'Peaceful, you know?'

'Mm. Could you have ended up somewhere like here, do you think?'

My head buried in the musty darkness, I paused. 'What? Lord and Lady, no. It's not for me — for the me I was before I met you, I mean. It's for the girls who are really mistreated, who are beaten and worked half to death and kept like prisoners, or worse.' Dragging the trunk across the scarred floorboards, I inched my way out again into fresher air. 'If that bastard Lem had taken to beating me, or tried to get me married off, then maybe. If I knew about it, and could figure some way to get here ...' Just thinking of the obstacles on that path was overwhelming. How would you even begin? 'What about you?' I said.

She laughed at that. 'Never in a thousand years. I'd sooner have died than let myself be taken off to the countryside. But then, I was like you — I hadn't yet been tipped out of the frying pan and into the fire. There's plenty of folks who don't have such luck. Compared to the path I was on before Gyssha found me, a place like this would have done me a world of good.'

I bit my lip then. There were words hovering on the tip of my tongue, but I didn't let them spill. *If you had to choose, which would it be? The nuns? Or Gyssha?* I fancied I already knew the answer. As much as she scorned her old mistress, Aleida loved witchcraft too much to choose a different path. 'I guess it's a godsend for those who need it,' I said. 'But what about those who'd rather be elsewhere? A pretty prison is still a prison.'

'Mm. All right, fine, I'll have a word with our lost little lamb out there.'

The trunk was small, but it was cursed heavy. I had to heave it little by little to the footboard, and then Sister Lodova helped me the rest of the way. She lifted it more easily, though she still grunted at its weight.

It was only a fraction of Gyssha's hoard, but I was still glad to see it go. Back at Black Oak, I'd glimpsed a little of what Gyssha had done to get hold of all that gold. There was not a piece of it that hadn't been tainted with blood and suffering and despair. Maybe now some good would come of it. Not enough to wash away the evil that had been done but it was a start.

While the nuns dealt with their bounty, Aleida beckoned me with a jerk of her head and turned towards Kara, who was still glowering against the far wall. 'Hey, girl,' she called, starting over. 'C'mere.' She was limping again, I noticed. She'd spent too long on her feet.

From the look on her face Kara didn't care for the summons, but she squared her shoulders and came over, anyway. 'Yes, miss?'

Aleida hooked her thumb into her belt while she studied the girl. 'So,' she said. 'You found that door a bit trickier than you expected, did you?'

Kara scowled. 'I don't know what you're talking about.'

'Yeah, you do. Just as well, kid, messing with anything inside would have been worse. Did it burn you? Or just scorch your sleeve?'

Kara pulled her sleeves down over her hands. 'Look,' she said, eyes sliding away. 'I just want to get out of here. I need to find my da.'

'You think he's in trouble?'

Hesitantly, Kara glanced up to meet Aleida's eyes. 'I know it.'

'How?'

Kara huffed an impatient sigh. 'I just do.'

'All right,' Aleida said. 'But he's not really a caravan guard, is he?'

Kara's eyes snapped to hers, and she lifted her chin defiantly. 'He is.'

'Pays well, does it?'

'We get by,' Kara said, guardedly.

'Enough to buy that sword you're carrying? It's good quality.'

'He got a bonus,' Kara said. 'For saving a rich merchant's life. And he bought it for me because he's gone so often, he wanted me to be able to defend myself.'

'I can see that. But listen, kid. Caravan guards don't often live to be old men. If he was killed on the road, would anyone think to send you a message?'

'He's not dead,' Kara said, clenching her jaw.

'How can you be sure?'

'I just know, all right?'

Aleida tilted her head to one side. 'You're very certain, I'll grant you that. But that doesn't mean it's true. So how do you know? Another feeling?'

Kara glowered under furrowed brows. 'You wouldn't understand.'

'I'm a witch. Try me.'

She looked away with a sigh of exasperation. 'I always worried that he'd die out there on the road somewhere and I wouldn't know. So he promised me, if that ever happened, he'd come to tell me. He'd send his ghost. And he hasn't done it, so I know he's still alive. And if you laugh at me, I'm going to knock your block off, all right?'

'I'm not laughing. I believe you. Trust me, stranger things have happened. Look, if you want me to take a chance on you, you're going to have to come clean. Tell me the truth.'

'I'm not lying,' Kara growled. 'He's a caravan guard. And if you get me out of here, I swear I won't give you an ounce of trouble. You won't even know I'm there.'

'Yeah, because you'll have made a runner before the sun's even set, won't you? Maybe your father was a caravan guard once upon a time, I can tell there's a hint of truth in there, but not anymore. Listen, kid, I'm not going to stick my neck out for some little girl who hasn't enough sense not to lie to a witch.'

'Oh, screw you,' Kara spat. She looked near to tears. 'You're just as bad as those toffee-nosed nuns! You think you're so much better than me? You wouldn't stand to be locked up in a place like this, would you? You'd tear down these godsdamned walls in a heartbeat if they tried! All I want is to help my father, and all any of you arseholes will do is pat me on the head and tell me to get on with my sewing! What would you do if it was *your* father missing?'

'Well,' said Aleida. 'For one thing I'd try telling the truth to the one person who's sincerely trying to help me.'

Kara pressed her lips tight together and glared at her.

'Aleida,' I whispered, and then winced. My voice came out sounding more like a plea than I ever intended. I felt halfway to tears myself. I could barely remember my father, he'd died when I was just a little girl, but if it was him out there I'd do just about anything to help him.

Kara stepped back, arms crossed, glaring at Aleida. 'Fine,' she said. 'Go then, I don't care. I don't need your help.' She turned on her heel and stalked off, cursing and muttering to herself.

I watched her go, my stomach in knots. 'We can't just leave her here, surely?'

'We can and we will. Look, Dee, if she had the sense to tell me the truth, I might have worked something out, but if she's just going to lie and lie and keep lying ... I'm not taking that on. It's just asking for trouble. Go and get the mare ready, would you? It's time to move on.'

I sank into a black mood as Maggie plodded away from the village and the abbey, back towards the forest. I chewed on my lower lip while my fingertips toyed with the tip of the wand at my belt. I didn't let myself look back at the abbey, but I couldn't help but wonder what Kara would be doing there now, or what it would feel like to be trapped inside those walls, knowing my father was out there somewhere, needing help, and no one cared but me.

I sighed through gritted teeth, shifting on the wooden board. 'Why didn't you make her tell the truth?'

'What good would that do?' Aleida said.

'But what makes you so cursed sure he's not a caravan guard?'

'Because I could tell she was lying,' Aleida said.

'If you already knew, then what does it matter that she wasn't telling the truth? Her father's still out there, he still needs help. He's still all the family she has in the world.'

'He's a bandit, Dee. He's spent most of his life stealing from people, and for all we know killing them as well. Say we did go and find him, what then? He'd go back to robbing people on the roads, and sooner or later someone's getting killed.'

'But you don't know that.' I protested.

She cut me off with a look. 'Yeah. I do.'

'But—'

'*Dee.* Don't tell me what I don't know.'

'Fine,' I snapped. 'So you expect her to just, what? Give up on him? Her own father?'

'I don't expect her to do any such thing. It doesn't change the fact that she's better off without him.'

That small handful of words brought a sudden flash of anger sweeping through me like a spark in dry grass. My fingers, still fiddling with the tip of my wand, flared with rushing heat, and I felt my wand spark up with a flash of searing rage.

Beside me, Aleida jumped and pulled away with a yelp that turned into a laugh. 'Oh, you got some real heat that time. Well done, Dee.'

I was too angry to take the compliment, and too angry to apologise. 'How can you say that? Don't you have—' I broke off, then, at the last minute thinking better of what I was about to say.

'Don't I have what?' She tossed her head, and I realised she knew perfectly well the words I'd left unspoken. 'Don't I have a father?' But of course she didn't, I knew that. Her mother was a prostitute, her father could have been anybody.

'If you did, maybe you'd have a little more sympathy,' I shot back.

She turned to me with a cool gaze. 'Maybe,' she said. 'Maybe not. She's still better off cutting her losses and moving on.'

'How can you be so cold?' I demanded. 'How can you say something like that? How did you feel when you went back to Stone Harbour to look for your kin, and found them all gone? Are you telling me that didn't hurt at all?'

'Sure it did — like pulling a rotten tooth. Better to get it over with than let it poison you slowly. Besides, it's not like she has any choice in the matter, is it? Whatever trouble her father is in, I'm betting one young lass alone won't be enough to solve it, sword or not.'

'Not if no one will help her.'

'And what if we did? Would we just turn him loose afterwards to keep attacking people on the road? Or do we deliver him to Lord Belmont's bailiff to be hanged? There's no future for her there. Besides, I have an idea what might have happened to him.'

'You what?' I said, my voice climbing.

She gave me an exasperated look. 'Dee, you need to take a step back and breathe for a minute. Stop imagining it's *your* father lost out there, and *think*.'

I frowned at her, equal parts puzzled and cross. 'If you're going to make me guess, we're going to be here a long time.'

She huffed an impatient sigh. 'The horse, remember? If there's one man turned into a beast there might well be others. Add those griffins to the equation too ... There's something going on here, I just don't know what.' She leaned back against the wall, holding the reins lazily in one hand. 'Oh, and come to think of it, I did see him once. My father, I mean.'

I pressed my fingertips to my temples, wincing. If she kept this up, swinging rapidly from one matter to the next without a breath in between, I was going to get a headache. 'You did? Did you talk to him? What was he like?'

She gave me a sidelong glance, as though dubious at my sudden enthusiasm. 'Oh, I never met him. My sister pointed him out to me one time. Well, they all thought he was my father. He had black hair, and skin like mine, and he'd always come and see Ma when he was in Stone Harbour. He was a sailor from Borraqis, you see.'

'Oh,' I said. 'That's ... quite sweet, actually. He must have really liked her.'

Aleida chuckled. 'Or maybe she was cheap. But they'd stay out all night drinking, so they must have been having some fun. Ma didn't want him knowing about me, though. If he'd been a local fellow it'd be different, she could have used me to wring money out of him for guilt, but a sailor can always find a different girl to take his coin.'

'You weren't ever tempted to sneak off and meet him?'

'Gods, no. There were all kinds of tales about what happened to girls who did that. I heard of one girl who got taken away to live with her father's family but since she was a whore's get she had to be their servant and spent all her days sweeping out fireplaces and scrubbing chamber-pots. You can bet Ma made sure we all knew that story.'

That was pretty much my life before I'd come to Aleida, so long as you added in changing babies' napkins and washing them out, too. 'It's not that bad,' I said with a sniff. 'At least no one tried to make me be a whore.'

'Well, true. But I was a wild little thing already, picking pockets all day and all night too, stealing anything not nailed down. I wasn't taking any chances of being chained to a sink and a scrubbing brush.' She turned to me then, with a measuring gaze. 'You were quite taken with her, though, weren't you? Kara, I mean.'

It took me a moment to bring myself to nod. Back at Burswood Farm my stepfather would have carried on all night about how I'd fallen for the girl's lies. I had to remind myself, sometimes, that for all Aleida's short temper and sharp tongue, she wasn't mean like Lem was. 'She just looked so ... fierce. With those divided skirts and her hair braided and that red tassel on the hilt of her sword. She looked like something out of a storybook. And when she came over to talk to me she was just so nice, but bold as brass, too. So interested in Maggie and the wagon and everything ...' I looked down at my feet, cursing myself. Of course she was interested. She'd been hoping she'd be able to ride away with us, or stow away in the wagon. 'She was like you. Walking around as though she owns the world. Like nothing can touch her.' But even as I said the words, I found myself wondering at them. It wasn't *true*, clearly. She was essentially a prisoner there in the abbey, but somehow that didn't make any difference to the air of freedom and independence that followed her like perfume.

Aleida was shaking her head. 'It's an act, Dee. Besides, you think she's untouchable? You've got far more power in you than she does.'

'But those bandits this morning—'

'If I hadn't jumped in you'd have found some way to handle them. And anyway, how do you think you looked to her?'

I looked down at my skirts, my worn boots peeking out from underneath. 'Umm ...'

'With your wand on one hip and your knife on the other, riding around in a traveller's wagon as an apprentice witch? You're not a scullery maid anymore, Dee. One day I'll get you to understand that.'

I was silent for a moment, thinking. 'It's so strange. Sometimes I feel like I hardly know myself. I feel like I'm living in a different world than the one I grew up in.'

'Well, you are,' Aleida said. 'There's no two ways about it.'

'Yeah,' I said. 'But you must be right about her. You're the one who can tell a lie when you hear it. I'm the damn fool who believed every word she said.'

'Mm,' she said, studying me with narrowed eyes. 'You know, you're probably about ready to learn.'

'Learn what?' I said, startled.

'How to recognise a lie. Here—' She pressed the reins into my hands. 'Take these. I'll be right back.'

She heaved herself up and staggered inside. I peered back to see her climb onto her bed and lift down her jewellery box from one of the overhead cabinets.

Something struck me then, an odd thought — after she'd run away from Gyssha, Aleida had gone back to her home at Stone Harbour to find her family, only to find them gone, vanished sometime in the ten years she'd been away. But that didn't seem right. They were her own flesh and blood, and she was a witch, after all. She could have found them if she'd really wanted to.

Aleida returned before I could follow that trail of thought any further. She sat heavily back on the footboard beside me, and passed me a ring.

Some of Aleida's jewellery was truly lovely but this was not one of those pieces. The plain silver band bore a stone of amethyst, but it wasn't cut or polished — it was just a chunk of raw stone, the tip of a crystal that had been broken off and held in place with a plain silver setting. I took it a little dubiously. 'How does it work?'

'Just put it on. You'll figure the rest out.'

I'd never worn a ring before. It felt strange and heavy on my finger. 'I'm still not happy about leaving her there like that.'

'You'll live,' Aleida said. 'And anyway, we've got bigger fish to fry. Kara is safe and sound where she is, but that poor sod stuck being a horse isn't, and his story has me curious.'

CHAPTER 3

At the edge of the forest, Aleida steered Maggie off the road and onto a swathe of grass between the fields and the woods. 'All right,' she said, reining in. 'We've got a bit of daylight left. You see to Maggie and get our fire going. I'm going to see if I can find our four-footed friend before the sun goes down.'

'Are you going borrowing?' I quickly asked. 'Can I help?'

'Not now, Dee. If I was just taking one beast to track him by scent, you could come along, but I'm going to have to move faster than that if I want to find him before the crows turn in to roost.'

I loved borrowing. Loved it. You can't imagine what it's like to swoop and dive like a swallow, to soar on warm, rising air like an eagle, or feel the explosive power of a horse's muscles as it leaps over fallen trees and streams. Back home at Black Oak Cottage I think I must have borrowed every animal within five miles, but birds were my favourite.

But I still couldn't do what Aleida could, which was jump from one beast to the next to find and follow the horse-man's trail, and then at the end of it find some way to communicate with the poor sod. That's why she wanted to find him before all the crows settled in for the night — crows can mimic a human voice and talk, after a fashion.

'Yes, miss,' I said with a sigh. 'Do you want me to set up the tent?'

She glanced around with a frown. 'It's not worth it. We won't be staying long.'

'Oh, I don't mind,' I said. 'It's nice to have the space.'

'All right then, if you want. I'll set myself up out on the grass, out of the way.'

She meant, so I wouldn't bother her with my fetching and carrying from the wagon. 'I'll fix us some dinner, too.'

'Keep it light,' she told me. 'We'll have some work to do once this fellow comes to find us.'

Slipping down from the wagon, Aleida hobbled a few dozen paces towards the forest and lay herself down on the grass, and with no fanfare at all, fell into a trance.

With a shrug and a sigh, I set about my chores.

We only slept in the wagon if the weather was bad, as a rule. It had everything we needed, but it was very cramped. If the weather was fair, we almost always camped outside. First came a frame of springy poles bent into a dome; and over that went colourful blankets with a waterproof oilcloth over the top, and another on the ground to keep the damp away. We had a little brazier for a fire and lanterns that hung from the roof beams, and colourful cushions to sit upon. It reminded me of a fortune-teller's tent I'd seen at the fair years and years ago. Aleida did tell fortunes, sometimes, but today the road was quiet and we were alone as the shadows grew long and the air became chill.

I lit the brazier, fetched water from a nearby stream and then stood outside the tent, watching darkness creep over the sky. And, as I often did in these quiet moments, I thought of my family back home, my ma and my little brothers and sisters. Just not my fat-headed stepfather. My next-oldest sister, Lucette, would be doing all my old work now, cooking and cleaning and mending at Ma's side. I wondered if she'd stopped complaining about it yet — it had only been three or four months since I'd come to Black Oak Cottage, so it was quite likely that she hadn't. I thought again of writing to them — I'd thought of it often over the last few months, ever since Aleida had started teaching me my letters. *But what would I tell them?* I asked myself. *That I'm learning to be a witch? That I'm travelling around the countryside in an old travellers' wagon, selling potions and charms? Tell them that I paid a ha'penny to see a stuffed griffin in a tavern?*

If I wrote any such thing, my stepfather would throw it into the fire in a fit of rage, without even reading it to the end. Mind you, he'd likely do the same if I wrote a letter full of boring, dreary lies.

With a sigh I shook myself, trying to put the thought out of my head, and went to check on my mistress.

She still lay in the long grass, fingers laced together and resting on her belly, and I settled down near her head.

There was no way of knowing where her mind was, or if she'd had any success in hunting down the tormented creature in the forest.

I hadn't been sitting there for long before I began to feel cold and damp. I hunched over my knees, gnawing on a thumbnail, looking out to the forest. It was growing darker by the moment, it seemed. The trees ahead of me made a wall of darkness and shadow.

The quiet stillness of dusk made the hair prickle on the back of my neck. I wasn't used to being alone, even at the cottage — if I wasn't working with my mistress she was still *there*, somewhere, and if she'd taken off our neighbours the Sanfords and my best friend Melly were only a mile or so away.

To be honest I didn't like to be alone back there, either. It hadn't bothered me at first, but then ... then I'd met a lad I'd really liked, with brown curls and freckles and a warm smile, but he was nothing but an illusion, and beneath the glamour of his pale, freckled skin and dancing brown eyes was a construct of green, mouldering bones and strands of glistening beads. He was built by Aleida's teacher, the old witch Gyssha, and I'd never have known if she hadn't let the illusion fall before using the thing to try and kill me.

I shivered in the evening chill. *I should probably go fetch her a rug,* I thought. If I was damp and cold, Aleida must be chilled to the bone.

Mother hen, she called me when I fussed over her, bringing her milk warmed with honey and spices on cold mornings, or her cloak when we were working late at night. She didn't understand — I'd spent most of my life looking after my little brothers and sisters, making sure they were warm and fed and happy. It was all I knew. Besides, she needed it. I'd never met anyone with a mind and will as strong as hers, but physically, she was rail-thin and quite weak. Frail, even.

I heaved myself up to go find a blanket, but when I stood, a flicker of movement overhead made me pause.

I stood still, head tipped back, gazing up at the dark sky. The patchy clouds from earlier in the day had thickened over the afternoon, and now there wasn't much starlight to be had.

It could have been a bird, I supposed. Not an owl, though, for it wasn't a flash of white I'd seen, but something much darker. A crow? At this hour? Aleida might keep one from its roost if she had a good reason to ... but why, when she could just come back to her body?

My searching eyes found nothing. *Just a trick of the eye,* I told myself.

I turned back towards the tent — just in time to see something dark swoop towards me out of the black sky. I glimpsed red eyes and long glistening teeth, and curved claws, each one as long as my finger, spread wide and ready to rake across my head.

With a shriek I threw myself down, flinging hands up to protect my head, while above me came a screech and the leathery flap of wings as the creature changed course and flapped away.

Hastily, I pushed myself up and snatched my wand and knife from my belt. 'Aleida!' I said, hoping she could hear me. You could, sometimes, when you were borrowing. It depended on how hard you were concentrating on the beast in your grip. 'Aleida, wake up!' I even nudged her with my toe, but then I had to turn my attention back to the sky.

On the far side of the wagon, I heard Maggie snort and stamp her foot — and then she gave a nicker of fright.

'Maggie!' I shouted, and started towards her — but after only a few paces I stopped again. I didn't dare leave Aleida here undefended.

Maggie snorted again, and then I heard the swishing of grass and the thudding of her huge feet, and she came trotting around the wagon towards me, ears flat against her head and her eyes showing their whites. There was a scratch on her neck, bleeding a thin trickle of blood, as black as ink in the dim light.

I was worried she'd trample Aleida, still lying prone in the grass, but I couldn't grab for her halter without dropping one of my weapons. Aleida still hadn't moved. 'Wake up!' I yelled again.

I heard the beast again, the leathery slap of wings, hidden in the darkness yet nerve-rackingly close — and then it landed with a *thump* on the roof of the wagon, and gave a screech that made me shudder and clench my teeth.

I'd heard a noise like that before. Months ago, when I'd first arrived at Black Oak Cottage, there'd been a … well, let's call it an incident, where someone opened a rift from our realm into another one, a realm of smoke and ash and fierce heat, and hunger and rage.

I clenched the handle of my wand so tight my knuckles ached. 'Well,' I said. '*You're* a nasty piece of work.'

The creature hissed as it clambered over the roof of the wagon. Its body was about the size of a large dog, with huge, leathery bat-like wings, tipped with claws that scraped and squeaked over the wood. It's face — it's whole body, actually, aside from those huge wings — put me in mind of a dog crossed with a monkey, though it had a long tail that lashed like a cat's, and huge eyes that gleamed faintly red. The fangs in its mouth were as long as a viper's. It clattered along the roof of the wagon and gave another shriek, a noise that made me want to clap my hands over my ears. Nothing in our world should make a sound like that.

It ranged back and forth along the roof of the wagon, its attention wavering between Aleida's still form in the grass and me, a few yards away. As it perched at the edge of the roof, gathering its haunches beneath it, I ran the few paces to my teacher's still form and raised my wand.

A spark of heat bloomed in my chest. It surged to my shoulder and down my arm, and the stone at the tip of the wand blazed with sudden light, blossoming to red and gold, a fireball that blazed through the air like a shooting star.

It struck just as the creature leapt, and with another shriek it twisted in the air, shying away so the fireball just grazed its shoulder instead of striking it full in the face.

I wasn't thinking; I was just *doing* — my arm swung again, again, with each one a fresh surge of heat through my chest and down my arm. 'Get out!' I heard my voice roar. 'Get out of here!'

As quickly as the creature ducked away from the first bolt, it climbed to evade the others. I'd borrowed bats, back home at Black Oak, I'd ridden with them while they hunted for insects at night. I'd seen for myself how dizzyingly agile they could be. For all its size, this beast ducked and weaved with ease, shrieking defiance as I sent more fireballs flying after it — until with one last screech it flapped away, climbing steeply upwards, and vanishing into the blackness of the night.

I stayed there, panting, breathing hard, heart thumping in my throat, not quite daring to believe it was gone, when a noise behind me made me jump almost out of my skin. I turned with a yelp, a fresh wave of heat setting my wand glowing again, to find Aleida heaving herself up.

She stretched, rolling her head to ease a stiff neck. 'Dee? What's going on?' Then she saw the wand in my hand, still smouldering with a spark at its heart, and frowned. 'All right, what'd I miss?'

My hands were shaking too much to cut the bread and cheese for our dinner, so Aleida did that while I told her about the bat-winged beast. 'It looked like the things that came out of the rift back at Lilsfield. I mean, not exactly like them, but the same sort of thing. It wasn't as big as the griffin we saw but it was still pretty damn big.'

Aleida just nodded along as she spread butter on the bread. 'But you saw it off, you said? With fireballs? Well done. See, I knew you could do it if it came to the crunch.'

She was completely calm about the whole thing, so much so that I had the sudden sickening thought that she was just humouring me. 'I really did see it,' I said with a lump in my throat. 'It was real, I swear it.'

She gave me an odd look. 'Dee. Of course you did. I believe you. I know those things are real.'

I gulped hard. 'Sorry. I just … while you were gone, I was thinking about back home at the farm. I was thinking about writing them a letter, and I realised they'd never believe a word of it. If I tried to tell them about that thing they'd probably say I imagined it, that it was just a regular bat and I got scared, or something stupid. They'd never believe what I saw.'

Aleida smiled to herself. 'There's a cure for that, you know. When you learn illusions, you can make one of the wretched things appear on the kitchen table. See how loud they argue with you then. Now, it didn't actually touch you, did it? Those things have some real venom if they bite.'

'No,' I said. 'There's just that scratch on Maggie's neck.'

'I saw that, it's nothing to worry about. I'll go put some salve on it, you try to settle your nerves. Have a bite to eat. I'd better cast some wards, too, I suppose. If it's alone it won't come back; but there's a chance it's got some friends nearby.'

'Friends?' I squeaked. 'How many of those things do you think are out there?'

'Oh, not any serious numbers,' she scoffed. 'Or we'd have heard about it back in the town — and those bandits who attacked us would be a scattering of bones out in the forest.' She passed me a wooden plate with bread, cheese and smoked sausage, and then picked up her staff to limp back outside.

Chewing a mouthful of crusty bread and sharp cheese, I followed her. 'But where did it come from?'

'You know where, Dee,' she cast over her shoulder, her voice sharp.

I cursed myself for asking a stupid question. 'I meant, why? How? Another ridiculous prank?'

'Ah, now you're asking the right questions. It could be, I suppose. But it's probably just an accident. Those things are like rats, they're always searching for food. Always scratching and picking and squirming. If there's a way through, they'll find it. But rifts never stay open for long.'

She'd talked about rifts before, since we'd had to clean up after the one back at Lilsfield. They could be made deliberately, but more often it was a side-effect of certain types of magic, just like an outbreak of dysentery could be a side-effect of a bad choice in digging a latrine pit. 'But ... did someone let it happen? The person who brought the griffins? The one who turned that fellow into a horse?' I found myself frowning then, remembering the mission she'd gone on before the sun set. 'Did you find him, by the way?' I'd been so worked up over the nether beastie that I'd forgotten to ask.

'Oh, yes. Hiding in some deep thicket full of brambles. He's coming. Dee, be quiet and let me get this done, would you? I need to get these wards sorted so I can have a rest before he gets here. This isn't going to be easy.'

'Yes, miss,' I said. 'Sorry.' I went back inside, feeling rather crestfallen despite her praise over the wand-work. *I should probably talk less and listen more*, I thought. That's what Ma always said. But I did wish I could have helped Aleida with the wards — she'd started to teach me about them, the spells of protection that would alert us if enemies came near, and could even place a shield over us if you had the time and the power to add that element to the spell. But usually she didn't bother, so I hadn't had much chance to practise.

I quickly finished the bread and cheese. It had been a long time since the pies at lunch, after all, and now that my nerves had settled, the effort of launching those fireballs had left me ravenous. I hadn't realised that Aleida hadn't prepared any food for herself when she'd made a plate for me, so I set her up a serving while I made seconds for myself, pausing briefly when I felt the wards go up. They felt like gossamer, like spiderwebs brushing over my skin.

She came back in while I was finishing my second slice of bread, and stopped, frowning. 'Did you have more to eat?'

I froze, the bread a half-chewed lump in my mouth, and then hastily swallowed. 'Yes? I-I'm sorry, should I not? We have plenty.'

She shook her head. 'No, it's not that. You can't do big workings on a full belly, Dee. A little, yes, but not like we'll have to do once the horse-fellow gets here. But it's my fault, not yours. I should have told you.'

'I … oh,' I said, and set my plate aside. The food in my belly swiftly turned into a leaden lump. Quickly, I stood, turning my back to hide the heat in my cheeks and set about tidying the already perfectly neat tent, swallowing hard at the sudden lump in my throat. 'I'm sorry, miss, I really am. If I'd known—'

'Don't worry about it,' she said. 'Like I said, not your fault.'

'But I ...' I trailed off, my throat too thick and close to speak.

I could feel her eyes on my back. 'It's not worth going and sticking a finger down your throat, if that's what you're thinking.'

I stopped what I was doing and bunched my hands in my skirt. There was nothing to tidy or fuss with, anyway. We hadn't been here long enough for anything to need straightening or setting aright.

'Dee,' Aleida said again. 'Seriously, it doesn't matter. We're not likely to get this sorted out in one night. You'll still be able to weigh in on the matter.'

'It's not that,' I said, and with the words the tears I'd been holding back began to spill. 'I just can't do anything right today. *Anything*. First with the bandits, I knew I should have my wand out, but I ... I just couldn't stop thinking about what would happen if I couldn't do anything with it. And then, at the abbey ... believed every word Kara said, every single one ...'

Aleida sighed. 'All right. But what about the rest of it? That fellow at the forge? You jumped in right away to try and keep the situation under control — and then you knew at first touch that something was wrong. The bandits, yeah, you mishandled that one, but then, just before with the nether beastie, you managed that one just fine.'

'So that's what?' I said. 'Two out of five? That's not good, no matter how you slice it. I just ... I feel like such a fraud.'

'A fraud?' Aleida said, eyes narrowing. 'Yeah, right. A fraud who can handle a critter from the nether realms with a solid round of fireballs. You're such a faker, Dee.'

I thought quite seriously about snatching up a cushion and throwing it at her. 'Is that your idea of how to make someone feel better?' I snapped.

'Well, I know anger's better than self-pity,' she said. 'As for mistakes, well, there's no avoiding them, in my experience. The trick is not to make the same one too many times. So, in that sense, I guess it's good to get them all out of the way early.'

'I'll keep that in mind,' I snapped.

'Good. Now I'm guessing that poor sod from the forge will be with us before too long. Go get the circle set up, will you?'

✤

I was fair seething as I laid out a circle with a length of rope and set out the candles and incense and so on. But by the time I was done I realised she had a point — that flash of temper really had driven away the swell of self-pity. On balance, I'd rather have had a hug than a poke with a needle, but she'd made it clear long ago not to expect any coddling from her.

I was just finishing the preparations when I heard a rustling in the darkness. The chestnut horse was picking his way towards our camp through the long grass. He held his head high, and his eyes showed white around the edges. He was scared, I realised. Terrified, maybe, and yet he'd come anyway. *Well,* I told myself, *Chances are he's got no hope in the world other than us.*

'Hello,' I said, and because of my flared temper the word came out much more brusquely than I had in mind. 'I'll go tell my mistress you've arrived. Wait here, or if you'd like, go get a drink of water before we begin, the stream's just down over there.' I pointed, and he flinched back from the movement, tossing his head up again and flicking his ears back.

A little bit more of my anger melted away. 'Don't be afraid,' I told him. 'We won't hurt you—' I cut myself off, then. In truth I had no idea how it would feel to be turned from man to beast and back again but I could imagine it wouldn't exactly be pleasant. 'I mean, we won't harm you; and we certainly wouldn't send you back to the men who had you earlier. Go and get a drink, and then ...' It took me a moment to find the words. After what had happened with Kara earlier, I didn't want to make promises I couldn't keep. '... then we'll see what's to be done.'

By the time he returned, Aleida had come out, and I was going around the circle, lighting candles and incense.

The fellow was not in good shape. He was heavy-set for a horse, with a barrel chest and thick neck, built for strength more than speed. His coat was streaked with old sweat and mud and there were many cuts and scratches on his legs, some old, some fresh. There were a few scars across his back and shoulders, too, large ones, as though he'd been raked by long claws. *Nether beast?* I wondered, *Or maybe one of the griffins?*

'Well then,' Aleida said, looking him over. 'You look like something the cat dragged in. Not been having a good time of it, have you?' She stepped back then, waving him towards the opening of the circle. 'All right then, in you go. Let's take a look at you.'

He hesitated, leaning away from us with a glance towards the dark forest.

'You've seen this sort of thing before, haven't you?' Aleida said. 'Well, go on. What's the worst that could happen?'

He gave a weary snort, and I knew then that he wasn't going to run. He was too tired, too desolate. He plodded through the gap in the rope, and swung around to face us.

At Aleida's gesture I closed the rope circle.

'Hold still,' she told him. 'This'll take a few moments. Dee, go to south. Might as well try before we declare it a hopeless case. No, not you,' she said when the horse snorted in surprise.

I did as I was told, but as soon as I drew my wand and knife and tried to summon power to assist, I realised it was hopeless. The food was a leaden lump in my belly, and I could no more draw up power than I could leap into the air and fly.

All I could do was watch as Aleida drew sigils in the still evening air to mark out the ritual space. Each one hung in the air, a glowing tracery of light, and the words drifting from her lips seemed to take physical form — there was a stream of mist coming from her mouth, twining its way around the circle and glowing like moonlight. The candle flames grew, stretching up until they were taller than the long white tapers that bore them. My skin prickled and my ears were ringing like a bell as the words of power reverberated in my head.

As a wall of energy rose up around the circle, I half-closed my eyes and steadied my breath, reaching inwards to a quiet place inside me. I was getting better at this part — when I first started learning Aleida would have to draw a sigil on my forehead with a ritual oil every time, but lately I'd found the trick of it. When I opened my eyes again, I could see the threads of power wrapped all around the unfortunate creature in the ritual circle.

Aleida sucked on her lower lip as she looked him over. 'Hmm,' she said, and slowly paced around him. When she stepped into the circle for a closer look, rippling lights appeared in the air around her, shimmering green and blue, pink and red. She paid them no mind as she peered at the threads of light wrapped around the beast, tracing them with her fingertips.

I wanted to ask her what she saw, what it all meant, but I'd made enough missteps for one day. I was determined not to make any more.

'Hmm,' Aleida said again, finishing her circuit. 'Interesting. No hedge-witch behind this one, was it?'

The horse shifted his weight from foot to foot, and snorted.

'Did you see the one who did it to you? Just snort for an answer, twice for yes and once for no. Did you get a good look at her?'

He snorted twice.

'It was a her, wasn't it?'

Two snorts.

'How can you tell?' I ventured to ask.

'It just has that feeling about it. The way the threads are wrapped and tangled ... men tend to be more direct.' She took a step back. 'So how did she do it? A magic circle, like this one?'

The horse hesitated, pawing the ground with one hoof, and then snorted twice.

'Ah, so not exactly like this one, but a circle nonetheless.'

Two snorts.

'And was it just you? Or were there others?'

He flattened his ears and gave a low nicker.

'Oh, fine,' she snapped. 'Were you alone?

One snort.

She raised one eyebrow. 'With strangers?'

He hesitated again, scratching at the ground with the tip of his hoof before dropping his head with another single snort. *No.*

'Friends, then.'

He gave two small snorts and hung his head low.

'Yeah,' Aleida said. 'A little while ago, wasn't it? Four months? Six? Something like that?'

Two more snorts.

'Mm. All right.'

I couldn't hold back the questions any longer. 'Have you ever seen anything like this before?' I asked in a soft voice.

She shook her head. 'Noooo, this is ... this is really something else.' She sank her hands into the tangle of threads, weaving between them like strands in a ball of yarn.

Her face thoughtful, she pulled one hand free and drew her ritual knife from her belt and raised it to her lips to breathe on the blade. Then, swiftly, she cut through the cord in her hand.

The horse snorted in alarm, throwing his head up. The cords wrapped around him shifted and pulsed, and the severed end of the thread Aleida held whipped out of her hand, hissing through the air as it convulsed like a cut snake. With a nicker of pain, the horse pulled away, only to slam into the invisible wall that was the ritual circle. He bounced off it and stumbled hard, almost going down to his knees.

'That hurt, did it?' Aleida said. 'This isn't going to be pleasant, I'm afraid.'

'Did it do anything?' I said. I hadn't seen what the cut ends did once they left her hands, but I couldn't see any sign of them now, and the cords wrapped around him didn't seem at all diminished. If anything they seemed thicker, stronger, almost *pulsing* with power.

'Nope,' she said. 'But I didn't expect it would. I just wanted to see what would happen.'

'Right,' I said, trying not to roll my eyes. 'I take it this is going to need a bit more than sage and salt water to cleanse?'

She chortled, like I'd told a good joke. 'Ha ha, yes. Yes, quite a lot more. Whoever did this had some serious power. It's not a dead spell, not a set and forget like a ward. It's like a living thing, it *reacts* like a living thing. What does that tell you?'

I shook my head. 'I don't know, miss.'

'Means it's drawing power from somewhere. If we want to have any chance of undoing it, we have to find the source and cut it off.'

At this, the horse snorted again, his head lifting and his ears pricking.

'Don't go getting excited,' Aleida told him. 'That's a big if. I'm not making any promises. But ...' She backed out of the circle, rolling her shoulders. 'I might be able to brute force it. Just for a few minutes, so we can have a proper conversation about the matter.'

I didn't like the sound of that. I hissed through my teeth, and Aleida turned my way with a sharp glance.

I wanted to say *Are you sure that's a good idea?* But I swallowed those words. She'd told me enough times never to ask those kinds of questions, never to voice my doubts. But some days I felt as though I was *made* of doubts and uncertainties — I didn't understand how I was supposed to keep silent when everything inside me was full of misgivings.

But I'd shamed myself enough for one day. 'Can I help?' I said.

Aleida gave me a withering glance as she sat on the damp grass and began to pull off her boots. 'Maybe if you didn't have a bellyful of food … Actually, scratch that, you're too green either way. It's easy to throw too much into something like this, Dee. Get the balance wrong and you'll have to spend the next week sleeping it off. Just fetch my walking stick for me, will you?'

I hurried off, afraid I'd come back to find her stripped to her skin. She did that sometimes, for difficult workings, though I doubted she'd do so in front of a stranger. When I returned with her staff she had just stripped down to her leather stays over her chemise, with her skirt and petticoat still on. She was still sitting in the grass with her legs splayed out to the side, and with my witch-sight enhancing my night vision I could clearly see the hairy dog's feet within the folds of cloth.

I held out the staff and my hand as well, and she took both to heave herself to her feet, then used the staff for balance. 'Don't say it, Dee,' she growled under her breath.

'I didn't say a word,' I protested.

'Yeah, well, I can still hear you thinking it.'

'I reserve the right to think what I want,' I said, tartly, and she chuckled.

'Fair enough. All right, let's do this thing.'

I moved back, trying to keep myself from scowling at her narrow back. Brute force didn't sound good. None of this really sounded good — but what was the alternative? Walk away and leave the poor sod in this state?

Aleida shook her hair back and squared her shoulders, planting her bare feet into the grassy earth, and raised her right hand.

White light flared around the beast within the circle. He tossed his head up in alarm, eyes showing their whites, feet stamping on the trampled grass.

'Just hold still,' I told him. 'Hold still and stay calm.' Then I turned back to my mistress, and started chewing on my lip once again.

Her breath was calm and steady — not laboured, but not relaxed, either. There was a purpose, an intent, with each rise and fall of her chest above her black leather stays.

The white light around the horse grew steadily brighter, moment by moment, until it hurt to look upon him, but the shape within that brightness remained stubbornly the same, until Aleida let it go with a sigh and a slump of her shoulders. 'All right, fine,' she said. 'We'll do it the other way.'

'Miss,' I said.

'Dee, hush.'

This time I didn't bother to hide my scowl. I moved to the side, so I could see her face, and watched as she closed her eyes and bowed her head.

This time, when her power rose I felt the strength of the earth flowing with it. The blades of grass around us bent towards her, not fluttering as though blown by the wind, but leaning slowly and steadily, as though gravity itself were pulling them towards her.

The strands of energy wrapped around the horse

throbbed, pulsed — and then they all turned to ash and fell away.

In the middle of the circle was a man, as naked as the day he was born. He fell to his knees with a sob, his skin streaked with dirt and filth, his brown hair shaggy and unkempt.

I didn't pay him much more mind in that moment, however, for my mistress swayed on her feet, grabbing her staff with both hands to keep from falling, and I hurried to steady her. 'Miss—'

'I'm fine, Dee,' she said. At the words, something on my hand hummed, tickling my skin, and without thinking I twitched. Probably some bug. 'But maybe you should fetch a blanket or something. Funny, I thought we still had a week or so before the full moon.'

I glanced over at the kneeling figure and quickly looked away. Full moon indeed.

Maggie's blanket was near at hand, and I confess part of the reason I didn't find one of ours was the prospect of washing it afterwards. A horse that smells like horses is one thing, but a naked man streaked with months' worth of dirt and sweat and stinking like a stable is a different matter.

By the time I'd dumped the blanket around his shoulders, Aleida was still leaning heavily on her staff, her dark skin sallow and sweat beading on her brow. 'Come on, big guy,' she said. 'I'm not sure how long we'll have before it all snaps back. Can you talk? What's your name?'

Trembling like the palsy, he clutched the blanket around himself and nodded. 'Y-yes, m-miss,' he said, his voice rough and ragged. 'They c-call me Toro.'

I saw her eyes grow narrow. 'Toro, is it? Strange sort of name.'

There were old scars across his broad back, long healed and bleached of colour. I saw him swallow hard as he straightened, sitting back on his heels with the blanket pulled tight around him. His face was battered, too, his nose crooked, and a fresher scar lashing across his cheek to disappear into his beard. His eyes were deep-set and fierce. I could imagine them full of rage sooner than full of laughter, but right now they showed nothing but worry and despair.

There was something very familiar about his face. Very familiar ... Then, with a start, I remembered where I'd seen it before.

'All right,' Aleida said. 'Time's a-wasting. What's your story?'

He just stared at her, mouth hanging open like a landed fish.

'Aleida?' I broke in. 'I've seen his face before.'

Her eyes slid to me, and she nodded to me to go on.

'You remember that poster at the blacksmith's forge? His face was on it.'

'Mm,' Aleida said. 'Well, Toro? Were you a bandit?'

He huddled low to the ground, like a dog expecting the whip. 'Yes, miss.'

'So what happened?'

He glanced around, eyes wide, face pale, but his jaw was clenched in a way that reminded me of Kara, sticking stubbornly to her story even when everyone around her insisted she was lying. But then he bowed his head.

He'd given up, I realised. The time he'd spent as a beast, running, hiding, fearing for his life, had beaten him down too far to cling to his lies. 'We met her on the road. A woman travelling alone, with two beautiful horses. Looked like easy pickings. But those horses — they fought like men would, aiming for weak points, feinting, driving us where they wanted us. And the woman. She just stood there and laughed at us. Laughed and laughed. And then ... she did something to us. She made us lay down our swords. She made us *obey* her.'

'Yep,' said Aleida. 'Sounds about right. What was her name? Did you ever hear it?'

He shook his head. 'No, miss. She talked to us for a bit; she wanted someplace to hole up. She made us tell her about all our places, you know, where we'd lay low after a job. But in the end she had us all follow her up to the ruins on the ridge. She kept us there for a few days, made us work for her, day and night, digging out the ruins, cutting down trees, building a wall. Then, when it was all done, she made a circle, and one by one she sent us inside.'

Aleida's face was flat as she listened to the tale. 'How many?' she said when his voice trailed away.

'Miss?'

'How many of you?'

'Eight,' he said, looking down. 'There were eight of us and she ordered us around like we was little children.'

By this point I was watching Aleida more than him. But her face was a mask, perfectly still. I couldn't read a thing from her.

'And she did you all at once?' she said. 'One after another?'

'Yes, miss.'

'And then what happened? Don't tell me she just let you go.'

He shook his head. 'No, she ... As each man got turned, she had the others lead him to one of the posts we'd set up, and chain him there. That was for the biggest beasts. She was happy about them, you see. But some of us she wasn't so happy about. Me and Knuckles and Fishbone, she didn't care about us. She just shoved us in the yard we'd built. At first we didn't understand what was happening, you see, we didn't *know*. Whatever it was she did to us, it stole our wits, left us blind and confused, but slowly, slowly it came back, and we could think again.

'It was too late for the other lads, she had them chained up good and proper, but the rest of us ... we couldn't talk, but we managed to work together enough to bust the godsdamned fence down and get away.'

'Three of you?' Aleida said.

Toro shook his head. 'No. Just two. Knuckles didn't make it. She, she turned him into a stag, you see, and I guess he didn't realise how big those damn antlers were. He got caught in a tree, and she got him. I heard him screaming back behind us.'

'What happened to the other one who escaped?' I broke in.

Toro glanced from Aleida to me. 'I-I don't know, miss. We got separated in the first few days. I haven't seen any sign of him, not since we escaped.'

'So for all you know she might have got him back, too,' Aleida said.

'I suppose so, miss.'

'But why?' I said. 'Why didn't she ...' I trailed off, unwilling to say the words.

'Why didn't she just kill them?' Aleida said. She shrugged. 'No idea. It'd be a hell of a lot easier. She must have had something in mind for them.'

The naked man kneeling on the grass, streaked with filth and stinking like a beast, began trembling harder.

'Something bad?' I said, hesitantly.

Aleida just gave me a humourless smile, a wry quirk of the lips. 'Blood sacrifice usually doesn't mean anything good — if that's what she's going for. It could be something else entirely. All right, Toro, what else can you tell me about this witch?'

'Nothing, miss. I swear I've told you all I know! She never said a word to us beyond giving us orders, but she ... she ... we should have known not to mess with her. Right from the start I knew there was something wrong about her. Something about her that was as wild as a winter storm.'

I missed whatever he said next as, beside me, Aleida swayed, her knees buckling. I leapt forward to steady her as she slumped forward. I caught her by the shoulders before she fell against the lit candle and the smouldering incense. As she hit the ground, the candles and the glowing sigils all shuddered and flickered as though in a sudden wind, and then snuffed out. There came a rush of air, a wave of bitter cold, full of the scent of summer storms, and the man screamed; a guttural, hollow bellow of pain. Then, in the midst of the circle, the horse stood once again, wheeling and plunging, ears flat to his head and eyes wide with fright.

Aleida's face was the colour of ashes. Then her eyes rolled back in her head and she was gone, lost in a faint as deep as the ocean.

CHAPTER 4

I laid her down on the grass and stepped back, raking my hands through my hair. 'Lord and Lady ...'

You idiot, I wanted to say. *You absolute dolt, what were you thinking?* My heart was beating hard as I cast around this dark, close world. There were nether creatures out there, and bandits, and somewhere, a witch who had turned a whole troupe of highwaymen into beasts. And here my teacher had overtaxed herself to passing out. *Lord and Lady, what do I do now?*

The circle broken, Toro inched closer, his head held low as he snuffled over Aleida's still form, and then raised his head to me, ears pricked.

I bit my lip, wrapping my arms around myself. This wasn't the first time this had happened, not exactly, though it was the first time she'd passed out completely. In the past when she'd overstretched herself it had just been a momentary faint, and after a few minutes she'd roused enough that I could help her inside. This time she was out cold and seemed ready to stay that way for a while.

'All right,' I muttered to myself. She couldn't stay out here, that much was clear, what with Nether beasties around and apparently a powerful witch, too. But I couldn't carry her; even as slight as she was, she was more than I could lift.

I retrieved Maggie's fallen blanket, and managed to roll her onto the cloth. So far, so good. Then, I started hauling it towards the tent.

I hadn't got far before the big chestnut horse circled around me, and with a nudge of his nose, pushed my hand aside and took hold of the old blanket in his huge yellow teeth.

Together, we made short work of the job and got her inside, behind the wards and out of the elements. I expected at any moment the tugging and shoving would make her rouse, but she never stirred.

When it was done I covered her with a blanket, and looked up to find the bandit still watching me, the human intelligence unsettling in those bestial eyes. 'Thank you,' I said. 'And I'm sorry we couldn't be more help. Could you stay here, for tonight? She might want to speak to you some more in the morning.' Or she might not. It was hard to tell sometimes, with her.

He gave a low nicker I took for assent, and turned away to graze on the dry autumn grass, and with a sigh I went to pack away the remains of the ritual.

I spent an uneasy night, tossing beneath the blankets and checking on Aleida. When I did sleep, I dreamed of things with wings and teeth stalking me through the darkness, while around me men and beasts wept and cried for help. It was only when I saw that my teacher had roused enough to roll onto her side and curl up beneath her blankets that I was able to get any real rest.

That ended around dawn when Aleida pushed herself up, grumbling something about coffee, and with a resigned sigh I kicked my covers off to sit up as well. 'I'll fetch some water and get grinding the beans,' I told her, pulling on fresh clothes. 'You need to eat something. You barely had anything last night, and don't you try and tell me that working didn't have you scraping the bottom of the barrel.'

She just sighed as she ground the heels of her hands into her eyes. 'It was nothing, Dee. Piece of cake.'

The amethyst ring she'd given me hummed on my hand, startling me and making me twitch. With a muttered curse, I flung the tent's curtain aside and stalked outside.

The world beyond the tent was quiet and dim, still cool from the night, though that wouldn't last long once the sun came up.

Maggie was pulling at the grass near the wagon, and a little further out a heavy-set chestnut horse grazed as well. Toro. He lifted his head when I emerged, and then hesitantly — shyly, I fancied — he started over with a low nicker.

I collected a bucket from the wagon and started towards the stream. 'Morning,' I said to him in short, clipped tones. I couldn't bring myself to call it a good one. I was in too much of a foul mood. *Why does she have to keep doing this? She should have known she was pushing herself too hard. She should have known when to stop and let it go.* I tried very hard not to think about how I had been the one to insist that we must do something. *She's going to really hurt herself one of these days, and then where will we be? Doesn't she know how much it scares me to see her like this?*

He followed me to the stream — not too closely, but at a companionable distance, and when I stooped to dip out a bucketful of water he stood back with his head up and ears pricked. It gave me the impression he was standing guard.

When the bucket was full, I set it down on the grass and kept staring out at the dry, stubbled fields, thinking. Worrying. It was only when Toro gave a soft, questioning snort that I realised I was toying with the handle of my wand. 'At what point does it become madness?' I said to him. 'When you keep doing the same thing over and over again, expecting something different to happen?'

He shifted his weight from foot to foot, and gave another soft nicker.

'Yeah,' I said. 'Exactly.'

I looked him over, arms folded across my chest. A powerful creature, solidly muscled; just like the man in the circle last night, the one who seemed so cowed and broken by months imprisoned as a beast, running in fear from wild creatures and men alike. My own problems, I remembered, were minor compared to his. 'How are you?'

I asked him. 'After last night? It can't have been pleasant, being shifted back and forth like that. Did it hurt?'

He snorted once, and the ring on my hand hummed again, making me twitch. It distracted me enough that it took me a moment to remember the instructions Aleida had given him — snort twice for yes, and once for no. I realised two things, then — first, he was lying, and second, this ring Aleida had given me worked on animals as well as people. Or maybe, just on animals who used to be people. 'Huh,' I said, and, stooping to pick up the bucket of water, I started back to the tent. 'Do you have any family around? Somewhere you'd have a safe place to stay?'

He snorted no, and added to it a shake of his head, which looked so comical I briefly smiled. 'Well,' I said, swapping the bucket to my other hand. 'I've got no blessed idea what we're going to do now. It's up to my mistress, I suppose.'

He snorted twice and dropped back, letting me return to the camp alone.

Inside the tent, Aleida was feeding twigs into the fire while she nibbled at a slice of bread and butter. I settled down across from her. 'So what are we doing?' I said, setting to work on the coffee beans. 'What's the plan?'

'The plan?' she repeated. 'The plan is to pack up and hit the road. That's it.'

I scowled at her. 'So we're not going to help them at all? Just, "too bad and good luck"?'

She watched me steadily as she chewed and swallowed. 'Well, what would you like us to do?'

I clamped my jaw shut at that. I knew full well why I'd woken up in such a foul mood. I just wasn't willing to put it into words. This situation didn't look good at all, and with Gyssha's death-curse hanging over Aleida's head I had great doubts as to whether she was in any state to deal with it.

Actually, no. Scratch that. I didn't have any doubts at all.

At my silence, Aleida went on. 'You do realise that that creature you feel so sorry for out there has likely killed dozens of people. If not more.'

I thought of his solid shoulders and arms, his scarred face and back. 'I know,' I said. 'But I still wish we could do something. This is just awful. Can you imagine it? Not just being homeless, with no shelter and no safety, but being so *alone*. Nothing to eat but grass, nothing to drink but water from streams, no matter how putrid and foul, knowing that if men catch you the best you can hope for is to be worked like a slave. It's just awful.'

'He's still alive, though,' Aleida said. 'You saw the prices on their heads. Lord Belmont and his men would have caught and hanged them sooner or later.'

I grimaced, trying not to think of it. Trying not to think of Kara, and how it would feel if it was my father strung up on the gibbet. He might be a bandit, a murderer and a thief, but I could see that Kara loved him. He was everything to her, the only family she had. 'It'd still be awful,' I said. 'But it'd be justice, at least. This ... this is just so bizarre. Such a strange and cruel fate. No one could have seen this coming.'

'I could,' Aleida said. 'If you tangle with a witch, strange and cruel is what you're gonna get. We're not known for our forgiving temperaments, generally speaking. If they didn't want to get turned into beasts, they shouldn't have attacked her.'

'Or anyone, really,' I said.

'Exactly.'

'But it's still not right, is it? You can't just go about punishing injustice with injustice.'

'So what would you do? Turn them back and then hand them over to the hangman?'

'Well ... It's probably what *should* be done.'

'Yeah, but are you going to be the one to do it?'

I pulled a face and shook my head. 'So what do you do? When there aren't any good choices, what do you do? Just walk away and pretend you didn't see anything?'

'Sometimes. At least that way you aren't making things worse.'

I didn't know what to say to that. I was silent for a long moment before another question occurred to me. 'Aleida?' I said, still grinding the beans.

'Yeah, kid?'

'Could you do that?' I'd said the same thing, yesterday, but it was a different question now that we knew what had really happened.

Aleida screwed up her face and shook her head. 'Not like that. That spell, that's something else, Dee. I mean, sure, if I wanted to badly enough and had enough time to put it all together, I could find a way ... but eight of them? Bam, bam, bam, one after another? Not a chance. There's not many who could, I'd wager.'

'Could Gyssha have done it?'

'No, never. Not her style at all. She'd make them *think* they're turned into beasts instead. Have a chap crawling about on the ground thinking he's a crocodile, chasing after dogs and chickens and trying to drag them into the pond. Much less effort and far more entertaining. Ugh, I can just imagine her cackling over it.'

The thought was enough to make my skin crawl. I'd only met Gyssha briefly, after she was already dead, but I'd seen enough of her to believe she'd do it, and that the result would be all kinds of ugly.

I shook my head, trying to clear that picture away. 'All right ... But what about this witch, then?'

'What about her?'

'Oh, don't play the fool!' I snapped. 'You know what I'm getting at! Shouldn't we find out why she did it?'

'You know why she did it, Dee. They attacked her. They got what was coming to them.'

'But why keep them chained up? Why bring the griffins? What's she doing that's letting the nether critters come through?'

'I don't know, Dee. And it's not our problem.'

'How can you say that?'

She heaved a sigh. 'Dee, put that thing down, you've ground those beans to powder. Now, look at me. You saw what happened last night. I can't break that spell. People who do this kind of thing don't take kindly to having others poke their noses into their affairs ... and we kind of already did that. So when I tell you that this is not our problem, what I mean is that we're going to pack up and leave this bandit-infested godsdamn forest far behind us, as quickly as possible. I'm going to send a message to those nuns and warn them that something strange is going on out here, and then we're gone. Is that clear?'

I wanted to argue. It didn't feel right, to know that something bad was happening here, and to turn our backs on it and walk away. Problem was, there was no part of her argument that I could refute. 'What about Kara?' I said. 'We can guess what happened to her father, we even have a fair idea of where he might be. Shouldn't we tell her?'

Aleida shook her head. 'She'll just be more determined to save him. If she tries anything around this witch, chances are she'll end up transformed right alongside him — if she's lucky. No, she's better off not knowing.'

I didn't like that either, but I could see there was no point in arguing. 'And Toro?'

She gave me an exasperated look. 'Lord and Lady, I don't know! I guess his best bet is to find a farm somewhere and let them take him in. If you'll forgive me, Dee, I'm more concerned with keeping our hides intact. He's the one who made his bed on a scorpion's nest, now he's got to lie in it.'

I just stared at her, open-mouthed. 'How can you be so ... so dismissive of all this? Doesn't it bother you? People are suffering.'

'Bandits, you mean.'

'They're still people! And what about Kara? What about whatever it is this witch is brewing up in that forest? How many more people are going to suffer because of that?'

She took the mortar from me and began to tip the ground coffee into the pot. 'There's nothing I can do about that.'

'But—'

'There's nothing we can do! And believe me, kid, I've spent a great deal of time learning how not to be upset over things I can't do anything about. A *great* deal of time. You've just got to trust me on this one, Dee.'

'I just don't understand how you can be so cold-blooded about it all!'

'Because I've been around long enough to know that cold-blooded wins over hot-headed every damn time. My mind's made up, let's pack all this up and hit the road.'

I stomped outside after that, leaving her to deal with the coffee. I didn't like the stuff anyway. Instead, I went around the back of the tent and started stripping off the oilcloth cover. I shouldn't have bothered with the effort of laying it out last night — it was bone dry, like everything else around here.

It was the good thing about being the apprentice, I decided. It didn't matter if I was happy with what we were doing. It didn't matter if I couldn't see a good way forward, if I couldn't think of any way to take an awful situation and make it better. It wasn't my choice to make. All I had to do was shut up and do as I was told.

I hadn't got far in the work when I heard muffled hoofbeats ringing out through the stillness. They were coming from the road. Abandoning my work, I sidled around to the edge of the tent, and saw a rider heading along the same road we'd taken out of town yesterday, moving at a smart trot. Once he rounded the corner of the field we were camped behind, however, he steered his horse off the road and started towards us.

I ground my teeth and swallowed my irritation as I peeled apart the layers of blankets over the dome-shaped frame to call inside. 'Aleida? There's someone coming. One man, riding a horse.'

I heard a sharp breath from inside. 'I'll be right out. Be sharp, Dee.'

I remembered what she'd said, about having already prodded this other witch by messing with Toro, and checked the wand at my belt. Not that it would do me much good.

The fellow was looking around with interest at our strange camp of domed tent and travellers' wagon. I quickly glanced around to see that Toro had hidden himself behind the wagon, so that only Maggie was visible, picking at the dry grass.

When he was still a few dozen paces away the man dismounted, though he laid a hand on a sword at his side. 'Hello?' he called. 'Ah, good morning, miss. Are you the ladies who called in at the Haven yesterday? Only Mother Ellendene said you might be camped out this way.'

Aleida emerged from the tent then, coffee cup in hand and a light shawl wrapped around her shoulders with the tails hanging down low enough to keep her wand and knife out of sight. 'That would be us,' she said. 'Good morning to you, too. Early to be out on the roads, isn't it?'

'It is, miss, but I'm carrying a message for Lord Belmont, so ride I must. But Mother Ellendene did ask me to give you the news if I happened to cross your path.'

She frowned. 'What news?'

'Well, it's not good, miss. Seems bandits came down from the forest last night and hit the Haven. Made off with all the coin in their coffers, but that's not all, I'm sorry to say. It seems they've abducted a young girl, too.'

Aleida clenched her fists, and from inside the tent I heard the fire *pop*, loud enough to startle the messenger's horse.

I drew a sharp breath. 'Kara? The blonde lass with the sword?'

'Yes, that's the one.'

'Was anyone hurt?' Aleida said.

'No deaths, but Sister Lodova has a broken arm after the scum threw her down. The women there said the young lass was trying to fight them off, but there were near on a dozen of them and they overwhelmed her and carried her off with them.'

I could just picture Kara, fierce and bold, drawing her sword against a dozen men. But I could just as easily see her sneaking down to open the doors late at night. She was desperate to get out of there. 'How'd they get in? Those new doors they had looked more than strong enough.'

'It's strong all right, but they got it open somehow. The way I heard it, they were already inside when someone spotted them prowling around and raised the alarm. Lord Belmont has me taking a message to Lord Haversleigh, asking him to keep watch on his end of the forest. But Mother Ellendene said you'd taken an interest in the lass, and she asked me to give you word of what happened, if our paths should cross. By the Lord and Lady, miss, this forest is no place for two women travelling alone, not if these wretches have stooped to carrying off young girls. You should head back into town, Mother Ellendene will be happy to put you and your servant up for a few days. Once these bandit scum are all swinging from the gallows it'll be safe to travel.'

'Mm,' Aleida said, narrowing her eyes. 'Gods, yes, the last thing I want is to be caught in the middle of this mess. Thanks for the news,' she said. 'Don't let us keep you.'

She watched him as he mounted up and rode away, standing perfectly still, perfectly calm and composed — until he reached the road. Then, her brow furrowed, and her hands bunched to fists at her side. 'That little idiot! That hare-brained, dim-witted, foolhardy little scrap! What in all the hells is she thinking?'

I didn't bother to answer that. We both knew what she was thinking — she'd told us herself. She'd do whatever she had to do to find her father. 'Aleida?' I said. 'Yesterday, she seemed awfully sure she could get out with or without us. Do you think she opened the gate herself?'

'Oh, I think there's every chance she did,' Aleida said. 'If you could mine stupidity that girl'd be worth a fortune! And here I thought those feckless nuns could be trusted to keep her out of trouble. Then again, I guess there's no ingenuity like a fool hells-bent on self-destruction.' She gave a hiss of pure frustration, and then unbunched her hands. 'All right, Dee. We need to get this camp broken down fast. I was going to send a note to those nuns, but I think it'd be better to take a pair of crows there and find out what they know.'

I cocked my head at her, puzzled. 'But ... I thought we were getting out of here.'

'Oh, we are,' she growled. 'We're just going to make a little stop along the way. That flea-brained little scrap may have stolen my money, but I'll be three-times cursed if I'm going to let her keep it!'

Before long, we were both flying towards the abbey on gleaming black wings while our bodies lay on the bed inside the wagon, safe behind the wards. It's glorious to fly — it doesn't matter if you're soaring on an eagle's wings, swooping and diving as a swallow or taking off in a goose's heavy body with laborious beats of powerful wings, it's always marvellous.

But that morning Aleida wouldn't let me enjoy the lofty heights and the morning's crisp breezes. She kept us both low as we winged our way across fields and lanes and hedges. After what she'd said about the possibility of this strange witch taking offence at our intrusion I didn't argue.

When we reached the Haven we first circled the walls. The gates stood open, but there was a small cluster of armed men outside — Lord Belmont's men, I guessed, looking at the colourful tabards they wore over mail shirts.

Following Aleida, I winged over the walls and glided down into the courtyard. The doors of the solar we'd visited yesterday stood open, even though the hour was still early, and Aleida glided right through them, swooping to perch on the back of the same battered couch she'd sat upon the day before.

Inside, Mother Ellendene sat at her writing desk, while Sister Lodova sat in an armchair nearby. The sister had her right arm splinted and resting in a sling, while Mother Ellendene sported a swollen eye and cheek and livid bruising across her face. She dropped her pen in surprise at the sight of two crows fluttering into her office as though they owned the place.

'I'd say good morning,' Aleida's crow croaked, black talons scratching over the carved wood of the couch's back. 'But clearly it isn't. I hear you had some excitement overnight.'

Sister Lodova stayed frozen and speechless, but Mother Ellendene just pursed her lips, and then heaved herself up. 'Mistress Blackbone, I presume?'

'However did you guess?,' Aleida said with a rustle of her black feathers. 'What happened last night?'

The mother superior shuffled over to the couch, moving stiffly when yesterday she'd seemed quite spry and hale. 'Well there's not much to tell. The gates were closed and locked last night as usual, but in the early hours of the morning a child going to the outhouse heard a disturbance and raised the alarm. At that point they were already inside and had a hold of young Kara. Sister Lodova and I tried to take her back ...' Mother Ellendene shrugged. 'But you can see for yourself how well that turned out. There was more than enough of them to keep our girls at sword-point while they pried up the flagstones and relieved us of all our coin. Then they left, taking the young lass with them.'

'Anyone else harmed?' Aleida asked, turning from one nun to the other with beady black eyes.

'A few of the girls tried to defend us, and took some bruises for their trouble,' Sister Lodova said, her face flat and stony. 'It's kind of you to call and enquire, Mistress Blackbone, but Lord Belmont's castellan has sent word to his master, and I'm sure he'll be taking the matter in hand.'

'I don't doubt it,' Aleida said. 'But that doesn't mean I won't take steps of my own.' She glanced across at me then, and gave me a nod.

I knew what that meant. 'You've told me the facts,' Aleida went on to the nuns, 'but what do you *think*? Did the girl set this up?'

I couldn't linger to hear the reply — I had a job to do. With a leap and a flap of wings, I took to the air and flew out of the solar.

Circling the courtyard, I spotted a little girl perched on a windowsill, playing with a dolly. She was about five, I guessed, a few years older than my youngest sister, Maisie. I was prepared to scout out Kara's room by myself, but I figured there was no harm in asking.

I glided down to land on the far end of the windowsill and the little girl yelped in surprise, clutching her doll close and pulling her bare feet in to hide them under her skirt.

'Good morning,' I croaked in the crow's harsh voice.

The little girl frowned at me. 'Birds don't talk,' she said in a scolding tone.

'I do, but I'm not really a bird. I'm trying to help my friend Kara. Do you know her?'

The lass nodded. 'She's mean sometimes. And Mam said she ran away.'

Well, that was a kinder way to put it to a little one than saying she'd been kidnapped. 'She shouldn't have been mean to you,' I said. 'But I'm worried she's got lost in the forest. My friend and I are trying to find her. Can you tell me where her room is?'

She studied me with a very serious little face. 'What's your name?'

'Dee,' I said. 'What's yours?'

'Jenna. Can I touch your feathers?'

I hopped closer and let her stroke my back, and then I spread my wings for her inspection. 'Gentle, now. I need those feathers to fly.'

'Kara's room is just down the hall,' she announced. 'But there's cats around. I'd better come with you.'

'Thank you,' I said. 'If you hold out your arm, I'll hop onto it.'

When she held out her hand, I jumped onto it with a flap and she gave a little shriek of surprise. I tried hard not to let my talons dig in, and kept my wings half-spread for balance as she slowly turned away from the window and started down the hall. I just hoped that no adults or older children would come across us, or there'd be quite some explaining to do.

She brought me to Kara's room without incident. It was a tiny chamber with a narrow rope-slung bed and a straw mattress covered with coarse, woven cloth. At the foot of the bed was a wicker trunk, and that was all — no ornaments or decorations, no rugs or wall hangings. Not even a candle stub. There was nothing in here to identify the room as Kara's. 'Are you sure this is the right one?'

'Of course,' she said. 'I'll open the shutters so we can see.'

Kara's boots were gone, I noted, once the early morning light spilled into the gloom. 'Can you open that basket-chest for me?'

Inside were only a few spare garments, very nondescript. Actually, they looked much like the plain dresses and chemises I'd seen people here wearing yesterday. So, she'd gotten dressed in her own gear, boots and all, before running to face the ruffians at the gate.

I hopped onto the bed. 'All right then, let's see if we can find some hairs.'

Together we fossicked through the sheets and found several long, blonde hairs. I could have carried them in my beak if I had to, but Jenna twisted them together for me into a neat little bundle. 'Here you go.'

'Thank you, sweet,' I said, taking it in one foot.

'Are you a witch?' she said.

'Yep. But I'm one of the nice ones.'

'But witches are all evil, aren't they?'

'Some are, but I'm not. Thanks for your help, I have to go now.'

'Wait!' she said, her voice wistful. 'Can I go with you? I want to fly and see everything, too.'

'Sorry, my sweet, no,' I said. 'Wait 'til you're big and grown, all right? Maybe then you can fly.'

I leapt from the windowsill and circled over the roof, dropping down into the courtyard again. I glided into the solar to make an awkward, hopping landing nearby with the tangle of blonde hairs clutched in one foot.

'Look, I don't care what you find,' Mother Ellendene said. 'I've sworn blind to Lord Belmont that young Kara couldn't have opened the doors, and I'll continue to swear it. I don't care if you get a signed blessed confession out of her, as far as I'm concerned she didn't do it. She wouldn't be the first young lass to make a foolish decision out of love and desperation, and I don't believe she deserves to have her life ruined for it.'

Aleida's crow shrugged with a flutter of wings. 'It's a fair call. But I'll tell you, I'd be more concerned about her surviving the next few days. Stupid decisions do have a way of compounding themselves to worse and worse situations.' She turned my way then. 'All done?'

'Yep,' I said.

'Good. Well, we'd best be off,' she said to the two nuns. 'But you mind what I said about that witch out there — I have a feeling she's naught to be trifled with.' Then, with a clack of her beak and a flutter of wings, she was gone, and I was right behind her.

Beyond the abbey, the sun was rising fast. Once we were clear of the walls, Aleida swung around so that she was behind and above me. It was an awkward spot; I couldn't see her at all and when I tried to twist around to glance back at her she just clacked her beak at me in irritation. 'Straight ahead, Dee! We need to get back swiftly.'

'But I can't see you.'

'Of course not, I'm guarding your blind spot.'

She never explained what she was standing guard against, but we returned to the wagon without any trouble. By the time I swooped in through the open half-door, Aleida was already back on her feet, bringing out a few crusts to thank the birds for their trouble, while I held on to my crow a little longer, until Aleida could retrieve my prize. She tucked my crow gently under her arm to untangle the hairs from my talons, and then I settled back into my body and opened my eyes.

It was always somewhat disconcerting, coming back to one's own flesh after borrowing, finding yourself suddenly larger and heavier and more ungainly than it seemed you ought to be. Sometimes you felt half-blind, what with eyes only on the front of your head and not the sides, and half-deaf, too, without a beast's fine-tuned hearing.

By the time I felt solid enough to sit up, Aleida was perched at the tiny table inside the wagon, with a book open in front of her and a feather quill in her hand. I shuffled across to peer over her shoulder and found her drawing out a rough map.

'Go get Maggie harnessed, will you, Dee?' she said. 'The nuns had a map of the region, and I need to get it copied down while it's fresh in my mind.'

'Yes, miss,' I said.

Outside, while I set about dressing Maggie in the collar, hames and breeching and all the rest of it, Toro came over with a soft snort, his ears pricked.

'Hey,' I said to him softly. 'How good's your hearing? Did you catch what that messenger said earlier?'

He gave a soft nicker, and I scowled, annoyed with myself for asking a foolish question. He could manage a yes or no easily enough, but an open-ended question was hopeless. 'Scratch that, let me start over. One of your bandit friends had a daughter — a girl called Kara. Do you know her?'

He fell very still, head up and ears pricked attentively, and gave two sharp snorts. *Yes.*

'Well, I'm guessing her father got taken by the witch at the same time you did. Was he the one who escaped with you?'

He snorted a no, and shook his head for good measure.

'Oh. Well, Kara went into town to buy some supplies and see if she could find any news of her da...' In brief words, I told him the tale of how she'd ended up in the Haven. 'Only she's determined to help her da if she possibly can, and told us she'd get out and hunt for him by hook or by crook. Well, she's gone and managed it — she was taken by this new pack of bandits last night ... only I'm not sure if she was stolen away or if it was just meant to look that way. Anyway, you'd know this forest pretty well, wouldn't you?'

He regarded me steadily for a moment, and then snorted yes again.

I glanced towards the wagon. 'So if we knew roughly what direction she'd gone in, you might know where the bandits would be holed up? You could help us find them?'

He shifted his weight from hoof to hoof, and tossed his head. He was thinking about it, I guessed, and not quite sure if it was a good idea. We were all but strangers, after all, and not exactly friendly ones. Just less unfriendly than the folks we'd helped him escape from yesterday.

Eventually, his huge head swung back towards me, and he snorted twice.

'Good thinking, Dee,' Aleida's voice said from above, making me jump. She was leaning on the wagon's half-door with her elbows on the wood and a silver bowl in her hands. 'I've got the compass and the map sorted. Let's get moving.'

Aleida had me take the reins, and we sat on the footboard with the silver bowl and her rough map between us. I peered at the page, trying to puzzle out the drawing. 'So the road heads roughly west until it hits ... what's that?'

'The locals call it the Scar,' Aleida said. 'Some rocky ridge that cuts through the forest.'

The compass, as Aleida called it, was pointing dead west. It was made up of a single feather floating on water in the bowl, with Kara's hair wound tightly around the quill. An enchantment made it point straight towards the hair's owner. 'Oh, that's a neat trick,' I said, looking down at it. Then, 'Huh …'

When my voice trailed off, Aleida glanced up at me. 'What?'

Part of me wished I hadn't said anything, but it was too late now. 'Simple spell, is it? Quick and easy?'

She gave me a puzzled look. 'Yeah?'

With a click of my tongue I urged Maggie onwards and steered her towards the forest. 'It's just that yesterday, we were talking about family; and I remembered that back when we first met you said you couldn't find your kin, after you left Gyssha.'

'Mm,' she said with a noncommittal tone. 'And?'

I turned to look her over. 'You could have found them, if you'd wanted to. Couldn't you?'

She leaned back, hands in her lap, looking out past Maggie's ears, and gave a quick sigh. She almost sounded amused. 'Yeah. You're right.'

I'd never expected her to admit it so readily. 'But, but … why? Your sisters, your mother — don't you want to see them again? Don't you care? I mean, do they even know what happened to you?'

She sat very still, the only movement her fingertips restlessly pressing against her thigh. 'They probably think I'm dead,' she said at last. 'It wouldn't be the first time someone hung themselves in a cell rather than face the axe. And I wasn't lying, it did hurt, going back to my old neighbourhood and finding them gone.'

'But you could have followed them. It would have been easy! I just ... I don't understand how you can be so cold-hearted.'

She patted my leg. 'I know, kid. I ... hmm.' Trailing off, she stood, head tipped up to peer at the sky, or what we could see of it through the huge trees that lined the road.

'What is it?' I said, and Maggie tossed her head, feeling my hands grow tight on the reins.

'An eagle, I think. Odd place for it.'

I frowned, puzzled. 'Is it? You borrowed an eagle yesterday.'

'Yes, but I found him hunting over the fields and brought him down under the trees. That's why it took so long. They don't soar over forests when the beasts they're hunting are on the ground under the trees.' She watched it for a moment longer, then opened the wagon door and picked up her skirts to step over the silver bowl. 'We'll have to talk about this later, I've got a few things to take care of. Follow the road, and keep your eyes peeled. Tell me if you see anything even slightly strange, all right?'

'Um, okay,' I said, glancing up at her. 'What are you doing?'

'Oh, a little of this, a little of that,' she said, and vanished inside, closing the door behind her.

I settled back, pursing my lips, and shifted the wand in my belt. I couldn't help but wonder if she'd just used that black speck as an excuse to leave the conversation behind.

Maggie tossed her head then, shortening her stride, and I realised my hands had grown tight on the reins. 'Sorry,' I muttered, making them soften.

I turned all my attention to our surroundings, then, thinking of the nether beastie I'd seen off last night and the mounted griffin back in the town — and the eagle, the one Aleida insisted was out of place. I'd seen how much damage her eagle had done the day before, and shuffled back a little so I was sitting closer to the wall of the wagon. At least the bird wouldn't be able to swoop down on me from behind.

Though I stayed alert, miles passed with no more excitement than the passing of an occasional woodcutter or swineherd, ushering his charges through the dark trees. I could hear Aleida pottering about inside, rummaging through crates and clinking glass bottles together — whatever it was she was doing, the rocking and bumping of the wagon didn't seem to be a bother.

The whole time, Toro had been trailing behind us, but when we reached a fork in the road and the floating feather guided us towards the left-hand path, he suddenly trotted forward and swung in front of Maggie, making her throw her weight into the breeching, jouncing the wagon to a sudden stop.

I leaned forward in consternation. 'What?' I said. 'What's wrong?'

He snorted, tossing his head, while above me the door opened. I glanced up to see Aleida looking out, irritation on her face. 'What—' she started, then pressed her lips together. 'Oh.'

A few moments later, we were both on the ground, watching the chestnut creature as he stamped his feet and lashed his tail in frustration, ears flat to his head.

After a few moments Aleida rolled her eyes and shook her head. Leaning on her staff, she hobbled past him to the edge of the road, where the ground was a little softer, and started scratching in the dirt with the tip of her walking stick. By the time I realised what she was doing, she was nearly halfway through drawing out the alphabet, letter by letter.

Toro realised it too, falling still with a nicker. Then he hurried over, nudging her aside to paw at the earth with one forefoot. In crude, misshapen lines, he scratched out a single word. AMBUSH.

Aleida came a little closer. 'Mm,' she said. 'I wondered if that might be the case. Whereabouts? Around this scar that cuts through the forest?' He answered with a quick double snort. 'All right. How far? Just stamp your foot. Six? Miles, I'm guessing? I see. That's maybe half an hour away, at this pace. And they'll have lookouts?'

Toro just twitched his shoulders, like he was trying to dislodge a fly. I took it for a shrug.

'Yeah, right,' Aleida muttered. 'Who knows what these idiots will do. Still, we should probably assume a basic level of competence.'

'But after yesterday they won't be foolish enough to attack us again,' I said. 'Surely?'

'Maybe. But maybe we want them to? Might be the easiest way to draw them out where we want them, it'd be a right pain to chase them down if they turn tail and run. Easy enough to cast a veil, if we look like wagoners hauling barrels of ale they'll be falling over themselves to come after us.'

'Is that easy to do?' I said, thinking back to the ritual last night, and how much it had drained her.

'Illusions are always easy, Dee,' she scoffed, but then she hesitated and looked up at the sky again.

I followed her gaze and saw it once more. The dark speck of an eagle, circling high overhead. Though the trees did arch over the road here and there, there were enough open patches that the bird could see us — assuming my teacher was right, and not just being paranoid.

'I should take a bird and go scout them out first,' Aleida said. 'Make sure Kara's actually with them before we go charging in. If they left her back at camp, that'll be our job half done. Hop up, Dee. Let's go.'

As soon as we set out Aleida ducked inside again, only to return moments later with a little basket of tiny glass flasks, each one sealed with cork and wax and holding about a dram of amber-coloured liquid. There were about eight or ten of them in total. 'Shove a couple in your pockets, Dee,' Aleida said as she started tucking the flasks away in her clothing.

I picked one up gingerly. 'What is it?' Knowing her, it wasn't anything I'd want to spill carelessly.

She gave me a tight smile. 'Just a little something. I don't want to have to do any fighting if I don't have to, so if swords come out, start throwing these around and they'll soon have other things to think about. Oh, and give me your hand, I'd best give you a charm against it.'

Taking my hand, she laid it on her knee and painted a sigil on the back of it with a tiny brush and some strange, glittering ointment. 'Oh!' I said. 'I know that one. Melusine's Shield, right?'

'Yep.'

We'd used that one before, back at the cottage when we'd burned off a load of noxious plants after clearing out the walled garden — it gave protection from agents in the air. 'So, what exactly is in those flasks?'

She gave a low chuckle. 'Oh, a bit of datura, some extract of ergot, a few other things. Short-acting though, so we'll need to move smartly.'

So, the brew would strike confusion and fear into anyone who came into contact with it. 'Do you need a sigil too?'

'Not for this little bit,' she said with a dismissive shrug. 'It's weaker than the one Gyssha hit me with back at the cottage. You'll be the same eventually, Dee. Now, I'd best go check the lay of the land.' She leaned back then, bracing herself against the wall of the wagon, and closed her eyes. Just like that, she was gone, flitting away on borrowed wings.

I gave her still form a sidelong glance, and gently pulled back on the reins, slowing Maggie's stride. If anything untoward happened now, it'd take more than a rap on the door to bring her back to my side.

She stayed that way for about ten minutes, and then she was back, as suddenly as she'd left, straightening and stretching with an arched back and her arms over her head.

'Any luck?' I said.

'Yep, they're up there, all right. Spread out to either side of the road. Looks like they're waiting for a target to roll on through.'

'What about Kara?'

She pulled a face. 'She's there, and she's in one piece. That's all I could tell from a quick pass. You go see for yourself, Dee. I'm going to get this illusion in place before we pass by their scouts.' She gestured for the reins and I handed them over, and then braced myself against the wagon just as she'd done, and went in search of a bird.

I found one quickly, a blackbird fossicking among the leaf litter a little way from the road, and soon I was in the air, following the road as it wound its way west.

The road had been sloping gently upwards for some time now, and after a few minutes in the air I saw outcroppings of rock appearing through the trees. I still found it amazing, this view from above with the earth laid out beneath us like a quilt laid over a bed. Through the forest there was a swathe of bare stone, and I understood why the local folk called it the Scar. A thick band of rock rose up out of the forest, milky white but streaked with darker lines, just like a long-healed wound. Around it the trees grew thinner, smaller, with less soil for their roots to anchor into. The road wove around the sun-baked outcrops, while here and there a small bridge crossed a fissure in the rock.

Once I was over the most exposed part of the road, I veered away and flew in a wide circle — and spotted the men hiding in the rocks almost at once. Though hidden from the road they were plainly visible from the air, even though some of them had constructed something like hunter's hides to let them watch the road without being seen.

On my second circuit I spotted Kara, wearing the same red divided skirts that had caught my eye the day before, and alighted on a boulder a short way away. Kara was sitting near a fellow I vaguely remembered from our encounter on the road yesterday, fidgeting nervously and looking around with every little sound. Kara, too, seemed discontent, sitting with her back to a huge boulder, holding her lips pursed tight as she threw pebbles against a rock face. A little distance away was yet another bandit, but he wasn't one I'd seen before. I'd have remembered if I had. He had tattoos across his face, circling one eye and scattered across his forehead and down his cheek. Tattoos themselves weren't that unusual, but these ones looked like the runes and sigils Aleida had started teaching me, not at all the usual sort of thing. Unlike the other men, there was no anxiety in his demeanour, if anything, he seemed rather bored. He looked hard-bitten and mean, more so than the ones who'd squared off with us yesterday, and his clothes bore the kind of stains that came from never having a proper wash. I was very glad, for that moment, that birds like this one didn't have much sense of smell.

I was about to head off again when another man approached, stepping lightly along the narrow path. The moment he straightened I recognised the kerchief around his neck and the leather hat on his head. When he reached the patch of shade where Kara sat, he swept off the hat to reveal a newly stitched wound across his cheek and forehead.

At his approach, Kara lifted her head, her face hopeful. 'Anything?'

'Not yet,' he said, and her scowl reappeared.

'Well, where are they? You said this wouldn't take long. You said—'

'Honeycake, you know what these blasted caravans are like. They take their own sweet time. It'll get here when it gets here.'

'Might even be tomorrow,' the nervous man grunted. 'Or the next day.'

Kara shot him a cold glare, and then glanced quickly at the tattooed man, her face wary. 'Holt,' she said, dropping her voice. 'You *promised* we'd find him.'

'I know! Kara, look, you have to bear with me. I gave you my word and I mean to keep it, but these folk …'

She heaved herself up, caught him by the edge of his jacket, and hauled him away along the path. The tattooed fellow leaned forward to watch the pair, as though keeping tabs on them. Since none of them had noticed me, I hopped across the rocks to follow.

'You should have told me about these new lads,' Kara growled at Holt. 'If I'd known they were joining you—'

'I told you, sweet, I didn't know! It'll be all right, I'll get them on board. You know me, I can talk them around.'

'How did they even know where to find us?'

Holt shrugged, looking away, and Kara punched him in the shoulder. 'Holt! You told them, didn't you? Lord and Lady ...'

'Kara, don't look at me like that! It's not that bad. They'll be useful, all right? None of my lads really know how to fight, and we've barely got any decent weapons. These folk are old hands, they know what they're doing. This caravan's got a hell of a payload, there'll be enough for everyone. I promised my lads, and you know I'm a man of my word.'

'A payload? I *gave* you a godsdamn payload!'

'You did, my sweet, but two is better than one, isn't it? We can't pass this up, who knows when we'll get another one as rich as this?'

Kara looked away with a hiss of frustration. 'Fine. But listen, Holt. Be careful, okay? I don't trust these men. I really don't.'

He grinned then, and lifted her chin with a curled finger. 'You only have to trust me, little kitten. The job'll be done before you know it, and then we'll go after your father.'

I'd heard enough, I decided. I leapt skyward, and winged my way back to the wagon.

When I released the blackbird and returned to my body, Aleida had finished the illusion. The wagon behind us was now a high-sided four-wheeled cart holding eight stout ale barrels, and Maggie had been transformed to a flea-bitten grey. Aleida wore a face that was passing-familiar to me — Old Grigg from Lilsfield, a mountain man with florid cheeks and a long and coarse grey beard. 'See anything interesting?' she said in Grigg's rumbling voice.

'I might have eavesdropped a bit,' I said. 'You were right, Kara went with them willingly. But I don't think everything's gone quite to plan. Looks like the bandits have a few newcomers, and they've got everyone's back up.'

'Newcomers?'

'Old hands, the leader said, with better weapons than the rest of the thugs. The one I saw look nasty, too, with these odd tattoos all over his face. Sounds like they're waiting for a shipment of some kind to come through. Kara and Holt were talking about a payload.'

'Tattoos, you say,' Aleida said. 'Interesting. And a payload? That makes sense. Well, if they've got any kind of discipline they'll let us pass through rather than risk their main target for a few barrels of ale. If they're greedy fools, on the other hand … If you were making a wager, Dee, where'd you put your money?'

'Oh, greedy fools, all the way,' I said. 'Want to take me up on it?'

She laughed. 'No dice. All right, when it happens, wait for them all to come down to the road before we start hurling the flasks.'

'Then what?'

'Then we find out what they've done with my money. And Kara, well, let's just see how this goes. Somehow I doubt she'll take kindly to being rescued.'

CHAPTER 5

It was, I must say, a rather odd feeling. It happened just the same as it had the day before — we rounded a corner, and there he was in the middle of the road, hat low over his eyes, handkerchief pulled up over his mouth and nose, gloved hand wrapped around the hilt of his sword. 'Stand and deliver!'

Aleida hauled back on the reins and leaned forward, peering at him as though near-sighted. 'What? What's that, young man? Come closer, and speak up.'

'I said, stand and deliver!'

I was wearing the face of Mistress Stafford, a very prim and proper matron who was Grigg's wife back at Lilsfield. Playing along, I leaned over to shout in my teacher's ear. 'He says it's a robbery!'

'Eh? What?'

'It's a robbery, you deaf old codger!'

'Tell 'im we don't want none.'

Holt pulled his kerchief down with a swift tug and

raised his fingers to his lips to give a piercing whistle. At that signal, the rest of the bandits materialised from their hiding places, swarming down to surround us.

Holt came closer then, drawing his sword. I could see the humour had faded from his eyes, replaced with something more vicious. Our voices were echoing over the rocks, and I did wonder just how far away this caravan they were waiting for might be.

He levelled the point of the sword right where Grigg's impressive gut ought to have been. 'I was going to only charge you a tax for the honour of passing through my domain,' he said. 'But given this display of insolence I think I'll take the lot. Now you'd best hop down, or I'll open you from gizzard to gullet.'

Aleida stared at the sword, as though only just realising what he held, and hesitantly reached out to touch it with one fingertip.

I felt a pulse of power, and in a flash the metal melted and flowed, rippling in the sun. Suddenly, what he held was not a sword at all, but a snake — grasped by the tail.

It lunged at him with shining fangs. With a shriek he threw it down, stumbling back — and at that moment, Aleida dropped the illusion, revealing the wagon and Maggie and herself, dressed all in black with her long black hair spilling over her shoulders and down her back like a waterfall of ink.

Swiftly, she hurled two of the flasks, one in front and one to the side. But I could hear voices behind us, from the rear of the wagon, and leaned around the side to throw one of mine back there. It shattered against a boulder and the amber liquid inside immediately bubbled away into a thick white vapour, hiding the men from sight. As the cloud enveloped them their voices changed from shouts and threats to screams and terrified babbling.

I turned back to see Aleida jump down from the seat, landing so nimbly and so lightly I could tell she'd used some power to negate Gyssha's curse and reshape her feet. She sauntered towards Holt with her ugly club of a wand in her hand, laughing a chill laugh while the bandit scrambled backwards on his hands and backside while the steel snake kept lunging and striking after him in the dust.

He'd escaped the vapour, unlike most of his companions. Right beside the wheel, one young lad was hugging his knees to his chest, rocking back and forth and whimpering. Another fellow had run head-first into a boulder beside the road and knocked himself out cold. A third was stripping off his clothes and shrieking something about spiders, and I could hear yet more of them gibbering from behind the wagon.

A movement from above caught my eye and I quickly looked up to see Kara's blonde head peering at us from a vantage point up the slope, her eyes wide as she recognised me and our wagon, and then she ducked out of sight again.

On the ground, Aleida closed with Holt just as the silver snake reached the end of its power. The sleek, gleaming shape withered limply to the ground, and then turned into water and melted away.

Holt stared at the spot in confusion, then looked up at her. 'You!' he said.

'That's right,' she said in a cheerful voice, and with a flick of her fingers, knocked his hat from his head with a gust of wind.

I saw the bandit's eyes grow narrow as he glanced around at the chaos we'd made of his ambush. There were only a couple of his men left unaffected by the vapours — one of them bore the same tattoos I'd seen on the man in the rocks. I held another flask ready to remedy that, should the need arise, but I doubt Holt realised that. All his attention seemed to be on Aleida.

With a startling swiftness, he drew his knees to his chest and then somehow turned the movement into a backwards roll. Next thing I knew he'd popped up on his feet again, with allies at his back.

Aleida hesitated, her knife in her forward hand, while the wand in her backhand began to glow. I stood up on the footboard, ready to throw the flask if they tried to rush her.

But the bandit leader raised his hands in a gesture of surrender. 'Wait! Fall back, lads, and put up your weapons.' He didn't even glance back to make sure they obeyed — they all did, except for the fellow with the marked face, who just lowered the point of his sword, watching Holt and Aleida both.

Aleida's gaze slid past Holt to the tattooed man, and she lifted her chin. 'Huh,' she said, looking him up and down. 'Well, well, there's something I haven't seen in a long time.'

Holt glanced between them. He seemed to me rather miffed that Aleida was focused on the other fellow, rather than paying attention to him. 'I'd have a care if I were you,' he began to say, but the marked man brushed past, ignoring him utterly as he watched Aleida with a predatory gaze. 'Little girl, you've never seen anything like me before.'

'I wouldn't be so sure of that,' Aleida said. 'Armund's Mark? What relic did you dig up to carve those into your skin?'

'Come here, sweet thing, and I'll tell you.'

'Oh, I don't think you'll find me very sweet,' Aleida said. 'Not at all. Would you like to try me?'

There was a rustle of movement behind me, and a quick cry of surprise. I glanced around to see a blur of movement, and Kara, sprawled in the road as though she'd been shoved down. Then, I felt power flex around me, like the air itself was squeezing me in a fist.

Where just one of the tattooed thugs had been facing Aleida, now five of them were mobbed around her, pressing close, reaching for her with scarred, calloused hands. They'd appeared in the blink of an eye, moving faster than humanly possible.

But while I'd been taken by surprise, it seemed Aleida knew what she was dealing with. She already had her hands raised, knife and wand crossed in a ward, raising a shield around herself. She held it just long enough for the thugs to realise they couldn't touch her — and then I saw fire bloom around her hands.

I was already raising an arm to shield my face when she dropped her ward and loosed a burst of flame, hot enough to blister the wagon's paint, and hurled them back.

Behind her, I stood, the last flask of her potion still in my hand. I couldn't see Aleida's face, but I could imagine the look in her eyes. She liked a good fight, my teacher. When things started to get dicey, she always got this mad, manic gleam in her eyes, and a wicked smile upon her lips. Could she deal with them all? Maybe. She sure *thought* she could. But all I could think of was last night, when she'd collapsed trying to undo the spell on Toro, and Aleida's warning that the other witch was likely out there somewhere, angry at our interference. It was no time for brawling with thugs on the road, especially ones who could move as fast as that. As Aleida's flames died away, I gritted my teeth and hurled the flask.

It shattered on the road at their feet, and the tattooed thugs retreated further, scrambling away from the thick white vapour.

Aleida just turned to me with fury in her eyes, the white vapour swirling around her like fog. 'Damn it, Dee! You're spoiling my fun!'

'Oh, I beg your pardon,' I snapped. 'I thought the plan was to get in and out quickly so we can be on our way! You know, before *someone* takes too much interest in our presence!'

'Oh,' she said, and took a quick glance skywards. 'Yeah, right. Good point.' She looked back at the marked men, who'd regrouped a dozen or so yards away, beyond the reach of the potion cloud.

Aleida reached up to the bracket on the front of the wagon and swung back up to her seat, keeping her eyes on the bandits. 'Kara?' she said without looking around. 'Hop up, girl. We need to talk.'

Kara had found her feet, and dragged Holt around my side of the wagon, away from the noxious cloud. 'Talk about what?' she demanded.

'We know what happened to your father,' I said to her. 'Come with us, and we'll tell you.'

Her eyes widened, but then she turned to Holt. 'Only if he comes too. We go together, or not at all.'

Aleida barked a laugh. 'I think that's the smartest thing I've heard you say yet. Fine, he can come. Get up here, both of you.'

Between reins and wand, I couldn't spare a hand to help her up. Not that she needed it, climbing up with ease, not getting even a little tangled in her divided skirts. Holt followed her without argument.

'Roll on, Dee,' Aleida said, still watching the marked men with her wand in her hand, the crystal still smouldering with a flickering flame at its heart. With a click of my tongue and a slap of the reins, I set Maggie moving once again, and left them in our dust.

❦

I concentrated on driving until we were past the rocks, leaving Aleida to watch behind. 'Toro still with us?'

'Yup. He's clearly got *some* sense. Those tattooed fools are hanging back, though. Must have realised they were biting off more than they could chew.'

Kara was peering around behind too, leaning past Holt to look back. 'Should have let her take them on,' she muttered, giving me a sidelong glance as she settled back into her seat.

Aleida gave a negative grunt. 'Nah. It was a good call, Dee, we've got bigger things to worry about. Sorry I snapped at you like that.'

I still didn't like it, but I was learning to shrug off her flashes of temper. 'What were they?' I said. 'Warlocks?'

'No, nothing like that. They're not really magic-users, despite what you just saw. It's the tattoos, they give them a few minor abilities. Very old spell, not terribly useful. Hardly anyone bothers with it anymore.'

Kara scoffed at that. 'Not terribly useful? Did you *see* how fast they moved?'

'If you're not ready for it they can be a pain, but they're not that hard to deal with.'

'What abilities?' I said, cutting in.

'Eh, nothing much. Some enhanced reflexes, strength and heightened healing, a bit of darksight. Sometimes they have resistance to mind control in there too.'

I turned to her with a frown. 'That doesn't sound like nothing much.'

'On the face of it maybe, but it's limited. They can move like that for a short time, but they won't be able to do it again in a hurry. Look, even ordinary folk can take them with a bit of planning and luck, but they're nothing to us.' She nudged me with her elbow. 'You could deal with them if you had to, and you're green as grass.'

'Oh, thanks,' I said sourly. 'Why do you say no one bothers with it? I mean, clearly they did.'

She shrugged. 'It *sounds* impressive, but living with it's a different matter. Those marks make you stand out like a sore thumb. They can forget about laying low somewhere or blending into a crowd.' She leaned around me to look across at Holt. 'Where'd you dig them up from?'

As Holt started to answer, Kara wrapped her hand around his arm and squeezed. 'Don't answer that,' she snapped. 'What do you care, anyway? I thought you had news about my father?'

'We'll get there. Let's get off the road first. Looks like we're nearly clear of the rocks. Take us over there, Dee,' she said, pointing to a gap in the trees up ahead. 'Back into the scrub.'

'You don't think they'll come after us?'

'Not unless they've got worms for brains,' she said.

Before long we were well hidden from the road, though close enough to hear if any other travellers came past. We all dropped down from the bench seat and gathered in a ragged circle, Aleida leaning against the wagon's huge wheel, Kara standing stiffly with her arms folded, and Holt looking like he didn't know what to do with himself since no one was paying attention to him.

Kara glowered at my teacher. 'Can we get down to business? You said you had word about my father.'

'First things first,' Aleida said. 'Where's my money?'

Kara clenched her jaw, and glared.

'Your money?' Holt said, looking bewildered. 'We never took anything from you!'

Aleida ignored him, and kept her gaze on Kara.

'It wasn't *yours*,' Kara said. 'You gave it away.'

'Oh, it's mine all right. And if you want to know where your father is, you'll hand it back.'

Kara blanched with anger, opening her mouth to speak, but before she could Holt caught her by the arm, squeezing hard. 'Kara! You never told me that money came from a witch!'

She yanked her arm away. 'And you never told me *she's* the one who gave you that cut yesterday!' She turned to Aleida. 'You can't take it back. I need it! Those toffee-nosed nuns don't need your help, they've got plenty of friends and favours to call on! I don't have anyone!'

'So that's why you took it?' Aleida said. 'To pay those thugs to help you?'

'Those marked men? No, not them.' She spat, and glanced at Holt. 'Him. To pay him, and his men.'

As one, we all turned to him.

'Look, it's not for *me*,' he protested. 'It's the lads! I promised them money when they agreed to follow me, and I'm a man of my word. Kara, sweet, I told you, I'd do anything for you, but my men … they've got families back home who need the coin. I can't ask them to work for free.'

Aleida heaved a sigh and turned back to Kara. 'Listen, kid. Dealings like this, the rule is you pay half upfront, and the rest when the job's done. If he's got all the money, you've got no leverage, and he'll just string you along. I'm surprised your da didn't teach you better than that.'

Kara looked down at her boots. 'I couldn't help it,' she muttered. 'The nuns buried all the coin under a bloody great flagstone, there's no way I could move it without him.'

Aleida's gaze slid to Holt. 'So. Where is it?'

He tried to smile, but there was something uncertain behind it. 'Here now, you can't just—'

'Oh, I can,' she said. 'And I will.'

Kara started to protest, but Aleida raised a hand and the girl's mouth snapped closed, and she fell silent.

'Well?' she said to Holt.

There was desperation in his eyes. 'I ... I ...' Power flexed around me, and he blurted, 'I don't have it!'

Aleida scowled at him, her face dark as thunder. Kara regained her voice. 'You *what?*' she demanded, rounding on him. 'What happened to it?'

'The ... those marked men. They took it. Last night, after we came back from the Haven. They just took it.'

With a hiss of rage, Kara punched him hard in the arm. 'You just let them do it? And you hid it from me? You godsdamned son of a bitch!'

Aleida rolled her eyes skyward. 'Oh, gods above, I'm dealing with amateurs.'

Kara and Holt didn't hear her, they were arguing too fiercely. 'I told you they were trouble,' Kara was hissing. 'This is all your fault! You should never have told them where we were!'

'Kara, I told you, I'll handle it. You have to trust me! I'll deal with them, I'll find your father. It'll all work out!' Then, looking thoughtful, he turned to Aleida. 'Actually, you could take care of them, couldn't you? Isn't that what you said?'

The look Aleida shot him was as cold as the heart of winter. 'Do I look like some godsdamn killer-for-hire to you?'

'Well, do you want the money back or not?' Kara said with narrowed eyes. 'We can't give you what we don't have. But if you help us get rid of them ...'

'You're offering to pay me off with my own damn coin? You've got balls, I'll give you that.'

Kara folded her arms tight across her chest. 'What about my da? You said you had news.'

This time, Aleida shrugged, leaning back against the side of the wagon. 'What about him? You not only stole my money, you went and lost it again the same night! Why should I tell you anything?'

Kara clenched her teeth, her face turning mottled red with fury. But before she could speak I reached for Aleida's arm. 'You can't just leave her hanging,' I hissed.

'Oh, I beg to differ.'

'He's her father! Just because you were raised by wolves doesn't mean the rest of us don't give a toss about our kin! Taunting her like that is just cruel! Besides,' I leaned closer and dropped my voice, 'it's not like she can do anything about it.'

Aleida started to pull away from me, and I saw her dark eyes tighten with anger. For a moment she looked about to speak — no, not speak. About to bite my head off. But then she fell still and blinked a few times, and just like that, the anger was gone. 'Oh. Yeah. That's a fair point.' She glanced at Holt. 'But let's just keep it between us for now. You there, you can go. Go on, run along.' She made a shooing motion with her hand and, looking bewildered, he obeyed, turning away to shuffle off through the dust and dry grass.

Aleida watched him go, and then turned to Kara. 'So, he promised, did he? I bet he promised a lot of things. Whatever it takes to get you into his bed, am I right? Well let me tell you one thing, girl — no man wants a girl's father lying in the tent next door and listening in when he's trying to get a bit of slap and tickle, you understand?'

Kara flushed furiously. 'I haven't—'

'Don't waste your breath trying to lie to me. Let me tell you, it's not worth it.'

'Oh, hold your wretched tongue!' she hissed, eyes blazing with anger. 'I'll do whatever it takes to get my father back, and Holt's the only godsdamn person in this wretched forest who's willing to help me! I'm not a fool. I know he's playing me. I'm playing him right back! And if you had only taken me out of the Haven like I wanted, the nuns would still have your precious money; so you're as much to blame for all this as anyone! Now, please,' she said with a crack in her voice. 'Please tell me about my da.'

Aleida tipped her face skywards with a puff of breath. 'Listen, kid, it's not good. Your father and his friends robbed the wrong person — they tangled with a witch. One with real power. She didn't take kindly to being assaulted on the roads, and she took the whole troupe prisoner.'

'But he's still alive. I *know* he's still alive.'

'Yeah, probably. I've got no reason to doubt you.'

'What has she done with them, then?'

'She's taken over some ruins up to the north,' I said. 'She dragged the lot of them up there, and worked some ritual to turn them all into beasts.'

Kara just stared at each of us in turn. 'What?'

'Yeah. It doesn't make a lot of sense, but that's what happened,' Aleida confirmed.

'But ... why?'

'Who knows? She must have had a good reason. Now, we know a few of them escaped — you haven't had any animals turning up back at your old house, acting strange, have you?'

Kara shook her head. 'No. None.'

'Right, I didn't think he made it out, but that pretty much confirms it; if he had he'd have gone to you by now.'

'By now?' Kara said, frowning. 'How long ago did this happen?'

'Months,' Aleida said. 'Four, or six.'

'That's about as long as he's been gone,' Kara said. 'So he's been there all that time? What is she doing with them?'

'Honestly, I have no idea,' Aleida said.

Kara took a step back, her eyes wide. 'She turned them into beasts ... but if we can get him out, you can turn him back, right? You said some others escaped, so it must be possible. Holt and his men can break him out, and then you can turn him back!'

Aleida shook her head, but Kara didn't see it. 'That ruin to the north, I know the one you mean. It's ten or fifteen miles from here. We could get there by tonight! If you can turn him back—'

'No.'

Kara broke off, staring at her. Then her eyes grew narrow. 'If this is about that blasted money ...'

'It's not. I can't break the spell.'

For a long moment, there was silence.

'Can't, or won't?'

Aleida said nothing. She just shrugged.

'I'll pay you,' Kara said through clenched teeth. 'I'll get the money. I'll kill those men myself if I have to.'

Aleida raised one eyebrow. 'Forget it, kid. You might be able to deal with one or two of them, if you were smart about it, but not all five. And it's not about the money, I honestly don't care that much; it's just the principle of the thing. And trust me, it's can't.'

Kara leaned back, studying her. 'Have you tried?'

Aleida looked away, raking her hair back from her face.

It cost her to admit she couldn't do it, I could see that. But what was pride when there were lives at stake? 'We tried,' I said. 'We managed it for a short time — no more than a few minutes. Long enough for him to tell us what happened.'

Kara leaned forward, her eyes intent. 'Who? Who told you?'

'He calls himself Toro,' I said. 'Do you know him?'

Kara gaped at me for a moment. Then her mouth snapped shut and she looked around wildly — and her eye fell on the ill-kempt chestnut horse that stood to the rear of the wagon, mostly out of sight, but with his ears pricked towards us.

She started towards him, hand resting on the hilt of her sword. 'Toro,' she said, and he gave a sharp snort, pawing the ground with one hoof.

'We met him in town yesterday,' I said. 'Well, I say met. Some of the village men were dragging him off, and we kind of got in the way. We could tell he wasn't really a horse, and, well, you heard the rest of it.'

Kara glowered at the beast. 'You escaped. You *escaped*, and left him there? You piece of shit! You godsdamned traitor! He was your friend! He was … he was …' For all her brow was furrowed and her eyes blazed with fury, tears were spilling down her face when her voice gave way. 'Why didn't you take him with you?'

Toro lowered his head with a low nicker.

Kara whirled to Aleida. 'Do it again.'

Aleida shook her head. 'I can't.'

'Don't give me that bullshit! Do it again! I need to talk to him!'

'I can't! I don't have it in me. I shouldn't even have done it the first time.'

'You're not strong enough, is that what you're saying? You're too weak?'

Again, Aleida shrugged, and Kara tossed her head in frustration. 'I have to talk to him, I have to.'

I was clenching my jaw hard enough to make my skull ache. I made myself let it go, and turned to my teacher. 'Isn't there something you can do? Not change him back again, but, I don't know, some spell or something?'

'What good would it do?'

'It's not for us,' I said. 'It's for *her*. We can't help her da, I get that, but if she can at least talk to someone who was there, ask him about it ... it's better than nothing, surely?'

Kara was listening, wiping tears from her cheeks. 'Please. You have to!'

Aleida looked from me to her and back again. 'Oh, Lord and Lady ...' She turned to Toro. 'Do you want this too?'

He snorted twice, before she'd even finished speaking. *Yes.*

'All right. Fine. You,' she pointed to the horse. 'Down. You need to be on the ground. I'm going to take you out of your body for a while, and there's a decent chance you'll fall — or I will.'

Toro snorted again. Then, he circled on the dusty earth, and carefully lowered himself until he lay on the ground, legs tucked to one side and his head and chest upright.

Aleida took a step towards him, then staggered when her leg seemed to give way beneath her. I hurried to steady her. 'Want your stick?'

'Just help me over to him first, then go fetch it. I'll definitely need it afterwards.' She leaned heavily on my arm, and then settled gingerly in the curl of Toro's legs, her back against his ribs. 'Can't believe I'm doing this,' she muttered, tucking her skirts around her feet to hide them. 'Right. Here goes.' She breathed out, her head sinking to her chest, and slumped as though the force that kept her up and breathing was suddenly ... gone.

Then, in the time it took to draw a sharp breath, her head lifted once more. Only her face … her face was different. The muscles slack, her mouth hanging open, her eyes wide and shocked. She looked down at herself, raised her hands to her face and then flinched back, as though they were something foreign and unexpected, and somehow terrifying.

Then, the horse swung his head around towards us and gave a sharp, impatient snort, and I understood at once what she'd just done. 'Kara,' I said, and nodded towards them. 'Go on.'

She looked utterly bewildered too, but she quickly shook it off. 'Toro?' she said.

Aleida's head came up, the eyes focusing on her. 'Kara.' The voice was deeper than Aleida's usual tones, rusty and harsh.

'What happened?' she said. 'What happened to him? Tell me!'

He rubbed his head, fingers tangling in Aleida's long hair. 'You've heard it already, lass. These ladies told you all there is to know.'

Kara narrowed her eyes. 'The hells they did. They said what happened, but not *why*. You all attacked a woman alone? Here, in our own damn neighbourhood? Don't shit where you eat; even I know that rule. *Why* would they do something like that?'

Aleida's eyes slid away. 'T'aint fit for your ears, girl.'

'I'm no fool,' Kara said through gritted teeth. 'I know what the others were like, Mattock and Grinner and the rest of those sods. They're the godsdamned reason

Da taught me how to fight. But my da wouldn't do that. He *wouldn't*. And there was a time I'd have sworn *you* wouldn't either.'

Aleida's gaze stayed off to the side, as though the one behind her eyes couldn't bear to look at Kara, this slender lass full of fury and determination. 'Your da didn't want to,' he said. 'You're right. He wouldn't. But the others … they made him come out to stop her on the road. They said he had to prove himself. Prove his loyalty to the troupe.'

Kara was seething, her breath hissing between her teeth. 'Loyalty? What bullshit is this?'

Aleida's eyes snapped up at that. 'No bullshit, girl. They knew he was pulling out, leaving us, and they didn't want to lose him. He was the best of us, you know — he knew people, people who'd tell us what caravans were worth hitting, what guards could be paid off, when things were getting too hot and it was time to make ourselves scarce. He was the reason we all lived as long as we have. We wouldn't last a year without him.'

Kara listened intently, pressing a knuckle to her lips while her left hand toyed with the hilt of her sword. 'But … leave? He never told me. Why? Where?'

'For you, lass. You're getting older now. He said it was time to start thinking about your life, your future. He didn't want you to waste any more years living in a hovel in the woods.'

Kara's eyes were wide with shock. 'No … no! I told him I didn't want that! I was happy here! I just wanted … I just wanted him around more. I didn't want him gone so much.'

'And how would you make a living?' Toro rumbled. 'Cutting wood? Gathering mushrooms? Poaching from Lord Belmont's lands? He was right, lass. He wanted more for you than this.'

'All right,' Kara said, her voice flat. 'So how did they find out? He wasn't stupid enough to tell them.'

Again, Aleida's eyes dropped, her gaze sliding away. 'No,' she said. 'No, I did.'

Kara stepped forward, her sword sliding out of its sheath. 'You? You son of a bitch, you *told them*?'

In the horse's body, Aleida tossed her head with a sharp snort. But I was already lunging forward to catch Kara's arm. 'Hey! No killing the messenger.'

She all but snarled at me, but she let me pull her back and took her hand from her sword. 'Why?' she said. 'Why would you betray him? You were his friend! At least, you used to be.'

Toro hung his head. 'It was the drink. Look, lass, I know what kind of man I am. I lose my mind when I drink, I always have. It's the reason I fell in with this cursed troupe in the first place, there was a noose awaiting me for what I did back home. And those bastards knew it, they knew there was nothing I wouldn't do for the grog. Your da was the only one who could keep a lid on things, he'd knock me on my arse if I was drunk, and keep them off my back if I was sober. But if he left me with them, I knew they'd be the death of me. Or I'd be the death of some poor sod in the wrong place at the wrong time. I couldn't take it. And the other lads, they could see something was amiss. So they got me drinking, and I spilled my guts. And then they got me to tell them what I swore I never would. I told them where you lived. So they told your father he had to stay, or they'd cut his throat on the spot, and then go pay you a visit. And then we saw this moll on the road, and Grinner hit on the idea to make him prove his loyalty.

'I knew it wasn't right. I knew it straight away. She wasn't normal, you see. She was dressed all in rags and scraps of leather, no proper clothes at all, and with these queer marks all over her skin. And those horses — two beautiful white horses, without a stitch of harness on them. It was just *off.* I knew it was going to go wrong, but all the others went down to nab her, so I went too, and then it all went to hell.'

Kara was still as stone, listening, her hands white-knuckled as they gripped her arms, folded across her chest. 'And then you escaped,' she said, her voice hoarse. 'But you didn't take him with you.'

'I couldn't,' he said, pleading in Aleida's voice. 'He was one of the big beasts, I don't know which one, I didn't see. All the big ones were chained up away from the gates. But me and the other two ... I got the idea she didn't think we were worth much. We barely got away as it was.'

He slumped then, abruptly falling forward as though taken by a faint. But then an instant later Aleida was back, sweeping her hair back from her face with both hands. 'All right, that's enough. Dee, bring me that stick.'

Kara was still, staring in shock as I stepped around her to help Aleida up and give her the staff. Toro stayed where he was, ears twitching, eyes showing their whites.

The poor sod was probably utterly disoriented. I knew I would be.

'You want some of your potion?' I asked Aleida quietly, but she shook her head.

'Just some water. Thanks, Dee,' she said, rolling her shoulders and stretching her neck.

I brought some for Kara, too. She looked like she needed it. She took the cup in both hands like a little child.

Aleida drank hers as Toro heaved himself to his feet. 'Well,' she said to him. 'I suppose that's one way to get sober. Look, you won't last out here. Maybe I can find a living for you somewhere, some kindly household that'll treat you decent while you work for your keep. Or you could stay with the girl, if she'll have you. It's up to you.'

His head low, Toro made a low nicker and turned away, his feet dragging in the dust.

As Aleida hobbled back to the wagon, Kara lifted her head. 'What do I do now?'

Aleida stopped to look her over, her eyes narrow and assessing. 'We're moving on. You ought to think about it too.'

Kara gaped at her. Then, her eyes filled with tears. 'Moving on? No! You can't!'

Aleida turned away with a sigh.

'Please!' Kara called after her. 'Please help me! You're the only one who can! Look, I'm sorry about the money. I'll find some way to get it back to you, I swear, just please help me save my father. I'll do anything you say, just tell me what to do!'

Shaking her head, Aleida started back towards the wagon. 'Just walk away. There's nothing you can do.'

Kara recoiled like she'd been slapped in the face. 'But... but you have to help me. You have to! You're a ... a—'

'What?' Aleida said. 'A good witch? I never claimed to be anything of the sort. Look kid, this is not my problem. As far as I see it, those sons of bitches got what's coming to them. If they didn't want to get turned into beasts and used for some ritual, they shouldn't have attacked a witch.'

Kara looked up at her with fury, and threw the cup down at her feet. 'You godsdamned hypocrite! Talking about my da like he's muck on your shoe! You're no better than he is, you sanctimonious harpy! I heard those wretched nuns gossiping about you, talking about all the things you've done!'

Aleida cocked her head to study her, like she was some curious specimen that had emerged in the gardens back home. 'Oh, it's true. It's all true, what you've heard. Listen kid, I'm going to give you some advice, though I know you don't care to hear it. It's a hell of a lot easier to avoid that life in the first place than it is to get in deep and claw your way out again. If you've got any coin stashed away, go and get it. Make your way to one of the big cities and find a sword-fighting school with a decent name. Look at you, you've got a pretty face, a good figure, got all your teeth — if you can fight worth a damn, the school will polish you up and get you a job as a bodyguard for some rich heiress, posing as her lady-in-waiting. You'll be living the high life, and getting paid to boot.'

'You can shove your advice up your arse!' Kara said. 'I'm not leaving here without him!'

'Up to you, it's your life. But there is one more thing ...' Aleida reached into the little pouch she carried on her belt, and pulled out a familiar thing: a little pot of shimmering ointment, and a tiny brush. 'Give me your hand.'

'I—' Kara started, her voice dripping fury, but then her mouth snapped shut, and she thrust out her right hand.

'Thank the gods for mind control,' Aleida muttered, opening the jar and swirling the brush in the ointment. 'Personally I wouldn't touch that sod Holt with a ten-foot pole; but you gotta do what you gotta do. This,' she said, painting a symbol onto the back of Kara's hand, 'will at least stop any other little souls getting tangled up in this mess. It's good for one year, all right? And that's assuming he hasn't already put a baby in your belly. If he did, it's too late for the ward to stop it, but the nuns back at Haven will take you in if it comes to that.'

The moment she finished, Kara snatched her hand away. 'Screw the nuns,' she said. 'And screw you.'

'Yeah, yeah. Good luck.'

In a flood of tears, Kara turned and bolted into the forest.

I frowned after her, biting my lip. My heart ached for her. I barely remembered my father, but I couldn't begin to count the number of nights I'd lain sleeplessly running over and over what memories I did have of him. I couldn't imagine how Kara must feel, finally learning the truth after worrying for so long, only to be told to give him up for dead — and to hear it so heartlessly, too.

On the other hand, the last thing I wanted was for Aleida to decide she had to go and confront this witch, whoever she was.

I felt torn in two, but there was one thing clear. Aleida seemed quite content with her decision, but Kara was distraught. 'I'm going after her,' I said to Aleida. 'I need to make sure she's all right.'

She nodded, as though she'd expected as much. 'Go on, then. Just keep your wits about you.'

CHAPTER 6

kara whirled when she heard me behind her, her hand flying to the hilt of her sword. 'What do you want?'

'I just wanted to make sure you're okay,' I said. 'I'm sorry we didn't have better news for you.'

She wiped tears away with an angry hand, and sniffed.

'What are you going to do?' I said.

'I am not giving up on him! I don't care what he's done or what you think of him, he's my father and I love him! I'm not giving up without a fight!'

'Of course not!' I said. 'I never thought you would. Look, Aleida … she never had a father. She doesn't know what it's like to lose one.'

'And you do?' Kara snapped.

'Yeah, I do. My da died when I was little. It was lockjaw, there was an accident while he was cutting wood.'

'Oh,' she said. Hesitantly, she turned away from me, heading back towards the bandits, but glancing back to see if I'd follow.

'I take it your ma's not around?' I said.

'She died a few years back. Da was away, and she just got sick one day. Real sick. Now it's just him and me.'

'What's his name?' I was trying to remember the woodcuts I'd seen back in town, and the names Toro had stammered out last night in the few brief moments he'd been back in human form.

'Brent,' she said. 'His name's Brent. But that's not what the others called him, they had nicknames they used out on the road, and that's what they put on that stupid wanted notice that was plastered all over town. There they called him Brute. Picture didn't look nothing like him, either.'

'It must be hard, living out there all on your own.'

Kara lifted her chin in a way that reminded me of Aleida. 'I'm used to it. It's just the way it's always been.'

'So what's your plan? How are you going to get the men to help you if the money's gone?'

She slowed, and stopped, wrapping her arms around herself. 'I don't know. If it was just Holt I could manoeuvre him to do what I want, but these outsiders have thrown everything awry. They want Holt to be their face-man, like Da was for his troupe. They can't show themselves much, what with those tattoos, your mistress was right about that. But Holt can talk to anyone.' She sighed, then, rubbing her eyes. 'Even if I can't turn Da back, if I can get him out alive, that's better than nothing. I don't care about leaving, if I get him out we can stay here forever. We just need to find a way to get rid of those outsiders.' She gave me a dark glance from under beetled brows. 'Is your mistress really going to walk away from all this?'

I shrugged. 'I honestly don't know what she'll do. This morning she swore blind that we were going to check on you and find the money and then be on our way, but now ...'

'*Check* on me?' Kara interrupted, heat in her voice. 'I don't need—'

'The nuns told Lord Belmont and his men that you'd been dragged off by the bandits,' I said. 'But that's how you wanted it to look, isn't it? Not a bad idea. If Belmont knew for certain that you'd opened the doors he'd put your face up on the wanted poster beside your father's.'

She was silent at that for a long moment. 'They lied for me? I never expected that.'

'I think they know you're in a tough spot,' I said. 'We do, too. Really.'

'You're not as heartless as your bitch of a mistress, then,' Kara said, and she rubbed a weary hand across her eyes and tipped her face up to the sky. 'Oh, Lord and Lady,' she groaned. 'Why couldn't Da have escaped instead of that wretch Toro? I can't believe he'd do that to Da. They used to be friends!'

'Did you know him well? I thought your da kept you away from the others.'

'Most of them, yeah, but Toro ... He used to have a wife, and a daughter. Her name was Abby, and she was my best friend when I was a kid. We were born in the same summer, and we didn't have to worry about keeping secrets since Abby's da was in the business, too. They'd come to stay with us, sometimes, when da and Toro were away for work. His missus had family over in Lord Haversleigh's lands, that's where they lived most of the time; but one day there was a fire ... half the village burned, or so I heard. I never saw him much after that. Ma told me he crawled into a bottle after they buried them, and never really came out again.'

'Oh, Lord and Lady, that poor fellow.'

Kara gave me a sharp look, opening her mouth to retort — but then there came a sound that made us both fall still. Twigs cracking, somewhere close.

Kara's eyes were wide as she met mine, and she reached for her sword-hilt.

A crash in the dry bushes behind me made me turn — and then something hit me hard from behind, sending me staggering. As I fell, an arm snaked around me, pulling me upright again and clamping me firmly against a man's chest, as solid as a tree-trunk. I tried to kick at him, but it was like trying to kick at a boulder, even with my hobnailed boots. He didn't seem to notice.

With a curse, Kara drew her sword. 'Let her go!'

I knew without looking around that it was one of the tattooed bandits, and I felt him laugh as the rest of the thugs emerged from the bushes to surround us. Silently, I cursed my teacher. Hadn't she said they wouldn't be able to move so quickly again without a rest? Then, with chagrin, I realised that one of the bandits *hadn't* used his burst of speed back on the road, after all.

'We should take her as well,' one of the others said,

nodding to Kara. 'That idiot Holt will soon fall into line when he knows we've got his girl.'

'Might be best,' another agreed. 'Don't want her telling the witch just where her little bird has vanished to. Let her think the lass's run off.'

I went for my knife, but before I could get to it the bandit caught my wrist and forced my arm up, grasping it in the same hand that kept me pressed against his chest. Then he plucked my dagger from my belt and threw it down in the dust.

I had an idea, then, thinking of the day before when Holt had swung himself up on the seat beside me. I twisted in the bandit's grasp, reaching for the wand that hung by my thigh.

He tightened his grip, squeezing me so hard I could barely breathe, and as my hand found the wand he found it too, crushing my fingers against the crystal at its tip with bruising force.

I felt power pulse, and with a blinding flash of light and a crack like thunder he was hurled away from me in a stinking cloud of scorched wool and hair.

With a ragged breath I pulled my wand free and stooped to snatch up my knife. That was Aleida's working, the one that meant only she or I could touch my wand. When she'd done it, I'd taken it as a defence against pickpockets, and though she'd never bothered to explain otherwise, the look she'd given me when I'd said as much now made sense.

As I moved closer to Kara she swung around, so we were back to back. 'Looks like you boys might want to rethink this whole thing,' Kara said to them. 'Looks to me like you've found more than you can handle.'

The men ignored her words, and drew their swords. The one who'd grabbed me picked himself up, shaking his head like a dog. 'Make sure you take them alive, lads. Don't have to be in one piece.'

I gripped my weapons tight and glanced upwards. How long before Aleida would come to check on us? I doubted we were close enough for her to hear the scuffle.

In the clear sky I saw the eagle's dark shape, much lower than before, clearly a bird now and not a distant dark speck. I looked away, but an instant later something dragged my gaze back.

Poised above us in blinding white and sun-lit gold was a magnificent creature — wings as long as our wagon, eagle's talons outstretched. It must have been soaring too high above us for me to hear the beats of its wings or to see its shadow outlined upon the ground, but now it was diving down from the heavens like an avenging angel — a griffin, swooping down upon us.

Every instinct within me screamed at me to run. Those eyes were full of ancient hunger, and they were fixed right on *me*.

I backed into Kara, pushing her off balance, and she cursed at me. 'Bloody hells, Dee.'

'Run!' I yelled, stepping around her, and bolted, not caring a whit about the bandits and their swords.

Above us, the griffin shrieked, like a demon freshly released from hell. I felt the buffeting of the wind as it spread those vast wings, beating the air to chase after me, and I knew how a hare felt when a hawk swooped down upon it.

The bandits moved to intercept me, but the sight of the griffin tailing me made them falter. I tried to dodge around them, but I'd forgotten what Aleida had said about their marks — enhanced reflexes, was that how she put it? The nearest of the bandits moved like a striking snake, grabbing me by the arm and swinging me around to his side.

But he hadn't reckoned on the griffin's bulk, or its speed. With a twist of its wings it changed course and slammed into both of us, driving us down to the ground. Those huge talons closed around the bandit's shoulders, and he cried out in pain as the creature's enormous bill-hook of a beak gaped wide above his head.

Squirming with all my strength, I managed to bring up my knife and wand to cross them in a ward, a bubble of force, just as the griffin's beak snapped closed. I hadn't given a thought to the bandit above me, but the shield saved him as well as the beak slid harmlessly off the impervious shell.

Then, with a screech of anger, the griffin pulled away. The others had regrouped to attack its hindquarters, and it turned to slash at them with sickle-sized talons.

I shoved the bandit off me, and tensed when I felt someone grab my shoulders — but it was Kara, dragging me up. 'Come on, run!' she screamed at me, and together we took off, heading for the nearest cover, a huge, sprawling tree. It wouldn't help us much against the bandits, but it would keep the griffin from swooping down upon us. 'What in the hells is that thing?' Kara demanded as we ran.

'They've got one at the tavern back in the village,' I said. 'Have you been to see it?'

'It's a fake,' she said. 'Those things are always fakes, Da says.'

'This one's not,' I said, glancing back. With powerful strokes of its huge wings, the griffin was lifting off the ground again, trying to escape the men and their swords. One man was lying wounded and bloody in the dust.

'Can you hide us or something?'

'No, I can't do veils yet. But Aleida will come, she *must* have heard all this fighting!' She had to be on her way already, surely? But then I bit my lip, hard, thinking of the eagle that had been soaring above us all morning. If this other witch had been watching us, then she must know I was only the apprentice. If she'd sent a griffin after me, then the gods only knew what she'd sent after my teacher, back at the wagon.

'I'm not waiting around to be rescued,' Kara said. 'Maybe we can lose these arseholes in the trees. Come this way, quickly!'

She ducked around the trunk of the tree, heading away from the bandits and the wagon, vaguely in the direction of the rocky scar — and the rest of the bandit troupe. Still, that was probably better than taking my chances with the marked men. I picked up my skirts, and we ran, darting from tree to tree.

We hadn't gone far when I heard a shout from the marked men as they realised we'd slipped away.

'Keep your head down,' Kara hissed to me, still heading back towards the rocks.

I could hear voices shouting somewhere nearby — not those of the marked men we'd left behind, but others. Holt's men, maybe? From somewhere above came the screech of a griffin — and then another, rising up in answer. *Oh gods, there's two of them.*

Kara halted, waving me to stop beside her. 'We're running out of cover.' Ahead of us was open ground, stubbed and studded with pale boulders, with only a scanty thatching of stunted trees and withered bushes. 'We'll have to run for the Scar. There's lots of narrow paths between those boulders — we'll crawl into a crack where they can't reach us.'

I bit my lip, saying nothing. There was another option, if I could make it work. But I hadn't been able to do it since that first desperate time, months ago in the mountains around Black Oak Cottage. I couldn't explain it to Kara though; I hardly understood it myself.

'Looks clear,' Kara hissed in my ear. 'Go!'

I followed on her heels, clutching my skirts to lift them clear of my feet. As we ran I caught a flash of movement from the corner of my eye and glanced around — only to falter as my heart leapt to my throat once again.

There was a huge, tawny beast charging towards us. Fierce golden eyes burning in a snarling face, surrounded by a dark mane, rippling with the wind as it sprinted, faster than a galloping horse. It was a lion, honest-to-gods, right in the middle of this tinder-dry forest where it had no business being.

Kara turned at my strangled cry of warning, and yelped in surprise. 'What in the hells?'

My legs faltered. It was pointless trying to run. The beast charged, breath grunting in its throat with every pulse of muscle. And just like the griffins, its fervent gaze was fixed right on *me*.

There was no time to think. Already the beast was leaping, and there was nothing I could do but cast the ward again and brace for impact.

There was no question of sending the creature bouncing back — it had to weigh as much as a small horse. It slammed into my shield and once again I was knocked sprawling on the dusty ground. But instead of those huge paws and wicked claws digging into my shoulders, they slid right off me. The lion hit the ground near as hard as I did, kicking up a cloud of dust.

Half-winded and coughing, I staggered up, while the lion found its feet with a sinuous twist of its spine. Kara darted in front of me, sword held low, while I struggled with the tangle of my skirts. With a guttural snarl, the lion swiped at Kara with a huge paw, and she answered it with two quick slashes of her blade, one to the swiping foot, the second across the beast's face, making it pull back with a growl. 'Dee, get up!'

'I'm trying! These blasted skirts!'

As we spoke, the lion feinted to one side, and when Kara swung to counter, the beast darted back, charging past her and towards me.

I was already summoning fire to my wand, feeling it sear down my arm and into my hand, and loosed it in a burst that made the beast think better of springing at me again — instead it shied aside with a snarl and the wafting stench of singed hair. On its flank I caught a flash of gold — it looked like a wax seal, the sort folk used on fancy letters, only made with solid gold and pressed into the fur.

I backed away, feeling Kara beside me. 'The rocks,' I hissed. 'We have to get to the rocks.'

'Yeah,' she said with a shaky voice. 'Find some crevice it can't fit through.'

I hoped that would be enough. I knew my fireballs wouldn't hold it off for long — an ordinary beast might be driven away with fire, but not this one. There was a man's mind behind those golden eyes, I was certain of it, and with that strange golden seal as well. The strange witch had sent him after us. After *me*.

I could hear other noises around us — shouting voices, and the thudding of galloping hooves, but I could barely make them out over the thundering of my heart in my ears. There came another roar, too, somewhere nearby, but I couldn't look around for the source, not while the lion crouched, ready to leap again. *Oh gods, what else is she going to throw at us?*

The lion crouched, snarling — and then a huge red blur slammed into the beast. It was Toro, galloping at full pelt directly for the beast. The impact sounded like a side of meat hitting a stone slab, and the pair of them went down, tumbling together in a tangle of limbs.

With a yell of dismay, I started forward, my head full of images of the lion's claws sinking into Toro's chestnut hide, those huge yellow teeth buried in his neck ...

But before I could take a step, I felt a hand on my shoulder, nails digging in. 'Don't move!' a familiar voice growled in my ear, and I shivered in relief. 'Aleida!'

Something cool settled over me, like gentle, tingling rain — a veil, hiding us from sight. 'Head for the rocks!' Aleida said, fingers digging into my shoulder to pull me away.

'But Toro! He'll be killed!'

'He's just distracting the beast so we can slip away. Once we're clear he'll leave it in the dust. Move!'

Kara didn't argue, she just headed for the shelter of the Scar, sheathing her sword as she went. I started with her, but dropped back when I realised Aleida couldn't keep pace, limping along with her staff. 'Where's Maggie?'

'She's safe, I turned her loose under a veil.'

The shouting voices were growing louder now, and at last the source of them came into sight, rushing towards us as they rounded the rocks — Holt and his bandits. The men must have trailed after us as we drove away from their ill-fated ambush, and met up with Holt after Aleida sent him away. But something had them retreating rapidly now, some helping their wounded fellows as they stumbled through the dust, shouting and hollering — and from behind them came another roar, loud enough to make my breath catch in my throat. It sounded bigger than the beast we'd just escaped from.

A moment later it came into view — a bear, huge, shaggy and hulking. It had to be nearly as tall as Toro, with rippling muscles under the thick brown fur, snarling lips baring teeth as long as my finger.

'Get into the rocks!' Holt shouted. 'Go!'

Aleida dropped the veil as we joined them, retreating between the warm milk-white boulders. If the men were startled by our appearance, it didn't bother them for long. From the sky above came a familiar shriek and Aleida and I both tipped our heads back to see griffins wheeling above — two of them this time.

'Damn it,' Aleida said. 'This is not going to cut it, Dee. You're going to have to get this one.'

I just blinked at her. 'What?'

She laid a hand on my shoulder, and the gesture was half a squeeze, half a shove along the path. 'Come on; you've got an ace up your sleeve, and now's the time to use it! Find us a pathway, now!'

The word struck a chill in my chest, like a band of ice around my ribs. 'I can't!'

'You can, you've done it before.'

'But I've tried and tried, and I've never been able to do it again.'

'Don't think, just do,' she said, while behind her the bear roared, shouldering between the narrow boulders after us. 'I'll keep them off your back. Go, Dee!'

She pushed her way back along the path as the bandits all crowded around, smelling of sweat and dust and blood. More than a couple of them were wounded. 'What's the plan?' one of them said. 'We've got to keep moving, find somewhere to hide.'

'Ain't nowhere those beasts can't get to,' another one babbled, cowering against the rocks.

'There's something wrong with those creatures out there. Something unnatural.'

I clenched my teeth and tried to block out the voices, weaving between the bodies until I found a wall of stone and pressed my palms against it.

It was smooth and warmed by the sunlight, dusted with orange lichen. I closed my eyes and leaned against it, trying to block out all the noise and chaos behind me as the bear roared and the griffin screeched, and the men around us yammered in confusion and dismay.

I felt a flicker of energy under my fingertips — my friendly little earth elemental. He'd taken something of a shine to me when I first arrived at Black Oak Cottage, and brought me little presents from time to time. I'd come to call him Facet, and he liked to join us when we went a-travelling. Now he hovered inside the stone, come to see what I was up to. 'Help me,' I murmured. *'Please* help me.'

A wordless question came back, just as it always did, and my heart sank. Every time I'd tried this since the day Kian lured me to the top of the waterfall, it always ended the same way. Facet didn't understand what I was asking. I pressed my forehead against the rock as behind me I felt Aleida loose the power in her wand, and heard the *whomph* of a fireball and the pained bellow of the bear. *Somewhere safe. We need to get somewhere safe, somewhere cool and calm and quiet where the beasts can't follow.* 'Please,' I said again, but I knew it was hopeless. I didn't know how I'd done it back in Lilsfield, and after all I'd learned about witchcraft I felt I understood it even less. But I could remember the chill of those dark passages, the sharp, earthy scent of clay in the air, the feel of the rough stone under fingers trailing along the wall.

Inside the stone, I felt my friend twitch as though startled ... and then the rock began to fold away.

I stumbled forward, opening eyes that were all but blind after the glare of the sun. The huge boulder slowly parted, like a loaf of bread being torn open. Inside, hanging in the air, was my friend, all his planes and facets rippling with light as they slowly spun through each other. He looked a little like the paper snowflakes children make for midwinter, only made of light and crystal and movement, while behind him a dark passage stretched down into the earth.

'Everyone in!' I shouted.

No one moved, until beside me Kara called, 'Holt, get them moving!'

'What? Oh! All right, you sons of bitches, everyone into the hole! Go, go, go!'

As the men filed past, I saw Aleida at their rear, her straw hat tipped back on her head and her staff raised high. Above her, the griffins wheeled and shrieked, one of them swooping down to alight on a boulder beside the path, while just past a cluster of rocks the bear snarled and struggled, fighting something I couldn't see. 'Aleida! Come on!' I shouted, not daring to take my hands from the rock. 'It's open!'

Casting a swift glance over her shoulder she started towards us, retreating step by step. She had to pass by the griffin, though, its bill-hook beak just above her head.

Then, before my eyes, my teacher blurred, like ripples in water will blur the image cast upon the surface. It lasted just an instant, and then my teacher let her staff fall, and, fleet as a deer, leapt up and sprinted out past the stones, out into the bare ground around the Scar.

Beside me, Kara gave a cry of dismay. 'What is she doing?'

The griffin perched on the boulder snapped its head around to follow her, its black pupils swelling huge, like the eyes of a hunting cat, and it leapt into the air with a mighty pulse of its wings. The one still aloft gave a shriek of triumph, and the two beasts took off after her in a flurry of wings and lashing tails.

It was enough to make my breath catch in my throat, my heart pounding beneath my stays, even though I knew exactly what she was doing.

Too late, I remembered that Kara had no idea. Beside me, she spat a curse, and then took off, sprinting after Aleida, even though by all appearances my teacher was yards away by now, with the griffins swooping down on her.

'Kara, stop!' I yelled, but while the words were still in my mouth, Kara slammed hard into something unseen in the path.

With a crackle like flames in dry grass, my teacher lost her hold on the veil that was hiding her from sight, and she and Kara both went sprawling over the rocks.

'Oh, for pity's sake,' Aleida groaned. 'Damn it, kid! Get up! Get back inside!'

Kara gaped at her in shock. 'But … you …'

'I'm a witch, you stupid child, or had you forgotten?' Snatching up her staff, Aleida tried to stand, only to stagger again as loose rocks rolled beneath her feet. 'Quickly, before they figure out it's just an illusion!'

Out past the rocks, the griffins had discovered just that — they were searching the dusty ground, like cats pouncing on a fragment of sunlight reflected off glass.

But I wasn't concerned about them. Just past the rocks, the bear lifted its huge head, fixing its gaze upon Aleida and Kara. I had no idea what Aleida had done to distract it, but from the looks of it that spell had died along with the veil when Kara knocked her to the ground. With a vicious snarl, the beast charged, moving far faster than a creature that size should ever move.

Aleida was backing away, her hand around Kara's arm, pulling the girl with her, just a few paces from safety.

But then Kara yanked her arm free, almost pulling Aleida off her feet again, and drew her sword. 'You go, I'll hold it off!'

'Don't be so bloody stupid! Get inside!'

I bit my lip, helpless to do anything but watch as I held the pathway open. Kara stood no chance, sword or not. Even if she could have struck the beast dead, she'd have been crushed as it fell. It'd be like being hit by a boulder.

But at the sight of her, standing fearless and defiant, the bear wrenched itself aside with a pained grunt, stumbling off the path and slamming into a boulder. With a snarl of protest and pain it snapped at the empty air, as though fighting something we couldn't see.

No, I realised. No, it was fighting itself, trying to advance and retreat at the same time.

Staring up at the huge beast, Kara slowly lowered her sword. 'Da?' she said. 'Da, is that you?'

In answer, the bear roared again, and lunged for her with claws and teeth, huge jaws gaping wider than her head — only to hit the ward Aleida cast behind her, slamming against an invisible wall.

'Get into the godsdamn cave, kid,' Aleida growled in her ear, and finally, Kara did as she was told, backing slowly away, unable to take her eyes off the huge, shaggy beast.

Step by step, they retreated, and the moment they passed the threshold, I let the door close. The rock flowed in behind me, cutting off the daylight.

In the absolute darkness, the only sound was Kara as she sobbed. 'Da ... Da.'

I could hear the voices of the men ahead of us, half panicked, half relieved. Holt hurried after them, but Kara didn't. She stayed where she was, her face blank with shock.

The shock lasted until Aleida moved past her, leaning heavily on her stick with each step. As she passed, Kara's hand lashed out and caught her by the sleeve. 'Take me back!'

Aleida stopped with a sigh. 'You're asking the wrong person. But either way, the answer is no.'

'But that was him! I know it was! Go back, we can bring him in here! We can get him away from her!'

'No,' Aleida said, firmly. 'Lord and Lady, do you know how close he came to killing you back there?'

'No!' Kara said. 'No, he stopped! He saw me and he stopped, you can't deny it!'

'Yeah. Once. And then the witch laid into him. She's riding him, Kara, he might have taken her by surprise the first time but she won't let it happen again.' She shook her sleeve free and limped along the path again. 'Come on. Can't be hanging around in between, it's not safe.'

She'd mentioned that once before, the last time I'd used a pathway. The only other time I'd done it, if you want to be accurate. I'd never got around to asking further, especially since I hadn't managed to open one again. And now didn't seem the best time. I hurried after her, my wand in my hand, for all the good it would do me. I wasn't sure fireballs would be any use against the sort of threats that lurked in ... whatever this place truly was.

Thankfully, it wasn't far to the shelter Facet had found for us. After only a hundred yards or so, the pathway brought us to a quiet cavern, a calm little bubble within the rock. There was a small stream flowing through it, and a kind of beach made up of round, water-smoothed stones.

We were the last ones to reach it. The bandits were there already, clustered around a few candle stubs someone must have been carrying in a belt-bag.

I waited in the end of the passageway until Aleida glanced back and beckoned me with a jerk of her head. 'Close the door, Dee. Don't let the flies in.'

I stepped away from the wall, and felt the rock melt closed behind me. I tried very hard not to think about what would happen if I couldn't manage to communicate to Facet that we wanted to go back. 'What happens if someone gets left in between?' I said, quietly. The bandits hadn't yet noticed that the doorway was closed.

'Well,' Aleida said, rubbing the back of her neck. 'It's a good way to get rid of someone you don't like, let's put it that way.' She limped over to a fallen slab of stone and sat gingerly, easing herself down to lean back against the wall.

Kara jammed her hands on her hips to glare at her. 'Are you just going to sit there? There are wounded men here!'

'You should probably go help them then,' Aleida said, closing her eyes and tipping her head back against the stone.

Kara started towards her, but I quickly stepped in front of her. 'I'll come help,' I said. With one more dark look for my teacher, Kara came away with me, heading towards the milling men.

They'd been a sorry-looking bunch to start with, and between our defence of the wagon and then the rout from the witch's beasts, each and every one looked bedraggled and forlorn. A number of them clustered around Holt, talking fiercely and sending wary glances our way.

It was probably wiser not to intrude upon those affairs. I turned away, but made sure I could keep watch on them from the corner of my eye.

Instead I turned to a lad who seemed to be the youngest of the troupe. He sat against the stony wall with his knees drawn up to his chest and his right arm cradled across his chest. He was deeply tanned with sun-bleached hair and he looked close to tears, but when I started towards him he lifted his chin and hurriedly sniffed them away.

'How bad is it?' I asked him, crouching down on my heels in front of him.

'Oh, it's, it's naught,' he started to say, but as soon as he tried to move he paled with a hiss of pain, just as the ring on my finger hummed again. 'Oh, well, it might be broken. I suppose. That rotten bear got me.'

'Mm.' It was certainly swollen enough. Not that I had a lot of experience with this sort of thing. 'Well, it looks to be straight still, that's a blessing.' I pointed to the stout stick lying on the rocks beside him. He didn't have a sword; that stick was the nearest thing he had to a weapon. 'You could use that as a splint for now. You'll need something for padding, though. Maybe if we cut the sleeves off your shirt? D'you want me to help?'

He glanced around furtively, then swallowed hard and nodded. 'Could you?'

He had to be close to my age, and decent-looking too, with the sort of muscle a lad gets from working in the fields — not that I was looking exactly, I just couldn't help but notice as I cut the sleeves from his shirt and tore them into strips. I tried to hold my tongue, but it didn't take long for my curiosity to get the better of me. 'Why d'you do this?'

He looked at me briefly before his eyes slid away. 'Do what?'

'Don't play the fool,' I said. 'Why do you rob people on the roads?'

He looked down at his good hand and flushed. 'It's easy money, Holt said. We weren't going to hurt anyone, not really. And I ... I need the coin, see? My mam is sick, she has been for months. We've been calling the physician out all the bloody time; but there's naught left to pay him with. We've got a cow, just the one, and my old man promised the physic we'd sell her once she's had her calf and pay him then. But if we do that there'll be no milk for my little brothers until the calf's old enough to breed, and that's if she even drops a heifer and not a bull, *and* if it lives; and I ask you, what's the calf going to eat if we sell her dam away? I thought, if I can get a little money we can hold the sawbones off for a bit longer, or maybe just buy a nanny goat so Mam and the boys can have some milk.'

I'd been waiting for the amethyst ring to hum at me, but it never did. 'I suppose there's not much honest work around these parts.'

He dropped his gaze. 'Not really. Not a lot.' There it was. The ring on my finger hummed like a bee. 'And then you and your missus came along and everything's gone to shit,' he went on, bitterly.

I sighed. 'Oh come on. You don't expect the people you rob to try and fight back? Maybe the money's not so easy after all.'

He glowered at me. 'It's all ruined now anyway. Only them who fight get a share of the spoils and I can't do a thing with this ruddy arm broken, here or at home. Why couldn't you just—'

'Just what?' I said. 'Let you rob us?'

He pressed his lips tight together and pulled the cloth I was winding out of my hand. 'I can do the rest meself.'

'If you like,' I said. 'I'll leave you to it, then.'

When I looked around the rest of the troupe, the only person who would meet my gaze was Kara. She glanced around with a frown and then came over to me, wiping bloody hands on a handkerchief she must have soaked in the stream. 'Maybe you should let me and Holt see to the rest of them,' she said. 'Might be best.'

'Yeah,' I said. 'Just can't imagine why they don't seem to like me.'

'It's just the way of things,' she said. 'You want them to be happy you trounced them and then got them attacked by wild beasts?'

'They didn't have to attack us.'

'You didn't have to trick them into it!' Kara hissed. 'All right, they're scum. You know it, I know it. My da is too. But he's still my da, the only one I've got!'

'I know,' I said. 'That's why we're still here.'

She pressed her lips together. 'When are you going to take us back?'

I looked across at Aleida. 'When she says it's safe. I'll go ask.'

'All right. Um, Dee?'

'Yeah?' I said.

'Thanks. And I'm sorry; I know I'm being a right bitch. I don't mean to be, I'm just … I've been so worried …'

'I know,' I said. 'I won't hold it against you. Let me go talk to my mistress, okay?'

The rocks slid and rolled beneath my feet as I went to where Aleida sat.

'Well, Dee,' she said as I crouched beside her. 'Were you touched by their gratitude?'

'I didn't help him for the sake of gratitude,' I said archly. 'Besides, it's our fault they got clobbered by those beasts, isn't it?'

'Not really,' she said. 'It was their choice to stick their noses into our business. They could have just stayed in the rocks and watched the whole affair from afar. Or, you know, stayed home in the first place instead of trying their hands at highway robbery.'

'So they deserve what they get, then?'

'Pretty much.' She cocked an eyebrow at me, studying me with her dark eyes. 'Oh, good grief, do you really feel sorry for them?'

I bristled at that — on the surface at least. Inside, my heart seemed to shrink, turning icy cold. 'Fine,' I snapped. 'I'm a soft-hearted fool with all the sense of a newborn lamb, and if I ever strayed out on my own I'd be robbed blind before I'd gone a mile.' I folded my arms tight across my chest and blinked back tears that stung in my eyes.

Beside me, my teacher was silent and still. 'That sounds like your blasted stepfather talking,' she said at last. 'Dee, what I said came out wrong, I didn't mean it that way.'

'How did you mean it, then?'

She rubbed her head again, wincing. 'I meant, you've got empathy by the wagon-load. It's something I don't have a lot of, and I know full well that's not a good thing. But too much can be just as crippling as too little, so maybe just have a care with it, all right?'

Now it was my turn to be silent, thinking her words over. 'I guess I'm just trying to understand why they're doing it,' I said. 'I mean, it's so stupid! They're like children playing a ridiculous game. Lurking on the roads, playing at being highwaymen like it's just a big lark! And it's not as though their mamas never taught them that stealing is wrong. What do they think is going to happen? It's like watching a puppy wander into the bull's pen; you just know the poor dumb beast is going to get the walloping of its life.'

'Exactly!' Aleida said. 'They're either going to kill someone or get killed themselves, and then Lord Belmont will come along and hang them. It's just … pointless. Then again, it's not like anyone ever needed a reason to do something stupid.'

I bit my lip for a moment, thinking. 'But you used to be like that, weren't you? Before Gyssha found you, you said you were a thief.' She'd told me that story once before — Gyssha had found her after she'd been caught stealing, and was in a dungeon waiting to have her hand cut off.

She shifted on the stones. 'I'd say it's not the same, but I bet every one of those fools has a reason why they're not like the others, why it's okay for *them*, just this once.'

'So why did you do it?'

With a low chuckle, she picked up a water-rounded pebble and rolled it between her fingers. 'My sisters taught me when I was just little — they practically raised me, you know, since Ma was either out working or drunk. We'd head down to the marketplace first thing in the morning to beg for food, or steal it if folk were stingy. They taught me to filch things from stalls and handcarts, or from the baskets of folk walking by. Most people won't beat a tiny child who gets caught thieving, and I learned pretty quickly to weep and wail and beg for mercy — and run for it as soon as I could wriggle free. My sisters made such a fuss when I got something good! They'd praise me to the moon!'

I found myself thinking of little Maisie, back home, and what I'd do if she woke up crying of hunger and there was nothing to eat. 'They were all you had,' I said. 'Just like Kara's da.'

She shrugged then, a faint smile on her lips.

Then I remembered the conversation we'd had earlier that day, and shook my head. 'I still can't believe you didn't find them after you left Gyssha.'

I regretted the words as soon as I said them, but that faint smile never left her lips. 'I guess I'm just cold-hearted, like you said.'

'Oh clearly,' I said tartly, turning back to the would-be bandits huddled together at the far end of the cave, as far from us as they could easily get, and I felt myself frown. 'I wish there was something we could do. I just know it's all going to go badly for them, and I wish someone could slap some sense into them and send them home before it gets that far. Before someone really gets hurt. Even their own stupid selves.'

'Mm,' Aleida said. 'You and me both, kid.'

I gave her a sidelong glance. 'Can't you do something? A compulsion, or something, to send them away?'

She heaved a sigh. 'Sure. I could make them pack up and go home. But the moment it wore off, they'd turn around and come back. Mind control is temporary, Dee, you can't just make someone be a decent person when they don't want to be. They have to decide that for themselves.'

I clenched my teeth in frustration, bunching my skirt in my hands. 'I just ... it feels like there should be *something* we can do!'

''Fraid not. See, this is why I prefer my way of dealing with it. It's not my problem. They've chosen the noose already, just like I chose the axe when I was a thief back in Stone Harbour.'

'But someone saved you from that fate.'

'Yeah,' Aleida said, gazing out over the water. 'And look where it got her. Honestly, Dee, I'm probably not the best person to talk over these questions of morality. It should be pretty clear by now that I'm bumbling around in the dark.'

'Not completely,' I said. 'I mean, you came here for the Haven, and that place was lovely.'

'Well, even a broken clock is right twice a day.'

I could see there was no use talking further on that matter. 'So. What do we do now?'

'Nothing, for a bit. I need to rest, and I expect this witch'll have those beasts searching around for a while, trying to figure out where we've gone.'

'She can't follow us in here, can she?'

'Nope. Even if she can use pathways, she'd never be able to find the exact one you used. Eventually she'll give up and call her beasts home, and then we'll be safe to come out.'

'And will that be the end of it?'

She grimaced. 'Maybe. If we just walk away, chances are she'll let us leave without any more trouble. We meddled in her business, she meddled in ours — we're even, more or less. That's assuming she's not a vicious snake like Gyssha was, of course.'

'I thought you didn't want to leave without the money,' I said, archly.

'There is that. Like I said, I don't *really* care. But I don't want those pricks to keep it, especially if it means the Haven's losing out. I could track them down when we get out and get it back.' She glanced across at me. 'Though I know already you won't like that. And I suppose I'm not exactly in a fit state to deal with them. Let me think on it a bit. We've got some time to kill, after all.'

'And what are we going to do about Kara?'

She pinched the bridge of her nose, squeezing her eyes shut. 'Ugh, Dee! You know she's not going anywhere willingly without her father, and I'd really rather not chain her up and drag her away. So what would you have us do, Miss Empath?'

I hugged my knees to my chest. 'I don't know.'

'Well, if you come up with any brilliant ideas, let me know.' She leaned back against the stone and heaved a sigh. 'Now, I really need to rest.'

'Yeah,' I said. 'All right. Let me tell Kara that we'll be here a little while longer.' She did care, at least a little bit, I was sure of that. She was just doing her best to hide it. I still couldn't understand how she could walk away from her family like she had but I knew there had to be a reason for it. She just wasn't willing to tell me.

Kara was standing by the pebbled shore with her thumbs hooked into her belt, looking over the dark water. She frowned as I relayed what Aleida had said about waiting for the witch to give up. 'I suppose that's best,' she said. 'Here's hoping those candle stubs can last us a while longer.'

I was too distracted to reply. Beside my foot, a little stone was emerging from the pebbles by the water's edge, like a mushroom heaving up from the soil. It wasn't round like the water-washed rocks around it, but merely roundish, with flat faces that glimmered in the faint light.

It popped free from the earth and rolled with a *clink* against the neighbouring stones. Kara glanced down, and then jumped back as a second little rock popped up beside the first. She gave me a wide-eyed look. 'I'll, I'll go tell Holt,' she said, and scrambled away.

I gathered up my skirts and crouched down to collect the stones. I couldn't see Facet, but I knew he was nearby, lurking somewhere under my feet. 'Thanks, friend,' I murmured. The stones didn't look like much, honestly. They looked to be plain black and opaque, like shining little lumps of coal; but Facet thought them worth giving as gifts and I wouldn't be so churlish as to refuse.

Rattling them together in my palm, I went back to Aleida and settled beside her. 'I'm going to check on

Maggie and Toro,' I murmured to her when she stirred and cracked open one eye. She gave a weary grunt of assent and settled back to her doze.

I closed my eyes and turned my attention to my breath, slipping bit by bit into a trance.

We weren't all that far from the surface, I realised as I stretched my senses into the rocks and earth around us. Only a few hundred yards — but it was a few hundred yards no human could traverse. Beyond this little bubble within the rock, there were only fractures and cracks for the water to flow through. But, following the flowing water for a-ways, I eventually found moist soil and plants, and from there earthworms and other small creatures, and finally I found my way to the surface. There, I found a sparrow fossicking for seed amid the patchy grass. Once I'd settled into the little fluttering body I didn't have to concentrate so hard on keeping myself in the trance.

The first thing I did was fly to the shelter of a tree and perch close to the trunk, where the branches would give me some protection. The very first lesson Aleida had taught me about borrowing was to be wary of beasts of prey. No matter how careful you were, how cautious and how watchful, we could never be as skilled as the beast itself at avoiding predators. All the same, I didn't think it wise to search further for a hawk or some other creature higher on the food chain. The witch had used an eagle to spy upon us earlier, and there was every chance the bird was still around. Something as small as a sparrow, staying sheltered under a canopy, would be safer than a hawk in the open air.

I set out carefully, flitting from tree to tree in an ever-widening circle, and before long I found myself beside the familiar white rock of the Scar. From there I started to explore in expanding circles, searching for any sign of our assailants, and eventually I found the tracks left by our hasty retreat.

There was no sign of the bear or the lion. One griffin remained, perched on a boulder near the place where I'd opened the doorway, as though standing guard. It didn't appear to notice the tiny sparrow hopping under the enormous rounded stones.

I was more worried about Toro, who'd risked life and limb to draw the lion away from us. But in searching for him, I found the troupe of five marked men, their faces sour and spiteful. A couple of them were wounded, with one of them moving very stiffly, dark blood crusting his shirt. They seemed to be heading back towards the Scar, and I wondered what they'd make of it when they found Holt's troupe vanished without a trace, and the griffin standing guard over our trail.

I winged past them and kept searching.

Back towards the road, I found Toro sheltering in a dense copse of trees. He was still blowing hard with his flanks streaked with sweat. He was covered with cuts and scratches, but it seemed that he'd taken no real harm. I flitted to a branch near his head and trilled at him, and he lifted his head with a snort of surprise, ears pricking towards me. Could he guess it was one of us? He must have no idea what had happened to us, and I could think of no way of telling him we were all safe underground. Any further communication was beyond me, however, and with another trill I took wing once again and fluttered away.

Heading back towards the Scar I found a patch of crushed grass smeared with blood — a place where the injured lion had lain and rested.

I retreated to a nearby tree and studied the sky. Was the eagle still out there? All morning it had been somewhere above us, but since I was so careful to keep under cover I couldn't see well enough to know if it was still there. Had it gone home along with the other two beasts, or was it still up there somewhere, watching?

There were flies buzzing around the spilled blood. My sparrow kept turning back to them, thinking of its belly, but my attention was drawn more to the gore smeared over the dry grass.

The lion must be in bad shape. I'd seen Toro trample him — hells, I was pretty sure he'd rolled over the beast when he'd come charging in, and being crushed by half a ton of horse was no joke, even to a lion. I'd known the beast was injured, but it only now occurred to me that he might be dying.

If I'd been in my own skin, I would have gnawed on a thumbnail as I sat and thought, watching bluebottles buzz around the drying smears. Aleida had said this might be the end of it, but we'd also reasoned that this witch had transformed her captives for some purpose. If the lion died before that purpose was fulfilled, would she still be willing to let us walk away?

I should probably return and tell Aleida, I thought. I nearly did it, too. But then I thought a little more. Aleida would still be resting, and it was probably worth knowing if the lion made it back to the witch's lair. He'd left a clear trail behind him, it would be simple to follow the tracks and see what was going on.

I studied the sky again. No black speck. I'd do it, I decided.

CHAPTER 7

I set out with renewed caution, fluttering from tree to tree. The lion had headed almost due north, leaving lots of blood behind him. If I was back home at Burswood Farm and sent to find a beast bleeding as much as this I'd expect to find it dead under a bush somewhere.

In the end I was nearly right.

I perched on a twig hiding under the leaves, holding very still as the lion lay in the dust. The only movement was the rise and fall of his ribs as he panted with shallow breaths.

About a hundred yards away stood the remains of a crumbling stone building. Perhaps it was an old hunting lodge, or a guards' post — there wasn't enough left of it for me to tell. A wooden wall had been built around it, but I use the words 'wall' and 'built' loosely. Some of the wood had been shaped into planks, but most of it was just sticks and branches, woven and knotted together with vines. At a glance it seemed like something built for privacy more than protection, but after spending the summer learning about Aleida's gardens and orchard I wouldn't like to test the idea. Smoke rose from somewhere behind the wall, and even from this distance, even with the sparrow's nose, I could tell that it didn't smell too good.

Up ahead the bear waited by the gate, swaying from foot to foot and making a low, guttural cry. He kept looking back at the fallen lion, but never came back to check on his companion. He just stood there, swaying and making a deep moan.

I flitted closer, moving from tree to tree, but when the gate began to move I dived into cover.

A woman heaved the gate open. It had no hinges, only more vines, but she moved it as though it weighed nothing at all. She said nothing, made no expression as she looked the bear over, but when her gaze fell on the lion her face twisted into a countenance of displeasure, and she stalked along the path towards him.

She didn't look old. That surprised me for some reason. I'd only briefly glimpsed Gyssha, Aleida's old teacher, and she'd been old and wizened, with skin like crumpled paper and limbs like sticks. This woman seemed to be of middle years, with sun-browned skin and muscular arms. She wore a leather jerkin that left her arms and shoulders bare, and a battered and filthy piece of cloth wrapped around her hips for a skirt, beneath which her feet and legs were naked. Her reddish hair was a mass of knots and tangles, and her arms were covered with little black marks; tattoos, but nothing like the ones worn by the marked men. These were a complex pattern of dots, triangles and lines, arranged in an odd geometry.

She walked up to the lion and prodded him with her foot. He stirred, raising his head in a snarl, but then let it fall again to lie still in the dust. Hands on hips, the witch paced back and forth, muttering in a voice too low for me to make out. She gestured to the beast to stand, and with a growl of pain it tried, only to fall back to the dirt. After a few mumbled curses, the witch stalked back to the walled yard. At her signal, the bear fell into step behind her.

While she was out of sight, I took the opportunity to move closer, darting from tree to tree before taking shelter on a branch hanging over the wall. I was on dangerous ground now, coming so close, but I wanted to know what had become of the rest of Toro's troupe.

Beyond the wall was ... filth. Filth and rot and decay. I don't know how else to describe it. Animal waste lay in piles, and strewn among the heaps of dung were mouldering bones, some still clinging to scraps of skin and hair. Just inside the gate was a stout wooden post sunk into the ground, attached to which were a few feet of stout chain and a heavy collar, lying empty, with the ground around it cleared of rubbish in a circle a few feet wide. There were other such posts around the yard but they all seemed to be abandoned, save another with an empty collar like the first.

There was one other exception to the trash and filth that littered the yard — the far corner away from the gate held a simple pen where two snowy white horses stood, watching with interest as their mistress returned. *Two beautiful horses*, I remembered Toro saying about their first encounter with the witch. Their coats were immaculate, and their pen looked like the cleanest spot in the whole place, including what I could see of the ruined building through the missing door.

I watched, hunkering motionless on my perch while the witch ducked through the doorway and returned with a coil of rope. She slung it over her shoulder and, with an imperious gesture, beckoned the bear to follow her.

A shadow overhead made me duck instinctively, and the eagle I'd been watching out for glided down towards her. With a quick glance upwards, the witch held out her arm and the eagle settled onto her bare skin, flapping vast wings to keep its balance. I winced at the thought of those huge talons, and the weight of that enormous bird, but the witch seemed not to notice either. When they reached the lion, the eagle flapped down to perch on the beast's hip, and the witch crouched down, uncoiling the rope. The lion snarled again, but the witch paid it absolutely no mind as she worked the rope under its front legs, wrapping it around the beast's chest. She was making a crude harness, I realised, to haul him the rest of the way home.

I glanced back to the ruined building. She'd be occupied there for a good few minutes. Long enough for me to scout inside and see what else I could learn. I took one last look at the peculiar group on the road to make sure no one was looking my way, and then I hopped off the perch and fluttered into the crumbling ruin.

Inside, the first thing I noted was a perch for the eagle — a stout branch wedged into a corner between cracks in the stone, with a veritable heap of droppings underneath. Nearby, also crammed under the remaining section of roof, was a pile of rags and old furs. It took me a moment to realise that it was the witch's bed, though it looked more like a nest, and didn't smell much better than the rest of the place.

A little deeper into the building, past a sagging, half-fallen roof beam was a set of stairs, leading downwards into a basement.

Wings fluttering, I hopped closer. There was a light burning down there — yellow lamplight gleamed over the old stones, slick with moss. I could feel *something* down there.

It was strange the way senses worked when borrowing. My own body was miles away, somewhere far underground, taking deep, slow breaths as I lay in a trance. I didn't entirely understand how I could sense magic and power even with my own flesh and blood, let alone with the tiny borrowed body of this little sparrow; yet I could sense the power welling up from below. I could feel it as clearly as you can feel heat from a hearthstone, or the sun on your face. The witch had a working afoot down there underground.

This was a bad idea, I knew it — but I was here now and I'd likely never get another chance to spy on her workings. Aleida would already be mad that I'd come this close — was I really going to go back and admit to what I'd done without learning anything about what the witch was doing here? There was no time to check what progress the witch had made out on the road and figure out how long I might have before she returned. It was now or never.

With the sparrow's tiny heart beating hard, I hopped down into the dank, musty darkness.

The staircase curved down in a tight spiral, and the witch's feet had torn the delicate moss away from the stone.

At the foot of the steps I fluttered down to a flagstone floor. There was a scattering of candles burning around the chamber, casting a flickering yellow light over the ... piles, on the floor. There were eight of them, and at first sight they reminded me of the wooden blocks my little siblings played with, stacked up to make houses or towers or whatever they took it into their heads to create. Only these towers were made of bones, carefully stacked like the beams of a log cabin. At the very top of each tower was a skull, staring towards the centre of the room with vacant eyes. The tower nearest to me had a skull as long as my arm, a grotesque thing of pitted, bubbling bone, a long snout and dozens of conical teeth. *Crocodile,* I thought to myself, remembering the greenish, knobbly creature in the bestiary. Another looked like the head of a bull, only the horns were not like any bull I'd ever seen. A few others were familiar creatures, but others came from beasts I'd never seen, some so strange that I couldn't begin to imagine what they must have looked like in life. As I moved past I noticed a glimmer from within the tower of stacked bone, and peering closer I found a large crystal inside the grisly structure, black as obsidian, gleaming darkly inside the shadows.

The piles were arranged in a careful pattern, laid out in curving lines that spiralled into the centre of the room. I hopped closer, trying to keep close to the piles of bones for cover; and trying to ignore the panic of the sparrow at being down here in the dark, away from the sky, and surrounded by the stench of blood and death.

As I rounded the pile of crocodile bones I saw something else — a symbol inscribed in the rock of the floor, glowing a deep and smoky red, a complex shape of lines and circles and dots.

There was one beside each pile of bones, each of them different, each of them glowing — except at the centre of the chamber, where the grotesque pattern had not been completed. There, I found four more symbols drawn onto the floor, but where the others gave off a sullen glow, these were drawn with a thick white paste. There was one in the centre too, larger and even more complex than the others. Her working was still underway, I realised. Whatever she was doing, she hadn't finished it yet.

All right, I decided. I'd seen enough. I took flight, but as I flapped up towards the rafters I heard a woman's voice drifting down from above and a low, rumbling growl from one of the beasts under her spell.

Time to go. Definitely time to go.

As I glided under the heavy roof beams an odd lump on one of them caught my eye. It was a mounded shape, like someone had coiled a rope and hung it across a rafter *just so*. Then, I saw the gleam of lamplight on a small black eye, and a flicker of movement from a darting tongue.

I folded my wings and dropped like a stone as the snake struck, mouth gaping wide and fangs glistening with wetness. The first strike missed by a hair's breadth — I felt the movement of the air over my back, and the spray of its venom settling over my feathers. Then, flapping hard, I shot up the stairwell and banked at the top, turning to dart through the doorway and out into the open air.

But the moment I saw the doorway I realised there was something wrong — a net of light was strung across the opening, like a spiderweb glowing in red and orange. There was no time to slow or change direction, I was moving too fast, and in any case staying inside was a death-trap with that snake behind me. I shot through the web.

I expected it to catch me and hold me fast, but I flew through the net without resistance — it shattered at my touch, though I could feel motes of power clinging to me. For a moment I was utterly disoriented — if it wasn't there to catch me, what purpose did it serve? I caught a brief glimpse of the witch, looking up at me with a satisfied smile. But then I was flying on, as fast as my little wings would take me.

Then, a shadow passed overhead, and I felt as though my heart would stop. *The eagle.* My sparrow knew what that meant as well as I did, and I felt his wordless desperation, his primal fear. I had to get to the safety of the trees, then we might stand a chance.

Or …

Or I could abandon ship.

My gut twisted at the thought. No, I'd brought the little creature into this mess, I couldn't just abandon it. I couldn't.

I couldn't.

I tried to lighten my hold on the sparrow, shift my senses back to my own body, safe in the cave miles away from here, but I couldn't shift away, I was bound to this tiny body, the labouring heart and heaving lungs. *That* was what that spell had done, I realised, not a web to catch this tiny bird but a web to bind me to the beast I'd borrowed.

If I could have, I would have screamed, but all I could manage was a tiny, terrified peep.

Then the shadow passed over me again and something struck me from above with crushing force.

There was blood in my mouth, blood in my throat, choking me. An awful pain in my chest, crushing, tearing. I couldn't scream, I couldn't breathe. I felt like my ribs had been turned to spears, all of them piercing through me.

There was something above me, *someone* — I could feel their warmth, their mass. 'Breathe,' said a voice. '*Breathe*, Dee.'

I knew that voice. My teacher. I tried to draw a breath, but my chest wouldn't work. My lungs felt like a punctured bellows. I was drowning in blood.

Aleida's hands were cupping my face, fingertips digging into my cheeks, and I could feel her breath on my skin. '*Breathe, Dee!* You listen to me, girl! Mind over matter, that's all magic is; your mind imposing its will on the universe. She's tricked you, you understand? She bound you to the bird and killed the bird, but it's the sparrow dying, not you!'

I gaped at her, trying to swallow, trying to gasp, but nothing worked. I could feel my mouth gulping like a landed fish, drowning in air. Hot blood soaked my chemise under my leather stays, and welled in my throat in a choking tide. I could feel the talons between my ribs, feel the broken bones. My vision was going dark, lungs starved for air, filling with blood.

'No!' Aleida yelled into my face. 'No! Don't let that bitch kill you, Dee! It's not real! Push it away, take a damn breath. You can do it. You have to trust me, you have to listen! Mind over matter, that's all this is. She's using your mind against you. You're just feeling an echo from the sparrow's body, don't fall for it! You can control it, push it away. Take a damn breath!'

But ... but ... I could feel the talons. I could feel the broken ribs, crushed to splinters. I could feel the mind starved of air and losing blood, starting to shut down. But I saw my teacher's face looming over mine, brows knotted in worry, eyes narrowed in rage.

I pushed the pain away, tried to focus. I could feel my hands slack on the rocks beneath me. Nestled in one palm were two small, rough stones. Faintly I remembered plucking them out of the pebbles at the water's edge. I clenched my fist, feeling them dig into my palm, and forced my chest to rise. It hurt, it hurt like a handful of broken glass. *No,* I said to myself. *It's not real. Don't believe it.* There were no talons between my ribs, no splintered bones. I clenched the stones tight in my palm, hard enough to bruise. *That* was the real pain, not this echo in my head. *Mind over matter,* I said to myself. *It's not real.* I took another breath, and began to cough and splutter over the blood in my throat.

Aleida had been straddling me, holding my face in her hands, but now she swiftly moved away and helped me turn over as I coughed and retched. She pounded me on the back as I vomited blood onto the stones.

When at last it was finished, she caught me by the shoulders and shoved me back against the wall. 'You absolute *idiot*! What in the hells were you thinking?'

'I — I just—'

'She almost killed you! Have you got wool for brains? Lord and Lady, what possessed you to do something so stupid?'

I squeezed my eyes shut, the taste of blood and bile still thick in my mouth. 'I'm sorry.'

'Sorry? *Sorry?* You'd bloody better be sorry, you little wretch! Why would you do something so bone-headed?'

All I could do was look at her with tears pouring down my face. My belly hurt from the force of retching up swallowed blood. My ribs stung and ached from the memory of the eagle's talons, and my shift beneath my stays was soaked and sticky. For a moment I tried to convince myself it was only sweat, but I knew better. It wasn't sweat, it was blood. I was soaked in it, surrounded by the iron stink of it, sticky and foul as it clotted against my skin.

'Well?' Aleida snarled, looming over me.

'I — I — I thought I could get in and out before she saw me,' I said with a gulp. 'She was outside, dealing with the lion, he was hurt too bad to make it back by himself. I, I knew it was a bad idea, I knew ... I'm sorry, miss.'

She sat back on her heels with a glare that made me wither. 'And yet you did it anyway! Damn it, Dee, she almost killed you! If I'd done something so stupid with Gyssha she'd have sat back and let me die! If you knew it was a bad idea, why in the hells did you do it? Listen to your godsdamn instincts, I've told you that a thousand times!'

I found myself nodding. 'I, I know, but ...'

'But what?' she demanded.

I looked away. Why *had* I done it? I knew it was foolish, but I'd done it anyway. Maybe I was stupid. Maybe I wasn't cut out for this life after all. 'I don't know,' I said in a bare whisper.

'Don't give me that horseshit,' she growled, raking her hair back with bloody hands, leaving red streaks along her temples. She glanced around and I remembered the rest of the bandits then, and stole a look across the cavern. They'd fallen very quiet, and were watching us while trying to make it look like they weren't. 'You'd bloody well better learn from this, kid. Your mind has power, don't ever forget that. You let yourself get bound up with the bird, and when she killed it your mind imposed those wounds on your real body. She damn near tricked you into letting your own mind kill you, and next time I might not be able to talk you down.'

All I could do was gape at her. '... how do you know?'

She gave me a look of utter disgust. 'I'm a witch, you little fool. And Gyssha knew every dirty trick the craft has to offer. Now, pull yourself together. It's time we got out of here.'

She started to pull away. Without really thinking about it, without any conscious decision to move, my hand shot out and caught her sleeve. 'Aleida, wait.'

She turned back to me, eyes narrow and sharp. 'What?' she demanded, and her voice made me wince.

'I saw something. Inside the ruins, I saw ... she's working some kind of ritual. It's something big.'

She pressed her lips together.

I don't care. I was ready for her to say the words, to brush it off. It wasn't our problem. Hadn't I heard her say that, over and over? We don't need to get involved.

But then, with a sigh, she settled back to the rocks. 'All right. Tell me.'

I described it as best I could with my heart still pounding beneath my ribs, my breath hitching in my chest and my bloody shift clinging to my skin. Her face was neutral as she listened without interrupting as I described the obelisks of crystal and bone, the sigils inscribed on the floor.

'These sigils,' she said when I ran out of words to say. 'What can you tell me about them?'

'Um ...' She'd taught me a little about sigils and runes, the elements that went into them, what they were called and how they were assembled. But all that knowledge had fled for the moment, and though I could picture it clearly I couldn't find the words to describe it.

Instead, I picked up a flat stone beside me. The blood on my skin was drying, turning thick and gummy, but it was still wet enough. I swiped my finger through it and started to draw lines and angles, curves and dots.

As I laid out the lines, my heart began to pound all over again, and I felt a flush of heat through my chest, surging through my veins. The stone was growing hot in my hands, throbbing as though it had a heartbeat of its own.

Then Aleida snatched it away from me. Quickly, she spat on the stone and scrubbed at the drying blood with her sleeve, clearing the symbol away. Then she licked her finger and drew a sigil of her own, one I recognised as a method of dispelling trapped power and releasing bound spirits. Then, she threw the rock away into the water with a splash that echoed around the cavern.

'Well,' she said. 'You've got a talent for sigils. You're sure you remembered that correctly?'

'I, I think so.'

'You *think*?' she demanded. 'Or you *know*?'

I dropped my gaze. 'I know.' I have a very good memory. One good thing that came out of the fact that I'd never gone to school. If I couldn't read, I couldn't rely on Ma's book of recipes or the list of chores chalked onto the wall, I had to just remember them. I was told once what I was supposed to do, and there was hell to pay if I forgot the smallest thing.

Aleida made a small noise in the back of her throat. A noise of concern.

'What is it?' I said. 'What does it mean?'

She didn't answer, frowning as she traced shapes on her thigh with the tip of her finger, silently mouthing words I couldn't understand.

'It's important, isn't it?' I said.

Her eyes cut to me, still glaring with fury. 'Well,' she said, after a pause. 'You've got good instincts when it comes to hunting out information, I'll grant you that. It's just that whole self-preservation thing that needs some work.' She stood then, wiping her hands on her skirt, and reached for her staff. 'Everyone up,' she said. 'Time to go.'

CHAPTER 8

I was still feeling shaky when I brought us all back into the sunlight. The bandits filed past me without so much as a glance in my direction. I wasn't sure how I felt about that. On the one hand, I didn't want them looking at me like a two-headed calf, but on the other, I *had* just saved their lives by bringing them to the refuge underground. It was pretty impressive, if you asked me.

When they'd all filed past, I let the doorway close and turned my back to the stone, only to find Kara waiting for me. 'Are you all right?' she asked in a low voice. She wasn't looking at my face, but lower. I glanced down, and saw that my shift above my leather stays was stained with drying blood. 'It's nothing,' I said.

She looked doubtful. 'If you say so. So, what now?'

I bit my lip. 'I don't—'

Aleida's shout interrupted me before I could finish. 'Dee! Get over here. The rest of you sods: go. Get lost.

Don't let me see your ugly faces again, or I'll do something we'll all regret.'

I met Kara's gaze, and we both shrugged.

Aleida was already walking away, leaning on her staff, and I hurried after her. As we departed, I heard muttering voices behind us, and someone growling at them to hush.

'Those marked men are around here somewhere,' I said. 'I saw them when I was scouting.'

'Screw those arseholes,' she snapped. 'They'll stay the hells away if they know what's good for them. Beyond that I don't care, we've got bigger things to worry about.'

'We do? But you said we'd walk away now. Tit for tat and the matter's settled, isn't that what you said?'

She ignored me and strode onwards, the hem of her skirts sweeping through the dust. For all she was limping with each step, her legs were so long I had to stretch mine to keep up.

Back at the wagon, she waved me inside. 'First things first, you need to get cleaned up. You smell like a butcher's shop.'

I was well aware of that fact. In the short walk from the rocks, I'd amassed quite the flock of flies. Flushing, I scrambled up the steps. It'd be a long time, I figured, until I heard the last of this misadventure.

She followed me up the steps and closed the door behind us, and as I started stripping off I heard her open the cabinet by the door, and heard the *clink* of glassware as she started riffling through the bottles within.

Any curiosity I had for what she was doing was quickly lost in a rising tide of dismay as I loosened my skirts and stepped out of the puddle of cloth. My overskirt had escaped the worst of the gore, but the waist of my petticoat was soaked, like it had been dipped in blood. And from there it only got worse. I loosened the laces of my leather stays, but at first they didn't budge — the clotted blood had all but glued them and my shift to my skin. I had to peel them away like the shell from a boiled egg, and I feared the memory of that sensation would make my skin crawl for years to come. I couldn't help but make a sound of disgust as I wriggled out of the stays, and then pulled the stiff and sticky chemise over my head.

I held it up, meaning to shake it out and fold it neatly out of sheer habit. But the sight of it, utterly soaked with blood, made me swallow hard.

'Could have been worse,' Aleida said from behind me. 'Between the shift and the stays, it's like you were wrapped in bandages. Kept the bleeding to a minimum.'

Hastily I bundled the shift up, hiding the worst of the gore inside. 'I'll never get those stains out,' I mumbled.

'We'll just dye it black,' Aleida said. 'That's what I always do.'

'And that'll look lovely with my brown leather stays.'

'We'll dye them, too.'

Quickly, I scrubbed myself clean, or at least as clean as a handkerchief and a little bit of water from the water butt could get me, before pulling on a fresh shift. I tried to clean the inside of my stays, too, but by then Aleida was tapping her foot impatiently, so I pulled them back on, damp enough to be uncomfortable and with the sinking knowledge that at the end of the day I'd have two bloodstained shifts to deal with instead of just one. 'Shall I call Maggie back? I can get her harnessed and get us back on the road.'

'We're not hitting the road.'

My hands froze tying the tapes of my skirt, and I swivelled to look at her. She was sitting at the tiny table, a glass with the dregs of something inky and black by her elbow. She'd found the two little pebbles Facet had brought to me in the cave and was rolling them back and forth across the table, tapping them against each other with a stony *chink chink chink.*

'B-but you said—'

She lifted her eyes to mine, and I fell silent.

'Are you ready?' She stood.

'No!' I said firmly. 'I am most definitely *not* ready. What are we doing? You said we'd leave, you said—'

'That was before that bitch tried to kill my apprentice,' she snapped. 'Dee, get your wand.'

Once again I hurried after her. She was still walking with her staff, but her stride was faster now, and I cursed myself for not taking notice of what she'd mixed herself from the bottles and flasks in the cabinet. 'Aleida, stop!'

She cast a dark glance back at me and kept moving. 'I'm giving the orders here, kid, not you.'

She was heading back towards the rocks, not to the witch's den, which lay miles away to the north. I suspected what she meant to do, and I wanted no part of it.

I stopped and watched Aleida's back.

She kept striding ahead of me, pushing onwards. But when she was a dozen yards away, she, too, came to a halt. 'Dee,' she said in warning tones.

'Why?' I said. 'Why are you doing this? Why fight her?'

She shook back her hair, and turned to me. 'Are you seriously asking me that? Seriously?' There was still blood streaked on her temples and in her hair. My blood.

But I stood my ground. 'I don't *want* you to. Not for my sake. Why can't we just walk away, like you said? If it's a matter of pride—'

'You think this is about *pride*?' She came stalking back towards me. 'Gods damn it, Dee, I don't want this either! Lord and Lady, I didn't come here looking for a fight! All I wanted was to try out a new path, offload some of Gyssha's filthy trophies, and see if I could make something, somewhere a little better! And now ...' She looked away, clenching her teeth. 'Look, it's not your fault. If a student makes a mistake of this scale, it's her teacher's failing. But what you did ... that witch has to be wondering if I sent you to scout the place out.'

'But we both know you didn't,' I said, twisting my skirt between my hands. 'Does it really matter what she thinks?'

'It matters because only the worst kind of witch would throw away an apprentice on a cursed suicide mission,' she snapped. 'So either she thinks I really desperately want to know what she's up to in there and I'm willing to sacrifice you to find out ... or I'm a completely useless blundering idiot with all the sense of a lamb that's been kicked in the head. Listen, Dee, if word gets out that this bloody witch tried to kill you, and I just walked away without calling her to account for it ... well, every witch who knew of Gyssha will come after us. Before winter's over we'll be fighting for our lives! Do you understand? Do you have any idea how many witches and wizards and warlocks there are out there who'd love to be the one who killed the last Blackbone, the upstart who put Gyssha in the ground? Do you?'

All I could do was stare at her, feeling hollow and sick. 'This is all my fault, isn't it?'

She huffed a sigh and turned away. 'No, it's mine. I just told you that, were you even listening? Look, I've been too soft on you. I couldn't bring myself to train you the way I was trained, I didn't want to be what Gyssha was. But that was a mistake. I'm going to put it right, you can be sure of that, but for now ... well, here we are.'

'But you can't fight her. You're too weak.'

'Ugh, Dee!' Aleida rolled her eyes. 'Are we going to have this conversation every single time I have to face off against someone? I know what I'm doing. This is what Gyssha trained me for; I have a few tricks up my sleeve, cursed or not. And, in any case, I don't like the look of that sigil you showed me. She's up to something, this witch, and I'm not leaving here until I find out what. Now, come on.'

She set off again, and this time I followed, although our little talk had done nothing to make me feel better about the situation. I didn't want to fight. The thought terrified me. It took me back to my first days at Black Oak Cottage, where we'd faced the black-robed warlock as well as the ghost of Gyssha Blackbone. As terrified as I'd been back then, this felt more grim. Back then the fight had come to us. This time, it was us looking for trouble, sticking our noses where they didn't belong. The thought was enough to make me grimace — it hadn't stopped me from venturing into the witch's lair in the first place, had it?

Aleida marched right up to a huge boulder of milky rock. 'All right, Dee. Take us in.'

'I beg your pardon?' I said. 'Don't I have to take us *to* somewhere?' Every other time I'd opened a pathway I'd had the destination firm in mind. Even if I didn't know exactly where that was, the *idea* of it was clear as crystal.

'Nope. You can just open the door and bring us inside, and decide on where you want to go later.'

I frowned at her. 'That's not how I've ever done it before.' All of the two times I'd managed it. 'Can ... can you—' *Can you show me?* That was what I meant to say, but the words died in my throat.

She'd never offered to show me how to open a pathway. We'd tried many times since that fight with Gyssha on the hillside. I'd even tried it by myself, when I was out wandering the forests back home at the cottage.

I raised my eyes to hers. 'You can't do it. Can you?'

She shook her head. 'No. It's not that common a talent. But you have an affinity for earth magic, what with your crystals and your little familiar spirit.'

'Facet?' I said. 'A familiar?'

Aleida sighed. 'Come on, Dee, time's wasting. I want us inside, away from prying eyes.'

I glanced around, looking for anything spying upon us. Of course it was hopeless. It could be something as small as a lizard or a skink hiding under the rocks. 'Oh,' I said. 'Right.'

I set my palm against the stone, and felt myself frowning.

'Don't think about it,' she said in my ear. 'Just do it.'

That's what she always said about working magic. Honestly, it didn't make much sense to me. How was I supposed to do something without thinking about it?

I remembered what she'd said a few moments ago: *I've been too soft on you.* And before: *If I'd pulled a trick like that when I was with Gyssha she'd have let me die.* I squeezed my eyes shut. Even if whatever she was planning went well, the next few weeks weren't going to be fun.

While I was lost in this thought, I felt the rock melt away beneath my hand.

'There we go,' Aleida said, striding into the darkness with a swish of her skirts.

I followed, letting the doorway close behind me, throwing us into darkness. Aleida pulled a candle from the little bag on her belt and lit it with a touch of her finger. Then, she set it down on the floor and crouched down on her heels. 'C'mere, Dee.'

I joined her, settling to my knees on the sandy floor. 'Isn't it dangerous, hanging about here in between? That's what you said before.'

'So you *do* listen sometimes. Let me worry about that. Now, tell me about that place. The witch, too. Start at the beginning, and tell me everything you saw, every little detail.'

I didn't like taking my mind back there, putting myself back in the little fluttering body of the sparrow I'd taken to its death. But I knew I'd get no sympathy. Hadn't she warned me against using prey animals for borrowing? And I'd known right from the start that venturing into the witch's lair was a bad idea.

I started with what I'd seen on the road, the lion dragging itself through the dust, and the witch coming out to meet it.

'What did she look like?' Aleida said.

'She had reddish hair, streaked with grey,' I said. 'A real rat's nest, looked like it hadn't been combed in weeks. She was dressed oddly, too — just a leather jerkin; not a corset, a jerkin like men wear, but with no shirt or anything under it. And a bit of cloth wrapped around her waist for a skirt.'

Aleida gave me a startled look. 'Did she have tattoos on her arms? All dots and triangles and things laid out in odd patterns?'

'Yes!' I realised then what that must mean. 'You know her?'

Aleida nodded. 'Yeah. Well, I know *of* her. Minerva. She's a strange one. Strange even for a witch, I mean. She's got a talent for beast magic, likes living in the wilds. Doesn't like people much. I can't imagine what she's doing here, this is far too close to civilisation for her liking.'

'Do you think it was her who brought the griffins?'

'Oh, most likely. Don't ask me why, though.'

'Not just a prank, then.'

She pulled a face. 'Minerva's not really the pranking kind. All right, go on. Tell me about the ruins.'

As I described the place, she drew it out with her fingertips, but instead of lines in the soft sand of the floor, she drew it with illusions, softly glowing threads that hung in the air. She quizzed me about the ritual this witch had laid out, too, and marked out the obelisks of crystal and bone. When I judged it as accurate, we both sat back on our heels.

'That sigil I drew,' I said. 'What does it do?'

She bit her lip, frowning at the diagram. 'It summons.'

'Summons? Summons *what*?'

She didn't answer. 'And the men she's killed … what are you doing, Minerva? Bones, bones are tied to life-force, but they're corporeal, too. You're summoning something and giving it a body … and from the sounds of it, not just any body. Crocodile, lion, bear. She chained them up securely, but she didn't care so much about Toro, or the other hoofed beasts. She's after predators.'

'What about the nether beastie I saw last night?' I said. 'Does that have something to do with it?'

'Oh! I'd forgotten about that. Yeah, probably …' she trailed off, frowning.

'Is she summoning something from the nether realms?'

She grimaced. And then she slashed a hand through the diagram, breaking it up into motes of light that drifted away and faded out, like sparks rising from a fire.

'Why would anyone do that?'

'Good question. Let's go find out.'

First, she cast a veil over me to hide me from sight. It felt cool as it settled across my face and shoulders, like walking through misty rain.

Then, she had me open a doorway right into Minerva's cellar.

'Are you sure?' I said.

'Just do it, Dee. Then stay inside, out of the way.'

'All right, good. If it goes badly I can try to pull you back in.'

Her scowl cut me dead. 'Lord and Lady, such faith you have in your teacher. Forget it. You're coming through with me. Open it. Now.'

I opened my mouth to protest, then hastily closed it again before I could make things worse. With her still frowning like thunder, I pressed my palm to the wall and took us into the ruins.

For all the struggles I'd had, all the times I'd tried and failed back home at the cottage, this time it came shockingly easily. I had the trick of it now, it seemed. The rock melted and flowed away, like a skin of ice melting from a pond. For the barest instant we could see the witch at work — the lion lay on the huge stone slab at one end of the room, lifeless and still. Minerva had her back to us, bent over the corpse with a knife in her hands, skinning the great beast.

The moment Aleida stepped through the portal, Minerva went stiff. Then, she spun and hurled the knife straight towards us.

With a wave of her hand, Aleida caught it in a net of force, like a spider's web woven from glowing strands. The knife hung there for a fraction of a second, spinning in place, and then shattered into a hundred gleaming fragments that shot towards Minerva like a swarm of wasps.

Flinging up her hands, Minerva cast her own net to catch the shards, but then stumbled back as Aleida followed them with a blast of fire. From somewhere above, beyond the stone walls, I heard an animal roar of fury and the sound of a beast throwing against its chain, but when I took a few quick steps towards the door, ready to cast a fireball of my own, there was no sign of any beast coming to her aid. *Of course not*, I told myself. *She's got them chained up tight.*

I pressed myself against the wall, clutching my wand as I felt Minerva calling in power, her face twisted in a snarl and her hands curled like claws. She spat a word, something that grated and rasped against my ears, and loosed a blast of wind. I felt the edge of it, and its touch was like a howling gale of sand and grit.

Aleida threw up a hand to shield her face, but the blast of air set her aglow — like when air from a bellows blasting into a forge casts up sparks from the fire, this blast of scouring wind stripped a thousand sparks and embers from her form. It tore away the spell she'd cast to give herself human feet, and she staggered, dropping to one knee, the hairy dog's feet that Gyssha's death-curse had given her in clear view beneath the hem of her skirt.

'Oho,' Minerva laughed, her voice rasping and coarse. 'Someone got you, didn't they? They got you good.'

Aleida forced a smile as she heaved herself up again. 'Not as good as I got her.' Then, Aleida's form *blurred*, just as it had when she'd cast an illusion to draw the griffin away just a few hours ago.

Minerva hesitated, power flaring at her hands. Her eyes darted around the room, anywhere but at the figure before her. She'd been watching, I realised. Aleida had suggested as much, but this confirmed it — when the beasts had attacked us, Minerva had been watching through some creature's eyes. She'd seen Aleida pull this move before, seen her use an illusion of herself to draw her target away and was searching for the real witch, hidden somewhere under a veil.

But while she searched, Aleida's figure circled around her, step by step. I could see her, just barely, a faint spectre. I wasn't sure how, or why — perhaps because we were kin in the craft? Aleida raised her left hand, and I felt power thicken the air.

The red-haired witch felt it too. With a snarl she held her hand out to the dead lion, palm up, and sharply raised it. 'Up.'

The dead beast on the slab began to stir, that huge head lifting sluggishly from the stone as it heaved itself up on cold, dead paws. 'Find her,' Minerva ordered the beast.

The sight of it stole my breath away, making my belly churn. The lion had been terrifying enough when it was hale and whole. This was worse — so much worse. Lord and Lady, she'd already gutted the thing.

I was so fixed on the awful sight, I didn't notice something stirring over Minerva's head. Neither did she — until thick, ropy vines plunged from the roof to seize her.

She tried to throw herself down, but it was too late — like an insect in a spider's web, she was caught fast. Vines — or were they roots? — twined around her arms, while another reached down to tear her wand from her hand, and yet another quested down to coil around her neck. As Minerva fought and clawed at them, the lion settled back to the slab, the animating force draining away.

The vines grew tighter and tighter, wrenching her arms back, winding around her ribs, choking off her breath. 'Blackbone,' she hissed. 'I know it's you! What are you playing at? Haven't I done as you bade me? Haven't I—'

I lost whatever else she said when a movement in the rafters caught my eye — something sleek and shimmering gliding along the moist and rotting beams. The viper! Had I even mentioned that to Aleida when I told her what I'd seen down here? I *thought* I had, but suddenly I was by no means sure.

And it was too late, now. The snake was right over her head and with mouth agape and fangs gleaming, it dropped right down upon her.

Aleida flinched and cursed as it sank those long teeth into her neck, right where it met her shoulder, and writhed, coiling its gleaming length around her neck as it bit again and again. Minerva's face turned to stone as Aleida gave a hiss of pain, and pulled the snake away, tearing it loose from her skin and gripping it in her fist. 'Tell your little familiar to calm itself,' she spat to Minerva. 'Or I'll wring its blasted neck.'

With those words I saw the older witch's face change. For an instant, her eyes widened — and then her expression seemed to soften, just a little. In it I saw something strange, something that seemed very out of place. Surprise, and maybe ... relief? She blinked at Aleida, and said, 'You're not Gyssha.'

The words seemed to hit Aleida like a blow, and she took a half-step back. Then, she lifted her chin. 'I should hope not,' she said, while the snake curled around her wrist, mouth gaping wide and the wickedly curving fangs dripping with venom. 'I said, call him off!'

Minerva clicked her tongue and, grudgingly, the little snake closed its mouth. It really was a beautiful creature — its body was only a little thicker than my thumb, and it was covered in odd ridged and pointed scales that made it look bristled rather than sleek and smooth.

'Gyssha would have broken his neck without a word of warning,' Minerva said. 'So who are you? I know you're a Blackbone, I can smell it, and if you were anything else you'd be frothing at the mouth and twitching on the floor right now, thanks to my friend. So where's your mistress, girl?'

'In the ground, where she belongs,' Aleida snapped. 'What does she have to do with any of this?'

For a moment the two witches stared at each other in silence. 'If Gyssha didn't send you, then what in the hells are you doing here?'

'What am *I* doing here? I was just passing through, minding my own godsdamn business, when you decided to set your beasts on me and try to kill my apprentice. So what in the hells are *you* doing here?'

There was another long, silent moment. Then, Minerva cleared her throat. 'Truce?'

Aleida dabbed at the bloody snakebite on her neck with her sleeve, and then shrugged. 'Yeah. All right.'

⁂

Aleida released the vines, and set the snake on the floor. The little snake swiftly returned to his mistress, slithering up her arm to coil around her neck beneath the mass of her faded red hair. He really was a beautiful creature, his scales coloured in red and orange, yellow and pink. He peered out at us, tasting the air with a flickering tongue.

Aleida had dispelled the veil she'd cast on me, and at my sudden appearance Minerva reacted with only mild surprise. 'Huh. Thought I'd killed the lass.'

'Mm, nearly. Wasn't me that sent her in here, I'll have you know. Little twit pulled that trick all by herself.'

'Hmph. She any good?'

My teacher waved the question away with a flick of her hand. 'She's green as grass. Maybe that walloping you gave her will shape her up a bit. Time will tell.'

That smarted. More than a bit, if I'm honest, and what was worse was that I couldn't refute it. I felt myself flushing, and my cheeks grew hotter still when Minerva laughed a dry cackle. 'Drink?'

'Sure. What have you got?'

'I don't know what it's called, whatever rotgut it is they brew around these parts. You, girl,' she jerked her head in my direction. 'Go fetch it from upstairs. Green glass bottle.'

I wasn't sure how to take that. I glanced at Aleida, and she gave me a nod.

I suppose that meant I had to do as I was told. I headed up the stairs, stepping carefully around the slippery moss and the pools of drying blood.

The hovel Minerva had cobbled together from the ruins looked no better through human eyes. The furs and rags of her bed still reeked, and the bones of rabbits and chickens, discarded from meals, didn't smell too sweet either. I stole a quick peek outside through the broken doorway, and saw the bear chained up near the front gate, swaying uneasily from side to side. There was a nasty, gaping cut across his face where one of the bandits had slashed him with a sword, but aside from that there were no major wounds. The other bandits had called him Brute, I remembered, though Kara said his real name was Brent. But whatever name he went by, Kara's da was safe enough, for now.

There were a few empty bottles scattered amid the refuse on the floor, but I found a full one tucked in next to the reeking bed, and brought it back downstairs.

'Seen you before, haven't I?' Minerva was saying. 'A few years ago.'

'Yeah,' Aleida said. 'Oretham, I think it was. Maybe eight years ago? I was just an apprentice.' The wound on her neck was barely bleeding now. There was a purplish stain around it, like an old bruise, but the mark was already fading. *I've got poison in my veins,* she'd told me once, and I guessed that meant she was invulnerable to the viper's venom, too.

Minerva grunted again as I offered her the bottle. She waved it towards Aleida. 'Guests first, that's what Granny Wormwood always said. I'd offer to prove it's not poisoned, but you bein' a Blackbone, it wouldn't make any difference.' They were lounging against the slab where the lion lay, a sad, discarded husk. Even knowing the sort of man he'd been in life, I still couldn't bring myself to say he deserved this fate, turned into a beast and then slaughtered in this desolate ruin.

Aleida took the bottle and pulled the cork out to take a swig. Then, she held it out to me.

I wanted to refuse. These witches had been doing their best to kill each other not five minutes ago, and now we were all standing around a dead man-beast-*thing* in a crumbling cellar set up for some sinister summoning ritual, having a drink together? It made no sense at all. I didn't much like the smell wafting from the bottle, either. It was a strong herbal scent; and I don't mean the savoury kind of herbs you'd use for cooking, but the sharp, bitter herbs from one of our medicinal brews.

But from the look in Aleida's eye I didn't dare argue. And I could kind of see her point, too; it'd be rude to refuse Minerva's hospitality, even after the fighting. Or perhaps more so because of it.

I took a swig, and immediately coughed and choked as the fiery stuff seared my throat.

Minerva fair doubled over cackling as she took the bottle from me. 'Ne'er mind, lass. It'll put hairs on your chest.'

Scowling, I held my tongue. It had been a long time since I'd had to just stand there and take it while someone prattled a load of horseshit about me, I realised. I'd fallen rather out of practice.

Whatever amusement I afforded her soon lost its sheen, it seemed, for she turned her attention back to Aleida, and the bottle as well. 'So the old hag really is dead? I see she got in a couple of good hits on the way out. Death-curse, was it?'

'Nothing all that serious,' Aleida said. 'I got you beat, didn't I? But it seemed like you were expecting her to pay a call. What's she got to do with all this?'

Minerva pursed her lips as she looked over the ritual. 'It's not your concern, girl. You ought to leave well enough alone.'

'If anyone's going to come looking for her, I want to know,' Aleida said. 'We've already had some trouble with deals she set up before I put her out of our misery. I'd sooner be forewarned.'

Minerva grimaced. 'You ought to know the old hag better than anyone. She always had plans afoot. And she told me the next time I saw her she'd be wearing a different face. But if you don't know what she was brewing up, you'd do better to keep it that way. I heard you ran off on her and I'm guessing you found some rock to hide under — if I was you, I'd go back to it. Keep your head down and wait for the storm to blow over. That's what I'm planning to do, once this work is done.'

'What storm? And what work is this, exactly?'

Minerva glowered at her. 'I'll thank you not to get in my way, girl. What I'm doing here is my own business.'

'"I've done as you bade me", isn't that what you said? Gyssha was behind this. I just want to know what *this* is.'

'You're just vowed and determined to make a rod for your own back, ain't you?'

'I'm a Blackbone, I'm not afraid of trouble. Or I wouldn't be here right now, would I?'

I wasn't sure if she was talking about killing Gyssha or facing Minerva here in the mouldering cellar. Either option seemed to apply.

'Fine,' Minerva said with a toss of her head. 'It's your funeral. I was off in the Northlands, minding my own godsdamn business when the Blackbone tracked me down. Now I weren't fool enough to try to fight her, and I sure as hells ain't silly enough to fight two of 'em. I thought they were just going to kill me, but instead they gave me a blasted compulsion to work this ritual and then swanned off again.'

Aleida frowned at her in puzzlement. 'Wait ... what?'

'You hard of hearing, girl?'

'*This* ritual?'

'I know. It's not like either of them couldn't do it with half the effort, but no. They wanted me to do it for them, and backed it up with a curse that's more than I can dispel. So here I am, like a good little worker bee, buzzing away.'

Aleida pinched the bridge of her nose. 'Wait, you said *two* of them. Who else? Gyssha and ... who?'

Minerva looked down, picking at her filthy yellow nails.

'What?' Aleida said. 'Scared to say it?'

'You don't want to know, girl.'

'I'm asking, aren't I?'

'You're a fool, is what you are.' She hesitated, sucking air between her teeth. 'It was Mae.'

Aleida shifted her weight, leaning back as she drew a sharp breath. 'Mae? *Mae?*'

'You heard me. I ain't saying it again.'

'But ... that doesn't make any sense.'

'Nothing about her makes sense,' Minerva said. 'You ever meet her, lass?'

Aleida shook her head. 'Gods, no. We crossed paths a few times, but I never met her. The last time I saw hide or hair of her, she and Gyssha were trying to kill each other. And now they've been working together? What in the hells?'

'I don't know,' I muttered. 'Seems to be about normal in these parts.'

Aleida chortled at that. Minerva, too, laughing in a dry cackle. 'Little girl has a lot to learn.'

'She does. If she lives long enough. But seriously, *Mae?* What's *she* playing at?'

'Damned if I know. And trust me, I wasn't about to go asking questions. I got more sense than to stick my nose where it don't concern me, unlike some I could name ... Actually, might be you have a point in wantin' to know. Might be that when Mae realises that Gyssha ain't around, she'll come looking to see what became of her.'

'Mm,' Aleida said, her voice flat. 'That did cross my mind.'

Minerva rolled her shoulders and pushed off the stone slab. 'Well, Blackbone? You came to settle the score for your lass there, and you got some news out of it to boot. Got what you wanted? 'Cause I got work to do.'

Aleida leaned back against the slab with a sigh. 'There is one more thing. The beast you've got up there. The bear.'

'What about 'im?'

'Would you trade for him?'

'Eh? Why? Why would you want 'im?'

Aleida looked away with a shrug. 'There's this girl, his daughter. She's been trying to find him for months now, and here I see you've got him chained up outside. She's got no other kin.'

'A girl?' Minerva squinted across at her. 'How old?'

'Sixteen or so.'

'*Sixteen?*' Minerva said, her voice dripping with scorn. 'If she were twelve, maybe I'd see your point, but sixteen? More than old enough to fly the nest. She don't need him.'

I felt my mouth opening. I saw Aleida's gaze flick my way, warning me to silence, but it was too late. 'And how old were you when you went out on your own?'

Minerva's strangely pale eyes caught mine, and I felt them boring into me. 'Seven or eight,' she said. 'I forget exactly. Not *your* father, is he, lass?'

I shook my head.

'Forget the *why* of it,' Aleida said. 'What would you take for him? Maybe we can find a price. Black Oak is mine now, I've got the orchard, the gardens ... or more bodies? By my count you're a few short to finish the ritual.'

Minerva just scoffed. 'I don't need nothin' I can't get for myself. Although ... Bodies, you say?' She glanced my way, and chuckled. 'I don't think your lass likes the sound of that.'

She read me like a book. I didn't like it at all. 'You can't!' I hissed.

'Shut up, Dee,' Aleida said. Then, to Minerva, 'She hasn't seen much of the world yet.'

'Who? Swineherds, woodcutters?'

'More bandits,' Aleida said. 'Taking out the old troupe left a bit of a void behind. Others have come in to fill it. I could give you five, easily. Real hard-bitten types, look like they've been in the game for a while. Even got Armund's mark carved into them. They'd give you a lot to work with.'

Minerva rubbed her chin. 'Hmm. I suppose ... no. No, too much work to prepare them for the ritual. I'm close now. I can finish this with what I have. I want to tie it up and get out of this wretched place.'

Aleida shrugged. 'Oh, well,' she said.

'At least you can tell the lass you tried.'

'Oh, yeah,' Aleida said. 'Yeah, I'm sure that'll go down splendidly.' With a shrug she took one last swig and passed the bottle back to Minerva. 'One for the road. Thanks for the drink.'

'Welcome. Now get the hells out of my den, missy. Take my advice, and get yourself and your lass well away from here, you don't want to be around when I finish this up.'

'Sure.' She turned for the wall, the same way we'd come in, and waved at me to come with her.

'And if you do get it into your pretty little head to come back and meddle,' Minerva called after us. 'Just you remember that I've tested your strength now. You might have killed Gyssha, but she took a chunk out of you on her way down. Don't think I don't know it.'

'Come on, Minerva,' Aleida called over her shoulder. 'Hasn't anyone ever told you that wounded tigers are the most dangerous?'

Minerva just laughed. 'And tell that young lass that if she's vowed and determined not to leave her father, she's quite welcome to come and join him.'

❧

I clenched and unclenched my fists as we walked back through the dark tunnels. 'How could you say that?' I demanded.

'Say what, exactly?' she said, distractedly.

'You know what I mean,' I said. 'Would you really have handed over those bandits when you know she's just going to kill them?'

'Of course. If she'd just taken the damn deal it'd be so much easier.'

'But you might as well kill them yourself!'

'Look, do you want to help Kara or not? And don't give me some blather about them still being people, or a life is a life. Those marked men are murderers, I'd put any money on it — and that's not the worst of it, I'd say. Damn it, I really thought she'd take them.'

'Why, because she's as heartless as you are?'

She ignored the dig completely. 'She's got a thing about bandits, old Minerva. You heard her say she's been on her own since she was just a little girl? From what I heard, her family was attacked on the road and she was the only survivor. Ran off into the woods to hide from them, and eventually fell in with a pack of wolves. Lived wild with them for years and years before old Mother Wormwood took her in and taught her witchcraft. Got to give her some credit, taking thieves and murderers for the work rather than innocent travellers; Gyssha never would have bothered with that distinction. But that's beside the point. Dee, it's just plain idiocy to say all lives are equal.'

'Is it? Is it really?'

'Of course it is. Look, if your house was on fire and you had the choice of saving your idiot stepfather or your little sister Maisie, who would you save?'

I clenched my teeth. 'Lem's a grown man. He could save himself.'

'Not if I've chained him to the godsdamned floor, and trust me, I just might. Is that what you're upset about? Not the other thing?'

I didn't need to ask what other thing she meant. 'Well, it wasn't a lie, was it? The ring didn't buzz. And these last few days have made it pretty clear I'm all but useless as an apprentice.'

'Oh, it buzzes for you? That's interesting, for me it turned hot. Dee, ragging on your apprentice is traditional. Apprentices are always lazy, stupid and ungrateful. Mistresses are cruel, demanding and expect miracles on a daily basis. Besides, nothing good comes of bragging about an apprentice. They'll either want to put you to the test or poach you away, and you, my sweet, are not ready for either of those. But forget the hypotheticals, we've got real problems to think about.'

I scowled at her back. 'Do we? I thought we were just going to load up and roll on out of here.'

For a moment she said nothing. She kept walking, head bowed. 'I'm wondering if we should. I really am. We could even take Kara with us. I could tamper with her mind a bit, give her a memory of nursing her father through a sudden illness, laying him to rest and all that. It wouldn't be perfect; deep down she'd know it was false, and she'd probably dream about searching for him for the rest of her life, but it'd do the job.'

I stopped, folding my arms across my chest.

She turned back to me. 'Dee ...'

'It's wrong and you know it,' I said. 'Just because you chose to walk away from your family, doesn't mean you can make the same choice for her.'

That earned me a flat, unfriendly look. 'Even if it means a little less suffering in the world?' She shook her head. 'But that's just an aside. No, I'm talking about that ritual she's working up. Lord and Lady, it doesn't make sense. Gyssha and *Mae*, of all people? What on earth were they playing at? The idea of those two working together ... Gods.' She shivered.

'Who is she?' I said. 'Someone like Gyssha, I take it.'

Lips pressed together, she shook her head. 'No. Not really. Look, you know what Gyssha did, tearing down kingdoms, destroying cities, starting wars. Mae's not into that at all. She ... Honestly, I don't really know *what* she does. She just ... appears sometimes. Mae o' the Mists, they call her. This fog springs up out of nowhere, so thick you can't see your hand in front of your face. There's a deathly silence ... and then it's gone, and everything's ... different. Or nothing is. It's kind of hard to explain.'

'Well,' I said. 'That doesn't sound ... bad, exactly.'

'She isn't ... exactly, not like Gyssha was. I mean, Gyssha hated her, but she hated everyone. That time they fought, it happened just because Gyssha caught wind of her and wanted to see what she could do. I tried to stay the hell out of it — Mae could have killed me then if she wanted to. I was six years under the wand, then, and no slouch, but that's nothing to her. I only caught the briefest glimpse of her and she clearly decided I wasn't worth bothering with.' She paused, biting on her lower lip. 'I think Mae is into some weird stuff — walking between the realms, into the void, that kind of thing. Gods only know. You spend enough time out there, it changes you. Whatever it is she's been doing, I doubt she's truly human anymore.'

'But if you knew why she was involved, maybe you could figure out what the ritual is about?' I asked. Despite everything she was telling me, I felt no closer to understanding just what was going on.

'Oh, gods, no,' she said, and started walking again. 'No, I figured that out ages ago. Well, you told me, really, with the nether beasts, but looking at the sigils in the basement there just confirmed it. That's why I'm trying to decide if we should stay and try to stop the ritual, or pull up sticks and get the hell away from here. She's summoning a hell-beast.'

CHAPTER 9

Back at the wagon, Aleida heaved herself up the steps and leant her staff in the corner. 'Coffee?' she said.

With a sigh I took out the mortar and pestle. 'Yes, miss. Um, Aleida?'

'Mm?' She rummaged through one of the cubbyholes beside the bed to pull out her runestones, and sat at the tiny table to shake them out of the bag.

'When you say hell-beast,' I said. 'Do you mean one of those things that came through the rift, back when the warlock died?'

'No, no,' Aleida said. 'Those were just critters. Nether beasties.'

'No, they weren't!' I said. 'One of those things was big enough to carry off a horse!'

'Dee,' she said. 'No. Look, the nether realms are in tiers, right? Like layers on a cake. That rift back at the cottage opened without any guidance or ritual to drive it, so it opened into the nearest of them. That's what you saw. And from the sounds of it, it's where that beastie you saw yesterday came from. But if you do the groundwork and really put your back into it, you can go deeper; and with months to set this up I'll bet Minerva's gone a long way down. How much do you know about demons, kid?'

'About as much as I'd like to,' I said. 'Which is not much at all.'

She gave a huff of amusement. 'Demons come from the deepest of the nether realms. They're a different order of being than the critters you've seen. They don't have bodies, exactly. Or maybe it would be better to say that the bodies they have can't survive here. If you want to bring one through, you have to give it a body.'

'Like the tree back home?' I broke in.

'That's one way of doing it, if you want to keep it bound to one place and harvest bits off it when you need them. But Minerva's giving it a body built from the strongest and fiercest beasts she can find.'

'Why would anyone do that?'

'Oh, you know, a bit of wanton chaos and destruction. And by a bit, I mean a lot. Really, quite a lot. This thing could raze a city inside of a few days. Kill every living thing that doesn't manage to flee. Shed poison into the air and the water, reduce forests and fields to ash and sludge. But whatever they meant to do with it, Gyssha was part of it, and she's gone now. I'm not sure what's worse — someone with a hell-beast and a plan to use it, or a hell-beast turned loose on the world with no plan and no one to control it.'

The coffee made, I poured her a cup and set it by her elbow. She barely acknowledged it as she laid out her rune-cloth and gathered the stones into the palm of her hand.

'What are you doing?' I asked. 'Well, I mean, I know *what*. Why are you doing that?'

For once, she didn't roll her eyes over asking a foolish question. 'Trying to get a read on what might happen. Minerva's probably doing the exact same thing right now.' She rattled the stones and scattered them over the linen kerchief. 'There's got to be some way to head this off.'

We both bent over to peer at them, but before I could make head or tail of it Aleida gathered the stones up to cast them again.

I pulled back to watch. As far as I knew, you weren't supposed to do that. The first reading was the true one, you can't just go casting the stones again and again to get the result you want. But I rather doubted that's what Aleida was doing. She was focused intently on her task, lips shaping words I couldn't hear.

That was how it always seemed to go, though. Ever since I'd become her apprentice, it seemed that the set of rules I learned one week was thrown out the next and replaced with something more confusing, less specific and with more uncertainty.

In the end, she pushed the stones away and leaned back with lips pursed. I gestured to the stones, offering to pack them away, and she nodded.

'What do they say?'

She didn't reply right away. Instead, she twisted around on the bench to look out the window behind her. Maggie had returned while we were calling on Minerva, and was patiently cropping the dry grass nearby.

'I might be able to stop it,' Aleida said. '*Might*. The summoning, I mean. I *could* kill Minerva … but I don't really want to. Aside from the fact that it wouldn't exactly be easy, she's not truly at fault here. She's not a witch of the dark path like Gyssha was, she's been forced into this.'

'How would we stop it?' I said. 'If she's been working on it for months, there'll be an awful lot of power bound up in it.'

'Mm. You're right, it's well advanced, it has a lot of … call it momentum, all stored up. Like a boulder poised at the top of a hill.'

I nodded, though I had only a loose idea of what the word meant. Sometimes I really hated Ma for not letting me go to school like my brothers and sisters. 'So what does that mean?'

'It means all that energy has to go somewhere …' She broke off with a shake of her head. 'It's not going to be easy. It might be more than I can manage with this curse hanging over my head. Releasing that power safely is a big problem, and rather out of my area of expertise. It's not something Gyssha ever cared about, so my training is more of the "let the chips fall as they may" school.' She looked out the window again. 'Mind you, we're more or less in the middle of nowhere. If we were going to just let 'er rip, there's worse places for it.'

'"Let 'er rip"? What would that look like, exactly?'

She shrugged. 'Oh, gods know. That's the fun part. But we're getting ahead of ourselves. There's no point worrying about what to do with all that energy when we still haven't figured out how to stop the blasted boulder from rolling. And even if we do thwart her, with that curse Gyssha and Mae put on Minerva she's still bound to do their bidding.'

'So, start all over again somewhere else?'

'Maybe.'

'What if ... what if we let the ritual complete, and then try to ... I don't know, shove the hell-beast back again?'

She gave me a wide-eyed look, and shuddered. 'Oh gods, no. That's not a good idea.'

'I thought those were your specialty?' I quipped. 'All right, it was just a thought.'

We fell silent for a moment as she looked out the window, drumming her fingertips on the tabletop. 'We should probably just get out of here.'

'Well, if you don't care about the folk who live here —'

She gave me a sharp look. 'I never said that. I said the bandits aren't my problem, and they're not, Belmont and his ilk are more than capable of dealing with them. But Minerva and her hell-beast make for a whole different kettle of fish, and the truth of the matter is that there's no one else in this corner of the world who's remotely equipped to face it.'

'The nuns at the Haven?' I suggested.

'Pfft, no. They've got all the offensive capabilities of a litter of baby rabbits; they couldn't even keep Holt and his merry band of idiots out.' She propped her head on her hand as she spoke, looking weary. I'd had my doubts about facing Minerva, and though she'd proved up to that task, this would be something far bigger.

She caught sight of my face, then, and grimaced. 'What is it, Dee? Spit it.'

'You tried to undo the spell Minerva cast on Toro,' I said. 'And it laid you out good and proper. Maybe you're right, maybe we should just leave.'

'Really? I thought you were all about doing the right thing, whatever the cost.'

'Within reason,' I said. 'Jumping in front of a tumbling boulder is a fool's errand, by any measure.'

'Well, I wouldn't be calling on my own well of power,' Aleida said. 'I'd have to go and raise some. But I haven't done much of that since I landed this curse. Just the once, really.'

I was about to ask when, but then I remembered — sunrise, the morning we'd set out to face the ghost of Gyssha Blackbone. 'Oh,' I said. 'Right. Is there anyone who could help?'

She shook her head. 'I don't really have those kinds of friends. Or any friends, except you.'

'What about Attwater?'

'*Attwater*?' Her eyebrows climbed to her hairline. 'He'd laugh himself silly and then find a handy mountain to hide behind. He can handle the smaller critters, but not something like this. I'd never ask it of him. Now, if we had a paladin, that might be a different matter, but there hasn't been one of those in over a century.' She fell silent for a moment, except for the drumming of her nails. 'So we should probably get going, right?'

'Yeah,' I said. 'Probably.'

'I mean, it's the only sensible option. That, or go and kill Minerva before she pulls it off.'

Killing Minerva might be logical, but I didn't like it one bit. Even though she had killed those men and kept Kara's father chained up like a beast. Like Aleida said, it was their choice to attack her. I shook my head. 'No. Like you said, it's not her fault. And I really don't want to see anyone dead.'

She glanced across at me, her eyes full of sadness. 'Sweet child,' she said. 'What on earth are you doing with me, then?'

'I was brought here, remember?' I said. 'To plague, pester and generally harass you, it seems. Maybe I'm supposed to lead you away from Gyssha's dark path, or something.'

'Well, you're about as far away from what Gyssha was as it's possible to be without being such a paragon of the noble virtues that I want to strangle you. So you've got that going for you, kid. I just hope it doesn't get you killed. But in any case, Gyssha's behind this, in some way, and as her heir and slayer it's my right to screw with her plans and schemes to my heart's content. And believe me, upsetting an apple cart of this scale would make my heart very content.'

I had to smile at that, but only briefly. 'We're not leaving, are we?'

'Oh, gods. How on earth am I going to stop this, Dee?'

'There has to be something we can do. There must be ...'

I fell silent, then. Outside the window, Maggie had stopped her grazing and lifted her head, ears pricked towards the road. But that wasn't all. I heard something. Shouting voices, and the ring of steel.

Aleida lifted her head.

'Did you hear that?' I said.

We set out swiftly on two pairs of wings, flying straight towards the road. We'd chosen Aleida's favourite beasts for borrowing, a pair of black crows.

The first clue to what was going on was the plume of smoke rising up from the narrowest part of the track, where it wound between pale, blocky boulders. The same place where the bandits had launched their ill-considered attack on us. Had that only been a few hours ago? I remembered, then, what I'd overheard when I'd flown this way before — a caravan, rich but lightly guarded, expected on this road today.

The smoke was coming from a rough barricade of dead, dry branches, bundled together into hurdles and set alight. On our side of the barricade there was a large caravan — only I could see now that it was truly no such thing. On each wagon, what looked from the outside like a heavy load of barrels and bales was only a façade made of barrels cut in half and nailed together, with an oilcloth thrown over the top for a roof. There was space inside each one for a dozen men. A trap had been set all right, but it was not Holt and his hapless comrades who had laid the bait.

From above, I could see it all at a glance — there were a few knots of fighting still, but some of the bandits had surrendered already, and those who hadn't were fleeing through the rocks, with soldiers hard on their heels.

Aleida circled the chaos once, and then settled on a boulder beside the road with a rustle of her black feathers. Feeling uncertain, I glided down to land beside her. We must have stuck out like sore thumbs here, black birds against the pale, smooth boulders, but none of the men paid us any mind over the shouts and grunts of effort and the ring of steel.

On the road, pinned against the boulders, the marked men were making their last stand. One of them was down, wounded but alive. It was the same man who'd tackled me earlier, his shirt still bearing stains of blood where the griffin's claws had dug into his back and shoulders, and he sat, legs sprawled, one hand pressed to his side as fresh blood seeped into the dust. He still held his sword, though, and the soldiers around him were wary, keeping their distance.

The rest of the marked men had been split into two groups, each outnumbered, and they cursed and swore as they slashed and parried.

Two men in merchant's garb stood back to watch with mild interest, chatting as though they'd happened to meet at a market on a fine day.

Aleida tilted her head to watch the soldiers with the crow's beady black eyes. 'Looks like it's just as well

Minerva didn't take the deal,' she croaked. 'I'd be truly cross if I'd managed to set it up only to have something like this spoil my plans.'

'It looks like they're playing with them,' I said. 'Like cats with a mouse.'

'In a way. They're not getting out of this, and everyone knows it. But they'd rather fight to the death than be taken alive, and if they can they'll take others out with them. The soldiers are just playing it safe.'

As I watched, one of the marked men lunged, striking out just a bit too far. The soldier who was his target nimbly darted back and one of his fellows lunged in and jabbed his sword into the bandit's thigh. In moments, the bandit was down in the dust, and the soldiers were upon him, disarming him and dragging him away.

'And there you see it,' Aleida said. 'Armund's mark. Sounds good on paper, but not as useful as you'd think when you're outnumbered and have your back to the wall. Say what you like of Toro's troupe, they did manage to survive a cursed lot longer than these idiots. Let's go, Dee, we've got work to do.' She spread her wings, ready to leap up and take flight, but a movement among the boulders caught my eye.

'Wait!' I said.

She settled back onto the boulder, folding her wings, and gave me a curious look.

The soldiers who'd set off into the boulders were returning, shoving their prisoners along ahead of them, all of them dusty and downcast and bloodied here and there. Among them, I saw the young lad whose broken arm I'd helped to bind underground. And near the rear, her blonde hair coming loose from its braid and the sheath of her sword empty at her side, was Kara.

⁂

I fair flew down the stairs of the caravan, tugging at my wand to free it from my belt. Toro had returned at some point while we were distracted — from the way he held himself, head up and ears pricked, he already knew something was afoot.

'Dee, wait!' Aleida called from behind me.

'I can't just leave her there!' I cried. 'I can't!' Even if the nuns back at the Haven swore she'd been kidnapped by force, no one would believe it now she'd been caught with the bandits unbound, unharmed and armed with a sword.

'Stop, Dee,' Aleida snapped from the doorway.

'We have to do something!'

'We will, all right? Just slow down, take a breath. We're not going in there unprepared. Come back here for a minute, I want you to carry the bag for me. Lord and Lady, I do not need this right now.'

Reluctantly I came back to the base of the steps, shifting my weight from foot to foot with impatience as she collected some flasks and vials from the cabinets and shoved them into an old satchel, except for one tiny bottle, which she tucked into the front of her dress before descending the steps. She was still walking on dog's feet, and thrust the bag towards me before collecting her staff.

'Hurry!' I said.

'Calm down, Dee. They're not going to just put everyone to the sword, this isn't wartime. They'll march them all back this way away from all the smoke and find a nice tree to hang them from. We'll meet them on the way.'

She set out, leading the way towards the road, and as we walked she fished out the tiny bottle. It was very beautiful, with the glass set into a kind of golden frame, to which the cap was fastened with a tiny chain, more like a scent bottle than the usual flasks and vials we used for potions. Aleida paused to unscrew the cap, and then dabbed a little behind her ears and inside her wrists.

'Perfume?' I said with incredulity.

'Yep. You, too.' She passed it to me.

It had to be a potion of some kind. The scent was strong, spicy and sweet ... and rather cloying, actually. I didn't particularly care for it; not that I was any great expert on the matter. All the same, I dabbed it on just as she had, and handed the bottle back. 'So what do we do?'

'Oh, *now* you want to come up with a plan. Just follow my lead, kid, and we'll pull this chestnut out of the fire.' She glanced up at the sky. 'Quickly, too. Gods, I could really do without this distraction; our clock is ticking, good and proper.'

'If she *does* get the ritual finished first, I can always open a pathway and take us out of here,' I said. 'Can't I?'

She grimaced. 'Maybe, maybe not. She's going to tear a hole between the realms, Dee, and the pathways exist in those same spaces. They'll be unstable, to say the least.

But you're right. Better to chance it than stay here and get a taste of hell on earth.'

'We'll know, then? If she's gone and done it, I mean?'

'Oh, yes. You couldn't miss it, trust me.'

In the end we had to wait for them, Aleida tapping her foot impatiently and checking the angle of the sun every few minutes. 'Hurry up,' she muttered. 'If I'd known they were going to take this long I'd have got some sigils drawn out in the dust — oh, and here they finally come. About bloody time.' With a sweep of her hand, she cast a veil over the both of us.

Along the dusty road they came in a long line, roped together with hands bound and feet hobbled, herded along by soldiers with their swords drawn. The two men in merchants' garb were walking alongside them, still chatting idly. One of them was older, portly with a steel-grey beard and thinning hair. The other was much younger, with thick black hair and olive skin and a large nose, hooked like an eagle's beak.

Aleida stood in the middle of the road, and when they were a dozen or so yards away, she dropped the veil.

The men at the head of the line faltered, cursing in surprise as she suddenly appeared. She was dressed all in black, from her boots and her dress and even the chemise peeking out above her leather stays. Even the muslin scarf around her shoulders and the hat on her head, pulled down to hide her eyes, a sly smile on her lips.

I couldn't help but glance down at my own dress, in a blue so faded it was most-way to grey, and felt glad I wasn't dressed in all black yet. I couldn't imagine standing in front of that long line of soldiers — there had to be more than two dozen of them, not counting the prisoners — and holding that small smile. But at the same time, a small voice in my head said, *Oh, good grief, are you* honestly *just going to stand there and pose?*

It seemed to work, though. The men leading the prisoners cut their pace. The bandits, of course, recognised her and began to mutter among themselves, until the guards cursed and slapped them into silence, and then turned to the two merchants, as though looking for orders.

The merchants had fallen silent too, and I could feel their eyes upon us. If I'd been out there alone I'm sure I would have melted away like fog in the sunshine to feel all those eyes upon me.

Aleida ignored the soldiers and their prisoners, and started towards the merchants, raising the brim of her hat with a graceful sweep of her hand. 'Lord Belmont, I presume?' she said to the elder man, and then turned to the younger. 'And you must be Lord Haversleigh. Good afternoon, my lords.' With that, she let go of her staff and picked up her skirts for an elegant curtsey, the sort that belonged more in a grand ballroom than on a dusty road with smoke hanging in the air. Meanwhile, her staff just stood there, perfectly upright, until she took hold of it again.

The men both bowed in return, seemingly out of reflex. 'Good afternoon,' Lord Belmont said in return. 'Madame—?'

'Indeed,' she said. 'A fine catch you've made there,' she said with a nod to the captured bandits. 'I knew those fools weren't going to last long, but I didn't think you'd have them rounded up quite so soon. Now, Lord Belmont, I simply must ask you for a favour.'

It was a curious sight to watch. Both men seemed perplexed but there was no hostility in their manner, even when Aleida linked her arm with Lord Belmont's and turned him towards the line of prisoners. Lord Haversleigh went with them, and though he looked suspicious he did not protest or intervene. I trailed along behind, and began to wonder if Aleida had left the veil hanging over me, after all. Squinting, I checked around me. Nope. She just had every one of these people in the palm of her hand, it seemed.

Aleida walked Lord Belmont to Kara. Her face was grimy, with tear-tracks cutting clean paths through the dirt. Between her teary eyes and her hair, which had come loose to spill around her shoulders, she looked much younger than she had before.

'My lord, I believe you know young Kara,' Aleida said.

With a gulp, Kara opened her mouth — but no sound came out. I saw the muscles of her throat tighten, saw her swallow hard, and realised that my teacher had no intention of letting her speak and spoiling everything.

'Of course,' Lord Belmont said with a sigh. 'When I got Ellie's message this morning I realised she was covering for the young lass. It's a shame she didn't stay in the Haven and make a better life for herself. I did hope the girl would have the sense to stay out of trouble ... but I'm not surprised to see her in this situation.'

'It is a pity,' Aleida said. 'So young, with her whole life ahead of her. And such a fierce spirit. You have daughters near her age, don't you, my lord?'

'I do, yes,' Lord Belmont said. 'They're good girls.'

'And are any of them fierce, like her? Tell me, would they sit quietly at home if it were their father lost and in danger?'

Lord Belmont blinked a couple of times, his eyes searching her face. He looked like a kindly sort, I decided, for all that deep frown-marks creased his brow. 'Well, my youngest ... she's the wild sort, truly. Madame, I never wanted to have the lass hanged, but to find her here, a willing participant with these pestilent bandits ...'

'I understand,' Aleida said. 'But she's just a child, a little girl all alone in the world, with no one to look to for guidance.' Kara's eyes were fair bulging out of her head at that, but she still couldn't speak, and Aleida just watched her with a cool gaze.

'Yes, yes,' Lord Belmont said. 'A most unfortunate circumstance.' There were beads of sweat on his face, and he dabbed at his brow with a lace-trimmed handkerchief.

'Perhaps,' Aleida said, 'she should be given another chance? She hasn't actually done any harm, has she? Your men found her hiding in the rocks, didn't they? It's not as though she were down there with the other cut-throats. It would be hard for the men here to see her strung up with the rest of them, don't you think? She's so young and so small, just like their own sisters and daughters back home.'

'Yes. Yes, of course. You there,' he called to the nearest soldier. 'Come cut the lass loose. She doesn't deserve to hang for this. She's just a little girl, after all.'

It was interesting to watch — she wasn't using mind control, I was certain of that. There was some magic at play, it was just of a very subtle kind. But it wasn't just the magic that I found fascinating — Aleida's whole manner had changed. I'd never seen her let a stranger stand so close to her, let alone link an arm through theirs or lean so close to talk. Her manner of speaking had changed, too, her voice and her words softer and more gentle than I'd ever heard from her. She was playing a part, I realised, a role she must have spent long hours practising and perfecting. Lord Belmont was taken by it completely, now — the beads of sweat were gone from his face, and as Kara rubbed her rope-marked wrists he was asking very kindly if she'd suffered any injuries in this unfortunate venture.

Lord Haversleigh, however, was a different kettle of fish. Without warning, he caught Aleida by the arm, gripping hard, and pulled her away from Lord Belmont. She stiffened at once, clenching her fist to pull away, but then I saw her draw a breath and make her muscles soften, wiping the look of affront from her face.

'You,' Haversleigh said. 'You're doing this, aren't you? You're doing ... something.'

'My dear sir, all I'm doing is taking pity on a foolish young girl who's made some bad decisions.' She edged closer to him. 'You're here for the five, aren't you, my lord? The thugs with the tattoos, is that right?'

'That's right. I've sworn a vow that they'll pay for what they've done, and if you think you're going to weasel them free—'

'Lord and Lady, never. I knew they were trouble from the moment I saw them. I'm just glad someone's come along to deal with them, there's no telling how much harm they'd have done to the country folk here if you hadn't come along with your men. Lord Belmont's grateful too, isn't he? He would have needed your men to drive the wagons into the ambush. If he'd used his own folk, the bandits would have recognised them and known something was amiss. It's really thanks to you that they've been captured at all.'

'I ...' Lord Haversleigh said. 'Well ...'

Lord and Lady, I thought. *You couldn't butter him up any more if you tried*. It was so unlike her I found it rather unnerving.

'Are you taking them back to your lands for trial, my lord?' she said.

'No, no. I had them in chains once before, you see, and they managed to escape. Some underhanded dealings. No, it's hanging for them, and for the rest of these louts too. As soon as my men find a suitable tree.'

I couldn't help myself then. I gasped, the sound escaping before I could quell it. Kara began to protest, too, but Aleida's head snapped 'round, like a hawk sighting prey, and Kara's voice died in her throat with barely a squeak.

'Very good, my lords,' Aleida said, slipping her arm free of Lord Haversleigh's grip, now quite slack. 'But I fear the sight might be too much for these young ladies. I'll take Kara into my own care; I assure you she won't cross your path again.' Her voice was soft, but her eyes were anything but. The warning in them was quite clear as she beckoned the girl with an imperious gesture.

Kara was looking around with wide eyes. She'd been bound near the end of the line, and just beside her was the young lad with the broken arm. He looked stricken and pale, tears coursing down his face with the news he was about to die.

Looking at the lad, and further along where Holt stood, head bowed and shoulders hunched, Kara ground her heels into the dust, set her jaw and shook her head.

'Aleida,' I said softly.

'Hush, girl,' she snapped. 'Kara, come *on*.'

Kara just shook her head harder.

'You can't just leave them all to die,' I said, rushing the words to get them out, in case she froze my voice like she had Kara's. I wasn't sure if speaking like this would break the spell the Lords were under, but I had to say *something*. 'Half these lads have never harmed anyone! That boy with the broken arm, he's only here because his ma's sick and his family needs money to pay the doctor. I bet he's not the only one seduced by that fool Holt.'

As I spoke, Aleida's serene mask all but melted away, and she turned to me with a glare that was equal parts incredulity and frustration. Beside her, Lord Haversleigh began to scowl, and Lord Belmont frowned in puzzlement, rubbing his brows as though his head pained them. With a quick glance back, Aleida raised her hand and both men froze, just like the innkeep had back in the griffin's chamber. 'Oh, for the love of life, Dee,' Aleida said through clenched teeth. 'Do you think this is *easy*? I'm not a godsdamned miracle-worker! If they didn't want to be hanged they should have thought of that before they turned to banditry!'

'That lad is just a boy!' I said in a fierce whisper. 'Are you going to leave a child to die because of a stupid mistake? That sounds ...' I faltered. The next few words felt rather like I was taking my life into my hands. But if I said nothing, I just knew she'd walk away and leave the rest of them to their fate. I had to try. 'That sounds like something Gyssha would do.'

She gave me a look of such vitriol then that I wanted to shrink away. I couldn't, though. I was too scared to move.

'You really want to save them?' she hissed. 'Fine. You do it, then.'

I gaped at her. 'But, I can't!' I stammered. 'I don't know how—'

'Figure it out.' She took a step back and stumbled, but managed to catch herself on her staff. Automatically, I reached to steady her, but her warning glare held me back as she wrapped both hands around the smooth wood of her staff and leaned heavily against it. 'Sink or swim time, kid. They're all yours.'

She released her hold on the two lords and gave me a tight little smile before fading from sight under a veil.

The two noblemen turned to me. The kindly aspect of Lord Belmont's face had turned stern, and Lord Haversleigh was watching me like a hawk.

I buried my hands in my patched skirts, and for a moment I wished the ground would open up to swallow me — only for a moment, though, for then I felt Facet thrumming beneath my feet and quickly pushed the thought from my mind lest he answer the call and open a pathway for me.

'Yes, lass?' Lord Belmont said, starting to frown. 'And who might you be?'

'I, I ...' Again, I stammered. *I'm just the servant girl.* That's what I always said, wasn't it? *I'm just a farm girl, I'm just the maid.* I glanced over at the line of men and boys in chains, the guards watching over them. All their eyes on me. I swallowed hard at the realisation that the only thing that stood between them and the gallows was me.

I didn't know how to answer the question, so I took a leaf from Aleida's book, and ignored it. 'Have mercy on them,' I said. 'Please.'

Lord Belmont's bushy brows furrowed in puzzlement. 'Mercy? Why?'

I bit my lip and looked away from his face, trying to find my teacher. I knew she was there — I could see her, just barely, a faint, translucent image, like a statue carved from fading mist. She gave me nothing, though, just watching me with narrowed eyes.

I had to say something. 'I don't want anyone to die,' I blurted out. 'I don't want anyone hurt. Please, isn't there some way this can all be put right?'

'Child, that's what we mean to do,' Lord Belmont said, his voice grave. 'They've broken the law of the land, threatened and robbed innocent travellers. How would you feel if it was you they stopped on the road, stealing your purse and all your goods, and maybe worse besides? Why do they deserve mercy?'

Again, I bit my lip. He had no way of knowing that they *had* tried to rob us. But even in the midst of it, I'd never truly been afraid. I'd known they couldn't touch me, that my teacher would keep us safe.

When I didn't answer, Lord Haversleigh's impatience broke to anger. 'What would you have us do, girl?' he demanded. 'Box their ears and send them to bed without their supper? They're grown men, not disobedient children! They chose their end when they took up swords against their countrymen — why should we let Justice turn her sword aside?'

Every argument I could think of died before it reached my lips. The would-be bandits weren't blameless. They weren't innocent. I couldn't even truly say they'd been led astray — even the youngest of them was old enough to know better. Deep down I knew that if it had been some other travellers on the eastern road yesterday instead of us, Holt and his men would have robbed them blind, at the very least.

'I don't have a good reason,' I admitted. 'But I'm asking for mercy all the same. My Lords, if you hang them all, then maybe that will see justice served — but it will also see a dozen or more families in your lands lose their brothers, their sons and their fathers. I lost my father when I was young, and it still pains me to this day. Maybe these men don't deserve your mercy and forgiveness, but their families also don't deserve to suffer for the choices they've made.

'Sirs, you may think me foolish. You may think this is childish, or that I'm just a soft-hearted girl with no experience of the world ... you might be right. But I have to believe there's some way all this can be put right, that everything can be fixed and put back where it ought to be. Some way that doesn't have every one of these young idiots swinging from a gallows. I don't want anyone to die, my lords, if there's anything I can do to stop it. I'm asking for mercy, for mercy's sake.'

Lord Belmont was thinking about it, watching me with serious eyes as he rubbed his bristling chin. My heart was beating hard, harder than it seemed it ought to, even with the nerves that gripped me. I felt flushed and a little faint, with the skin of my neck and my wrists tingling unpleasantly, prickling so fiercely it almost felt like a burn.

Lord Haversleigh looked down the length of his hawkish nose. 'I've heard enough of this tripe,' he said. 'If you think I'm letting those marked men slip away from me again—' With one hand he gestured to his men, and with the other, he grabbed me by the arm, about to pull me aside and shove me towards the two men who started over.

But as soon as he touched me, Aleida was there, her veil dropping away like a cloak slipping from her shoulders. 'Now now,' she said lightly, laying one long-fingered hand on Lord Haversleigh's arm. 'Don't go touching what doesn't belong to you. That's how folk lose their hands.'

She was barely touching him — just her fingertips rested on his forearm, but at once he began to tremble, and I felt his grip go weak. His breath ragged and with sweat beading on his brow, he released my arm.

'You lads fall back,' Aleida said, watching Haversleigh's men from the corner of her eye. 'Back where you were. There's good boys. Now, my lord.' She linked her arm through Lord Haversleigh's, shoving her staff towards me to hold. 'Which of the prisoners hail from your lands?'

'The five tattooed wretches,' Lord Haversleigh said. His voice was slow, almost slurred, and his glare had become a glassy stare. 'The others are Belmont's folk.'

'Just the five? Well, you needn't trouble yourself in that case, my lord. My apprentice's plea for mercy was never meant for them. What about you, Lord Belmont?' she tipped her head back, raising the brim of her hat enough to look him in the eye. 'Have you been moved by her words?'

'Mercy, for mercy's sake?' His expression was sombre, even sad. 'It's true, there's little enough of it in the world. And there's an argument to be made that too heavy a hand when it comes to discipline can do as much harm as too light. Very well, young lady — those who've only committed robbery will be sentenced to a flogging and fine, or to labour in my fields if they can't drum up the coin. The ones who've had a hand in murder, however ... they will hang.'

'Seems fair,' Aleida said. 'Satisfied, Dee?'

'Murder?' I said, feeling like I'd been slapped. 'They've killed someone?'

'A farm lad, some months ago. A foolish young man who got mixed up in some underhanded dealings. He was found on the roads, beaten half to death, and lasted another week before he breathed his last. My castellan and guard captain have been looking into the matter — they tell me he joined this band of wastrels, only to back out again once he'd thought better of the whole affair. It seems they gave him a thrashing for it, and took it too far.'

'Oh,' I said. I didn't know what else to say as I looked along the line of young men and boys, all chained together, the young lad with the broken arm on the end. He was the only one of them I'd really spoken to, other than Holt.

'Dee?' Aleida prompted me. 'This is what you wanted, isn't it?'

I swallowed hard, and nodded. 'Yes. Yes, thank you, Lord Belmont.'

Aleida held her hand out for her staff, and I passed it over. 'Well, gentlemen, I'll let you get about your business. Come along, girls.'

She turned away, and the moment she released Lord Haversleigh's arm he staggered back, shaking his head like a flystung horse.

'Watch him, Dee,' Aleida muttered as she veered towards the five outsiders. 'This could still go sour. Tell me if he signals to his men.'

Glancing back, I saw Lord Haversleigh talking to Lord Belmont, the hawk-nosed man gesturing angrily, a frown of confusion on his brow, while Lord Belmont laid a fatherly hand on his shoulder. 'All right for now,' I said. 'But we should probably go, quickly!'

'In a moment. There's something I have to do first.'

The five marked men were chained separately from the others, with double the guards even though two of men were badly wounded and barely staying on their feet. As she drew near, the leader turned to her, despite the guards barking at them to hold still.

'Get us out of here,' the tattooed man said — the same one who'd stood beside Holt when we met them on the road that morning. 'We'll make it worth your while. Never mind that business earlier, we'll make it square.'

'What, with that money you stole from me?' she said with a faint smile.

'You let them hang us, you'll have no hope of getting it back.'

'Oh, I wouldn't be so sure of that. In any case, maybe I'll consider it a price worth paying.' Leaning on her staff, she quickly drew a sigil in the air with her finger, and then released it with a flick of her hand, shattering it into myriad fragments that settled over the brutes, glowing briefly before dying away.

'Hey!' Lord Haversleigh called out, striding towards her. 'What are you doing?'

'Don't get all worked up, now, my lord,' she said. 'I'm not going to rob you of your prize. In truth I can't do anything about the sods without my bloody apprentice having a conniption fit, so honestly, you're doing me a favour. Goodbye, lads,' she said to the five as she turned away. 'Rest in peace, and all that.'

As she limped away, I caught Kara by the sleeve and pulled her after me. 'Come on!'

'But, my sword!'

'Don't push your luck,' I said. 'Let's go.'

⁂

As soon as we were out of sight of the road, Aleida sat heavily on the ground, her legs folding beneath her. She was breathing hard and trembling badly.

'Oh gods,' I said, hurrying to her side. 'Can I help?'

'Oh, I think you've done enough,' she gasped. 'Good gods.'

'I've done enough?' I said with indignation. 'You just dumped me in there!'

'Yep. That was weak, Dee. You had Belmont, but you fumbled Haversleigh completely. He was this close to clapping you in chains.'

'I had no idea what I was doing! What was that, anyway? Mind control?'

With a withering look, she raised a hand, and a fat blue spark flared at her fingertip, buzzing like a hornet before it leapt across to sting me on the arm. I jumped back with a yelp of protest.

'Not mind control,' she said. 'We talked about that in the cave. Or is your head too full of lambswool to remember?'

I shrank back, wounded and still indignant — but then I remembered. Mind control only works as long as you hold the spell in place. I remembered something else she'd said, too. *I've been too soft on you. That was a mistake, and I mean to correct it.* 'Then what was it?'

'You tell me.'

When I didn't reply, she raised her hand again, bringing to life another blue spark.

'The perfume?' I blurted out. 'I know it was a potion of some kind.'

'Oh, so you do have some wits rattling about in that little head. It's called Persuasion. Subtle, but powerful — you can't just tell people what to do, you have to talk them into it, but if you play your cards right you get them to do all kinds of things, and they'll walk away thinking it was their own idea.'

'You could have told me that!'

'And you could have kept your mouth shut instead of meddling with affairs you don't understand!' She squeezed her eyes shut, pressing the heel of her hand to her forehead with a groan.

Kara fidgeted nearby, her hand hovering where the hilt of her sword should have been. She'd watched the whole exchange, but wisely, I thought, decided not to comment upon it. 'What do we do now? Are you just going to let Belmont take them to the fort?'

Aleida lowered her hand to give the girl an incredulous look. For a moment I thought she was about to speak, but then she turned away again with a shake of her head.

I wiped sweating hands on my skirts. 'Did you know they'd killed someone?' I demanded.

Kara grimaced. 'Holt said it was some other lads. Not

him. And it wasn't meant to be like that; they got carried away.'

Aleida laughed, a low cackle. 'Oh, other lads, was it? Not your beau. Because of course the leader of the troupe is going to let someone else decide who gets a beat-down, and how much. Your swaggering skunk of a swain is going to hang, little girl.'

'Don't call me that!' Kara snapped. 'And he's not my beau, or anything like that! He's just … useful. That's all.'

The ring on my finger hummed, but this time I managed not to startle at the feel of it. Even without the ring, I reckoned I'd have known it was a lie. Kara's face was still pale from shock, and there were fresh tears in her eyes. She dashed them away quickly with the back of her hand. 'And now what am I going to do? They were going to help me rescue my da. Now I've got nothing! Those bastards even took my sword!'

'Oh, would you shut up,' Aleida growled. 'I've had enough of your bleating! All you've done is hang around begging other people to do the heavy lifting for you; first Holt and then me and Dee. Oh, I saw you strutting around with that bloody sword at your hip, but have you ever pulled it in a real fight? Well, have you? Or have you only ever squared off against scarecrows and empty air?'

Kara didn't reply. Her mouth hung open, speechless, her face slowly turning red with fury.

'It's true, isn't it?' Aleida said. 'You've never been in a real fight in your whole blessed life. It's all an act. You're just a poser, like that idiot Holt, like you're living in a bloody fairy tale. For all your squawking about your precious father you've not made one move in his direction, have you? We told you hours ago exactly where to find him, and what have you done? Just sat on your lily-white hands and waited for someone else to go and save him.'

'You shut your wretched mouth!' Kara said.

'Why don't you come over here and make me?' Aleida spat back. 'Come on, put your money where your mouth is. 'Cause it seems to me that you're more than willing to shed other people's blood for your father's sake, but you draw the line at risking your own. You're just like him, aren't you? Let other folks do the hard work, then swoop in at the end to snatch your prize. I should have let Belmont keep you, you'd be more use feeding worms in the graveyard than you'll ever be in life. And that goes for your wretched father, too.'

Kara moved towards her, fists bunched. 'Don't you dare say that about him. Don't you dare!'

Quickly, I stepped between them, hand on my wand.

'If you really cared about him, you'd *do* something,' Aleida said. 'Anything. Whatever it took. But never mind, I'm sure he'll understand. Tonight, after Minerva cuts his throat and his ghost comes to tell you it's finally over, you'll be able to explain that you just couldn't do it. It was all too hard. He'll understand. You're just a little girl, after all.'

'Rot in hell, you putrid old sow,' Kara said in a whisper, tears spilling down her cheeks. Then, she turned and ran, vanishing into the dry brush.

I wanted to go after her. I tried to follow, but my feet were rooted to the spot. I wanted to call out her name, but my voice was frozen.

'Gods, Dee,' Aleida said in a small voice. 'Please don't fight me. I can't afford to waste the strength.'

My mouth snapped closed, and I whirled to face her. She wasn't looking at me though. Her head was hanging down, black hair dragging in the dust.

'Why would you say that?' I demanded. 'How could you be so cruel?'

She didn't say anything; she just sat in the dust and shrugged.

'She's going to do something stupid,' I said.

'Yeah, that's the general idea.'

I dropped to my knees. 'She's going to go to Minerva!'

'I hope so. Listen, Dee, we need to buy some time. I let on that I give a shit about Kara when I asked Minerva to spare her father. Minerva's witch enough to know we're coming to mess with her ritual, she needs to slow us down. Kara hates me with a passion now; Minerva will see that and find a way to use her against us, but she'll have to break off finishing the rite to figure out a plan.'

I realised my fists were clenched and aching with strain, and I made myself release them. 'You ... you planned all this?'

'*Planned* is a little strong. Had the idea while you were dithering around with Belmont and Haversleigh. Good to know I've still got the touch ...'

Knowing those vicious words were chosen with care didn't make me feel any better about the matter. But that horse had bolted, and there was no use shutting the gate now. 'Well, if time is so valuable we'd best not waste it. Here, I'll help you up.'

But Aleida shook her head at my proffered hand. 'No, not yet. Just a little longer.'

She wasn't in good shape. She looked exhausted and frail. If we were back at the cottage I'd be urging her to bed, building up the fire and pouring her a cup of the restorative potion we now brewed by the kettle. 'You can lean on me,' I said. 'You need your potion. And I'm sorry I spoke out of turn and interrupted the working, you were right to be cross at me. I should have known better. I'll try not to do it again.' I crouched down to pull her arm across my shoulder, but again she refused, warding me off with a raised hand.

'No, Dee. Just wait. It shouldn't be long.'

'*What* won't be long?'

She ignored the question, sweeping hair back from her face with a shaking hand and glancing back towards the road. 'Lord and Lady, Haversleigh, how long is this going to take?'

I remembered, then, the five outsiders, and the sigil she'd drawn to mark them all. I'd only glanced at it, I'd been too worried about Lord Haversleigh and his men to pay much attention; but I could remember some of it. There was the element that meant life-force, and another that would direct energy towards the one who cast it. And encircling them all, binding them together ... that one represented death. They were going to be hanged, Lord Haversleigh had said. 'Aleida? Lord and Lady, those bandits ... What did you do?'

'I did what I always do,' she muttered. 'I did what had to be done to have any chance of getting out of this mess in one piece.'

'By draining their life-force as they die? How could you?'

She lifted her head, and pierced me with her gaze. 'For pity's sake, Dee, what do you want from me? Save every life, defeat the evil witch, all without shedding a single drop of blood? You don't get to do something like this and walk away squeaky clean! There's a price to these things! Look, you wanted to save those idiot bandits and I let you, even though it meant holding every one of those men-at-arms off your back while you fumbled with the job. But this is what it cost me.' She slammed a palm against the dusty ground. 'I'm sorry if I can't give you everything you want all tied up with a pretty bow! But the truth is you can't drain a swamp without getting covered in muck, and you can't heal a wounded man without getting blood on your hands. I'm not a godsdamned miracle-worker!'

I fell to my knees at her side, wrapped an arm around her heaving shoulders. 'You're right. You're right. I'm sorry.'

'Look, I know I've spent half my life going deeper and deeper down the wrong path,' she said, voice rasping in her throat. 'I know I'm heartless and cold and have all the empathy of an abandoned brick but that's what it's taken to get me where I am, and if I'm to have any hope of stopping this bloody hell-beast it's because I am what Gyssha made me, and I'm damn good at it. All right? It's because I can switch it all off and be what I need to be. So just ... let me do it. Please?'

'Of course,' I said. 'I'm sorry. I shouldn't ... I mean, you're the teacher. I'm just your apprentice. I shouldn't keep hounding you, about your family, about all of it.'

She leaned her head against my shoulder, chest heaving above her stays. 'My blasted family ... It really bothers you, doesn't it?'

I nodded. 'I, I just can't get past it. I think about mine every day. I know they wouldn't understand any of this, but I can't imagine never seeing them again. And the way you talk about Kara and her poor father ...'

'Look, you want to know the truth? You're right, I could have found them. It'd be easy. Even easier than the spell I used to lead us to Kara. I even started to cast it back there at Stone Harbour ...'

She trailed off, and though it cost me every ounce of self-control I had, I held my tongue.

'But then I got to thinking ... what would happen when I found them?'

'They'd have been so glad to see you,' I said. 'They'd be over the moon! They think you're dead. Aleida, if my da somehow came home one day, after all these years ...'

She bowed her head with a weak chuckle, but the sound carried more rue than humour. 'Dee ... How in the hells do you have such a rosy view of the world, after all the shit your stepfather's heaped on your plate over the years? Look, you want to believe your life would have been different if your father had lived, I understand that. And who knows, maybe you'd be right.

'But my sisters, my mother — wherever they are, they're the same people they were when I left. The same ones who told me all my life that I was destined to spread my legs for any filthy, stinking brute who offered a bit of coin. Sure, they'd have been happy to see me ... for maybe two or three days. Then they'd be after me to start bringing in money, just like it was before. "You've got to pull your weight, Ally. You're such a spoiled brat. You think you're better than us? Oh no, Ally's too good to lift her skirts in some filthy back alley."' She pressed a hand to her forehead, hiding her eyes.

Those awful words made me shrink inside. 'But ... you've got plenty of ways to bring in money now,' I said. 'You wouldn't have to—'

'To whore for it? No, that's true. It'd be *easy* — I mean, I'd make these pathetic bandits look like boys scrounging for dropped coppers on market day. I could bring in more money than these idiots will see in their whole lives. All I'd have to do is walk up to some rich bastard with a fat purse and he'd hand it over with a smile. He wouldn't even remember doing it. I could change their lives, make them live like kings — for a few days. Then the money's gone and they're back where they started.'

'But it wouldn't have to be like that,' I said. 'What if you set them up with a little shop, or a rooming-house, or something —'

She laughed again, more mirthful this time, but it was a bitter kind of humour. 'Oh gods, I'd like to see that — they'd have the place up in flames before the week was out. They couldn't handle it, Dee, they wouldn't know the first thing about running the place. And I'm no better, I'd have no hope of leading them through it ... and in any case, doing any such thing would have made it easier for Gyssha to find them. I couldn't have stayed, you must see that. At best I'd swoop in for a night or two, turn their world upside-down, and then vanish again. They couldn't understand what I am now, what I've become since I left them. They'd never understand why I couldn't just go and steal another purse of coin for them, and then another and another.'

I pressed my lips together, thinking hard. Trying to find the right words, the ones that wouldn't sound hopelessly naïve and romantic, like I thought life was some storybook tale. 'I, I just ...' I trailed off. The words wouldn't come.

'Dee, look, you don't understand; and that's all right. I didn't, until the moment came. I got halfway through casting the blasted spell before I really thought it through, before the gods or fate or whatever it was showed me where it would lead. Call me heartless if you want. Call me cold as ice, I don't care. It's the truth. And it's better this way.'

She leant against me, trembling with strain, and I wanted to weep at the hopelessness of it all, at how *lonely* it must have felt. 'Oh, Lord and Lady ... I'm so sorry.'

'What?' she said, and glanced up, her eyes bone dry. 'Oh, gods, don't go getting all maudlin on me. It's fine. Witch wins over thief and whore any day, dog's legs or not. Or are you telling me you plan on going back to your wretched scullery one day?'

'Of course not! It's just—'

'Just nothing. Listen, kid—' Then, with a breath she stiffened, all her muscles going tense beneath my arms. 'Oh gods,' she gasped. '*Finally*!'

I felt the rush of it, pure, crackling power, blinding, scorching in its brilliance. All I could do was watch as the force of it drove her to the ground and left her gasping in the dust.

Then, in the span of just a few moments, it was done. She pushed herself up, the tremor gone, her golden skin a healthy shade once again. Her hands were steady as she swept her filthy hair back from her face. 'Gods, that's better. Sorry, Dee, I'm kind of at the end of my rope here, and this day is a long way from over.'

In my mind's eye, I couldn't help but picture those men, hands bound behind their backs, feet swinging in the air, faces purple and bloated. The thought of it turned my stomach. But if I took a step back from that twisting, sickening feeling, I could see the cold calculus of it. Those men were going to die anyway. Justice had come to them. And if that was the case, why shouldn't we make use of what was left to stop the cataclysm heading our way?

Or try to, in any case.

'It's all right,' I said. 'You do what you've got to do. I understand.'

'Do you? One day, maybe, but I'm not sure you're quite there yet. Anyway, we've got to get moving. I've got an idea, and there's a lot of work to do.'

CHAPTER 10

Back at the wagon, Aleida sat heavily at the little table again, pulling down a book from the cabinet and taking out her writing box as well. The little roundish pebbles I'd collected in the cavern were still sitting by the windowsill, and once again she rolled them back and forth under her fingertips, rattling them across the table like the world's worst marbles. 'All right, Dee, I think this could work, but it's going to take a bit of effort. The only way I can pull this off is if I tap into a source of power.'

My mind was still reeling with all she'd just told me, but with a deep breath I tried to push it all aside and focus. 'Makes sense,' I said. 'What source?'

She abandoned the stones for a moment to point downwards with her free hand.

It took me a moment to understand what she meant. 'The *earth*?'

'Mm.'

'So ... how does that work, exactly?'

'Exactly? How about we just stick to the basics for now, hmm? It's not as simple as drawing power from the sunrise, like I did back at the cottage. You have to build a focus and open a conduit. It needs to be strong enough not to burn up under the flow, and you need to make sure it won't feed you more than you can handle and burn *you* up as well.'

'That sounds dangerous,' I said, doubtfully.

'It is, but it's my only chance at stopping this thing.'

'And if you draw too much, what happens? Aside from hurting yourself, I mean. Can you leave the place a wasteland?'

'In theory. Practically, you could never draw that much, it'd be like drinking the ocean. The Lords of the Earth would step in and put a stop to it long before it went that far.'

I blinked, thinking back to one of the books she'd given me to study. 'Lords of the Earth — elemental spirits, right? A kind of guardian?'

'*Major* elemental spirits — these are the big guys. They don't pay us any attention under normal circumstances, but they really don't take kindly to this sort of thing. If I can keep the flow relatively low they'll stay out of it, but if I have to dig deep ...' She pulled a face. 'But, like I said, it's our best bet.'

'All right. What can I do?'

She tapped the pebbles again. 'Do you know what these are?'

I shook my head. 'No idea. Facet dug them up for me, down in the caves.'

'Here.' She tossed one to me. 'Hold it up to the light.'

Puzzled, I did as I was told — and then found myself frowning. I'd thought of them as just little black pebbles, oddly shaped with lustrous, glassy sides. But when the sunlight streamed through it, the stone gleamed, transparent and blue.

'It's a sapphire,' she said. 'A gift from the earth. I'm going to need more of them, I'm afraid. Lots. You'll have to go find some for me.'

'A *sapphire*? Oh, um, okay. How many?'

'At least three dozen. More if you can manage it.' Dipping a quill into the ink, she started to scrawl something out on a sheet of paper. 'You'll have to work a ritual. Summon some earth sprites, bind them to do your bidding and send them out to find them. But *quickly*. That hot-head Kara will buy us a little bit of time, but we really can't be standing around twiddling our thumbs.'

'But ... summoning sprites? I've never done anything like that before.'

'No, but you saw me do it back at Black Oak Cottage when I was hunting for Gyssha. You've got a good memory, Dee, you'll manage. The sigils you'll need are slightly different, since we're dealing with earth spirits and it's autumn now instead of spring, and the moon's waxing, but I've drawn them out for you.' She handed me the paper, ink still wet and gleaming. 'I'd try near a stream if I were you, I'm pretty sure that's supposed to be a good place to find sapphires. Or is that just for gold?'

'You're not coming with me?'

'No, I've got to figure out the conduit, and I need peace and quiet so I can concentrate. This one's for you, Dee.'

'I … okay. I'll need an offering, though, won't I?'

'Yep. Metal would be best, I think. Rare, refined metals are a treat for these little creatures. The chest on the shelf by my bed has some money in it, go fetch it.'

I brought it over, a lovely thing inlaid with brass and mother-of-pearl. At the top was a tray that held an array of jewellery, but Aleida lifted that out to get to the coins underneath. Quickly, she counted out a good handful of silver, and a couple of hefty coins of gleaming gold. 'Always good to keep some pure coins on hand — trust me, you don't want to go offering them dross that's mostly brass and nickel.' Watching her, I pulled a face, remembering the stolen money, lost now that the marked men were dead. This did not seem like the right time to bring it up.

When she'd stacked up all the coins, I bit my lip to see them. That was more than we'd paid for Maggie and the wagon, by quite a lot. 'Are you sure?'

'Just get it done, Dee. Time is of the essence. Oh, and take care — chances are Minerva will send her bird by to see what we're up to.'

I left the wagon with a satchel over my shoulder, coins bouncing heavy against my hip. Toro was there, hanging around again, and as I turned away from the wagon, he fell into step beside me with a querying snort.

I wasn't sure what to make of the fellow, to be honest. After everything I'd learned, about Minerva and her past, about the old bandit troupe and how they'd met their doom,

I just couldn't see him the way I had before. Before that had all come out, he'd seemed a victim in all this, a tragic figure. Now it seemed to me that he was safer in this form than any other — no longer a slave to the drink, no longer a loose cannon to be nudged and spun by the other bandits who knew his weaknesses and used them without pity. I could understand why he stayed so close to us and our wagon, too. A beast of burden in the human world and a beast of prey in the forest. At least we hadn't threatened to mutilate him and put him in harness. I couldn't imagine how it felt, to have spent months voiceless, vulnerable and stewing in guilt, knowing that it was his fault alone that Brute had been caught up in this mess with Minerva, when all his friend had wanted was a better life for Kara. He might have done awful things, but it didn't mean he deserved the fate he'd been dealt. I couldn't help but feel pity for him. 'I've got a job to do,' I said. 'Do you want to come along? I could use a second pair of eyes to keep watch.'

He gave an assenting snort, his ears pricked towards me.

'Actually, you might be able to help me. I need to find a stream nearby. Can you show me the way?'

With another snort, he stopped. When I kept moving, his head snaked forward and he caught my sleeve with his lips. Then, with a nudge of his nose, he manoeuvred me around to his shoulder, and sank gingerly to his knees in the dust.

I bit my lip as I laid a hand on his broad, smooth back, and heard Aleida's voice in my ears again. *Time is of the essence.*

I clambered onto his back and took two good handfuls of his tufted mane. 'Not too fast, okay? I'm not a great rider. Especially not bareback.'

He gave a snort, and set off through the dust.

$$\backsim\!\!\infty\!\!\backsim$$

Don't think, *just do.*

That's what Aleida had told me over and over again since I'd begun my apprenticeship, and I let the words echo through my head as I drew a circle in the dust with a broken stick, and copied out the sigils Aleida had scrawled for me. I'd have been happier if I couldn't also hear my ma's voice. *I wish you would just* think *for a moment before you acted, Dee.*

Once everything was laid out — candles, coins and the symbols drawn on the dry earth — I closed my eyes and, with an effort, pushed both voices out of my head, and cast my mind back to that morning on the misty field behind the cottage, and the day witchcraft had stopped being something full of incomprehensible terror, and had become something full of promise and wonder.

On the first attempt I stumbled over the words, my voice cracking and faltering. I broke off with a curse and stomped my feet in the dust, pulling myself away from the ritual before I could mar the work. *Don't think, just do. Isn't that what I did when I took that sparrow into Minerva's den? And exactly how well did that turn out, hmm?*

With a little growl I went back to my station. I emptied my lungs and drew a slow breath, tasting the dust and dryness of the air, the parched land crying out for winter rains.

This time, when I said the words, they came steadily and easily, spilling from my lips like jewels as I felt power condense around me.

Facet was there before I even completed the first part of the ritual, and no sooner had I finished the incantation than other little beings started to appear. The first, clambering up from the dry stream-bed, was made up of a handful of water-washed pebbles arranged in a line like a snake; each stone of its body rolling across the ground in a little puff of dust. When it reached the circle the stones all stacked up in one neat, pile, largest to smallest, right on top of one of the silver coins.

Others appeared soon after, more shimmering, crystalline beauties like Facet and other strange rocky characters like the pebbles, and others as well — some that seemed to be made of dirt or sand, and even one that was made entirely of the roundish pebbles that Aleida insisted were sapphires. One that was particularly beautiful looked like a mobile blob of quicksilver, oozing from coin to coin, its sleek silver surface untarnished by dust. I watched it with fascination, but some instinct told me to keep my hands away.

I was so fascinated, watching the creatures, that I didn't notice at first what was happening to the coins. They'd slowly grown pitted as the sprites swarmed over them, moving from one to the next like a litter of puppies convinced that the *next* dish was somehow better than the one they were currently gorging upon. Hastily, I closed the circle, trapping the little beasts within. There were about a dozen of them, and I had no idea if that was a good number or a poor one.

They paid it no mind, until all the silver was gone. Then, they all fell still, as still as … well, stone. It was unnerving, really. Nothing can sit there and play dead like a rock can, and it made me wonder how many times I might have walked past a stone sprite only to have it up and roll away the moment my back was turned.

I pulled out the stone I'd brought from the wagon, and set it down in the circle. The sprites remained perfectly still, but I had the impression they were studying it closely, and with a degree of puzzlement. It was nothing particularly interesting to them, especially compared to the refined metals I'd just given them. 'I need more of these,' I told the sprites. 'Many more — as many as you can bring me. Um, please?' Then, hoping devoutly that I'd performed the binding correctly, I broke the circle. In the blink of an eye, the sprites were all gone.

Had it worked? I didn't know how to tell without calling them all back again. I supposed I'd just have to have faith that I'd done it properly.

I shuffled my feet in the dust, and wondered how long I should give them. We couldn't afford to wait too long, but I couldn't call them back too soon, either. With nothing to do but wait, my mind turned to ruminating on what was to come. Another fight. Another battle. Another friend turned against me. I thought of Kara, turning in desperation to the same witch who'd cursed her father, who'd sent him out to attack us just because we took too close an interest in her affairs. I wasn't sure I'd have the courage to do that. But then, courage was one thing Kara had never lacked.

I glanced across at Toro. 'Were you ever scared? When there was a big fight coming, I mean, back when you were a bandit?'

He lifted his head, pricking his ears, and then he snorted a yes.

'What did you do?' Then, I remembered the conversation we'd had when Aleida loaned him her voice. 'Oh, right. You used to drink.'

Another yes, and he dropped his head again, pawing at the earth with one hoof.

I sat down, knees bent with an arm hooked around them. ' I'm not sure I'm cut out for this,' I said. 'I don't want to fight anyone. I don't know the first thing about it. And I don't want anyone to get hurt. Least of all me.' That last part was meant to be a joke, but it didn't quite come out that way. 'I mean, just look at Kara. She's so splendid, with her sword and her braided hair and her red trousers ... And then there's Aleida.' It scared me sometimes, how cold she could be, the choices she was willing to make without hesitation or remorse. That smile she'd worn when she cast her spell over the thugs before they were taken away to be hanged. I didn't think I could ever do something like that. I didn't ever *want* to.

I laid my wand in my lap and traced a finger over the crystal's glassy faces. Despite everything I'd seen and done, inside I still felt like the pot-girl and nursemaid

I'd been back at home, like I was a farm beast that had wandered astray and found itself somewhere it had no business being. I couldn't help but remember what Aleida had said to me when I protested the path that we were on, and the moves she was proposing to make. *Sweet child, what on earth are you doing with me?* I honestly wasn't sure. I did love this life that I'd found myself in — right up until we hit those moments of sheer terror and looming danger, like the one that lay ahead of us tonight, and then I longed for home, for the chipped sink in the kitchen and the laundry copper and the floor that needed endless scrubbing.

A little distance away, Toro lifted his head, ears pricking to alert. I straightened, and found my hand on my wand without any thought of doing so.

He was watching the sky, I realised, and I heaved myself up in time to see Minerva's eagle flapping overhead, moving with determination but flying quite low over the trees. It held something in its claws, something long and slender with a red blob swinging from one end.

It was the red that gave it away — Kara's sword, the red tassel still swinging from the hilt. 'Oh,' I said in a low voice. 'Oh, that doesn't bode well.'

Toro made a low rumble of agreement in his throat, and backed away under the cover of the trees. Then he pointed his long nose at the ritual circle laid out in the dust, and scraped his hoof restlessly against the ground.

'No, it's too soon to call the sprites back,' I said. 'Last time, Aleida gave them half an hour or so. It's barely been ten minutes.'

He made a dissatisfied sound, but dropped his head again in submission.

I joined him under the tree, and tried not to think about what Kara must have promised for Minerva to take the time and trouble to fetch her sword.

Shortly after the eagle disappeared from sight, a strange noise began to echo across the forest, a low, distant rumbling. It made Toro startle, and set my heart to beating harder, making me tense. But though I listened with all I had, even holding my breath to hear more clearly, there was nothing else. Just a distant grinding noise, like an enormous millstone.

After five or ten more minutes, growing more and more uneasy, I couldn't stand it any longer. 'All right,' I muttered. 'I'll call them back. I hope by all the gods that it's been long enough.' Quickly, I laid out the rest of the offering, and started the incantation to call the sprites back.

They were none too swift about it, unfortunately. Facet was the first to arrive, and he brought six of the odd, dark pebbles with him, popping them up out of the ground like sprouting seeds before drifting over to the gold coin to take his reward. The rest returned, one by one and taking their sweet time, and I anxiously counted the pebbles they brought. Each of the little creatures brought at least three, but the undisputed champion was the little quicksilver sprite, who brought nine of the things before muscling his way through the rest of the group to reach the gold coin. The other sprites edged aside to let it through, even though it was smaller than the rest of them.

Even Facet gave ground, which struck me as something of interest, though I was rather too preoccupied to dwell on it for long. Somewhere in the distance, that deep rumbling sound was still carrying on.

I gathered up all the stones, piling them into a handkerchief, and the knot of worry in my chest eased a little as the count steadily climbed. Forty, fifty, nearly *sixty* of the things!

'All right, we're done,' I said to Toro as I scuffed out the circle and the symbols drawn in the dust. 'Will you let me on your back again? We should get back as fast as we can.'

He tossed his head in something I took for a nod, and with the aid of a rock beside the dry stream I scrambled onto his back again.

Now, looking back, I admit that I wasn't as watchful as I should have been. I was filled with relief that my first ritual alone had worked, and that I'd collected nearly double the number of stones Aleida had asked for. My mind was also bending to what lay ahead, the fight to stop Minerva's portal before it opened and brought a hell-beast through to our realm. Whichever way you look at it, I wasn't doing what I *should* have been doing, which was to focus on the here and now — though exactly how much good it would have done is anybody's guess.

We were trotting back towards the wagon, me doing my best to grip Toro's sleek, slippery sides with legs that were not at all accustomed to the task, when there came a sudden shriek from above us. It was an awful, ear-splitting noise, a sound that pierced right through my thinking mind and spoke directly to the primal part of me, striking it with a wordless, visceral terror.

Toro shied violently and launched into a gallop with a powerful kick of his hind legs, surging forward with breathtaking force. Once again, I felt the cold shadow of enormous wings pass over us and threw myself down against his neck, remembering too clearly the feeling of sickle-like claws slipping between my ribs. By some miracle I kept my seat, gripping his flanks with all my strength and burying my hands in his mane, as he desperately ran for the cover of the trees.

It never occurred to us — and it really should have — that the damn things might hunt in *packs*.

Toro swerved between the trees, trusting the branches arching overhead to stop the griffin from swooping down upon us. He leapt over a fallen branch, threading and weaving between a couple of trunks, while every twist and turn threatened to send me sliding off over his shoulder — and then there came another screech, dead ahead of us. I caught the briefest glimpse of huge, golden eyes and a gaping beak, and massive white wings spreading wide.

Toro threw himself aside, and this time I had no hope of holding onto my perch. I flew over his shoulder, and tumbled to a landing right at the griffin's feet. It reared back to swat at me with one of its taloned forefeet, pinning me to the ground, and looked at me quizzically along that bill-hook of a beak. The only reason I wasn't screaming in fright was because the fall had driven all the breath from my body, and with the weight of it pinning me down I simply couldn't draw breath.

Somewhere I could hear Toro's panicked whinny as he realised he'd lost me. Then came the thundering of hooves, getting closer.

The griffin's head snapped around, pupils shrinking to pinpricks — and then with a flash of his chestnut hide, Toro slammed into the beast's shoulder, half a tonne of solid muscle and power and fury. Just as when he'd charged the lion, they both went down, tumbling together in a flurry of legs and feathers and fur.

I scrambled up, snatching for my wand and knife. The heavy satchel was wrapped around me, pulling me off balance, but I couldn't risk losing it. There came a strange chittering behind me, and I whirled to find the other griffin stalking towards us on foot. A gleam of gold caught my eye — another one of those golden seals, pressed into its neck. I understood what it meant, now. Minerva owned this beast, it was bound to follow her will. The one behind me must have one, too.

I pressed my back to the tree and raised my wand, feeling fire and fury course through me, as hot and bright as molten metal. 'Fire!' I snarled, and the stone at the tip of the wand glowed like iron fresh from the forge, red as cherries and blazing with heat, sending a fireball the size of my head roaring towards the griffin. It splattered against the beast's neck and shoulder, splashing over the white plumage like liquid flame, and with a screech of alarm the creature threw itself to the ground again, rolling to smother the flames.

I kept the fireballs going as I pushed away from the tree. I could only spare the briefest glances for Toro, struggling to stand again. I hoped he hadn't broken a leg, risking a move like that. And for the second time today, too. 'Up! Get up!' I screamed at him. He was bleeding from several cuts along his flank and down his leg, but thankfully those long limbs seemed able to bear his weight.

The air was full of the stench of burning feathers, but the nearer griffin had managed to put out the flames, and the second one hung back, wary. It turned those yellow eyes towards Toro, rearing back on its haunches as though to pounce, but I warned it back with a shout and another fireball. I was so focused on the two griffins that I barely even noticed the golden brown shape weaving and flitting through the branches overhead.

It was a mistake on my part. It was Minerva's eagle, and though it was enormous by earthly standards, it paled to insignificance next to the massive griffins, each one of them nearly as tall at the shoulder as Toro himself.

With a few flaps of its wings, the eagle launched itself towards Toro, and alighted on his withers, talons sinking in as Toro gave a squeal of pain and bucked to rid himself of the unwelcome passenger. But the eagle was gripping tight, and with wings spread for balance it lowered its head towards Toro's shoulder.

Too late, I noticed the gleam of gold in its beak. The same gleaming golden seal that the griffins bore, that Brute the bear and Grinner the lion had carried when they attacked us that morning.

'No! Get off him!' I threw another bolt of fire, not even thinking of how it would burn Toro as well as the eagle — but the bird was already leaping away with a powerful flap of its wings, and Toro ...

He fell, legs folding beneath him. He rolled to his side, thrashing and kicking. *Convulsing.*

I backed away, gripping my wand tight, heart thundering in my throat. 'Oh gods, no.' Minerva had him, and only the gods themselves knew what she had in mind for him.

I didn't want to leave. But I knew I had to. The rocks of the Scar were near, I could feel them. I had no idea if Minerva wanted me dead or her prisoner, but I had no intention of giving her either.

With clenched teeth, I set my wand glowing again, and with a steady stream of fireballs to keep the beasts at bay, I beat my retreat.

I came out of the pathway down where the road cut through the rocky scar, as far as I could get from the beasts under the trees while still being somewhat near the caravan. I only knew how to use pathways through bare, exposed rock — if there was some other way of opening a door, I didn't know it. Once I was out in the fresh air and dying sunlight again, I set out for the caravan, hiking my skirts so I could run.

Aleida was waiting for me in the clearing beside the wagon, leaning on her staff and looking grim. 'What happened?' she said as I came near, breathing hard. 'I started over, but once you ducked into the pathway I figured you'd be heading back here. You hurt?'

I shook my head, still panting. I'd have liked to know how she knew I'd retreated through the pathways, but that was a question for another time. 'No, but she's got Toro. Minerva, I mean.'

She pulled a face. 'I was afraid she'd come after him, now that we'd flushed him out for her. Is he dead?'

'No, no … They could have killed us, I think, but they didn't seem to want to. There were two griffins, and the eagle. It had one of those seals in its beak, you remember, the golden ones?' Quickly, I told her what had happened.

'Mm,' Aleida said when I was done. 'So she's got control of him now. Interesting the eagle went straight to him and not you. Perhaps the seals don't work on humans? That would explain why she went to the trouble of transforming them. I've been wondering why she'd go to so much effort just to kill them anyway.'

'I thought they were after me.'

'I expect they would have taken you to her if they could. Did you get the stones?'

I nodded, and opened my bag to show her the bundle of them, wrapped up in the handkerchief. 'Nearly sixty.'

'*Sixty?* Lord and Lady, Dee. That's perfect. Okay, let's go. You can catch your breath while I'm setting everything out.'

'Can I just get a drink of water first?'

'There'll be water where we're going. Come on.'

The job took longer than I'd expected. Aleida had me open a pathway again, and bring us to a cavern underground, where we laid out an array of leaves and twigs, seeds and stones, anointed with oils and candlelight, all set out in a complex pattern. We built three of them in total, and the work went a little quicker once my hands stopped shaking from the fight and I was able to help.

'Is that the last of them?' I spoke quietly, but my voice still echoed over the rocks and the still water. It was lucky that we had the means to lay them all out underground, Aleida had explained. They'd have a little more power this way, and there was no chance of them being disturbed, whether by Minerva's eagle or wild creatures or even the nether beasties that we knew were scattered through this tinder-dry forest.

'Yep, that's the lot. Now there's just one more thing.' She pulled a familiar little jar from her belt, along with a tiny brush. 'Turn around, and drop your dress down from your shoulders a little. I'm going to give you some armour, and that's the best spot.'

I did as I was told, sweeping my hair away too, and tried to hold still against the tickling touch of the brush and the cool, tingling ointment she painted onto my skin. 'When you say armour ...'

'It's called Steelskin,' she said. 'There, done. Give me your hand, I'll show you what it does.'

Turning, I offered my hand. She seized it, turning it palm up, and drew her knife across my palm, pressing hard. I pulled away with a yelp of surprise, but she held my wrist tight. It took me a long moment to realise that it didn't pierce my skin. It didn't so much as scratch. 'Oh,' I said.

'Be warned, it only keeps you from being cut,' she said. 'You'll still bruise, and a hard enough blow will still break your bones. And sorry in advance, by the way.'

'For what?'

'You know how when you get a sunburn, your skin peels? Well, in about three days, you're going to get that all over. And I mean *all* over. Now you do me.' She handed me the brush and ointment, and pulled a slip of paper from her pocket with a sigil drawn upon it. 'This one.'

I hesitated. 'What if I get it wrong?'

'*Don't.*'

I swallowed hard and opened the pot. 'All right. You're going to have to crouch down, though, or I can't reach. Is this the same one?'

'No, different.' She knelt on the ground and tugged her dress down to expose her golden skin. 'This one's called Salamander's Kiss. Stupid name, if you ask me, but I didn't invent it.'

Real salamanders lived in the water, but someone had decided that a certain type of fire sprite should be called a salamander as well. 'Defence against fire?'

'That's right.'

'Why don't we have the same one?'

'Because I'm going to be in the thick of things, and you've got another task to do.' The sigil drawn, she stood again, pulling her dress up and fastening the buttons. 'You're going to keep Kara off my back. Toro, too.'

'Are you serious? You want me to fight Kara?'

'Yep. I'm going to have my hands full with Minerva. Kara's yours.'

'But I don't know how to fight! Her da's been teaching her for years, and she has her sword back! I saw the eagle carrying it.'

'Dee, if you're wearing Steelskin, all she's got is a stick. And you do know how to fight, you did a damn good job against Gyssha's construct back at the cottage a few months ago. But I've got a couple of other things that might help ...'

'That's really not the same thing,' I protested as she pulled a pair of rings from her pocket. 'And I don't want to hurt her.'

'Dee, that's good and all, but if she gets past you and gets to me, I *will* put her down. I know you like her, that's why I'm leaving her to you. Listen, she's not going to go too hard on you, did you get a look at her hands? Those pretty little knuckles have never taken much of a pounding. Now, here.' She grabbed my left hand and pushed a ring onto my finger. 'This one's a shield. This one' — she pushed another onto my right hand, next to the amethyst she'd given me yesterday — 'will give your fireballs a bit more of a kick. If she does get past you, just start throwing fire at her. They won't touch me but they'll force her to back off.'

'Okay.' The ring bore an angular shaped stone that flickered with streaks of orange and red. The shield ring had a dull grey stone that looked a little like quicksilver turned solid. I could feel power in the stone, and after a couple of tries I managed to activate the enchantment within. The shield sprang up around my hand, a glowing, translucent disk a good two feet across.

'There you go,' Aleida said. 'You're not wearing earrings, are you? Best take them out.'

'I'm not,' I said. 'I can't, my ears aren't pierced.'

'Oh. We ought to do something about that, one of these days. Ready?'

I shook my head. 'No. Do we really have to do this? I don't want to fight anyone, I really don't.'

'That's too bad,' she said, flatly. 'You want to stop this, don't you? Or would you rather load up the wagon and drive away? Because it's not too late.'

I shook my head. 'No,' I said in a small voice. 'We can't just let it happen.'

'Exactly. If you want to make a difference, you have to be prepared to get your hands dirty and take a few knocks.' She looked down at me, sadness in her dark eyes. 'Look, Dee, I'll be honest; you're probably going to get clobbered. There's just no way to do this without taking that risk. But you'll need to pick yourself up and keep going. I'll patch you up once it's all over.'

I looked down at the rings and my wand, and bit my lip. *Lord and Lady, what am I doing here? I'm not a fighter.*

Her face thoughtful, Aleida reached into her bag again and pulled out a little glass vial, sealed with cork and wax. Inside was something dark brown and oily. 'Damn it. All right. I'm in two minds about this, but what the hell, we're probably going to need any advantage we can get.' She passed me the vial. 'Drink it.'

I hesitated. 'Don't you need it more? I don't want to take something you could use.'

'I've already had some, this is for you. Drink it, and you could smash your thumb with a hammer and barely even notice. It's dangerous, mind you, it'll let you ignore an injury that could kill you. So take care, all right?'

I took the glass tube and broke the seal with my thumb. Then, with a shrug, I drank it down. It was thick, like molasses, bitter and sweet at the same time, and when it hit my throat it burned with a searing heat.

'Ready?' Aleida said.

'No, but we're out of time, aren't we? Aleida, will you promise me something? Promise to get her da out of there, if you can?'

'No, Dee. It's going to take everything I have to stop this ritual. *You* get him out. Once he's out of danger, Kara will stop fighting you. Your job is to get them out and get them to safety, all right? Leave the rest to me.'

⁂

To my relief, Aleida didn't ask me to bring us right into the basement again. I didn't ask why, but she volunteered the explanation anyway. 'It's never a good idea to use the same trick twice. She'll be prepared for it this time, and I don't know her well enough to know what she's likely to spring on us.'

'All right then, but where?'

'There's more rocky outcrop north of the place, as I recall. Bring us out there.'

When we stepped out into the deepening dusk, Aleida cracked her knuckles and stretched her arms over her head. 'Well, well. Someone's been doing some renovations.'

The fading light had cast everything in shadows, but that was less of a barrier now than it had been a few months ago, before I'd begun my apprenticeship. The crude fence around the ruins was gone, utterly, and the ruins themselves seemed to have been reduced to a heap of rubble, arranged in an oddly regular dome-shaped structure. I remembered the distant rumbling I'd heard when I was summoning the sprites, utterly forgotten after the griffins attacked. 'Is it just me, or does it seem odd that she'd spend time and effort rebuilding the place instead of finishing the ritual?' I said.

'When she knows we're coming to jam a stick in her wheel?' Aleida said. 'Building defences is no wasted effort. Gods only know what's changed inside.' She tucked her skirts up into her belt to keep them out of the way of her feet, and then pulled out her wand. Her knife she left in the sheath for now, since she needed her other hand for her staff. 'Nothing interesting out here. Let's go in.'

I followed after her, my palms sweating on the oiled wood of my wand and turning the leather-bound hilt of my dagger slick. 'It's awfully quiet.'

'Mm. That won't last.'

Cautiously, we circled around the heap of rubble to find that one side of it was open, with a path descending to what had once been the basement of the ruins.

Kara was there, perched upon a boulder with her legs crossed and her blonde braid snaking across her shoulder, her sword lying in her lap. Behind her, the mouth of the cavern glowed a deep, sooty red, and I could hear a faint roar rising up from below, something between the crackling of a huge fire and the rush of fast-flowing water.

At the sight of us, Kara swiftly stood, barely even touching the ground. It just made me admire those divided skirts of hers all the more. I could never manage a move like that with all these skirts and petticoats getting in the way.

'Hey kid,' Aleida said. 'Let me give you a tip. Next time, find a hiding spot and attack from behind. It's more effective when you're outnumbered.'

'Thought about it,' Kara said. 'But I figured you'd know I was there.'

'True,' Aleida said. 'Also, I suspect you're not quite as hardened as you'd like us all to think, hmm? Never got that pretty sword all bloodied up, have you?'

'There's a first time for everything,' Kara said.

'What deal did she cut you, kid?'

'What do you care?'

'If I didn't care, I wouldn't ask. Your father's life, is it? A transformation, too, or you just going to live with a bear from now on?'

'It's none of your concern,' she said through gritted teeth.

'You know, you're right. I've got bigger fish to fry. I'd step aside if I were you. I don't really want to hurt you.'

'Good,' Kara said, drawing her sword. 'That gives me an advantage.' She jumped down from the boulder, landing lightly in the path.

Aleida gave her a faint smile as she swapped her wand to her left hand. 'I said I didn't want to. I didn't say I *wouldn't*.' Then, with a gesture like pushing open a door, she shoved Kara aside, throwing her into the rocks strewn beside the path. 'All yours, Dee,' she said, and with a swish of her skirts, started down into the cavern.

I stood there, hand on my wand as Kara gave a shriek of frustration, trying to free herself and her sword from the rocks. If I was going to press my advantage it would be now ... but I couldn't bring myself to do it. I didn't want to fight her.

I offered her my hand. 'Kara—'

She slapped it away. 'Get away! What are you doing? We're fighting! I have to stop you.'

I backed away as she struggled to her feet and took a fresh grip on her sword. She held it angled across her body, knees bent, boots planted in the ground. Then, drawing a deep breath, she raised it, lifting her hands to her shoulder as though ready to swing it down. To swing at me.

'You don't have to do this,' I said.

There were tears in her eyes. 'You don't know anything!' she spat. 'She'll kill him! She said I have to keep you from stopping the ritual, or she'll kill him!'

'Okay, but what if I can get him out? What if—'

'You can't! Just ... stop talking! Stop acting like we're friends! I can't ...'

I shook my head. 'We're here for her, Kara, not you. But I'll get your da out of here if I possibly can. I'll—'

I didn't get a chance to finish. I saw the movement in

her eyes. She gulped hard, hands tightening on the hilt of the sword, and swung it down.

I stepped in close. It was probably a bad idea — without the spell Aleida had cast on me it would have been disastrous; but I'd been a farm girl for most of my life, and one thing you soon learn is that if a beast is going to kick you it's better to be close where the blow doesn't have as much force.

Kara's eyes widened for an instant, and her swing faltered. Then her gaze narrowed, her eyes filled with anger, and she brought the sword down on my shoulder.

Her hesitation had robbed the blow of most of its might, but it still should have cut deep, especially when she pulled the blade back towards her. It slid over my skin with a kiss of heat, and sliced right through the shoulder-seam of my dress.

I clapped a hand to the cut with a little cry of dismay. 'Oh, for pity's sake, not another one.'

Kara gave me a look of wide-eyed disbelief. Gently, almost hesitantly, she pressed the tip of the sword against my shoulder, and pushed. The skin blanched around the point, but did not part under the wicked edge of the blade. 'Oh, what?' she said with indignation. 'Witchcraft!'

'Well, honestly,' I said. 'What else did you expect?'

The next thing I knew, I was stumbling backwards. Kara had drawn up a foot and kicked me in the chest. Then she was gone, running down towards the cavern where my teacher had gone.

Oh, dear. That was exactly what I was supposed to prevent. 'Kara!' I pushed myself up, and ran after her.

CHAPTER 11

*T*he site of the ritual was ... different, to say the least. For one thing, the floor inside seemed to have sunk by several dozen yards. What had been a fairly cramped space was now a veritable cavern — Black Oak Cottage and all its outbuildings could have comfortably fit inside. A long, spiralling path wound down the inside of the walls to reach the floor, which was strewn with rocks and rubble, except for the old flagstones where the sigils and obelisks were laid out. Minerva stood at the far side, surrounded by shifting, swirling lights of red and orange and yellow, making her red hair blaze like coals in a forge. Beside her were two pale shapes crumpled on the ground. They were so pale they seemed to glow, and for a moment I frowned at them in confusion. But then I realised what lay behind her.

Behind her was Kara's father, the enormous bear, bound with rusted chains. The posts that anchored the chains also supported a flimsy-looking structure of wood and vines, a kind of net that was straining to hold back a mass of rock and rubble, poised over the bear's shaggy back. I took it in with a sinking stomach. It would take only the smallest disturbance, it seemed to me, to bring that huge rockfall down upon him.

I didn't have time to look more closely. Kara was already heading down the spiralling path, and ahead of her I saw Aleida, making her way down to the cavern floor, the stone of her wand all aglow as wisps of light and smoke wreathed around her.

Kara heard me behind her and whirled, hurling a fist-sized stone. Her aim was good, I had to admit. It came straight towards my head, but I brought up my shield ring and it bounced away. Over the roar of magic down below I heard her give a shriek of frustration.

'Kara, stop! Just let me talk!' I shouted.

'I'm not here to *talk*,' she snarled back. 'I'm here for my father! And you've made it clear you don't give a shit about him!'

'Have I?' I demanded. 'When? Tell me when!'

She glanced down at Aleida. 'She said—'

'That was *her*! She's here for Minerva, but I'm here for you! I want to get him out too, it's Minerva who wants to kill him! We're not enemies, Kara, we want the same damn thing!'

Eyes narrowed, she stooped to pick up another rock, but this time she just weighed it in her hand. She was no fool. She wasn't going to keep trying an attack that was proven not to work.

That might just be my chance to get through to her. 'There's got to be some way we can get him out of here, we just need to stop fighting and *think*!'

She scowled at me, gripping the stone, and then her eyes flickered to something behind me.

I didn't dare look around. It could just be a distraction. My shield ring was only useful if I could see the stone coming; I wouldn't put it past her to draw my attention away.

But then I heard it, over the roar of power from the ritual below and Minerva's voice, unnaturally loud as she chanted her incantation. *Hoof beats.*

I raised the shield at the same time as I twisted to look behind me. I felt the stone strike, but it barely registered. All my attention was on the dark shape charging towards me, the golden seal on his shoulder gleaming even in the darkness of the cavern. *Toro.*

I hurled a fireball. I didn't aim it, there wasn't time, and in all honesty I didn't want to hit him, I just wanted to turn him aside. But I'd forgotten about the other ring Aleida had given me.

Fire seared through my arm with all the swiftness and fury of a lightning bolt. The heat of it radiated back at me like the blast of a furnace, and it roared like a dragon as it spat a jet of fire towards the charging horse.

With a squeal of fright, Toro swerved violently away, barely missing the full brunt of the flames. Instead it just scorched his flanks with a reeking waft of burnt hair. As soon as the flame was gone, he veered back, heading for me once again.

I was already backing away, but my steps brought me to the edge of the drop. There was no other escape. Running down the spiralling path was out of the question, I was no match for him when it came to speed.

There was only one other choice. I turned, and jumped.

A hail of gravel fell with me as I slithered down. I landed hard on the path below, losing my balance as my legs crumpled beneath me. Above there came a snort and a rattle of loose stone as Toro broke off the charge. Then, hoof beats retreating, fading away. I felt odd, overcome by a tingling kind of numbness all over my legs and arms where I'd skidded over the jagged rocks. *Oh*, I thought, remembering the potion Aleida had given me, and tried to put it out of my mind.

While I was still trying to stand in a tangle of skirts, Kara slipped down the steep slope with far more control than my ungainly descent. Before I could find my feet, she slammed into me, shoving me back against the rocky wall. Her arm was across my throat, and the other reached for my right wrist, for my wand.

With a yell I drove the heel of my hand into her chin and cheek, pushing her head back and forcing her away. When that wasn't enough to make her let go, I buried my hand in her hair and pulled instead, as hard as I could. With a shriek she released me and swung a fist, but my shield ring was already raised. The force of it bursting out of the stone threw her back, sending her sprawling across the path.

Then I heard it again. Thundering hooves in the darkness. Toro had circled around the cavern to come after me again. I could see him now, charging ahead at a flat gallop, and downhill to boot.

And Kara lay sprawled on her back in his path.

I darted forward, grabbed her under the arms, and *hauled*. Never in my life had I been so glad that my daily chores included so much heavy lifting and hauling. Kara couldn't have weighed any less than I did, but I managed to heave her up and out of the way of those charging hooves.

Unfortunately, the only way to avoid him was to go down again, and with even less control than before. Together, we tumbled down the rocky slope, landing in the path again in a small avalanche of jagged, crumbling rock.

Sobbing from fright and pain, Kara pushed herself up. 'What's he *doing*? I thought he was with you.'

'Minerva got him,' I said. 'That golden seal the other beasts had? He's got one too, now. He's fighting for her.' I glanced down at my wand, gripped so tight my knuckles ached. Aleida would tell me to use it, but when she gave me that ring I hadn't thought about how much hotter and faster it would make my bolts of flame. I'd seen bad burns before, and I could imagine just how much damage one of those bolts would do if it hit with full force. I could picture it clearly, and wished I hadn't.

Kara reached for her sword-hilt and bit her lip, eyes searching my face. 'If she's got him ...'

'He'd have trampled you to get to me,' I said. 'Don't think he won't hurt you just because you're both fighting for Minerva.'

'I'm not fighting for her!' Kara spat. 'I'm here for Da.' She took her hand away from the hilt and grabbed for my sleeve. 'Come on, climb! We need to get back up above him!'

It was easier said than done. The loosely packed gravel fell away under our hands and feet, and for every inch we gained it seemed we fell back double.

As I fought my way upwards, I glanced across the cavern, trying to pick out Toro's gleaming hide through the darkness. Aleida had reached the floor now, I saw, and had begun her attempt to counter the ritual, but I couldn't make out anything more than a swirling haze of shifting light and the feel of power in the air, wrapping around me like spider webs in the dark.

Then something else caught my eye. It lay on the path below, right where we'd fallen. Small enough to fit in the palm of a hand, with a jewel-like gleam of gold and jade.

'Dee, come on!' Kara screamed at me. But then she saw it too, and cursed. 'Oh, hells!'

'What is it?' I said. It looked like a seal, for pressing wax onto paper. Or for pressing odd lumps of gold onto a beast's fur to seal it to the will of the witch. 'Kara?'

'I stole it,' she admitted. 'I saw it in that rats' nest of a bed she had and snatched it up while she and her beasts were elsewhere. I thought it might be useful.'

I gave her a wide-eyed look. 'Yeah,' I said. 'I think it might be. We have to get it back.'

She scrambled back down to get it, and the small rockslide she made brought me back down too. And Toro was still thundering towards us.

Climbing wasn't working. Time to try something else. I shoved my wand into my belt and cupped my hands into a stirrup. 'Here,' I said. 'I'll give you a leg-up.'

She wasted no time asking questions. She just stepped into my hands and leapt off them, all but knocking me over in the process. But it was enough for her to scramble up to the level above, where she lay on her belly to reach down for me. 'Grab my hand!'

With her help I clambered up, both of us covered with dust and grit, Kara scratched and bleeding from the sharp stone. From below I heard Toro scream with rage, and spin on his haunches with a clatter of hooves.

'Again!' Kara shouted, and we started up the next wall.

'Does this mean we're on the same side now?' I said as she made the stirrup this time.

'Shut up,' Kara said. 'Just promise me you'll save him.'

'I promise,' I said, scrambling up and reaching back for her. 'I have an idea.'

There were two souls to save — Toro and the bear. Best to do the bear first, I thought, Minerva had him pinned as her hostage. Toro was at risk too, since she'd figured out I cared for him, but Brute was the one she could kill with a flick of her fingers.

I stood on the edge, looking down to take stock. Aleida was in the depths of the cavern now. The opalescent light that surrounded her was spreading, intruding upon the deep, smoky red of the lines and symbols laid out on the floor. I didn't understand what she was doing, but it seemed to be having some effect, beating back Minerva's work and supplanting it. But the spreading lights weren't the only thing that was different from earlier. I frowned down at the scene, the obelisks of stone gleaming darkly, the bones shining bright white. Then I figured out what had changed — earlier, there had been four sigils marked in blue near the centre of the spiralling shape. Aleida had told me earlier that each of those sigils marked a life sacrificed to fuel the ritual, and back then Minerva had needed more to bring it to fruition. Now there was only one left.

One must have come from the lion. The others ... I bit my lip, turning back to the two pale shapes that flanked Minerva, and finally realised just what they were. Her white horses, crumpled and still. The realisation of it shook me. I'd spent most of my life on a farm, the idea of slaughtering beasts was nothing shocking to me. Horses, though ... they were different to the regular beasts of field and fold. For most folk a good horse was like a good dog, they would hold a special place in the heart of even the toughest old farmer. Were they just beasts, or something more, like the transformed bandits? Impossible to know, now.

I shook myself to dispel the chill of it, and pulled myself to focus. It didn't matter how or why, what mattered was that now she only needed one more life to spill out on the stones.

We had to get Brute out of there.

Kara was waiting for me, fidgeting but quiet, letting me think. I backed away from the drop and thumped her on the arm. 'Come on.'

I ran to the wall and pressed my hand against the crumbling stone, calling on the pathway.

Nothing happened.

'Oh, for pity's sake. Come *on*!'

Nothing. I could feel the power tugging on the stones, I could feel them shifting and twitching at my touch, but the doorway never came. 'Facet!' I cried. 'Are you there? Why isn't it working?'

He was, of course, and he rose out of the ground, rippling with shifting light. But there were no answers in his crystalline planes.

'Dee?' Kara said. 'What's going on?' There was a dangerous note to her voice. If I couldn't do it, I knew she'd turn on me again. Her loyalty wasn't with me, not really.

I squeezed my eyes shut, trying to think. Why wasn't it working? Well, every other time I'd opened a pathway it had been through solid rock. This rock was anything but solid. It was crumbling like a dried-out cake. Minerva had probably done it on purpose, I realised, so we couldn't surprise her again by appearing at the heart of her lair. Perhaps we could run outside to the outcrop I'd used to bring us here, but I wasn't sure Kara would follow me that far, and it still left the problem of how to snatch Brute out from under Minerva's nose.

Unless ... unless I could make the rock solid again. I didn't know a lot of magic, but fire was an easy one, and what was fire but heat? I had an affinity for earth magic, that's what Aleida said, *and* I had a ring that was supposed to give me a boost to the fire I could summon.

It was our best chance.

I pushed back my sleeves and pulled out my wand. 'Stand back,' I said. 'Keep watch for Toro, let me know if he's coming.'

Kara looked me over with a searching gaze, and nodded, drawing her sword. 'You won't have long.'

'I don't want him hurt!'

'Then you'd better be quick!'

She was right. I bit back a curse and then turned my attention inward, drawing a breath to steady myself and calling up a page from the book of sigils Aleida had given me to study. There was something there I could use, if only I could remember it correctly.

I anchored the picture in my mind and summoned power to my wand. Once again, I felt heat searing through me in a scorching wave, but this time, instead of loosing it in a ball of flame, I held it in, and used it like ink to inscribe a sigil in the air, and with a flick I released it upon the stone.

There was a flash and a blast of heat, a scorching wave of it. For an instant the rock glowed and rippled, turning glassy, and then it was done. Over the roar from below, I could just hear a faint tinkling noise, a tiny *plink, plink, plink* as the rock began to cool.

I could also hear hoof beats. 'Dee,' Kara said in a low voice.

Swallowing hard, I reached for the rock. It felt like reaching into an oven. 'Oh gods,' I whispered. 'Open, please open.'

The rock folded away in front of me. I didn't even have to touch it.

'Kara, come on!' I shouted, and ran inside.

The sudden silence was deafening, and I was sweating uncomfortably in the cool, damp air underground.

'Now what?' Kara said, shifting her weight from foot to foot.

'Let me see that seal,' I said, holding out my hand.

As soon as I touched the seal, I sighed in relief. It was enchanted, I could feel the power inside it, and I'd handled enough enchanted devices now to understand how to use it, if not how it worked.

'All right, all right,' I muttered. 'I think I know how to do it. Once we've got him loose you're going to have to draw his attention so I can get him free. I—'

I broke off as a tremor rippled through the dark cave, sending a rain of dust down over us.

'What—' Kara started, but I was already cursing, remembering what Aleida had said earlier. The pathways might be destabilised by Minerva's ritual.

'We'd better be fast,' I said, turning towards the nearest wall.

I tucked the seal into the front of my dress, and pressed both hands against the wall, closing my eyes. I was getting the hang of this — I ought to be, it felt like I'd been doing it all day. *Brute*, I thought, thinking of the great shaggy beast trussed in chains. I had no doubt he was standing on more of that loose, crumbling rubble, but Minerva had spent a lot of power reshaping this place. Just how far beneath us did that gravel go? I was about to find out. 'You'd better back up,' I said.

The doorway opened, and suddenly our quiet, calm cavern was full of dust and smoke and falling stones and the roar of power. I heard Minerva's voice, and Aleida's. Minerva's rose to a scream of rage as the very ground beneath her feet heaved and crumbled away.

I had opened a doorway directly beneath the huge bear. He fell, still wrapped and bound by chains, and his massive weight pulled down the flimsy structure holding back the mound of rocks and boulders. His fall brought them all tumbling down upon us.

But it didn't matter. As soon as he was through, I slammed the doorway shut, sealing out the avalanche.

Choking, blinding dust and grit filled the chamber as the force of the fall sent bear and rocks all sliding in a heap across the floor. It must have been disorienting to say the least, and I took full advantage. I threw myself at him, leaping half onto his great shaggy back as I fumbled for the seal in my bodice.

Kara wasn't ready for it at all. She stumbled back, face drained of blood. 'Hey,' she said weakly. 'Hey, you sorry excuse for a bearskin rug. Hey, Da.'

With a low rumble in his chest, the bear struggled to his feet. The chains that had wrapped around him were broken — no, not broken, *cut*. The ends of them were perfectly smooth, like glass, where the closing door had severed them. They slithered off him like clanking snakes. He didn't seem to even notice my weight upon his back as he kept advancing upon his daughter, the rumble in his chest growing to a snarl.

The seal was in my hand now. Winding fingers into his shaggy coat, I reached down. It didn't fit at first, but I kept trying, turning it in my hand and praying that I wouldn't drop it.

'Da,' Kara said, still backing away. Her hand went for her sword-hilt. 'DA!'

I felt the seal *click* into place, fitting perfectly over its gleaming golden impression on the bear's shoulder. The gold disk came free and fell to the ground with a musical chime, and the great shaggy body beneath me collapsed in a puff of grit and dust.

I gave them no time to rest, or catch their breath. As soon as Brute was able to stand, I was opening the doorway again. All I could think about was that Aleida was there, facing Minerva with no one to watch her back, and the best remaining sacrifice for Minerva to call upon was still charging around the spiralling path, searching for us — Toro. There was also the fact that the rock around us was still trembling and shaking every few moments. We had to move.

I opened the doorway as I had before, into the solid rock beneath the loose gravel floor of the cavern, and clambered over the rattling stones to climb out. Stepping through, the shift from entering a hole in the wall on one side to exiting through a hole in the ground was every bit as unsettling as I'd imagined. The world swung crazily around me, sending my belly into knots and giving me a sudden wave of dizziness.

But that wasn't the worst of it. Not by far.

The power bound in Minerva's ritual roared in my ears like a waterfall, the kind of sound you felt rather than heard. The air was full of portent, like a summer storm right before the first lightning bolt comes crackling out of the sky. I had an inkling, then, why Aleida had been so hesitant to take this path — in trying to stop Minerva's ritual she'd only been feeding more power into the spell. The air itself felt charged and ready to ignite.

Kara and Brute came through behind me, whimpering at the strangeness of our passage back into the world. I'd brought us out behind Aleida, and she cast me a brief glance over her shoulder, her brow knotted and her dark eyes troubled, a look of urgency etched on her face.

At my shoulder, Kara hissed in unease. 'She doesn't look happy. And that's a damn big knife she's got there.'

It took me a moment to realise that she was talking about Minerva. The witch's face was twisted in fury. She was gleaming with sweat, her tangled hair slick with it, her bare arms raised high. The knife in her left hand was as long as my forearm, the curved blade already stained with blood. She was still chanting, a shrill note to her voice now, a note of summons.

A flash of movement along the wall caught my eye. Toro, charging down the spiral path to answer her call.

'She needs one more to finish the ritual,' I shouted. 'We have to stop him!'

'Right. You've got a thing for rocks, don't you, Dee?' Kara said. 'Can you bring the path down? Cut him off?'

'She'll make him jump!'

'Doesn't matter. Just bring him near us, and then Da can pin him while we get the seal off. You can do it, can't you, Da?'

The bear rumbled in reply.

It was a good plan, assuming Toro didn't break a leg in the process. Hells, even if he did, better that than dead and fuel for the ritual. 'All right,' I said. 'Okay.' I jammed my wand back into my belt and ran for the wall. I didn't have long.

I dug my fingers into the wall. Any other time it would have torn my skin to ribbons, but between the sigil and the potion Aleida had given me it felt like sinking my hands into a bucket of smooth, round pebbles. I thought back to how it had felt to try to climb this crumbling, shifting mass, how easily it had slipped and slid away beneath me. Rocks knew how to fall, it was part of their very nature. *Come down*, I thought to the tiny, clinking pebbles. *You know you want to, you know it's where you'll be before too long. Just come on down!*

At first there was just a trickle, a brief shower cascading over my feet. Then, they all came at once. With a yell, I beat a hasty retreat. Kara and Brute, too, as the spiralling pathway simply melted away, like a child's mud pies under rain from a watering can. Aleida cast another quick glance around, her brows knotted even deeper, and with a gesture split the avalanche to flow around her. For a moment she was lost amid a swirling cloud of dust, the haze turning the hellish red glow dim and murky.

Then, with a crash, Toro was there, falling in a tangle of legs and stones. From behind me came a rumbling growl, a sound that sent a flicker of terror through my heart, despite everything else going on around me, and Brute charged past me like a boulder hurled from a catapult. Toro was struggling to find his feet, but Brute was there first. Easily twice Toro's weight, Brute slammed against his flanks, heedless of the flailing hooves, and knocked him sprawling onto the stones.

Before I could truly take stock, Kara was already running past me. 'Now, Dee, now!'

'Oh, you don't say,' I muttered under my breath, and fumbled in my dress for the seal. In the moments it took me to get there, Kara was already kneeling on Toro's neck, pinning his head to the ground. I had to squeeze in beside her to reach the seal, but in an instant it was done, and I felt Toro go limp beneath us. He was free.

Minerva's chanting abruptly stopped, the echoes of her voice dying away. Aleida, too, though she finished the phrase of her incantation first. My mistress didn't look well — she was leaning heavily on her staff, her face sallow and drawn, her shoulders slumped. I hadn't noticed before now how badly she was tiring, and it sent a sudden spike of fear through me. The webs of crystal and power we'd laid out — weren't they working? Or was it simply not enough? Maybe Gyssha's death-curse had weakened her too much. I scrambled up and ran to stand behind her, afraid of what Minerva would do next. Was she beaten? I wanted to believe it, but I didn't quite dare.

Minerva's weathered face was full of fury as she slowly lowered her arms, eyes boring into Aleida as though they could burn a hole right through her.

'I'm not surprised you're a meddler, girl,' Minerva said. 'Bein' your mother's daughter and all. Following in Gyssha's footsteps, aren't you?'

'Is that what you think?' Aleida said.

'Are you sure this is the path you want to take? You may have got lucky against Gyssha but if you keep on this road, sooner or later you'll find yourself facing the Misthag herself.'

'That's naught to concern you,' Aleida said.

'P'raps not. What does concern me, lass, is that I still need one more life to finish this ritual, and you've stolen away the one I had marked for it. Though come to think of it, that little matter concerns you, too.' Minerva started forward, padding across the stones in long, languid strides, moving like a great cat. She didn't look weary at all, even after all the effort it must have taken to shape this cavern out of the earth, to sacrifice her horses and bring the ritual to its climax. Despite the sweat on her face and in her hair, she looked as fresh as a daisy.

Aleida shifted her weight and staggered, grabbing for her staff with her free hand, her head hanging low. From the line of her skirts I could see that she'd lost her human feet; she was balancing on those dog's paws once again.

'Hit you hard, didn't she?' Minerva said. 'If you were anyone else, I'd say you deserved it, turning on your own mother like that; but I do see why you'd want Gyssha

Blackbone dead, mother or not. So I'll throw you a dash of mercy, girl. I need a life, but it needn't be yours. Give me one of them, and I'll let you go. Your apprentice too, maybe, if she doesn't try to fight me.'

'Dee, get them out of here,' Aleida said.

I hesitated, hand on my wand. *I'm not leaving you.* I didn't say it aloud, but I reckoned I thought it hard enough for her to hear.

Minerva laughed, a low cackle. 'Well, never let it be said I didn't try.'

Aleida laid her temple against her staff, head bowed, her tall figure stooped like an old woman. 'If you want me, Minerva, come and get me.'

Minerva took a step forward … then stopped, her eyes narrowed. I had a flash of memory, of Aleida standing in the road just a few hours before, waiting for the lords and their prisoners to approach, posing with her hat pulled down over her eyes. From this angle, I could just make out that her eyes were half-open, and she was watching Minerva from beneath her lashes. Waiting for her to draw near.

Slowly, Minerva backed away. 'Oh, I see. I see what you are. Trying to lure me in, like a plover feigning a broken wing. Gyssha *did* teach you well.' She raised a hand, scraping damp hair back from her face, then pulling the whole knotted mass of it forward across her shoulder. Her eyes flicked to me. 'Here's a lesson for you, girl, the second I've taught you today. Never let yourself be backed into a corner with no escape. Always have a little something tucked up your sleeve.' She pulled her hand from her hair, bringing a thick lock with it.

No, I realised, not a lock of hair. Not with those bright colours. It was her snake, that gorgeous viper that had nearly caught me when I came a-spying in her den, its scales rippling with red, yellow and orange, like flames made flesh. I saw its tongue dart out, tasting the air, as it wrapped its body in coils around her wrist.

Then, she brought up the knife in her other hand.

Somewhere in the distance I heard myself scream. A cry of warning or a cry of protest, I couldn't say. All I could think about was that beautiful creature, and how it had silently dropped on Aleida when she came to confront Minerva in her den. I couldn't say how much her familiar knew of witches, if it *knew* that it had risked its life when it attacked my mistress — but whether it knew or not, its loyalty to its mistress was unfailing, even here at the last.

I flinched away. I couldn't bear to see it. *Oh mercy, her own familiar.*

Beside me, Aleida's hand shot out and power *flexed* around me, squeezing me breathless. *So much power.* Our spell laid out deep beneath the earth had worked, after all. Aleida had just been measuring it out in careful doses, making it look as though she were using all her strength while she secretly kept the rest in reserve.

But it was too late. Blood dripped from the blade, and the tiny body fell writhing to the stones.

Minerva threw down the knife as the earth beneath us began to tremble and shake. It seemed to me that there were tears on her cheeks, washing rivulets through the dust and sweat on her skin. 'You see what comes of meddling, you stupid girl?' she howled at my mistress.

'These fools you spared are going to die anyway. The beast is coming.'

The shaking beneath our feet grew. Within the span of a few breaths, I could no longer stand. Aleida staggered and fell to her knees, head bowed and shoulders slumped in defeat. Her hair fell across her face and in a small voice I heard her say, 'Fuck.'

Then, the roof started to fall around us. Aleida cast a glowing dome above us as the others scrambled close, Kara and the beasts wide-eyed with fear.

'Her own familiar,' I heard myself say. I was still in shock from the flash of the knife, the anguished writhing of that tiny body. 'She killed her own familiar. How could she?'

Aleida glanced up at me with a grimace. 'For some folk that's half the point of keeping them. It's a reserve you can call on if you find yourself caught short, like a few coins sewn into the hem of your skirt. The horses must have been familiars too, or maybe more transformed folk; ordinary beasts wouldn't feed enough power to the ritual.'

'Where is she?' Kara said. 'What's happening?'

'You heard her, girl,' Aleida said. 'It's coming. Don't worry about Minerva, she's done with us. She's heading out, look.' She nodded across the cavern. There was a flash of white and gold against the far wall, a familiar silhouette. A griffin. I hadn't noticed it before, and it took me a moment to realise it must have been hidden behind the mound of rock towering over Brute. While I squinted through the dust and falling grit, I could just make out Minerva climbing onto the beast's back.

'She's going to escape!' Kara said. 'Stop her!'

'There's no point,' Aleida said. 'Let her go.' She turned to me, dark eyes anguished. 'I did everything I could, Dee, I swear. But it was just like with Toro, every thread I pried loose snapped back as soon as I moved on to the next. I don't know how she's done this, *what* she's done to anchor it, but I couldn't bring it down ...' Her voice trailed off as she watched the griffin. It had taken wing and was circling the cavern, Minerva on its back with one fist buried in the feathers of its neck, the other holding a wand aloft. I felt a surge of power, and above us the night sky split open to reveal a ribbon of cold, clear blue — some distant sky. Not ours, I'd guess.

'It wasn't enough?' I said. 'The webs we laid out, the power from the earth ... it wasn't enough?'

'It's not a question of power. I could have overloaded the working and brought it apart, but it would have razed everything from here to the Haven.'

We both watched as Minerva's griffin glided through the slit in the sky without a backwards glance, and the ribbon sealed shut behind her.

'You just let her go?' Kara said. 'You didn't even try to stop her!'

'Kara, hush,' I said. 'She doesn't matter anymore. Aleida, what do we do? What's the plan?'

She shook herself, and heaved herself up with the aid of her staff, wiping dust and sweat from her face with her sleeve. 'Dee, you need to get them out of here.'

'But the pathways — they're unstable.'

'If they stay here, they'll die. It's coming, Dee. Just get them out.'

'What about you?'

She glanced away. The shaking had died away a little while we spoke, but now it was returning — different, this time. Now it was not so much a rumble but a growl, as though the earth itself was snarling. 'I'm staying,' she said. 'I'm not letting it through without a fight.'

Biting my lip, I nodded. 'Okay. I'll take them somewhere and then come back.'

'No, stay away. This is more than you can handle. Get somewhere safe, I'll find you when this is done.'

'But how? You can't use pathways. And how will you even find me?'

'Dee, we're kin now. I can find you anywhere. Just go! Do it now, this is only going to get worse.'

'What about Maggie? And the wagon?'

'There's no time! Maggie will have to take her chances, and the wagon is just stuff. We can replace it. Go!'

Behind her, the earth was cracking open, like mud drying in the sun. Deep red light streamed out between the cracks. The ground *heaved*, and the fissures exhaled a blast of hot, acrid air, stinking of rotten eggs and foulness.

I backed away. 'Just … be careful, okay?'

Aleida smiled. It wasn't reassuring in any way. There was a crazed, manic quality to her face that reminded me of the morning in Black Oak Cottage when she'd announced we were going out to hunt down the ghost of her old mistress. But what could I do? I'm just an apprentice, after all.

I grabbed Kara by the arm and pulled her after me. 'Come on!' I called to the beasts, shouting now to be heard over the raging snarl of the earth. 'We have to go!'

CHAPTER 12

O pening the doorway was a struggle, and that
was only the start. Inside the rock was hot like a
blacksmith's forge; and wracked with quakes and tremors
that sent grit and stone raining down upon us. Within
moments I could feel sweat running down my neck and
over my forehead, but the searing heat of the air seemed
to dry it out as quickly as it came.

I trailed my hand along the stone as I hurried through
the scorching darkness, feeling Facet flitting through the
stone to keep pace. I had the idea to take us all to Black
Oak Cottage, for lack of anywhere better to go, but as
the heat wrapped around us I had to change the plan. We
couldn't stay here that long. We had to get out, or we'd be
roasted alive.

I stopped, pressing both hands to the wall, while
behind me Brute panted like a dog and Kara shifted from
foot to foot, sweat dripping down her face. 'Dee ...'

'I know,' I said. 'I know. I'm getting us out.'

Facet was just under my hands, rippling with worry and confusion. I wasn't sure he understood the danger we were in, but like a pet he could sense my distress. 'Help me find a doorway, please!' I whispered to him. 'We can't stay here!'

I could feel his wordless refusal through the stone. He didn't want to, he couldn't, it was wrong. He was trying to explain why, but I couldn't understand.

'You have to!' I pleaded. 'We'll die if we stay here, it's too hot for us!' I was starting to feel faint, my stays too tight around my chest, my head pounding. I couldn't breathe. Kara slumped against the wall next to me, head bowed and sweat soaking through her shirt and trickling down her neck. Still panting, Brute gave a low moan of distress and pressed his head against her.

'Now!' I demanded. 'Please!'

Thrumming with anxiety, he relented, and with his help I forced a doorway open, pushing with all my strength.

We stumbled out into chill night air, like a splash of ice water after the heat of the caves. Kara and I stumbled through, but the beasts had to squeeze and squirm through the narrow opening, first Toro and then Brute, with a grunt and snarl of pain as he left chunks of fur behind on the rough stone.

Outside, we collapsed onto soft sand, our skin steaming in the cold air. My vision had narrowed to a dark tunnel, and all I could do was gulp down breath after breath and listen to my heart pounding in my ears. Small tremors shook the ground, but I barely noticed, still recovering from the assault of the heat. I could feel Facet in the ground beneath me, still flushed with ... worry? Fear? It was hard to put into words what he felt, this little sprite that I'd somehow befriended, he was so alien and set apart from my world of flesh and bone.

But as my vision cleared and my desperate need for air abated, I pushed myself up, trying to figure out where in the hells I'd brought us.

Blinking, I rubbed my stinging eyes.

The sky overhead was black. Utterly black, and devoid of stars. The sand beneath us was red, a deep, rusty hue, and that made me frown. Red never looked red at night, I'd spent enough time back at home searching for my little brothers' toy soldiers in the yard after dusk to know that. This sand should be as black as the sky above.

I heaved myself up, and what I saw made my heart leap and flutter with sudden anxiety. There was enough light to see by, even without stars or moon, though exactly where it was coming from, I couldn't say. We were on a plain, largely flat but studded with strange dents and pockmarks, like the earth itself had been afflicted by the pox. In the distance I could make out dark streaks that might have been distant cliffs. But far closer than that, and far more ominous, was a huge cloud, clinging to the desert floor perhaps half a mile away. Hundreds of yards across, it was black as soot, seething and swirling and flickering with lightning

Kara sat up with a groan, pushing sweaty hair back from her face, and swore a soft oath. 'By all the gods, what in the hells is that?'

I didn't answer. In my chest my heart was sinking, my belly tightening to a hard knot. This place ... this place was familiar, and yet not. Months ago, when I'd first arrived at Black Oak Cottage, Gyssha's ghost had used my body to open a portal to one of the nether realms, and the glimpse I'd caught had haunted my nightmares ever since — a world of searing heat and blood-red sand, full of creatures that gibbered and howled and hungered, creatures like the one that had come out of the woods to stalk us last night while Aleida was seeking out Toro.

I tried to dismiss the thought. Months ago when I'd caught a glimpse of another world through a rift, the sky had been a harsh yellow, blasting with heat and full of shrieking horrors. This world was cold and empty, but I couldn't help but remember what Aleida had told me about the realms, the difficulties of telling just *where* in all creation we might be. It could just be night-time in that same roasting world. The bestiary had told me that, in our world, creatures of the desert avoided the baking heat of the sun, but from what I'd seen of the denizens of the nether realms, they seemed to revel in it.

'Dee?' Kara said again. 'What is that? Where are we?'

Never ignore your intuition, that's what Aleida so often told me. It would explain why Facet had been so reluctant to let us through, too. 'Um ...' I said. 'Nowhere good, I'm afraid.' Shakily, I got to my feet, pulled my wand from my belt, and set out.

'Where are you going?' Kara shouted.

I didn't answer her. I couldn't have explained it if I tried. But that storm ... I knew down in my bones that it was important. It had something to do with Minerva's ritual.

I didn't expect the others to follow me, but they did. I glanced back to see Kara and Brute walking together, Kara with her fingers entangled in the bear's shaggy coat. But Toro broke into a trot until he reached my side, and swung his head across to sniff at my shoulder, ears pricked towards me.

'Are you all right?' I asked him. 'I didn't want to hurt you back there. I didn't want to hurt anyone.'

He snorted a yes, and shook his head with a low nicker.

'I'm sorry I let her get to you,' I said. 'I should have been better.' *I will be better.*

He made another nicker, a questioning sound, ears pricked towards the storm.

'I don't know,' I muttered. 'We shouldn't be here, but here we are. Maybe there's something we can do. Some way to help.'

His head snaked out, catching my sleeve in his lips. I stopped, and with a toss of his head, he dropped to his knees once again.

I hesitated, worried for the scratches on his withers where the eagle had dug in its talons. But he knew his own mind, I reasoned, and he was as deep in this as any of us.

I clambered onto his back, and held tight as he heaved himself up again, and set out towards the storm at a canter.

As we drew near, I saw something ahead of us, jutting out of the sand. A pillar of stone. No, an obelisk, like the ones in the basement, surrounded by grotesque towers of bone. This was bigger, though, as thick at the base as a good-sized tree, and tall enough that I had to reach up to touch the tip while mounted on Toro's back. It thrummed with power, and when I stretched my hand towards it, the air around it felt as thick and sticky as treacle. We could feel the wind from the storm now, howling around us and blasting us with ash and grit.

Small tremors had been shaking the ground ever since we arrived, but now a bigger one set Toro staggering and me snatching at his mane to keep my seat. Moments later, another one had me sliding to the ground for safety, while Toro stood straggle-legged to keep his balance. With it came a deep, earthen roar, and a deep red glow appeared within the storm, like someone had cracked open the door to a furnace. I couldn't help but recoil from it, raising a hand to shield my face from the gritty blast of the wind. As I did, I caught a brief flicker of light wrapping around the vast, swirling cloud.

It took me a few tries to bring it back into sight — I had to squint my eyes just *so*, and turn my head like *this* — but then, I saw it clearly. Lines of force, wrapped all around the storm, anchored firmly to the ground at one end, and reaching up into the black sky from the other, all woven together like threads in cloth. One of the threads reached into the ground right at our feet — right at the obelisk of black stone, humming with power.

Kara and Brute caught up with us as I was examining the stone. Markings were scored into the smooth, glassy faces, some of the same sigils I'd seen in the basement earlier.

'Minerva did this,' I muttered, talking mostly to myself. 'It's part of the ritual. She must have made these, sent them here somehow ...'

In a flash I remembered what Aleida had said, last night when she was trying to undo the spell that transformed Toro. She'd said almost the same thing just moments ago. *Every thread I pried loose snapped back as soon as I moved on to the next. I don't know how she's done this, what she's done to anchor it, but I couldn't bring it down.*

Something was holding those spells together, something she couldn't reach. I thought of the webs of crystal we'd made in the caverns deep below the surface. Deep down where they couldn't be found, so Minerva's eagle couldn't find them and destroy them.

'It's an anchor,' I breathed. 'Lord and Lady ... She must be awfully good at portals, bringing the griffins through; hells, she opened the one she escaped through like it was nothing. *That's* why Aleida can't break the spells. They're anchored in another blessed realm!'

All the while, the earth still shook and rumbled in pulses, and the red glow within was growing brighter and brighter. But there was another light, now, as well as the constant flicker of lightning. There was a glow far above — a clear, brilliant blue, and at the centre a knot of shifting, opalescent colours. The same ones that had wreathed around Aleida as she fought in vain to break up Minerva's spell. She was still trying, I guessed, pouring more and more power into the work. But I could see she was doomed to fail — as long as the anchors here supported the portal, she'd never be able to destroy it.

I turned back to the obelisk. 'Help me! We need to tear it down!' I dropped to my knees, clawing at the soft sand, only to have Brute push me aside with his giant head and start digging with his enormous paws instead. After a moment, Toro circled around and leaned his shoulder against the pillar, pushing and heaving with his half-tonne of bulk. Between the two of them, there was nothing Kara and I could do but stand back and watch with growing anxiety as the red glow stretched upwards, higher and higher. It was not just soot and ash swirling through the storm now — here and there were huge dark chunks of something jagged and crumbling, tossed around like dry leaves. They were pieces of earth, I realised, broken loose and hurled in the howling wind, while the red glow intensified with every moment.

With a grunt of satisfaction Brute backed out of the hole he'd dug and circled around to the other side of the obelisk, nudging Toro out of the way. He reared up on his haunches, pressing his front paws near the tip of the obelisk, and with a great heave, pushed the thing over.

With a boom of thunder, the line of power tore loose, snapping back like the tail of a whip. Kara flinched back from the noise, but she set her jaw in determination, her hand once again winding into the fur of her father's coat. 'We have to do all of them, don't we? Just one didn't make much difference.'

'Mm, I think so,' I said. There were dozens of chunks of earth floating through the storm now, and I could see more of them at the base as the wind pried them from the ground.

'Well then—' Kara began, but then she broke off. 'Wait. What's that?' She slithered down into the hole and retrieved something from the sand. It was a brass chain, tarnished and corroded, strung with some kind of tooth, jagged like a saw blade. The beasts crowded around her to sniff at it, Brute making a low rumble in his throat.

'Let me see,' I said, and Kara handed it over. I could feel traces of power wrapped around it, but I couldn't have said what they were for. 'Did this belong to one of your friends?' I said. Toro stamped and Brute growled, as though to protest my choice of words, but then Brute nodded, a veritable pantomime of the human gesture. 'I'll hold on to it,' I said, tucking it into the pockets tied around my waist, under my skirts. 'It might be important.'

As the words left my lips, another tremor set us staggering, and the roar of the storm swelled, Kara and I both clapping hands over our ears. Through eyes squinting against the grit and dust blasted by the wind, I saw … something … erupt from the earth. Something huge, wreathed in red light and swirling ash. For a moment I couldn't make sense of it — it was just a vaguely egg-like shape, if an egg could be jagged and ridged and studded with knobs and spikes. But then the massive shape split open, revealing a mouth with row upon row of viciously pointed teeth. A multitude of spikes studded its broad blunt nose, scattered amid dozens of knobbly growths I took for warts — until I saw them rippling open, blinking in the harsh light and scouring sand. Eyes. Dozens of eyes.

'Lord and Lady,' Kara whispered beside me.

'We have to take down those stones,' I said as the ground shook again. The beast was fighting to push its way through to our realm, and those black gleaming eyes were all fixed on the sky above, straining and striving to reach the portal through to our realm. 'We should split up; you go with your da, I'll go with Toro. Collect the trinkets if you can, we might need them later. Go!'

Wide-eyed, she nodded, and set out into the blasting wind, her father hurrying after her.

Toro nudged my elbow with a snort, starting to kneel again. But before he could, I stepped up onto the fallen obelisk, using it as a mounting block to climb onto his back. 'Quick!'

I expected him to head in the opposite direction from Kara and Brute, but instead he whirled on his heels and galloped past them, leap-frogging ahead to the next stone.

When we reached it, I slithered down from his back with my wand already in my hand. *Don't think,* I told myself. *Just do.* I'd done it before, after all, when I'd brought the path in Minerva's den crashing down. Before my mind could run away with thinking of all the ways it could fail, I crouched down to press my hands against the red sand, the wand as well. 'Move,' I said.

Beneath my hands the grains of sand rippled, trembled, and then they flowed aside like water, parting in a deep trench, a furrow as neat as any made by a plough.

With a snort of surprise Toro whirled on his hindquarters, set his shoulder against the stone and leaned upon it with all his considerable weight. It toppled with a *thud* and a puff of dust, tearing another strand of support loose from the storm. Moments later there came another, cracking like an enormous whip, while the hell-beast at the storm's heart bellowed with rage.

I started to climb up on the obelisk again when I remembered to check the base, where I found a pipe, carved from smooth, slick stone. It was uncomfortably warm, like the sand around it — significantly hotter than the sand at the surface, even at only a few feet in depth. I tucked it into my pocket as well and climbed back onto Toro's back.

As we galloped onwards, again leap-frogging ahead to two stones away, I wound my fingers tight into Toro's mane and squinted up at the storm. I could see the rift in the sky above, full of shifting lights like the play of colours on mother-of-pearl. At the very edge of the tear in the sky I could just make out a small figure, her hair and dress streaming in the wind, her wand a pinprick of light in her hand. As I gazed up at her, I felt a peculiar prickle of sensation over my skin, a distinct sense of being watched.

When we reached the next obelisk, she was waiting for me — sort of. It was Aleida's shape, but made up of red dust and ashes caught up from the storm, swirling around inside her form like a whirlpool of coloured sand in a glass bottle. 'Dee, what the hell?' her shape said as I slithered down over Toro's shoulder. 'What are you *doing?*'

'It wasn't my idea!' I said. 'The pathways were like a furnace, we had to get out. Facet didn't want to let me through but I made him open the door and, well, here we are. And then I saw all this ... Aleida, I've figured out

why you couldn't undo Minerva's spells. Somehow she
had them anchored here in another realm.'

'So I see,' she said, looking around with blank
red eyes. 'Well, Dee, I … oh shit. I gotta go. Back in a
moment, I hope.' With that, she dissolved, blowing away
in a stinging blast of grit.

I gaped for about half a second, and then looked up.
I could still make her out, just, silhouetted against the
opalescent light, but hanging over her was something
else. Something huge and dark, solid as a mountain.

With a sharp snort, Toro nudged me with his nose,
hard enough that he almost knocked me over. I shook
myself and swept a handful of hair back from my face.
'Right. Right.' It didn't matter what was happening up
there, not really — there was absolutely nothing I could
do about it. I needed to focus on the task at hand.

This time, when I ordered the sand to move, it blasted
aside in a veritable fountain, spraying high into the air. In
moments the obelisk was toppled, and in the dirt beneath
I found a belt-buckle of tarnished silver. I only glanced at
the thing for a second before shoving it into my pocket,
long enough to see that it was engraved with an image
that was, frankly, obscene. 'I sincerely hope that wasn't
yours,' I said to Toro as I mounted up again.

I looked up again as we rode on — Aleida was still
there, and the huge dark shape, too. It seemed to me that
she had her head tipped back to look at the thing, but at
this distance I couldn't be sure. But I could only spare her
the briefest glance, for on this plane things were getting
worse. The hell-beast let loose another shattering roar,

and with a tremor that set Toro stumbling, the huge creature heaved its body out of the ground. It was truly massive — the whole courtyard at the Haven wouldn't have been big enough to contain it. It looked like a giant lizard, but with three sets of legs along its long, snaking body, its back covered with horny plates and wicked spikes, and its long tail tipped with a boulder-sized club. It raised its ugly head to the tear in the sky above and gave a bone-shaking roar of rage and fury.

Then, it started to climb, clawing its way up through empty air, straining towards the rift into our world. 'Oh gods,' I said, though the howling wind stripped the words away as though I hadn't spoken.

I'm not sure what made me glance back to check on Kara and Brute. It can't have been anything I heard — I couldn't hear a thing over the hellish noise of the storm and the beast. I couldn't even hear the thumping of my heart in my ears. But I did glance back, for whatever reason, and saw the two figures being mobbed by dark flapping shapes. *Oh no.* Whether I said the words or only thought them, I didn't rightly know. *Oh hells!*

'Stop!' I howled to Toro, pulling on his mane, but he was thundering on to the next stone, head and neck surging forward with each stride, powerful muscles bunching beneath me. He must have felt the shift in my weight as I craned to look behind, for he tossed his head and glanced back — and then abruptly turned, swinging around to gallop back the way we'd come.

Kara and her father were surrounded, at the centre of a dark cloud of flapping, squalling beasts. Kara had her sword out and was slashing at the creatures that swooped down on her, reaching out with their long, vicious claws. Her father was standing up on his hind legs, swatting and snarling at anything that came within reach. There were half-a-dozen beasties on the ground around them, but dozens more were circling above them, buffeted by the storm. While we galloped I saw where the creatures were coming from — they were rising out of the ground itself, clawing their way up through the sand, shaking it off before they leapt into the air with their dark eyes glowing with reflected light from the storm.

As Toro charged towards Kara and Brute, another glow appeared on the red earth, a pinprick that swelled larger and larger. My heart sank. *What now? What else can possibly go wrong?*

It swelled until it was roughly the size of our wagon, and then popped like a soap bubble. Inside was Aleida, and the huge dark shape I'd glimpsed through the rift above. At this range, it looked like a heap of boulders, stacked together in the vague shape of a human trunk and arms, though in place of legs was just one huge rock.

Aleida hurried towards the mob of nether beasties, staff in one hand and her wand in the other, and let loose a jet of flame, driving the creatures off. Behind her, the stone-man raised its massive arms and pounded its fists together.

I felt the shockwave ripple through the air, striking my skin like a stinging slap. But the nether beasties, it seemed, felt it as something else entirely. In a wave, they simply fell from the air, raining down like stones.

Aleida and I reached them at the same time. As she blasted the creatures nearest to Kara and Brute, Toro and I circled around to deal with the rest, and once again I felt the scorching blast of the ring.

'By all the hells, Dee,' she shouted. 'I've never met anyone with such a talent for being in the wrong place at the right time!'

I let that pass without comment. 'Who's your friend?' I shouted back instead, nodding past her to the hulking creature of stone.

'It's a mountain lord. Remember what I said about drawing too much power? Well, luckily it's decided this is a fight worth having. Come on, the beast is nearly through — we have to move!'

She turned her face to the howling storm and forged into the stinging wind. Behind her, where the bubble of blue light had appeared, there was a perfect circle of dark, crumbling stone, the same stuff that had made up the ground of Minerva's cavern. The sight of it made me wonder if, back in our world, there was now a perfect circle of red sand.

The mountain lord rolled after her, the huge boulder of its lower body rolling across the red sand. As it passed me, the stone of its head turned my way, and I met the blue pools that were its eyes. For a moment, my head was full of the roar of waterfalls, the dizzying heights of stony cliffs, the biting cold of rarefied air. Then, the elemental looked away, releasing the hold it had on me, and I was left with the distinct impression that I'd been examined, assessed and found at least somewhat acceptable.

Without a word, the rest of us followed them. Kara was splattered with blood, but aside from a few scratches she seemed unharmed — most of the gore had come from the flapping horrors, I guessed. Her father hadn't been so lucky; I could see fresh blood matting his fur, and he was limping on one front paw as he loped along at Kara's side.

Up ahead, Aleida had her wand in one hand and her staff in the other, held wide as an arc of power rippled and shimmered around her. Her voice was chanting an incantation, the droning words lost in the howl of the wind. Above us, the shifting pearly hues wreathed around the portal intensified, and I saw the edges of the rift ripple and waver. She was fighting to close the fissure, sealing the beast out.

The hell-beast gave an ear-rending screech and strained upwards, redoubling its efforts to reach the portal. Ahead of me, the mountain lord halted, and leaned down to the ground, pressing both its stony fists to the desert floor. I felt power ripple around me, *squeezing* me like a huge snake wrapping me in its coils, and then it stretched away from us like the roots of a plant. Up ahead, thick ropes of power burst out of the red sand and shot up towards the beast, wrapping around it like vines, hauling it back towards the desert's barren floor. For a moment, the beast faltered, falling back, but then it clawed its way upwards once again, surging ahead with a force that dragged the Mountain Lord skidding and grinding across the red sand.

I watched with a sinking feeling as the beast fought its way upwards. The portal was shrinking, but it wasn't closed, not by a long shot. And it wouldn't shut, I realised — three interwoven strands of power still reached up into the sky. We'd taken down five of the pillars, but it wasn't enough.

I turned to Kara. 'We have to finish those pillars! Come on!'

She turned to me with wide eyes, and nodded. 'Let's go!'

We both scrambled onto Toro's back, Kara in front and me clinging to her waist, and as soon as we were seated he was off, his hooves pounding in the soft sand and Brute charging alongside us. He kept pace easily, despite his wounds. Never in my life would I have imagined a creature so large could be so fast.

At the first pillar I was sliding down while Toro was still moving, and parted the sand. Kara helped pull me back up again while Brute reared up to knock the stone over. As it fell I heard the hell-beast raging, but we were already riding on again. Holding tight to Kara's waist as we charged across the sand, I snatched a glance at the struggle at the heart of the storm. The portal had shrunk — now it was barely as big as the beast's head, but the beast was only yards beneath it, straining and striving to climb the empty air.

Then we were at the second-to-last stone. Again I ploughed a furrow in the sand and scrambled back up to my perch, leaving the rest of the work to Brute. It was only as we were galloping away that I realised I'd forgotten all about the trinkets buried beneath them. Exactly why they mattered, I couldn't have said, but some niggling sense deep within me insisted that they did. My stomach sank, but there was no turning back. There was no time.

The last stone. I slid to the ground with shaking legs, and for the last time I willed the sand to move. Brute wasn't here yet — I glanced back to see him charging towards us, more flapping horrors beating around his head. There was no time to wait, no time to help him. All that mattered was the stone. Kara and Toro were already straining against it, heaving it over. I ran to join them, but I couldn't help but glance back at the storm, at the hellish creature determined to reach our world.

The stone fell with a dull *thump*, and with the snap of a gargantuan whip, the last of the ethereal supports melted away. With that sound, the storm died. The wind simply stopped dead, like closing the door on a gale. The sudden cessation of noise left me reeling, my ears ringing, as all the sand and grit that had been carried on the wind rained down in a shower. Suddenly I could hear Aleida's voice, still chanting, and above us the hissing crackle of the portal.

The beast had its head through the rift, along with one great clawed foot. The webbing of power that had lifted it this far was gone, but it didn't matter anymore, it seemed. That vast body twisted, clawing at the empty air, but with its head and one foot inside the portal it could still climb through ...

But as Aleida's voice rose to a shriek, I saw the portal cinch tight like a noose. The huge body stiffened, writhed with a muffled shriek, and then it fell, an empty space where that hideous head had been.

The quake as it hit the ground made me stagger. A moment later came a gust of wind, bearing with it a blast of sand and an awful, sulphurous stink. The beast didn't lie still as it fell, but writhed and twitched like a headless snake, claws and club-tail scything through the sand.

For a moment that was the only sound, and then the alien world around us erupted into shrieks and jibbers as all the circling beasties swooped towards the fallen hell-beast.

I heard someone shrieking my name. Then, Kara was at my side, mounted on Toro's back, screaming at me to climb up behind her. Brute was there too, more blood in his fur now, something clutched in his mouth. It was silver, curiously bright in this dark world. As I scrambled up behind Kara he lifted his great head and pressed it into my hand. It was a flask, a silver flask. Just why it was so important to him I couldn't begin to imagine, but I shoved it into my pocket along with the other trinkets. I could still hear someone calling me, and realised it must be Aleida, on the far side of the fallen beast.

The moment I was settled, Toro took off once more, galloping across the sand, weaving between the flapping horrors that joyfully shrieked and howled as they clawed their way up through the sand to join the chaos.

We met her on the far side, leaning heavily on her staff as she backed away from the fallen beast. Her eyes lit up when she saw me, her face flushed with triumph. 'Did you see it, Dee? Did you see that? Took its head right off! Like a cork from a godsdamned bottle!'

'Yes, yes,' I said. 'That's amazing, good work! Now can we get out of here?'

'Gods, yes. Back to where I came in. Quickly!' She

turned away, leaning on her staff, only to stagger after a couple of steps. 'Oh, for pity's sake ...'

Once again I swung down from Toro's back. 'What's wrong?'

'Ugh, I'm cut off. Godsdamned elementals, they're very literal, you know. I convinced him to give me power to deal with the beast, and now it's dead he's not letting me have any more.'

The words sent a chill through me. 'But he's going to take us home, right?'

'Oh, yes. I was *very* clear about that, believe me.'

'All right, good. You'd better get on Toro if you can't walk. Kara, help me!'

Brute caught up with us as Kara and I got Aleida up on Toro's smooth back, though Kara was left frowning at the strange feel of Aleida's feet, their true shape hidden beneath the folds of her skirts. As I helped heave my teacher up, I felt something shift in my overloaded pockets, topple out and fall, and once Aleida was settled on her perch I stooped with a curse to pick it up from the sand. The flask. It was engraved, I realised, with a picture of a bull. 'Oh,' I said. 'Toro, this was yours!' Perhaps that was why Brute had been so insistent on bringing it to me.

'What's that?' Aleida said sharply as we started towards the circle of crumbling stone. The elemental was already there, waiting for us with the calm patience of mountains.

'A trinket. There was something buried under each of those stones. Something personal, I think? I can feel power clinging to them, it's odd.'

'Mm,' Aleida said, frowning. 'Interesting. Actually, that would explain how she was able to anchor the spell here, and why I couldn't undo the blasted thing. Very interesting. Come on now, hurry!'

I was going as fast as my weary legs would take me. But we were close now, just a few dozen yards away.

There came a sound from behind us, a kind of startled grunt. I glanced back, and saw that Brute had fallen behind. He was stopped still, biting and clawing at his foot.

No, not his foot. There was something wrapped around it, something dark, like vines or rope.

'Uh oh,' I said.

Aleida looked behind. 'Oh hells. Dee—'

'On it,' I said. 'Kara, stay with Aleida!'

Kara frowned and glanced back. 'Da? Da!'

'Stay!' I roared at her. I wished there was time to explain. *She's weak, and she's drained, she needs someone to stay with her!* But there was no time for that. I turned on my heel and sprinted for the bear, hoping just for once that Kara would do as she was asked.

Up close, I could see why Brute had fallen behind. The thick black cords had caught him just like a snare, and despite his powerful claws and teeth, more of them were reaching up out of the warm sand to wrap around him, two more for every one he tore loose.

I met his wide, panicked eyes as I pulled out my wand once again. 'Hold still,' I said to him, and crouched down beside his feet. 'This might hurt. I'm sorry.'

I jammed the tip of the wand into the sand, right into the knot of vines or tentacles or whatever the blasted things were, and once again I thought of fire, and felt the ring on my finger throb with heat.

I loosed everything I could muster into the sand, sending a scorching spear of heat into whatever hellish creature was lurking down there.

With a bellow of pain Brute pulled back, wrenching himself away, while from under the sand I heard a piercing shriek, much muffled, and the sudden sickening stench of roasted beastie. Sand heaved beneath us as the thing down there writhed in agony. It bowled me over, sending me tumbling — but Brute was free, and so was I. Picking up my skirts, I ran back towards Aleida and the others, Brute beside me breaking into a lumbering run that would have swiftly outdistanced me if he hadn't checked his pace to keep from leaving me behind.

Ahead, Aleida and Kara were in the stone circle, shouting and hollering. Toro was charging back towards us, coming to bear me back to them faster than my own legs could carry me.

Then, I felt something bump against my thigh and fall. The flask, fallen out of my pocket again. Before I could react, it struck my foot and bounced away across the sand.

Cursing, I tried to stop and turn back. The shouts of encouragement up ahead turned to yells of protest as I darted after the tarnished silver flask.

Then, I saw the thing that had come out of the sand after us. I'd never seen an octopus before I'd leafed through Aleida's bestiary with its beautiful illustrations, but that's what this thing looked like, if you could imagine an octopus crossed with a gnarled and ancient tree, crawling after us with dozens of contorted, leathery roots.

Before I could properly take in the awful sight, Brute and Toro were there, one snarling in rage, the other tossing his head with a shrill, demanding neigh. In the background I could hear Aleida hollering. 'Get back here, Dee! Now, damn you!'

The flask was still yards away, but Brute cut me off from reaching it, swerving into my path like a furry wall. Toro caught my dress in his yellow teeth and pulled me hard towards his shoulder, while Brute shoved his head between my legs, hoisting me bodily towards Toro's back. 'No!' I protested. 'The flask, get it! We have to get it!'

Brute's roar drowned out my words, and Toro wheeled beneath me, bolting back towards the others, Brute barely half a pace behind.

At Aleida's side, the mountain lord had raised its fists, and a glowing sphere had appeared in the air around it, for the moment nothing more than a soap bubble, but growing brighter with every passing second.

Fingers buried in Toro's mane, I squeezed my eyes shut and bowed my head, the taste of failure bitter in my mouth. I felt power wash over us, soft and cool as silk. 'I'm sorry,' I sobbed to the man beneath me, bound into this bestial form. 'I'm sorry, I'm sorry, I'm so sorry ...'

Coming back to our world was like coming home. The smell of it, the touch of the air, the feeling of the earth beneath my feet. When I slithered down from Toro's back I would have loved nothing more than to just lie there and embrace it, even if we were back on the horrible, crumbling stone that Minerva had contrived to build her cavern. Although I would have been happier about it if the hell-beast's severed head hadn't been sitting there, its jaws and tongue still twitching.

I turned my face away and tried to put it out of my mind. I had more important things to attend to.

The mountain lord was departing, sinking away into the brittle stone, the hell-beast's head and foot descending with it. 'Wait!' I shouted after the elemental. 'I need to ask you something! Wait!'

'Dee, no!' Aleida called after me, but I ignored her, stumbling towards the disappearing being.

It halted its descent, and slowly turned towards me with those cold blue inhuman eyes, and I faltered.

Behind me, I heard Aleida stagger to her feet and come after me, leaning heavily on her staff. 'Damn it, Dee.'

The elemental's gaze flickered her way, before settling back on me. Then its voice echoed inside my head, like the grinding of stone. *Speak, child.*

It took me a moment to muster my thoughts. 'Please,' I started. 'Please, we left something behind. Something important.'

The stone head, so small compared to the bulk of its body, tilted to one side, like a quizzical dog. *You are all here, are you not?*

'It was a flask, a silver flask,' I said. 'We need it! It's important!'

'Listen, kid—' Aleida began, but those cold blue eyes flicked her way again, and her voice choked off.

No. You have spoken enough, witch; now you will be silent. The child will speak.

'It's important,' I said again. 'I think … I think it's the key to undoing what was done to them. The transformation spell.'

The token, yes. It is lost.

'But we have to get it back! What was done to them — it's wrong! They've done bad things, I don't deny it, but this isn't justice! This is, this is horrible!'

The mountain lord said nothing. It just watched me with those cold eyes. Then it started to sink away into the earth again.

'Wait!' I shouted. 'Please! I'm asking for mercy!'

As the elemental disappeared, its voice echoed through my head once more. *What is justice? What is mercy? These are nothing to the mountains and the earth. You must ask the lords of your kind, child. This one cannot help you.*

Beside me, Aleida doubled over with a cough, raising a hand to her throat. 'Lord and Lady, Dee,' she rasped. 'You'll be the death of me, I swear.'

I couldn't look away from the place where the being had vanished. 'He didn't, he didn't even try.'

'I was trying to tell you. He doesn't care. He didn't help us for our sake. It, I mean. It's not a he any more than it's a she. Look, the hell-beast would have corrupted the earth itself with its presence; that's the only reason I was allowed to draw that much power and drive it back.

You did your best, Dee, and you did a damn good job, but you can't win every time. You just can't.'

With a low nicker, Toro came around behind her. At the sight of him, my eyes filled with tears.

Toro nudged at Aleida's shoulder. She waved him away, but he nudged her again, nearly knocking her over. She glared at him, but then she turned back to me and her face softened. 'Oh, fine,' she growled. 'But if you make me fall on my face I'll see that you regret it.' She leaned back against his shoulder and wrapped an arm around his neck to steady herself. Her head bowed, her chin sinking to her chest — and an instant later, lifted again. 'Don't weep for me, lass,' he said in Aleida's voice. 'You've a kind heart, but I don't deserve your mercy. I truly don't, not after all I've done. Dragging Brent back in when all he wanted was a better life for his lass is the least of it all.'

His head fell again, and Aleida was back, rubbing her eyes. 'Hey, kid. You okay?'

I shook my head, tears spilling over my cheeks. 'We can't just leave him like this. I could go back there, maybe. I could find it—'

'Dee, *no*,' Aleida said, her voice full of steel. 'You are not throwing your life away for him!' Standing by her shoulder, Toro snorted in agreement, stamping his hoof in emphasis.

'But—'

'Over my dead godsdamned body, you understand? The fact that you all even made it there in one piece is a miracle, and getting back again ... Listen, you don't even know how lucky you are to have pulled that off.'

I scowled up at her. 'But Minerva managed to go there and plant them all.'

'Minerva's got forty years of experience on you. And before you ask, no, I'm not doing it either.'

I felt myself flush. 'I wasn't asking.'

'Not yet, but you'd get there eventually. Dee, the only reason you were able to travel there as easily as you did was because Minerva's ritual already bridged the gap between the realms. If we wanted to go back there we'd probably have to use that wretched demon tree to open a portal.'

'Oh gods,' I said.

'Yes, exactly. It's not going to happen.'

I felt my shoulders slumping in defeat. 'But the elemental said something about asking human lords for help ... what about that? Who are they?' It wasn't referring to Lord Belmont and his like, I was sure of that much.

'Oh, you know. The gods, that kind of thing.'

I stared at her. 'What do you mean, the gods? Are they, are they real?'

She chortled at that, and slipped an arm around my shoulders. 'Yeah. Yeah, kid, they're real.'

'And they could turn him back?'

'Could, maybe. But they won't. Not with all the harm he's done. It takes more than one good turn to atone for years and years of murder and pillage.'

Something in her voice made me turn to her, but her eyes were down, her head bowed. I started to speak, I even opened my mouth — but then I realised I had no idea what to say. Instead I looked across to Kara and Brute, still huddled together where the mountain lord had brought them back to our own world. Brute had his huge paws wrapped around Kara's small shoulders while she buried her face in his fur and sobbed.

Aleida squeezed my shoulder and pulled away. 'You two okay?' she said, hobbling towards them. 'Well, I know you're cut up like a fresh-ploughed field, big guy, but from what I can see they're all skin-deep. I can sort you out once I've had a chance to catch my breath. Kara, you in one piece?'

Kara turned to her, tears wet on her cheeks, but her eyes were guarded. 'I ... I'm fine. Look, miss, I'm sorry about going behind your back to the other witch, but if you've got a bone to pick with me, leave my da out of it. It was me that did it, not him.'

Aleida barked a laugh. 'Ha! Don't worry yourself over it, kid, you're good. You did everything just right.'

That set Kara frowning. 'What?'

I could just imagine how the girl would react when she figured out what Aleida meant, so before she could head any further down that path I swallowed hard on my tears and dug into my pockets, pulling out all the trinkets we'd collected. 'Brent, here, one of these is yours, right?' I spilled them out over the ground, the necklace, belt-buckle, and then the pipe.

As soon as the pipe appeared, Kara snatched it up. 'This one! This is his! But why? What does it matter now?'

Aleida leaned down to pluck it out of her hand. 'Minerva used them as a focus for the transformation spell. Burying them in another realm was a bit of a master-stroke, if I'm honest, though it's a lot of trouble to go to.'

'Almost like she knew someone was going to come along and interfere?' I said, looking up at my teacher.

She gave me a thoughtful look. 'Dee, have I mentioned how glad I am that you're not stuck in some backwater kitchen down on the plains? Your intuition is too bloody good to be wasted in a scullery.' She frowned at the pipe, and waved a hand over it. Then, she swayed violently and with gritted teeth pressed the heel of her hand to her forehead. 'Oh, for pity's sake. I can't do it.'

Kara swallowed hard. 'I don't mind,' she piped up. 'I mean, I'm just glad he's alive. If it can't be undone ...'

'Oh, hush, girl. I just mean right now.' She handed it to me. 'But you probably can, Dee. Cleanse and banishment to start with, and see how you go from there.'

'Um, all right,' I said. 'But maybe we should get back to the wagon first? Only last time ...' My voice faltered, but I pushed on. 'Last time he was, well, buck naked. And it'd be a long walk on bare feet.'

'Bear feet, ha ha,' Aleida said. 'Yeah, fair point. Well, the big lunk's lasted this long. Another hour or so won't kill him. Let's go.'

EPILOGUE

The next morning, I awoke to Aleida's voice outside the window of the caravan. 'Well?' she was saying. 'What's your plan, then? Kara and her father are heading out of here, if I have any say in the matter, and we'll be on our way, too. Do you want to see if they'll take you with them? Or I can find you a nice quiet farm somewhere, like I said before. Hells, the Haven would probably take you in, for that matter.' From the sound of it she was leaning against the wagon, right near my head.

In answer, there came a rumbling snort. Toro's snort.

'No? None of these? Then what? You want to stay with us?'

He gave two snorts for yes.

'Well, you were damned useful last night, I'll grant you that,' Aleida said. 'But listen, I'm not collecting waifs and strays here. This life is no walk in the park, and you'll have to earn your keep. If you get injured I'll do my best to fix you up, but there's limits to what I can do, and you'll be risking life and limb. But then again, I suppose you're no stranger to that sort of thing.'

Once again, he snorted yes.

'Why, though? The girl? Taken rather a shine to Dee, haven't you? Don't think I don't see it. I know you went with her when she went to find those stones for me, and I know why, too.'

I squirmed out of the covers and sat up — at least, I tried to, only to clamp down hard on an inadvertent moan. *Everything* hurt, and I could barely move, but with teeth clenched I managed to haul myself up.

From outside there came another low nicker.

'Mm,' Aleida said. 'It's like that, isn't it? Somehow she manages to see the good in people. Despite all evidence to the contrary. Actually, it's not a bad idea; she could use someone to help her keep out of trouble, and despite your best efforts you haven't managed to pickle your brains entirely. All right, let me think it over.' The wagon rocked slightly as she pushed away from the wall and walked away with a swish of her skirts.

A moment later, she was inside, closing the door behind her. 'Oh, you're awake. Did you hear all that? What do you think?'

I blinked at her. My first instinct was to deny I'd been listening in, but I quickly thought better of it. 'You're really considering it?'

She shrugged. 'Like I said, he was useful. And honestly, kid, you've got a talent for getting yourself into trouble. I can't always be there to watch your back and swoop in when things go awry. So what do you think?'

I hugged my knees to my chest. 'I don't know. What if he gets hurt? Or killed? I'd hate to be the cause of it.' I knew it was rubbish even as I said it. He'd be safer with us than he would be anywhere else. To other folk he was just an animal.

'Is that the real reason you're hesitating?'

I bit my lip, and shook my head. 'I just … I feel awful. I wanted to save him so badly. I had that flask in my blessed hand!'

'And, what? You're afraid if you see him every day you'll remember that feeling of failure?'

I nodded.

Aleida shrugged. 'Well, kid, it's up to you. We don't owe him anything. If you're not comfortable keeping him around I'll leave him with Sister Ellendene. The Haven could use him and they'll treat him well.'

'Sister Ellendene?' I said. 'We're going back to the Haven?'

'Yeah. I need to make them forget they ever saw us. The folk up at the fort, too. Sooner or later someone's going to come looking for their hell-beast, and we need to cover our tracks. Luckily I didn't use too much of my own power here, just what I drew from the earth, so they won't be able to track us through that. I'll see to the nuns, and then pay a visit to Lord Belmont, and that should take care of it.'

Someone, she said, but I knew the name she left unspoken. Mae o' the Mists. 'What about Kara, and her da? Will you make them forget, too?'

She looked away, frowning. 'I probably should,' she muttered. 'But, no, it'll cause too many problems. Bad things can come from messing with folks' memories like that. It won't matter a jot to the nuns, but making Kara forget all this is a different matter.' While she spoke, she was pouring something from the little kettle that had been simmering on the oil-burner, and she mixed in a few drops of this and that from the cabinet. Then she set it on the little shelf beside me. I'd slept in her bed last night, since she had been up pottering about, too jittery to sleep after the fight. I wasn't sure she'd been to bed at all. 'Here you go,' she said. 'Drink up, it'll help.'

I wrapped my hand around the teacup. Even that little movement hurt. My knuckles ached fiercely, but then I remembered how hard I'd gripped the wand, and supposed I shouldn't be surprised. 'I don't suppose you've got any more of that stuff you gave me last night?'

'Nope. Definitely not.'

Her voice was so firm I looked up at her in surprise.

'It's not something to be used lightly, Dee. Given how things went, I'm glad I brought it, but we won't be using it again for a *long* time. It's dangerous. Take too often and you'll start craving it, and before long you can't function without it. I'm not going to let you go down that path, kid.'

Her sombre tone gave me pause — usually the only time she was so serious was when I'd gone and done something stupid. 'Is ... is that something Gyssha did to you?'

She gave a brief smile, a wry quirk of her lips. 'Went and showed my hand, didn't I? Should have made a joke of it instead. This is mostly willowbark, with a couple of other things to speed healing. Gentle as a spring breeze.'

'Aleida?' I said, as she started to turn away.

'Mm?'

'Where do you think she went? Minerva, I mean.'

She pursed her lips, looking out the window. 'Hard to say. Mae can't be too mad at her, she did complete the ritual, after all. But I get the feeling she won't be back around here any time soon. She set up her escape route early on, bringing those griffins through like that. I wouldn't be surprised if she's decided to leave this realm behind for good. She'll be happier out there, anyway.'

'I just can't believe she killed her own familiar,' I said. 'He was so beautiful. Does it, well, harm a witch if they do something like that?'

Aleida shook her head with a sigh. 'No. Well, unless you count the guilt of harming the little creature that loved and served you. I don't like to have familiars, myself. I don't ever want to find myself in a position where that's an option. That, and the fact that if someone's coming after you, taking out your familiar is one of the first things they'll do. I wish it hadn't come to that with Minerva, but she was too afraid of Mae to risk failure. It's a lesson worth remembering, Dee — desperate people do desperate things. Now, get yourself up and moving, you'll feel better for it. Kara and her father have some breakfast cooking, and it'll be ready before too long.'

I tried not to dawdle, but just pulling on my clothes was an ordeal, and my hands hurt too much to pull the laces on my stays tight. When I was as presentable as I was going to get, I gingerly descended the stairs, hobbling like an old woman.

Kara and her father were crouched beside the fire, while Aleida sat on the wagon's steps. I inched past her and made my way to the back of the wagon, where Toro was half-heartedly plucking at the dry grass. At the sight of me he lifted his head with a low nicker and pricked his ears my way.

'If I could go back and get it for you, I would,' I said.

He flicked his ears back, and shook his head.

I folded my arms across my chest. 'You don't want me to? Why? I don't understand.' I glanced back towards the wagon, wondering if Aleida would come translate for him again. She was still sitting there on the step, but I made myself turn away without calling out to her. I needed to figure this one out on my own.

I shuffled closer, and gingerly pressed my fingertips to his cheek. I closed my eyes, remembering the first time I'd seen him, panicked and fighting for his life against the ropes dragging him into the blacksmith's yard. I'd tried to slip into his mind then, to calm him before someone could get hurt. Now I tried again, bracing myself for the bewilderment and disorientation.

The moment my mind brushed his I felt him go tense with the shock of it.

Can you hear me? I thought to him.

... Yes. Yes, lass, I can hear you.

For a moment I was silent, trying to organise my thoughts. *I'm sorry,* I said at last. *I'm so sorry. I can't imagine how you must hate me.*

Hate you? Good gods, lass, why would I ever hate you?

Because I almost had it! I had it and then I lost it and now we'll never get it back.

Listen to me, lass. I didn't say those things last night just to make you feel better. It was the truth. If you turned me back, I'd just be the same as I was before — a vicious drunkard with a price on his head. I'd fall back into that life. It's all I know.

But this isn't fair!

There's naught fair in the world, girl. If things were fair, I'd have died in that fire years ago, instead of my wife and our little girl. She'd be about your age if she'd lived, lass, and I hope she'd have grown up as brave and kind-hearted as you. I've spent the last ten years trying to drown the memory of what I lost, but now it's time to honour them instead. I'll serve you faithfully, if you'll have me, miss; I'll do all I can to aid and protect you. Maybe it'll go some way to redressing the evils of my life.

There were fresh tears on my cheeks. I stepped back from him, blotting them away with my sleeve. 'I'm not giving up,' I said to him. 'One day, I'll find a way to change you back. But I promise I won't do it unless you wish it. And I'll tell Aleida I want you to stay with us.'

He snorted, ears pricked and alert, and dropped his head to rub his face against my shoulder. Then, with a flick of his nose, he nudged me back towards the fire with another low nicker. From the scent hanging in the air, breakfast was nearly ready, and my belly was growling with hunger.

Aleida glanced up at me as I hobbled past. 'What's the word, Dee?'

'I'd like him to stay with us. If that's all right with you, I mean.'

'Your call.'

Over by the fire, Kara glanced up, her face curious, while Brent lifted slices of bacon from the pan over the coals. In the end I hadn't done the working to turn him back all by myself — Aleida had lent a hand. Back in his natural shape, Kara's father seemed nearly as big as he had been as a bear, with a thick, reddish beard and long, unkempt hair. Aleida had found him a smocked shirt and some ragged breeches from a stash of odd clothing she had in the wagon.

'Holt?' Brent was saying to Kara, his voice incredulous. 'Holt, that strutting, perfumed cockerel? I never trusted that puffed-up braggart, Kara. If I'd ever seen him sniffing around you I'd have thrashed him within an inch of his life!'

'Oh, Da.' Kara looked away to hide the flush on her cheeks. 'I needed *someone* to help me get out of the Haven and away from those nuns. Don't worry yourself over it, I just led him on to get what I wanted.' She cast a sidelong glance our way, as though pleading not to betray her lie.

'And where is he now?' Brent said darkly.

'In the fort, awaiting trial for murder,' Aleida interjected. She'd pulled out her tobacco pouch and was carefully preparing her pipe. 'Lord Belmont picked him up along with the rest of his crew yesterday. Hey, got your pipe on you, old chap?' she waved the pouch at him.

'Oh,' he said with surprise. 'Thank you kindly, mistress. Kara—'

'You go, Da,' she said. 'I can handle this.'

'I'll help you,' I said, hobbling over to take over the pan of bacon.

Kara gave me a shy smile. 'Sorry about last night. About fighting you, I mean. You're not hurt, are you?'

Aleida's brew was working, I felt a great deal better than I had when I woke up. 'Don't worry about it,' I said. 'It's fine.' I looked her over out of the corner of my eye as I shook the pan. She still looked marvellous, all the more wild and fierce for her rumpled clothes and tangled hair. 'Umm, Kara?'

'Yeah?' she glanced up.

'I really like your trousers,' I said.

'Oh!' she looked down with a flush and ran her hands over the red cloth. 'They're great, aren't they? Da hates them, but I told him that's too bad, if he's going to be off gallivanting around the countryside all the time I'll wear what I blessed-well like. You should make yourself some, they're so much better than skirts for doing work around the yard, and for riding. Fighting, too.'

I started to speak, the words in my mouth unbidden. *Oh, I'm not a fighter.* But I thought better of it. It wasn't true, after all, not a bit. 'Maybe I will,' I said. 'They might come in handy.'

Kara smiled, but then her face turned thoughtful, and she glanced up at Aleida. 'Um, miss?' she said. 'Remember yesterday, you were telling me about some sword-fighting schools where I might be able to find a place?'

'Mm?' Aleida said, glancing up from packing her pipe.

'Do you think you could tell me where to find them?'

'Sure,' Aleida nodded. 'You'll need a letter of introduction. I could fix one up for you but I think it'd be better coming from the sisters back at Haven.'

'Oh gods, you don't expect me to go back there, do you? I'm not leaving Da again, and he can't show his face in town!'

'Don't worry about that,' Aleida said. 'I'll go with you, I need to stop by anyway. Your father can hide in the wagon, I'm not going to turn him over to Belmont's men ... well, not as long as he swears to put all this banditry behind him.'

'I'll give you no arguments there,' Brent said. 'I've spent the last few years trying to figure out how to get out of the life without getting Kara and myself killed over it. I'm out and done, and most grateful for your aid.'

'Glad to hear it,' she said. 'I'm going to hold you to it, you know. Last night, when Dee and I turned you back, I added a little something to the spell.' Stooping, she picked up a twig from the ground, and breathed on it to set it alight. 'If you ever raise a hand to someone for any reason other than defence of yourself or others, you'll find yourself back in the form Minerva gave you.' She wasn't even watching him as she said it. All her attention seemed to be on lighting her pipe with the burning twig.

Beside me, Kara fell tense and still. But Brent just paused briefly in packing his own pipe, raising his eyes to her. 'What about teaching others to fight? I had a thought, if Kara gets into some fighting school, perhaps I could get a place too. Some honest work for once.'

'You can teach,' Aleida said with a nod. 'Just keep hold of your temper. The moment you strike out of anger, you'll feel the curse upon you, but you'll have the chance to back down.'

'A curse?' Kara snapped. 'You've got no right—'

'Kara, hush,' Brent said. 'It's fair. More than fair.' He handed the pouch back to Aleida. 'I give you my word, that life is behind me. Can I trouble you for a light?'

Aleida handed him the burning twig. Beside me, Kara let out her breath in a soft hiss, and with a shake of her head, went back to her work.

'It's a shame about the money for the Haven,' I said. 'We never did get a chance to find out where those marked men hid it.'

'Oh,' Kara said, ducking her head as though to hide a smirk. 'That's a shame. I suppose it's lost for good.'

But Aleida just laughed. 'Oh, right. I'd forgotten about that. Glad you mentioned it, Dee, we can pick it up on the way.'

I glanced up at her from across the fire. 'You know where it is? How?'

'While you were off spying on Minerva and trying to get yourself killed, I borrowed a beast to track their scent. It's not too far away.'

'Good,' I said. 'But there is one other thing I'd like to do, too.'

'Oh? What's that?'

'One of the bandit lads — the one whose arm I helped fix up? He said his ma is sick, and they can't afford to pay the doctor. I thought maybe we could stop in and help.'

'And how do you propose to find them?'

I raised an eyebrow at her. 'Witchcraft? Or we could just ask. I mean, you said you were going to the fort anyway.'

She huffed a sigh. 'Oh, fine. You know, this is going to take all day.'

'Did you have somewhere else to be?'

'Yeah. Far away from here, before a certain person comes sniffing around after a certain hell-beast. But that's fine, you've got your pathways all under control, once we're done here we can go pretty much anywhere.' She turned her dark eyes to me, pipe in one hand as smoke wreathed around her face. 'So the question is, kid, where do you want to go?'

THE END